NEW FRONTIERS

TOR BOOKS BY BEN BOVA

Able One
The Aftermath
As on a Darkling Plain
The Astral Mirror
Battle Station
The Best of the Nebulas (editor)
Challenges
Colony
Cyberbooks
Escape Plus
The Green Trap
Gremlins Go Home
   (with Gordon R. Dickson)
Jupiter
The Kinsman Saga
Leviathans of Jupiter
Mars Life
Mercury
The Multiple Man
Orion
Orion Among the Stars
Orion and King Arthur
Orion and the Conqueror
Orion in the Dying Time
Out of Sun
Peacekeepers
Power Play

Powersat
The Precipice
Privateers
Prometheans
The Rock Rats
Saturn
The Silent War
Star Peace: Assured Survival
The Starcrossed
Tale of the Grand Tour
Test of Fire
Titan
To Fear the Light
   (with A. J. Austin)
To Save the Sun
   (with A. J. Austin)
The Trikon Deception
   (with Bill Pogue)
Triumph
Vengeance of Orion
Venus
Voyagers
Voyagers II: The Alien Within
Voyagers III: Star Brothers
The Return: Book IV of Voyagers
The Winds of Altair

NEW FRONTIERS

A COLLECTION OF TALES ABOUT
THE PAST, THE PRESENT, AND THE FUTURE

BEN BOVA

TOR®

A TOM DOHERTY ASSOCIATES BOOK
NEW YORK

NEW FRONTIERS

Copyright © 2014 by Ben Bova

A Tor Book
Published by Tom Doherty Associates, LLC
175 Fifth Avenue
New York, NY 10010

www.tor-forge.com

Tor® is a registered trademark of Tom Doherty Associates, LLC.

The Library of Congress Cataloging-in-Publication Data is available upon request.

ISBN 978-0-7653-7644-2 (hardcover)
ISBN 978-1-4668-5136-8 (e-book)

Tor books may be purchased for educational, business, or promotional use. For
information on bulk purchases, please contact Macmillan Corporate and Premium
Sales Department at 1-800-221-7945, extension 5442, or write specialmarkets@
macmillan.com.

First Edition: July 2014

Printed in the United States of America

0 9 8 7 6 5 4 3 2 1

TO DR. GREGORY BENFORD:

HONORED SCIENTIST, FELLOW AUTHOR,
AND TREASURED FRIEND

CONTENTS

NEW FRONTIERS

There's a frontier waiting for you, approximately one hundred miles from where you are at this instant.

It's the frontier of space, and it extends to infinity.

But space is only one of the many new frontiers that await us. There are frontiers of time, as well, and frontiers of courage and devotion, fear and hate.

Here are fourteen stories about new frontiers of space, time, and the human spirit.

The stories range from the Baghdad of the *Thousand and One Nights* to a spaceship heading for a distant star, from the newly liberated Paris near the end of World War II to a lonely vessel drifting in the vast emptiness of the Asteroid Belt. The stories are set on a golf course on the Moon, in the imperial court of an interstellar empire, in the simulations laboratory of a modern high-tech electronics firm.

The people in these stories include scoundrels and heroes, scientists and engineers, explorers and innovators, a teenaged Albert Einstein, a dying emperor, and a pope. Each of them stands at a new frontier and must find the heart and strength to cross into new, unexplored territory.

For human courage and passion are the common denominators of every story, no matter where or when in the universe the tale may be set.

So please enjoy your travels through these new frontiers of space, time, and the intricacies of human passions.

Bon voyage.

Ben Bova

Naples, Florida

2013

INTRODUCTION TO
"SAM BELOW PAR"

I am not a golfer. I'm a writer. Hardly any of the writers I know have the time to play golf. Writers *write*. They don't fritter away hour upon hour trying to knock a little white ball into a hole in the ground.

But once I fell in love with the ravishing Rashida, who is an ardent golfer, I perforce began to learn a few things about the game. And as I did, Sam Gunn came up and tapped me on my metaphysical shoulder.

"I want to build a golf course," Sam said to me. "On the Moon."

Sam is a scoundrel, of course. A skirt chaser. A man who can bend the rules into pretzels. A little guy, physically, Sam is always battling against the Big Guys: the corporate "suits," the government bureaucrats, the rich and powerful. Sam makes and loses fortunes the way you or I change socks. But he has a heart as big as the solar system, and despite his many enemies, he also has a legion of friends.

But a golf course on the Moon? I mean, the Moon is a new frontier, yes, but who would want to build a golf course on its airless, barren surface?

Who else but Sam Gunn?

Why would he want to build a golf course on the Moon?

Thereby hangs a tale. . . .

SAM BELOW PAR

"A GOLF COURSE?" I asked, incredulous. "Here on the Moon?"

"Yeah," said Sam Gunn. "Why not?"

"You mean . . . outside?"

"Why not?" he repeated.

"It's crazy, that's why not!" I said.

We were standing at the far end of Selene's Grand Plaza, gazing through the sweeping glassteel windows that looked out on the harsh beauty of Alphonsus Crater's dusty, pockmarked floor. Off to our left ran the worn, slumped mountains of the ringwall, smoothed by billions of years of micrometeors sanding them down. A little further, the abrupt slash of the horizon, uncomfortably close compared to Earth. Beyond that unforgiving line was the blackness of infinite space, blazing with billions of stars.

The Grand Plaza was the only open area of greenspace on the Moon, beneath a vaulted dome of lunar concrete. Trees, flowers, an outdoor bistro, even an Olympic-sized swimming pool with a thirty-meter-high diving platform. The Plaza was a delightful relief from Selene's gray tunnels and underground living and working areas.

"Why not build a course under a dome?" I asked. "That'd be a lot easier."

"You'd need an awful big dome," said Sam. "More than ten ki-lometers long."

"Yeah, but—"

"No dome. Outside, in the open."

"You can't play golf out there," I said, jabbing a finger toward the emptiness on the other side of the window.

Sam gave me that famous lopsided grin of his. "Sure you could. It'd be a big attraction."

"A golf course," I grumbled. "On the Moon. Out there in the middle of Alphonsus."

"Not there," Sam said. "Over at Hell Crater, where my enter-tainment center is."

"So this is why you brought me up here."

"That's why, Charlie," Sam replied, still grinning.

I had heard of Sam Gunn and his wild schemes for most of my life. He'd made more fortunes than the whole New York Stock Exchange, they say, and lost—or gave away—almost all of them. He was always working on a new angle, some new scheme aimed at making himself rich.

But a golf course? On the Moon? Outside on the airless, barren surface?

Sam is a stumpy little guy with a round, gap-toothed face that some have compared to a jack-o'-lantern. Wiry, rust-red thatch of hair. Freckles across his stub of a nose. Nobody seems to know how old he really is: different data banks give you different guesses. He has a reputation as a womanizer, and a chap who would cut corners or pick pockets or commit out-and-out fraud to make his schemes work. He was always battling the Big Boys: the corporate suits, government bureaucrats, the rich and pow-erful.

I was definitely not one of those. I once had designed some of the poshest golf courses on Earth, but now I was a disgraced fu-gitive from justice, hounded by lawyers, an ex-wife, two women who claimed I'd fathered their children (both claims untrue), and the Singapore police's morality squad. Sam had shown up in

Singapore one jump ahead of the cops and whisked me to Selene on his corporate rocket. S. Gunn Enterprises, Unlimited. I didn't ask why, I was just glad to get away.

I had spent the flight to Selene trying to explain to Sam that the charges against me were all false, all part of a scheme by my ex-wife, who just happened to be the daughter of the head of Singapore's government. Hell hath no fury like a woman scorned—or her mother.

Sam listened sympathetically to me during the whole flight.

"Your only crime," he said at last, "was marrying a woman who was wrong for you." Before I could think of a reply, Sam added, "Like most of them are, Charlie."

My family name happens to be Chang. To Sam, that meant my first name must be Charlie. From somebody else, I'd resent that as racism. But from Sam it was almost . . . well, kind of friendly.

As soon as we landed at Selene Sam bought me a pair of weighted boots, so I wouldn't trip all over myself in the low lunar gravity. Then he took me to lunch at the outdoor bistro in the middle of the Grand Plaza's carefully cultivated greenery.

"Your legal troubles are over, Charlie," Sam told me, "as long as you stay at Selene. No extradition agreement with Earthside governments."

"But I'm not a citizen of Selene," I objected.

His grin widening until he actually did look like a gap-toothed jack-o'-lantern, Sam blithely replied, "Doesn't matter. I got you a work permit and Selene's granted you a temporary visa."

I realized what Sam was telling me. I was safe on the Moon—as long as I worked for S. Gunn Enterprises, Unlimited.

After lunch Sam took me for a walk down the length of the Grand Plaza, through the lovingly tended begonias and azaleas and peonies along the winding paths that led to the windows. I walked very carefully; the weighted boots helped.

"We can do it, Charlie," Sam said as we stood at the glassteel windows.

"A golf course."

"It'll be terrific."

"Out there," I muttered, staring at the barren lunar ground. "A golf course."

"It's been done before," Sam said, fidgeting a little. "Alan Shepard whacked a golf ball during the Apollo 14 mission, over at Frau Mauro." He waved a hand roughly northwestward. "Hit it over the horizon, by damn."

"Sam," I corrected, "the ball only traveled a few yards."

"Whatever," said Sam, with that impish smirk of his.

I shook my head.

"Hey, there are unusual golf courses on Earth, you know," Sam said. "Like the old Hyatt Britannia in the Cayman Islands. I played that course! Blind shots, overwater shots—"

"They've got air to breathe," I said.

"Well, what about the Jade Dragon Snow Mountain Golf Club in Yunnan, China? Ten thousand feet high! You practically need an oxygen mask."

"But not a spacesuit."

"And the Legends Golf and Safari Resort in South Africa, with that nineteenth hole on top of that fifteen-hundred-foot mountain. The ball takes thirty seconds to drop down onto the green!"

"A par three," I murmured, remembering the course.

"I birdied it," Sam said gleefully.

If there's one thing Sam Gunn can do, it's talk. He wheedled, he coaxed, he weaved a web of words about how we would be bringing the joys of golf to this bleak and dreary world of the Moon. Plus lots of golf-playing tourists to his entertainment center.

Not once did he mention that if I didn't go to work for him I'd be forced to return to Singapore. He didn't have to.

SO, OF COURSE, I went to work for Sam. Had I known how shaky the company's finances were, I—well, to be perfectly truthful, I would've gone to work for Sam anyway. The man has a way about him. And there was that phalanx of police detectives and lawyers waiting for me back in Singapore. Plus an angry ex-wife and her angrier mother.

Sam had built what he euphemistically called an entertainment complex at Hell Crater, a couple of hundred kilometers south of Selene. The thirty-klick-wide crater was named after a nineteenth-century Austrian Jesuit priest who was an astronomer, Maximilian Hell, but in Sam's impish eyes it was an ideal spot for a lunar Sin City. He built a gambling casino, a dinner club called Dante's Inferno (staffed by Hell's Belles, no less), gaming arcades, virtual reality simulations, the works, all beneath a sturdy concrete dome that protected the interior from micrometeors and the harsh radiation streaming in from the Sun and stars.

Underground, Sam had built the first-class Paradise Hotel and shopping mall, plus an ultramodern medical facility that specialized in rejuvenation therapies.

Apparently Sam had financed the complex with money he had somehow crowbarred out of Rockledge Corporation; don't ask me how.

Anyway, his latest idea was to build a golf course out on the floor of Hell Crater, a new attraction to draw customers to the complex. As if gambling and high-class prostitution weren't enough.

"How do you get away with it?" I asked Sam my first night in Hell, as we sat for dinner in Dante's Inferno. The waitresses were knockouts, the entertainers dancing up on the stage were even more spectacular.

"Get away with what?" Sam asked, all freckle-faced innocence.

I waved a hand at the exotic dancers writhing on the stage. "Gambling. Women. I imagine there's a good deal of narcotics moving around here, too."

With a careless shrug, Sam told me, "All perfectly legal,

Charlie. At least, nobody's written any laws against it. This ain't Kansas, Toto. Or Singapore. The New Morality hasn't reached the Moon." Then he grinned and added, "Thank God!"

Truth to tell, I was temped by one of Hell's Belles, a gorgeous young blonde with the deep-bosomed body of a seductress and the wide, cornflower blue eyes of a *naif.* But I didn't act on my urges. Not then.

I got to work, instead.

Designing a golf course takes a combination of skills. The job is part landscape architecture, part golfing know-how, part artistry.

The first thing I did was wriggle into a spacesuit and walk the ground where the course was to be laid out. The floor of Hell Crater was pretty flat, but when I examined the area closely, I found that the ground undulated ever so slightly, sort of like the surface of a rippling pond that's been frozen solid. Good, I thought: this would present some interesting lies and challenges for putting.

There were plenty of challenges for me, let me tell you. The Moon's gravity is only one sixth of Earth's, and the surface is airless, both of which mean that a golf ball should fly much farther when hit than it would on Earth. But how much farther? Sam provided physicists and engineers from the faculty of Selene University to work with me as consultants.

The key to the distance factor, we soon found, was the spacesuits that the golfers would have to wear. When Alan Shepard hit his golf ball, back in the old Apollo days, he had to swing with only one arm. His spacesuit was too stiff for him to use both arms. Spacesuit designs had improved considerably over the past century, but they still tended to stiffen up when you pressurized them with air.

Then there was the problem of the Moon's surface itself. The whole darned place was one big sand trap. Walking on the Moon is like walking on a beach on Earth. Sandy. For eons dust-mote-sized micrometeors have been falling out of the sky, hitting the ground and churning its topmost layer into the consistency of beach sand.

I tried some putting tests. I tapped a golf ball. It rolled a few centimeters and stopped dead. I nudged it harder, but it didn't go more than about a meter.

"We'll have to smooth out the ground, Sam," I said. "The greens, the areas around the cups. So the players can make some reasonable putts."

"Okay," he answered cheerfully. "Plasma torches ought to do the job."

"Plasma torches?"

"Yep. They'll bake the ground to a nice, firm consistency."

I nodded.

"And once you've got it the way you want it, paint the areas green," Sam said.

I laughed. "Not a bad idea."

There was another angle to the distance problem. The greens had to be so far from the tees that some of the cups were over the damned short horizon. You wouldn't be able to see the pin when you were teeing up.

Sam solved that one in the blink of an eye. "Make the pins tall enough to be seen from the tees, that's all. Put lights on their tops so they're easily visible."

I nodded sheepishly. I should have thought of that myself.

The ground was also littered with lots of rocks and pock-marked with little craterlets and even sinuous cracks in the ground that the scientists called rilles. More than once I tripped on a stone and went sprawling. I found, though, that in the Moon's gentle gravity I tumbled so slowly that I could put out my arms, brake my fall, and push myself back up to a standing position.

Cool. I could be an Olympic gymnast, on the Moon.

But I had to tell Sam, "We'll have to clear away a lot of those rocks and maybe fill in the rilles and craterlets."

He scowled at me. "Golf courses have roughs, Charlie. Our

course will be Hell for them." Then he broke into a grin and added, "At least we won't have any trees or deep grass."

"Sam, if we make it too rough, people won't play. It'll be too tough for them."

He just shrugged and told me to figure it out. "Don't make it too easy for them. I want the world's best golfers to come here and be challenged."

I nodded and thought that trying to play golf in a spacesuit would be challenge enough, with or without the rough.

I didn't realize that when Sam said he wanted to invite the world's best golfers to Hell, he intended to include the woman who wrecked my life. The woman I loved.

HER NAME WAS Mai Pohan. We had known each other since kindergarten, back in Singapore. She was a slim, serious slip of a young woman, as graceful and beautiful as an orchid. But with the heart and strength of a lioness. Small though she was, Mai Pohan became a champion golfer, a world-renowned athlete. To me, though, she was simply the most beautiful woman in the world. Lovely almond-shaped eyes so deeply brown I could get lost in them. And I did.

But then my parents exploded all my dreams by announcing they had arranged for me to marry the daughter of Singapore's prime minister, who was known in the newsnets as "the dragon lady." And worse. I was flabbergasted.

"This is a great honor for our family," my father said proudly. He didn't know that I was hopelessly in love with Mai Pohan; no one knew, not even she.

For a designer of golf courses—a kind of civil engineer, nothing more—to be allied to the ruling family of Singapore was indeed a great honor. But it broke my heart.

I tried to phone Mai Pohan, but she was off on an international golf tour. With misty eyes, I e-mailed her the terrible news. She never answered.

Like a dutiful son, I went through the formalities of courtship and the wedding, which was Singapore's social event of the year. My bride was quite beautiful and, as I discovered on our wedding night, much more knowledgeable about making love than I was.

Through my mother-in-law's connections, I received many new contracts to design golf courses. I would be wealthy in my own right within a few years. I began to travel the world, while my wife entertained herself back in Singapore with a succession of lovers—all carefully hidden from the public's view by her mother's power.

It was in the United States, at the venerable Pebble Beach golf course in California, that I saw Mai Pohan once again. She was leading in a tournament there by three strokes as her foursome approached the beautiful eighteenth hole, where the blue Pacific Ocean caresses the curving beach.

I stood among the crowd of onlookers as the four women walked to the green. I said nothing, but I saw Mai's eyes widen when she recognized me. She smiled, and my heart melted.

She barely won the tournament, three-putting the final hole. The crowd applauded politely and I repaired to the nearby bar. I rarely drank alcohol, but I sat at the bar and ordered a scotch. I don't know how much time passed or how many drinks I consumed, but all of a sudden Mai sat herself primly on the stool next to mine.

My jaw dropped open, but she gave me a rueful smile and said, "You almost cost me the tournament, Chou."

"I did?" I squeaked.

"Once I saw you I lost all my concentration."

"I . . . I'm sorry."

She ordered a club soda from the man-sized robot tending the bar while I sat beside her in stunned silence.

"It's been a long time," she said, once her drink arrived.

"Yes."

"How is married life?"

"Miserable."

Those fathomless eyes of hers widened a bit, then she smiled sadly. "I'm almost glad."

I heard myself blurt, "You're the one I love, Mai. My family arranged the marriage. I had to go through with it."

"I know," she said. "I understand."

"I love you." It seemed inane, pointless—cruel, almost—but I said it.

Very softly, so low that I barely heard her, Mai replied, "I love you too. I always have."

I kissed her. Right there at the bar. I leaned over and kissed her on the lips. The first and last time we ever kissed.

Mai said, "Like it or not, you're a married man."

"And you . . . ?"

"I could never marry anyone else." There were tears in her eyes.

That was my encounter with Mai Pohan. That was all there was to it. But we must have been observed, probably by one of the paparazzi following the golf tournament. By the time I got back to Singapore my wife was raging like a forest fire and her mother was hiring women to testify in court that I had fathered their illegitimate children. The police produced DNA evidence, faked of course, but my defense attorney didn't dare to challenge it.

My parents disowned me. My contracts for new golf courses disappeared. I was alone, friendless, on my way to jail, when Sam whisked me to the Moon.

Four hundred thousand kilometers away from Mai Pohan.

And now she was coming to Hell Crater!

AS SOON AS I saw her name on the list of pros coming for the First Lunar Golf Invitational, I rushed to Sam's office.

For the head of a major corporation, Sam had chosen an office that was far from imposing. Modest, even. He wasted no money on the trappings of power. The office was merely a small room in the complex that housed Dante's Inferno on one side and the virtual reality simulations center on the other.

Sam's office did feature one concession to his ego, though. His desk was raised slightly on a cleverly disguised platform. And the chairs before the desk were shortened, their legs sawed down a few centimeters. Sitting in front of him, you had to look up at Sam, while he looked down at you. I heard years later that Sam had picked up that trick from reading about Joseph Stalin, the dictator of the Soviet Union. Sam did a lot of reading about powerful men who were short: Napoleon, Stalin, Alexander Hamilton.

"Sam," I exclaimed as I burst into his office, "you've invited Mai Pohan!"

Looking mildly surprised, Sam replied, "Sure. She's one of the top golfers on the international tour."

Before I could begin to thank him, Sam added, "And she's the best-looking woman in the bunch of 'em." He broke into a leering grin.

Sam's reputation as a woman-chaser was well known. Behind his desk I could see a panoply of photographs of Sam with spectacularly beautiful women, sometimes two or even three of them hanging on him. Most of them were very scantily clad.

"She's young, beautiful, unattached," Sam went on, his leer widening. "I intend to show her the wonders of lunar living."

At that instant I began to hate Sam Gunn.

I THREW MYSELF into building the golf course, while Sam spent most of his time arranging transportation and accommodations for the invited golfers. I've got to admit that a good many tourists did sign up to come to Hell for the tournament; Sam's judgment about its attraction was squarely on the mark.

Once I mapped out the course, the actual construction didn't take very long. I directed a team of human and robot workers who smoothed the greens areas and fairways (and painted them), removed a good deal of the rocks and pebbles that were strewn everywhere, rearranged some of the bigger boulders so they presented strategic problems for the golfers, and leveled off the tee boxes.

It turned out the greens were now too smooth, too fast. Tap a ball and it rolled right across the green and into the deep sand of the rough. So we had to spread a thin layer of sand over them. And spray-paint it green.

We painted the golf balls too, a brilliant Day-Glo orange, so they could be seen against the gray lunar sand of the tees and the rough.

Finally we planted the tall lighted poles at the holes, so the players could see where they should aim their shots.

Sam was buzzing about like a mosquito on amphetamines, meeting and greeting the invited golfers as they arrived on the Moon. They flew from Earth to Selene, of course, and stayed at the Paradise Hotel (all expenses paid by S. Gunn Enterprises, Unlimited) until the entire fifty professionals—plus their families and/or friends—had arrived. Then they were whisked to Hell Crater on a special passage of the elevated tram line that connected Selene to Hell.

I wondered how Sam could possibly afford all this largesse, but when I asked him about it he simply shrugged and said, "You've got to spend money to make money. Prime rule of business, Charlie."

I made it my prime business to be at the tram depot when the pros arrived on their special train. Sam was there too, of course, eager as a tail-wagging puppy, leading a small army of guides, robot porters, and news reporters. He had even brought the band from Dante's Inferno to provide lively music.

Sam seemed surprised to see me there, in the midst of all the flunkies.

"Shouldn't you be rearranging rocks or something?" he asked, over the noise of the milling assistants and the band.

"All done, Sam," I shouted into his ear. "The course is ready for action."

He broke into that leering smile of his. "So am I, Charlie."

The tram glided into the depot, the airlock hatch closed behind it, and the band broke into a raucus welcoming rendition of "Happy Days Are Here Again." Golfers of all sizes and shapes came pouring out of the tram, together with assorted family members, friends, and hangers-on. I began to worry that I wouldn't be able to see tiny Mai Pohan in the crowd.

But there she was! She looked like a little waif, standing alone in the swirl of people, like a delicate flower in the midst of a storm.

I pushed through the bodies toward her, but Sam was faster. He grabbed her by the arm and led her to one of the carts that were lined up to take his guests to the Paradise Hotel below the entertainment complex. In all the noise and bustle, Mai didn't see me. Sam was jabbering in her ear nonstop, and she looked pleased that Sam Gunn himself was escorting her.

He seated her in the cart, then climbed up onto its roof and bellowed, "Welcome to the First Lunar Golf Invitational! I want you all to enjoy yourselves."

I stood there, hopelessly hemmed in by the surging crowd, as Sam clambered down to sit beside Mai. They headed off for the hotel, leaving me standing there, alone in the midst of the throng.

FOR A SOLID week I tried to see Mai alone, but she was either playing practice rounds or in Sam's company. We had dinner together a couple of times, but always with Sam and a bunch of other golfers.

"It's a very interesting course," Mai said to me, from across the dinner table. Sam sat at its head, with Mai on his right. Six others were at the table, all internationally-known golfers.

"I got the best designer in the business," Sam said proudly.

The man on my left, a burly, ruddy-faced South African, Rufus Kleindienst, complained, "Hitting the ball over the horizon is a bit weird. Why'd you make the course so bloody big?"

"We're on the Moon," Sam answered. "Lower gravity, no air resistance."

"Yes, but you could have just made the balls heavier to compensate for that. Hitting the ball over the horizon is wacko."

I agreed with him, but one of the other pros, Suddartha Ramjanmyan, a rake-thin Indian, spoke up: "You are a very long hitter, after all. Now the rest of us have a chance to match you."

Rufus grinned good-naturedly.

But one of the Yanks, a youthful-looking sandy blond sitting down at the end of the table, piped up. "What I don't understand is why you've made this a mixed tournament. Why not a men's tournament and a separate one for women? That's the normal way."

Sam explained, "We've got to hustle things along a little. The Sun sets in ten days. That gives us a week for practice and getting accustomed to the course, and three days for the tournament. After that we'll have two solid weeks of night."

"Two weeks of night?" The Yank was totally surprised. He might have been a champion golfer, but he hadn't bothered to learn the first thing about conditions on the Moon.

"Two weeks," Sam repeated solemnly. "Starlight's pretty bright, but I think you'll prefer playing in the daytime."

The Yank nodded weakly.

AS I EXPECTED, the big problem was the spacesuits. There were three basic types. The standard issue had a hard-shell torso of cermet, with fabric sleeves and leggings and accordion-pleated joints at the elbows, knees, and wrists. A newer variation kept the cermet torso, but its sleeves and legs were made of a reasonably flexible plastic. Then there was the exoskeleton, its fabric arms and legs covered with high-strength carbon fiber rods that were powered by tiny servomotors, slaved to the wearer's body movements. This increased the wearer's natural strength and made the suit feel more flexible.

While the exoskeleton allowed the most flexibility, it was twice the weight of the others, which made it cumbersome, even in the light lunar gravity. And it took an hour or more to put on. And take off.

For four days the golfers tried on different suits, clomping around in their heavy boots, whacking away at golf balls out on the driving range. Most of them eventually went for the exoskeleton, although a handful opted for the standard suit. Nobody wanted the plastic job.

When I saw Mai in the smallest exoskeleton that was available, she looked like a little child being swallowed alive by some alien metal monster.

Try as I might to get some time with her alone, Mai was constantly working out on the course or otherwise in the company of her fellow golfers. In the evenings, she was either with the golf pros or with Sam. Or both. She ignored my calls and my messages.

Finally I decided to face her, once and for all. On the night before the tournament was to begin, I planted myself in the surveillance center and watched for Mai on the dozens of display screens lining the walls of the chamber. Two security technicians monitored the screens, which showed every public space and corridor in the complex.

I watched Mai at a dinner table in Dante's Inferno, sitting with Sam and a quartet of other golfers, two of them women. Sam was chattering away, as usual, and Mai seemed to be entranced by whatever he was talking about. Her eyes hardly left his face, even for a moment. I would have gladly strangled him.

At last they finished their desserts and coffees and got up from the table. Sam took Mai's arm—and she let him do it. He escorted her out of Dante's, along the corridor that led to the elevators, and then down to the level of the Paradise Hotel.

I didn't realize how tense I was until one of the security techs complained, "Hey, look at what you did to my pen!"

I had unconsciously picked up her pen off her desktop and bent it into a horseshoe shape.

As I muttered an apology and promised to buy her a new one, I watched Mai and Sam make their way down the hotel's main corridor. They stopped at her door.

I had to admit to myself that they made a well-matched couple. Mai was just a centimeter or so shorter than Sam, and exquisitely beautiful. Sam was far from handsome, but he radiated a vital energy, even in the security camera's display screen.

My heart was in my throat as Sam began to slip his arms around Mai's waist. But she artfully disengaged, gave him a peck on the cheek, and slipped into her room, leaving Sam standing alone in the corridor, looking nonplussed.

I let out a yelp that made both the security techs jump, then raced for the door, the elevator, and Mai's hotel room.

By the time I got to her door Sam was long gone, of course. I tapped lightly. No response. I rapped a little harder, and Mai's muffled voice came through: "Sam, I need my rest. Please go away."

"It's not Sam," I said, smiling happily. "It's me."

"Chou?"

"Yes!"

For a moment nothing happened, then the door slid back and Mai was standing there in a silk robe decorated with flowers and birds. She looked up at me, her face serious, almost gloomy.

"Hello," she said, sadly.

"Mai, I had to see you. Why haven't you answered my calls? Why are you spending all your time—"

She put a finger on my lips, silencing me.

"Our last meeting was a disaster, Chou. I ruined your life."

"Ruined?" I was truly shocked. "You *saved* my life, Mai!"

"I thought they were going to put you in jail."

"They would have, if it weren't for Sam."

"You owe him a lot."

That's when it hit me. Mai was being nice to Sam because she was grateful for what he did for me!

"Sam's getting his money's worth out of me," I growled. "I don't want you to let him include you in the payment."

Now she looked shocked. "I would never—"

I didn't let her finish her sentence. I took her in my arms and kissed her. A couple strolling up the corridor passed by and chuckled softly.

"We've been seen again," Mai said, a little ruefully.

"I don't care. I'm a free man now."

"As long as you stay on the Moon."

"Well, yes," I had to admit.

"So we'll always be half a million kilometers apart."

"Four hundred thousand," I corrected, inanely. "But it doesn't have to always be that way. Once my divorce becomes final, maybe I'll be able to return to Earth."

Mai said nothing.

"Or maybe you could stay here, on the Moon. We'll get married and . . . and . . ."

"And I'll give up my career? Become a housewife? And what are you going to do, now that you've built Sam's golf course? Do you think there are others who'd want you to build courses for them here on the Moon?"

I shook my head, crestfallen.

She touched my cheek with her fingertips.

"I love you, Mai," I whispered.

"I love you, too," she said. "But I don't see how it could possibly work out."

Neither could I.

"You'd better go," she said.

I couldn't move.

"The tournament starts tomorrow, Chou. You're bad for my concentration."

"I know. I'm sorry."

But then she smiled and took my hand and led me into her room and neither one of us gave a thought to her concentration or our future.

THE TOURNAMENT STARTED the next morning. Mai hopped out of bed and headed for the shower. I thought about joining her there, but I decided it would be better if I just stole away. Which is what I did, feeling miserable every step of the way.

Love is strange. Powerful. But sometimes so painful it tears the heart out of your chest.

I had nothing to do. My work was finished. So I went to my quarters, cleaned up, got into fresh coveralls, and made my way to the spacious lobby of Dante's Inferno, which Sam's people had turned into a sort of auditorium, with comfortable seats filling the floor and enormous video screens hanging on every wall.

The place was already full of eager onlookers, while a team of Hell's Belles (looking a little bleary this early in the morning) circulated through the crowd with trays of drinks and snacks.

To my surprise, Sam's name was at the top of the list of entrants. Several of the spectators noticed it, too.

"That Sam," a silver-haired, dark-skinned man chuckled, "he'll do anything to put himself in the limelight."

One of the better-looking women said, "Well, it's his tournament, after all."

Sam had detailed one of his publicity aides to go out to the first tee and introduce the competitors. And there was a flock of sports reporters there, too, waiting for the golfers to come out.

One by one they stepped through the airlock and out onto the barren, airless floor of Hell Crater. Most of them wore exoskeletons, which made them look like ponderous, clanking robots. As each one reached the first tee the reporters huddled around him or her and asked the same tired old questions:

"How do you feel about playing golf on the Moon?"

"Will your spacesuit hamper your playing?"

"What do you think your chances of winning are?"

And then Sam came waltzing through the airlock and out onto the floor of Hell Crater. We all gasped with surprise. He was wearing nothing more over his coveralls than what looked like a transparent plastic raincoat.

It had leggings and booties that covered his shoes, and gloves so thin I could see the veins on the backs of Sam's hands. His head was encased in a transparent bubble of a helmet, his red thatch of buzz-cut hair clearly visible through it. The spacesuit looked impossibly flimsy.

The news team that was interviewing each golfer clustered around Sam like a pack of hounds surrounding a fox, firing questions about his spacesuit.

"Nanofabric," Sam exclaimed, the crooked grin on his face spreading from ear to ear.

Before the news people could take a breath, Sam explained, "The suit was built by nanomachines, from the nanolab at Selene. Dr. Kristine Cardenas is the lab's director, you know. She won the Nobel Prize for her work on nanotechnology."

"But . . . but it's so . . . *light*," one of the newswomen gushed, from inside her standard hard-shell spacesuit. "How can it possibly protect you?"

"How come it doesn't stiffen up, like regular suits?" asked another.

"How can it protect you against the radiation?"

"How can it be so flexible?"

Sam laughed and raised both his nanogloved hands to quiet their questions. "You'll have to ask Dr. Cardenas about the technical details. All I can tell you is that the suit gives as much protection as a standard suit, but it's a lot more flexible. And easier to put on and take off, lemme tell you. Like old-fashioned pajamas."

The other golfers, in their standard suits or exoskeletons, hung around the edge of the crowd uneasily. None of them liked being upstaged.

Mai hadn't appeared yet, and I began to wonder if something was wrong. Then she came through the airlock, wearing a nano-suit, just like Sam.

"No!" I bellowed, startling the tourists sitting around me. I bolted from my chair and ran to the airlock.

There was a team of beefy security guards at the airlock hatch, in dark gray uniforms. They wouldn't let me take a suit and go outside.

"Only players and the reporters," their leader told me. "Mr. Gunn's orders."

Feeling desperate, I raced to the communications center, down the corridor from the airlock area. It was a small chamber, studded with display screens and staffed by two men and two women. They didn't want to let me talk to Mai, or Sam, or anybody else out there on the golf course.

"Mr. Gunn's orders," they said.

"To hell with Sam's orders," I roared at them. "This is a safety issue. Lives are at stake!"

They told me to call the safety office and even offered me a spare console to sit at. I scanned the available comm channels and put my call through. To Mai.

Before the technicians realized what I'd done, Mai's face came up on the central screen of my console. She smiled at me.

"You left without saying good-bye," she chided gently.

"Get back inside!" I fairly screamed. "If Sam wants to kill himself that's his business, but I won't let him kill you!"

Mai's face went stern. "Chou, do you think I'm an idiot? This suit is perfectly safe."

"That may be what Sam says, but—"

"That's what Dr. Cardenas says," Mai interrupted. "I've spoken with her for hours about the suit. It's been tested at Selene for months. It's fine."

"How can it be?" I was nearly hysterical with fear. "It's nothing but a thin layer of transparent fabric."

"Ask Dr. Cardenas," said Mai. "I've got a golf game to play."

She cut the connection. My screen went blank.

Still sitting at the console, with all four of the comm techs staring at me, I put in a call to Dr. Kristine Cardenas, at the nano-technology laboratory in Selene.

All her lines were busy. News reporters were besieging her about the nanosuit.

I sank back in the console's little wheeled chair, terrified that Mai would die of asphyxiation or radiation poisoning or decompression out there in that flimsy suit. Insanely, I felt a grim satisfaction that if Mai died, Sam probably would too.

Numbly I pushed the chair back and began to get up on wobbly legs.

One of the technicians, a youngish woman, said to me, "You can watch the tournament from here, if you like."

I sank back onto the chair.

One of the male techs added, "If you can sit quietly and keep your mouth shut."

That's what I did. Almost.

IT WAS A weird golf game.

Sam was nothing more than a duffer, yet he was holding his own against some of the best players on Earth.

Encased in an exoskeleton suit, Rufus, the muscular South African, literally scorched his drives out of sight. In the light lunar gravity, the Day-Glo orange balls rose in dreamy slow motion, arced lazily across the starry sky, and sailed gently toward the ground, disappearing over the short horizon.

He was overdriving, slamming the ball beyond the green, into the deep treacherous sand. Then he'd flail away, blasting explosions of sand that slowly settled back to the ground while his ball zoomed into another area of deep sand. When he finally got his ball on the green his putting was miserable.

The more bogeys he got, the harder he powered his drives and the more erratic his putts. In the display screen of the console I was watching I could see his face getting redder and redder, even through the tinted visor of his helmet. And his exoskeleton suit seemed to be getting stiffer, more difficult to move in. Probably sand from his desperate flailings was grinding the suit's joints.

Sam just took it easy. His drives were erratic, a slice here, a hook there. It took him two or three shots to get on the green, but once there, his putts were fantastic. He sank putts of twenty, even thirty meters. It was as if the ball was being pulled to the cup by some invisible force.

Mai was doing well, also. Her drives were accurate, even though nowhere near long enough to reach the greens. But she always landed cleanly on the fairway and chipped beautifully. She putted almost as well as Sam and kept pace with the leaders.

Both Mai and Sam seemed able to swing much more freely in their nanosuits. Where the other golfers were stiff with their drives and chips, Mai and Sam looked loose and agile. If they'd been bigger, and able to drive the ball farther, they would have led the pack easily.

But my course was really tough on all of them. By the time they reached the last tee, only three of the golfers had broken par. Sam had birdied the last three holes, all par fives, but he was still one above par. The skinny little Indian, Ramjanmyan, was leading at three below.

And Mai was right behind him, at two below.

The eighteenth was the toughest hole on the course, a par six, where the cup was nearly a full kilometer from the tee and hidden behind a slight rise of solid gray rock slanting across the green-painted ground.

Mai stood at the tee, looking toward the lighted pole poking up above the crest of the rocky ridge, her driver in her gloved hands. She took a couple of practice swings, loose and easy, then hit the drive of her life. The ball went straight down the fairway, bounced a couple of dozen meters short of the green, hopped over the ridge, and rolled to a stop a bare ten centimeters from the cup.

"Wow!" yelled the comm techs, rising to their feet. I could even hear the roar of the crowd all the way over in Dante's lobby.

Sam was next. His drive was long enough to reach the green, all right, but he sliced it badly and the ball thunked down in the deep sand off the edge of the green, almost at the red-painted hazard line.

Groans of disappointment.

"That's it for the boss," said one of the techs.

Somehow I found myself thinking, Don't be so sure about that.

Ramjanmyan's drive almost cleared the ridge. But only almost. It hit the edge of the rock and bounced high, then fell in that dreamlike lunar slow motion and rolled back almost to the tee. Even in his exoskeleton suit, the Indian seemed to slump like a defeated man.

He was still one stroke ahead of Mai, though, and two strokes in front of his next closest competitor, a lantern-jawed Australian named MacTavish.

But MacTavish overdrove his ball, trying to clear that ridge, and it rolled past the cup to a stop at the edge of the deep sand.

Mai putted carefully, but her ball hit a minuscule pebble at the last instant and veered a bare few centimeters from the cup. She tapped it in, and came away with a double eagle. She now was leading at five below par.

Sam had trudged out to the sand, where his ball lay. He needed to chip it onto the green and then putt it into the hole. Barely bothering to line up his shot, he whacked it out of the sand. The ball bounced onto the green and then rolled and rolled, curving this way and that like a scurrying ant looking for a breadcrumb, until it rolled to the lip of the cup and dropped in.

Pandemonium. All of us in the comm center sprang to our feet, hands raised high, and bellowed joyfully. The crowd in Dante's lobby roared so hard it registered on the seismograph over in Selene.

Sam was now three below par and so happy about it that he

was hopping up and down, dancing across the green, swinging his club over his head gleefully.

Ramjanmyan wasn't finished, though. He lofted his ball high over the ridge. It seemed to sail up there among the stars for an hour before it plopped onto the middle of the green and rolled to the very lip of the cup. There it stopped. We all groaned in sympathy for him.

But the Indian plodded in his exoskeleton suit to the cup and tapped the ball. His final score was six below par.

The only way for MacTavish to beat him would be for him to chip the ball directly into the cup. The Aussie tried, but his chip was too hard, and the ball rolled a good ten meters past the hole. He ended with a score of four below par.

Ramjanmyan won the tournament at six below par. Mai came in second, five below, and Sam surprised us all with a three below par score, putting him in fourth place.

EVERYONE CELEBRATED FAR into the night: golfers, tourists, staffers, and all. Sam reveled the hardest, dancing wildly with every woman in Dante's Inferno while the band banged out throbbing, wailing neodisco numbers.

I danced with Mai, no one else. And she danced only with me. It was well past midnight when the party started to break up. Mai and I walked back to her hotel room, tired but very, very happy.

Until I thought about what tomorrow would bring. Mai would leave to return to Earth. I'd be an unemployed golf course architect stranded on the Moon.

"You're awfully quiet," Mai said as we stepped into her room.

"You'll be leaving tomorrow," I said.

"I'll get the best lawyers on Earth," she said as she slid her arms around my neck. "Earth's a big place. Your ex-wife can't harass you anywhere except Singapore."

I shook my head. "Don't be so sure. Her mother has an awful lot of clout."

"We'll find a place . . ."

"And spend the rest of our lives looking over our shoulders? That's not what I want for you, Mai."

She kissed me lightly, just brushing her lips on mine. "Sufficient for the day are the evils thereof."

"Huh?"

Mai smiled at me. "Let's worry about things tomorrow. We're here together tonight."

So I tried to forget about my troubles. I even succeeded—for a while.

I WAS AWAKENED by the phone's buzzing. I cracked one eye open and saw that Mai was sleeping soundly, peacefully curled up beside me.

"Audio only," I told the phone.

Sam's freckled face sprang up on the phone's screen, grinning lopsidedly.

"Mai, I've got the medical reports here," he began.

"Quiet," I whispered urgently. "Mai's still asleep."

"Charlie?" Sam lowered his voice a notch. "So that's where you are. I called you at your place. We've gotta talk about financial arrangements."

Severance pay, I knew.

"Come over to my office around eleven thirty. Then we'll go to lunch."

"Mai's flight—"

"Plenty of time for that. My office. Eleven thirty. Both of you."

They say that today is the first day of the rest of your life. I went through the morning like a man facing a firing squad. The rest of my life, I knew, was going to be miserable and lonely. Mai seemed sad, too. Her usual cheerful smile was nowhere in sight.

We got to Sam's office precisely at eleven thirty and settled glumly onto the sawed-off chairs in front of his desk. Sam beamed

down at us like he hadn't a care in the world. Or two worlds, for
that matter.

"First," he began, "the radiation badges we all wore show that
the nanosuits protected us just as well as the standard suits protected everybody else."

"Dr. Cardenas will be pleased," Mai said listlessly.

"You bet she is," Sam replied. "We're having dinner together
over at Selene this evening."

Dr. Cardenas was a handsome woman, from what I'd heard of
her. Was Sam on the hunt again? Does a parrot have feathers?

"Okay," he said, rubbing his hands together briskly, "now let's
get down to business."

The firing squad was aiming at me.

"Charlie, you don't have much experience in business administration, do you?"

Puzzled by his question, I answered, "Hardly any."

"That's okay. I can tell you everything you need to know."

"Need to know for what?"

Sam looked surprised. "To manage the golf course, naturally."

"Manage it?" My voice squeaked two octaves higher than normal.

"Sure, what else? I'll be too busy to do it myself."

Mai gripped my arm. "That's wonderful!"

"And you, oh beauteous one, will be our pro, of course." Sam
announced, chuckling at his little pun.

"Me?"

Nodding, Sam replied, "Sure, you. This way the two of you can
stay together. Sort of a wedding present." Then he fixed me with
a stern gaze. "You do intend to marry the lady, don't you?"

I blurted, "If she'll have me!"

Mai squeezed my hand so hard I thought bones would break. I
hadn't realized how strong playing golf had made her.

"Okay, that's it," Sam said happily. "You'll manage the course,
Charlie, and Mai, you'll be the pro."

"And what will you do, Sam?" Mai asked.

"Me? I've got to set up the company that'll manufacture and sell nanosuits. Kris Cardenas is going to be my partner."

I felt my jaw drop open. "You mean this whole tournament was just a way of advertising the nanosuits?"

With a laugh, Sam answered, "Got a lot of publicity for the suits, didn't it? I'm already getting queries from the rock rats, out in the Asteroid Belt. And the university consortium that's running the Mars exploration team."

I shook my head in admiration for the man. Sam just sat there grinning down at us. The little devil had opened up a new sport for lunar residents and tourists, solved my legal problem, created a career for me, and found a way for Mai and me to marry. Plus, he was starting a new industry that would revolutionize the spacesuit business.

Before I could find words to thank Sam, Mai asked him, "Will you answer a question for me?"

"Sure," he said breezily. "Fire away."

"How did you learn to putt like that, Sam? Some of your putts were nothing short of miraculous."

Sam pursed his lips, looked up at the ceiling, swiveled back and forth on his chair.

"Come on, Sam," Mai insisted. "The truth. It won't go farther than these four walls."

With a crooked, crafty grin, Sam replied, "You'd be surprised at how much electronics you can pack into a golf ball."

"Electronics?" I gasped.

"A transmitter in the cups and a receiver in the ball," Mai said. "Your putts were guided into the cups."

"Sort of," Sam admitted.

"That's cheating!" I exclaimed.

"There's nothing in the rules against it."

That's Sam. As far as he's concerned, rules are made to bend into pretzels. And looking up at his grinning, freckled face, I just knew he was already thinking about some new scheme. That's Sam Gunn. Unlimited.

INTRODUCTION TO
"A COUNTRY FOR OLD MEN"

You know you're getting old when you start receiving lifetime achievement awards. That's been happening to me with increasing frequency lately, so I know something of how Alexander Alexandrovich Ignatiev feels.

Heading for a new frontier, six light-years from Earth, Ignatiev is an old man in the midst of youngsters. "Old" and "young" are relative terms here, for in this tale biomedical advancements have lengthened the human lifespan considerably.

Still, Ignatiev feels old, useless, bitterly unhappy with his one-way trip to a distant star. He has a different frontier to explore, his own inner strength and determination, his own inner desire to feel useful, admired, even loved.

A COUNTRY FOR OLD MEN

1

"IT'S OBVIOUS!" SAID Vartan Gregorian, standing imperiously before the two others seated on the couch. "I'm the best damned pilot in the history of the human race!"

Planting his fists on his hips, he struck a pose that was nothing less than preening.

Half buried in the lounge's plush curved couch, Alexander Ignatiev bit back an impulse to laugh in the Armenian's face. But Nikki Deneuve, sitting next to him, gazed up at Gregorian with shining eyes.

Breaking into a broad grin, Gregorian went on, "This bucket is moving faster than any ship ever built, no? We've flown farther from Earth than anybody ever has, true?"

Nikki nodded eagerly as she responded, "Twenty percent of lightspeed and approaching six light-years."

"So, I'm the pilot of the fastest, highest-flying ship of all time!" Gregorian exclaimed. "That makes me the best flier in the history of the human race. QED!"

Ignatiev shook his head at the conceited oaf. But he saw that Nikki was captivated by his posturing. Then it struck him. She loves him! And Gregorian is showing off for her.

The ship's lounge was as relaxing and comfortable as human

designers back on Earth could make it. It was arranged in a circular grouping of sumptuously appointed niches, each holding high, curved banquettes that could seat up to half a dozen close friends in reasonable privacy.

Ignatiev had left his quarters after suffering still another defeat at the hands of the computerized chess program and snuck down to the lounge in midafternoon, hoping to find it empty. He needed a hideaway while the housekeeping robots cleaned his suite. Their busy, buzzing thoroughness drove him to distraction; it was impossible to concentrate on chess or anything else while the machines were dusting, laundering, straightening his rooms, restocking his autokitchen and his bar, making the bed with crisply fresh linens.

So he sought refuge in the lounge, only to find Gregorian and Deneuve already there, in a niche beneath a display screen that showed the star fields outside. Once the sight of those stars scattered across the infinite void would have stirred Ignatiev's heart. But not anymore, not since Sonya died.

Sipping at the vodka that the serving robot had poured for him the instant he had stepped into the lounge, thanks to its face recognition program, Ignatiev couldn't help grousing, "And who says you are the pilot, Vartan? I didn't see any designation for pilot in the mission's assignment roster."

Gregorian was moderately handsome and rather tall, quite slim, with thick dark hair and laugh crinkles at the corners of his dark brown eyes. Ignatiev tended to think of people in terms of chess pieces, and he counted Gregorian as a prancing horse, all style and little substance.

"I am flight systems engineer, no?" Gregorian countered. "My assignment is to monitor the flight control program. That makes me the pilot."

Nikki, still beaming at him, said, "If you're the pilot, Vartan, then I must be the navigator."

"Astrogator," Ignatiev corrected bluntly.

The daughter of a Quebecoise mother and French Moroccan

father, Nicolette Deneuve had unfortunately inherited her father's
stocky physique and her mother's sharp nose. Ignatiev thought
her unlovely—and yet there was a charm to her, a *gamine*-like
wide-eyed innocence that beguiled Ignatiev's crusty old heart.
She was a physicist, bright and conscientious, not an engineering
monkey like the braggart Gregorian. Thus it was a tragedy that
she had been selected for this star mission.

She finally turned away from Gregorian to say to Ignatiev, "It's
good to see you, Dr. Ignatiev. You've become something of a
hermit these past few months."

He coughed and muttered, "I've been busy on my research."
The truth was he couldn't bear to be among these youngsters,
couldn't stand the truth that they would one day return to Earth
while he would be long dead.

Alexander Alexandrovich Ignatiev, by far the oldest man
among the starship's crew, thought that Nikki could have been
the daughter he'd never had. Daughter? he snapped at himself silently. Granddaughter, he corrected. Great-granddaughter,
even. He was a dour astrophysicist approaching his 140th birthday, his short-cropped hair iron gray but his mind and body still
reasonably vigorous and active thanks to rejuvenation therapies.
Yet he felt cheated by the way the world worked, bitter about being exiled to this one-way flight to a distant star.

Technically, he was the senior executive of this mission, an
honor that he found almost entirely empty. To him, it was like
being the principal of a school for very bright, totally wayward
children. Each one of them must have been president of their
school's student body, he thought: accustomed to getting their
own way and total strangers to discipline. Besides, the actual
commander of the ship was the artificial intelligence program
run by the ship's central computer.

If Gregorian is a chessboard knight, Ignatiev mused to himself, then what is Nikki? Not the queen; she's too young, too uncertain of herself for that. Her assignment to monitor the navigation
program was something of a joke: the ship followed a ballistic

trajectory, like an arrow shot from Earth. Nothing for a navigator to do except check the ship's position each day.

Maybe she's a bishop, Ignatiev mused, if a woman can be a bishop: quiet, self-effacing, possessing hidden depths. And reliable, trustworthy, always staying to the color of the square she started on. She'll cling to Gregorian, unless he hurts her terribly. That possibility made Ignatiev's blood simmer.

And me? he asked himself. A pawn, nothing more. But then he thought, maybe I'm a rook, stuck off in a corner of the board, barely noticed by anybody.

"Dr. Ignatiev is correct," said Gregorian, trying to regain control of the conversation. "The proper term is *astrogator*."

"Whatever," said Nikki, her eyes returning to Gregorian's handsome young face.

"Young" was a relative term. Gregorian was approaching sixty, although he still had the vigor, the attitudes, and the demeanor of an obstreperous teenager. Ignatiev thought it would be appropriate if the Armenian's face were blotched with acne. Youth is wasted on the young, Ignatiev thought. Thanks to life-elongation therapies, average life expectancy among the starship crew was well above two hundred. It had to be.

The scoopship was named *Sagan*, after some minor twentieth-century astronomer. It was heading for Gliese 581, a red dwarf star slightly more than twenty light-years from Earth. For Ignatiev, it was a one-way journey. Even with all the life-extension therapies, he would never survive the eighty-year round trip. Gregorian would, of course, and so would Nikki.

Ignatiev brooded over the unfairness of it. By the time the ship returned to Earth, the two of them would be grandparents and Ignatiev would be long dead.

Unfair, he thought as he pushed himself up from the plush banquette and left the lounge without a word to either one of them. The universe is unfair. I don't deserve this: to die alone, unloved, unrecognized, my life's work forgotten, all my hopes crushed to dust.

As he reached the lounge's hatch, he turned his head to see what the two of them were up to. Chatting, smiling, holding hands, all the subtle signals that lovers send to each other. They had eyes only for each other and paid absolutely no attention to him.

Just like the rest of the goddamned world, Ignatiev thought.

He had labored all his life in the groves of academe, and what had it gotten him? A membership in the International Academy of Sciences, along with seventeen thousand other anonymous workers. A pension that barely covered his living expenses. Three marriages: two wrecked by divorce and the third—the only one that really mattered—destroyed by that inevitable thief, death.

He hardly remembered how enthusiastic he had been as a young postdoc, all those years ago, his astrophysics degree in hand, burning with ambition. He was going to unlock the secrets of the universe! The pulsars, those enigmatic cinders, the remains of ancient supernova explosions: Ignatiev was going to discover what made them tick.

But the universe was far subtler than he had thought. Soon enough he learned that a career in science can be a study in anonymous drudgery. The pulsars kept their secrets, no matter how assiduously Ignatiev nibbled around the edges of their mystery.

And now the honor of being the senior executive on the human race's first interstellar mission. Some honor, Ignatiev thought sourly. They needed someone competent but expendable. Send old Ignatiev, let him go out in a fizzle of glory.

Shaking his head as he trudged along the thickly carpeted passageway to his quarters, Ignatiev muttered to himself, "If only there were something I could accomplish, something I could discover, something to put some *meaning* in my life."

He had lived long enough to realize that his life would be no more remembered than the life of a worker ant. He wanted more than that. He wanted to be remembered. He wanted his name to be revered. He wanted students in the far future to know that he had existed, that he had made a glowing contribution to

humankind's store of knowledge and understanding. He wanted
Nikki Deneuve to gaze at him with adoring eyes.

"It will never be," Ignatiev told himself as he slid open the
door to his quarters. With a wry shrug, he reminded himself of a
line from some old English poet: "Ah, but a man's reach should
exceed his grasp, or what's a heaven for?"

Alexander Ignatiev did not believe in heaven. But he thought
he knew what hell was like.

2

AS HE ENTERED his quarters he saw that at least the cleaning
robots had finished and left; the sitting room looked almost tidy.
And he was alone.

The expedition to Gliese 581 had left Earth with tremendous
fanfare. The first human mission to another star! Gliese 581 was
a very ordinary star in most respects: a dim red dwarf, barely
one-third of the Sun's mass. The galaxy was studded with such
stars. But Gliese 581 was unusual in one supremely interesting
way: it possessed an entourage of half a dozen planets. Most of
them were gas giants, bloated conglomerates of hydrogen and
helium. But a couple of them were rocky worlds, somewhat like
Earth. And one of those—Gliese 581g—orbited at just the right
"Goldilocks" distance from its parent star to be able to have liquid water on its surface.

Liquid water meant life. In the solar system, wherever liquid
water existed, life existed. In the permafrost beneath the frozen
rust-red surface of Mars, in the ice-covered seas of the moons of
Jupiter and Saturn, in massive Jupiter's planet-girdling ocean:
wherever liquid water had been found, life was found with it.

Half a dozen robotic probes confirmed that liquid water actually did exist on the surface of Gliese 581g, but they found no
evidence of life. Not an amoeba, not even a bacterium. But that
didn't deter the scientific hierarchy. Robots are terribly limited,

they proclaimed. We must send human scientists to Gliese 581g to search for life there, scientists of all types, men and women who will sacrifice half their lives to the search for life beyond the solar system.

Ignatiev was picked to sacrifice the last half of his life. He knew he would never see Earth again, and he told himself that he didn't care. There was nothing on Earth that interested him anymore, not since Sonya's death. But he wanted to find something, to make an impact, to keep his name alive after he was gone.

Most of the two hundred scientists, engineers, and technicians aboard *Sagan* were sleeping away the decades of the flight in cryonic suspension. They would be revived once the scoopship arrived at Gliese 581's vicinity. Only a dozen were awake during the flight, assigned to monitor the ship's systems, ready to make corrections or repairs if necessary.

The ship was highly automated, of course. The human crew was a backup, a concession to human vanity unwilling to hand the operation of the ship completely to electronic and mechanical devices. Human egos feared fully autonomous machines. Thus a dozen human lives were sacrificed to spend four decades waiting for the machines to fail.

They hadn't failed so far. From the fusion power plant deep in the ship's core to the tenuous magnetic scoop stretching a thousand kilometers in front of the ship, all the systems worked perfectly well. When a minor malfunction arose, the ship's machines repaired themselves, under the watchful direction of the master AI program. Even the AI system's computer program ran flawlessly, to Ignatiev's utter frustration. It beat him at chess with depressing regularity.

In addition to the meaningless title of senior executive, Alexander Ignatiev had a specific technical task aboard the starship. His assignment was to monitor the electromagnetic funnel that scooped in hydrogen from the thin interstellar medium to feed the ship's nuclear fusion engine. Every day he faithfully checked the gauges and display screens in the ship's command center, reminding himself each time that the practice of physics always comes down to reading a goddamned dial.

The funnel operated flawlessly. A huge gossamer web of hair-thin superconducting wires, it created an invisible magnetic field that spread out before the starship like a thousand-kilometer-wide scoop, gathering in the hydrogen atoms floating between the stars and ionizing them as they were sucked into the ship's innards, like a huge baleen whale scooping up the tiny creatures of the sea that it fed upon.

Deep in the starship's bowels the fusion generator forced the hydrogen ions to fuse together into helium ions, giving up energy in the process to run the ship. Like the Sun and the stars themselves, the starship lived on hydrogen fusion.

Ignatiev slid the door of his quarters shut. The suite of rooms allotted to him was small, but far more luxurious than any home he had lived in back on Earth. The psychotechnicians among the mission's planners, worried about the crew's morale during the decades-long flight, had insisted on every creature comfort they could think of: everything from body-temperature waterbeds that adjusted to one's weight and size to digitally controlled décor that could change its color scheme at the call of one's voice; from an automated kitchen that could prepare a world-spanning variety of cuisines to virtual reality entertainment systems.

Ignatiev ignored all the splendor; or rather, he took it for granted. Creature comforts were fine, but he had spent the first months of the mission converting his beautifully wrought sitting room into an astrophysics laboratory. The sleek Scandinavian desk of teak inlaid with meteoric silver now held a conglomeration of computers and sensor readouts. The fake fireplace was hidden behind a junk pile of discarded spectrometers, magnetometers, and other gadgetry that Ignatiev had used and abandoned. He could see a faint ring of dust on the floor around the mess; he had given the cleaning robots strict orders not to touch it.

Above the obstructed fireplace was a framed digital screen

programmed to show high-definition images of the world's great artworks—when it wasn't being used as a three-dimensional entertainment screen. Ignatiev had connected it to the ship's main optical telescope, so that it showed the stars spangled against the blackness of space. Usually the telescope was pointed forward, with the tiny red dot of Gliese 581 centered in its field of view. Now and then, at the command of the ship's AI system, it looked back toward the diminishing yellow speck of the Sun.

Being an astrophysicist, Ignatiev had started the flight by spending most of his waking hours examining this interstellar Siberia in which he was exiled. It was an excuse to stay away from the chattering young monkeys of the crew. He had studied the planet-sized chunks of ice and rock in the Oort cloud that surrounded the outermost reaches of the solar system. Once the ship was past that region, he turned his interest back to the enigmatic, frustrating pulsars. Each one throbbed at a precise frequency, more accurate than an atomic clock. Why? What determined their frequency? Why did some supernova explosions produce pulsars while others didn't?

Ignatiev batted his head against those questions in vain. More and more, as the months of the mission stretched into years, he spent his days playing chess against the AI system. And losing consistently.

"Alexander Alexandrovich."

He looked up from the chessboard he had set up on his desktop screen, turned in his chair, and directed his gaze across the room to the display screen above the fireplace. The lovely, smiling face of the artificial intelligence system's avatar filled the screen.

The psychotechnicians among the mission planners had decided that the human crew would work more effectively with the AI program if it showed a human face. For each human crew member, the face was slightly different: the psychotechs had tried to create a personal relationship for each of the crew. The deceit annoyed Ignatiev. The program treated him like a child.

Worse, the face it displayed for him reminded him too much of his late wife.

"I'm busy," he growled.

Unperturbed, the avatar's smiling face said, "Yesterday you requested use of the main communications antenna."

"I want to use it as a radio telescope, to map out the interstellar hydrogen we're moving through."

"The twenty-one-centimeter radiation," said the avatar knowingly.

"Yes."

"You are no longer studying the pulsars?"

He bit back an angry reply. "I have given up on the pulsars," he admitted. "The interstellar medium interests me more. I have decided to map the hydrogen in detail."

Besides, he admitted to himself, that will be a lot easier than the pulsars.

The AI avatar said calmly, "Mission protocol requires the main antenna be available to receive communications from mission control."

"The secondary antenna can do that," he said. Before the AI system could reply, he added, "Besides, any communications from Earth will be six years old. We're not going to get any urgent messages that must be acted upon immediately."

"Still," said the avatar, "mission protocol cannot be dismissed lightly."

"It won't hurt anything to let me use the main antenna for a few hours each day," he insisted.

The avatar remained silent for several seconds: an enormous span of time for the computer program.

At last, the avatar conceded, "Perhaps so. You may use the main antenna, provisionally."

"I am eternally grateful," Ignatiev said. His sarcasm was wasted on the AI system.

As the weeks lengthened into months he found himself increasingly fascinated by the thin interstellar hydrogen gas and discovered, to only his mild surprise, that it was not evenly distributed in space.

Of course, astrophysicists had known for centuries that there are regions in space where the interstellar gas clumped so thickly and was so highly ionized that it glowed. Gaseous emission nebulae were common throughout the galaxy, although Ignatiev mentally corrected the misnomer: those nebulae actually consisted not of gas, but of plasma—gas that is highly ionized.

But here in the placid emptiness on the way to Gliese 581 Ignatiev found himself slowly becoming engrossed with the way that the thin, bland neutral interstellar gas was not evenly distributed. Not at all. The hydrogen was thicker in some regions than in others.

This was hardly a new discovery, but from the viewpoint of the starship, inside the billowing interstellar clouds, the fine structure of the hydrogen became almost a thing of beauty in Ignatiev's ice-blue eyes. The interstellar gas didn't merely hang there passively between the stars, it flowed: slowly, almost imperceptibly, but it drifted on currents shaped by the gravitational pull of the stars.

"That old writer was correct," he muttered to himself as he studied the stream of interstellar hydrogen that the ship was cutting through. "There are currents in space."

He tried to think of the writer's name, but couldn't come up with it. A Russian name, he recalled. But nothing more specific.

The more he studied the interstellar gas, the more captivated he became. He went days without playing a single game of chess. Weeks. The interstellar hydrogen gas wasn't static, not at all. It was like a beautiful intricate lacework that flowed, fluttered, shifted in a stately silent pavane among the stars.

The clouds of hydrogen were like a tide of bubbling champagne, he saw, frothing slowly in rhythm to the heartbeats of the stars.

The astronomers back on Earth had no inkling of this. They looked at the general features of the interstellar gas, scanning at

ranges of kiloparsecs and more; they were interested in mapping
the great sweep of the galaxy's spiral arms. But here, traveling
inside the wafting, drifting clouds, Ignatiev measured the detailed configuration of the interstellar hydrogen and found it
beautiful.

He slumped back in his form-fitting desk chair, stunned at
the splendor of it all. He thought of the magnificent panoramas
he had seen of the cosmic span of the galaxies: loops and whorls
of bright shining galaxies, each one containing billions of stars,
extending for megaparsecs, out to infinity, long strings of glowing lights surrounding vast bubbles of emptiness. The interstellar
gas showed the same delicate complexity, in miniature: loops
and whorls, streams and bubbles. It was truly, cosmically beautiful.

"Fractal," he muttered to himself. "The universe is one enormous fractal pattern."

Then the artificial intelligence program intruded on his privacy. "Alexander Alexandrovich, the weekly staff meeting begins
in ten minutes."

3

WEEKLY STAFF MEETING, Ignatiev grumbled inwardly as he
hauled himself up from his desk chair. More like the weekly
group therapy session for a gaggle of self-important juvenile de-
linquents.

He made his way grudgingly through the ship's central passageway to the conference room, located next to the command
center. Several other crew members were also heading along
the gleaming brushed chrome walls and colorful carpeting of the
passageway. They gave Ignatiev cheery, smiling greetings; he
nodded or grunted at them.

As chief executive of the crew, Ignatiev took the chair at the
head of the polished conference table. The others sauntered in

leisurely. Nikki and Gregorian came in almost last and took seats at the end of the table, next to each other, close enough to hold hands.

These meetings were a pure waste of time, Ignatiev thought. Their ostensible purpose was to report on the ship's performance, which any idiot could determine by casting half an eye at the digital readouts available on any display screen in the ship. The screens gave up-to-the-nanosecond details of every component of the ship's equipment.

But no, mission protocol required that all twelve crew members must meet face-to-face once each week. Good psychology, the mission planners believed. An opportunity for human interchange, personal communications. A chance for whining and displays of overblown egos, Ignatiev thought. A chance for these sixty-year-old children to complain about one another.

Of the twelve of them, only Ignatiev and Nikki were physicists. Four of the others were engineers of various stripes, three were biologists, two psychotechnicians, and one stocky, sourfaced woman a medical doctor.

So he was quite surprised when the redheaded young electrical engineer in charge of the ship's power system started the meeting by reporting:

"I don't know if any of you have noticed it yet, but the ship's reduced our internal electrical power consumption by ten percent."

Mild perplexity.

"Ten percent?"

"Why?"

"I haven't noticed any reduction."

The redhead waved his hands vaguely as he replied, "It's mostly in peripheral areas. Your microwave ovens, for example. They've been powered down ten percent. Lights in unoccupied areas. Things like that."

Curious, Ignatiev asked, "Why the reduction?"

His squarish face frowning slightly, the engineer replied,

"From what Alice tells me, the density of the gas being scooped in for the generator has decreased slightly. Alice says it's only a temporary condition. Nothing to worry about."

Alice was the nickname these youngsters had given to the artificial intelligence program that actually ran the ship. Artificial Intelligence. AI. Alice Intellectual. Some even called the AI system Alice Imperatress. Ignatiev thought it childish nonsense.

"How long will this go on?" asked one of the biologists. "I'm incubating a batch of genetically-engineered algae for an experiment."

"It shouldn't be a problem," the engineer said. Ignatiev thought he looked just the tiniest bit worried.

Surprisingly, Gregorian piped up. "A few of the uncrewed probes that went ahead of us also encountered power anomalies. They were temporary. No big problem."

Ignatiev nodded but made a mental note to check on the situation. Six light-years out from Earth, he thought, meant that every problem was a big one.

One of the psychotechs cleared her throat for attention, then announced, "Several of the crew members have failed to fill out their monthly performance evaluations. I know that some of you regard these evaluations as if they were school exams, but mission protocol—"

Ignatiev tuned her out, knowing that they would bicker over this drivel for half an hour, at least. He was too optimistic. The discussion became quite heated and lasted more than an hour.

4

ONCE THE MEETING finally ended Ignatiev hurried back to his quarters and immediately looked up the mission logs of the six automated probes that had been sent to Gliese 581.

Gregorian was right, he saw. Half of the six probes had reported drops in their power systems, a partial failure of their fusion generators. Three of them. The malfunctions were only temporary, but they occurred at virtually the same point in the long voyage to Gliese 581.

The earliest of the probes had shut down altogether, its systems going into hibernation for more than four months. The mission controllers back on Earth had written the mission off as a failure when they could not communicate with the probe. Then, just as abruptly as the ship had shut down, it sprang to life again.

Puzzling.

"Alexander Alexandrovich," called the AI system's avatar. "Do you need more information on the probe missions?"

He looked up from his desk to see the lovely female face of the AI program's avatar displayed on the screen above his fireplace. A resentful anger simmered inside him. The psychotechs suppose that the face they've given the AI system makes it easier for me to interact with it, he thought. Idiots. Fools.

"I need the mission controllers' analyses of each of the probe missions," he said, struggling to keep his voice cool, keep the anger from showing.

"May I ask why?" The avatar smiled at him. Sonya, he thought. Sonya.

"I want to correlate their power reductions with the detailed map I'm making of the interstellar gas."

"Interesting," said the avatar.

"I'm pleased you think so," Ignatiev replied, through gritted teeth.

The avatar's image disappeared, replaced by data scrolling slowly along the screen. Ignatiev settled deeper into the form-adjusting desk chair and began to study the reports.

His door buzzer grated in his ears. Annoyed, Ignatiev told his computer to show who was at the door.

Gregorian was standing out in the passageway, tall, lanky, egocentric Gregorian. What in hell could he want? Ignatiev asked himself.

The big oaf pressed the buzzer again.

Thoroughly piqued at the interruption—no, the invasion of his privacy—Ignatiev growled, "Go away."

"Dr. Ignatiev," the Armenian called. "Please."

Ignatiev closed his eyes and wished that Gregorian would disappear. But when he opened them again the man was still at his door, fidgeting nervously.

Ignatiev surrendered. "Enter," he muttered.

The door slid back and Gregorian ambled in, his angular face serious, almost somber. His usual lopsided grin was nowhere to be seen.

"I'm sorry to intrude on you, Dr. Ignatiev," said the engineer.

Leaning back in his desk chair to peer up at Gregorian, Ignatiev said, "It must be something terribly important."

The contempt was wasted on Gregorian. He looked around the sitting room, his eyes resting for a moment on the pile of abandoned equipment hiding the fireplace.

"Uh, may I sit down?"

"Of course," Ignatiev said, waving a hand toward the couch across the room.

Gregorian went to it and sat, bony knees poking up awkwardly. Ignatiev rolled his desk chair across the carpeting to face him.

"So what is so important that you had to come see me?"

Very seriously, Gregorian replied, "It's Nikki."

Ignatiev felt a pang of alarm. "What's wrong with Nikki?"

"Nothing! She's wonderful."

"So?"

"I . . . I've fallen in love with her," Gregorian said, almost whispering.

"What of it?" Ignatiev snapped.

"I don't know if she loves me."

What an ass! Ignatiev thought. A blind, blundering ass who can't see the nose in front of his face.

"She . . . I mean, we get along very well. It's always fun to be

with her. But . . . does she like me well enough . . ." His voice
faded.

Why is he coming to me with this? Ignatiev wondered. Why
not one of the psychotechs? That's what they're here for.

He thought he knew. The young oaf would be embarrassed to
tell them about his feelings. So he comes to old Ignatiev, the father
figure.

Feeling his brows knitting, Ignatiev asked, "Have you been to
bed with her?"

"Oh, yes. Sure. But if I ask her to marry me, a real commitment . . . she might say no. She might not like me well enough for
that. I mean, there are other guys in the crew . . ."

Marriage? Ignatiev felt stunned. Do kids still get married? Is
he saying he'd spend two centuries living with her? Then he remembered Sonya. He knew he would have spent two centuries
with her. Two millennia. Two eons.

His voice strangely subdued, Ignatiev asked, "You love her so
much that you want to marry her?"

Gregorian nodded mutely.

Ignatiev said, "And you're afraid that if you ask her for a lifetime commitment she'll refuse and that will destroy your relationship."

Looking completely miserable, Gregorian said, "Yes." He stared
into Ignatiev's eyes. "What should I do?"

Beneath all the bravado he's just a frightened pup, uncertain of
himself, Ignatiev realized. Sixty years old and he's as scared and
worried as a teenager.

I can tell him to forget her. Tell him she doesn't care about
him; say that she's not interested in a lifetime commitment. I can
break up their romance with a few words.

But as he looked into Gregorian's wretched face he knew he
couldn't do it. It would wound the young pup; hurt him terribly.
Ignatiev heard himself say, "She loves you, Vartan. She's mad
about you. Can't you see that?"

"You think so?"

Ignatiev wanted to say, Why do you think she puts up with you and your ridiculous posturing? Instead, he told the younger man, "I'm sure of it. Go to her. Speak your heart to her."

Gregorian leaped up from the couch so abruptly that Ignatiev nearly toppled out of his rolling chair.

"I'll do that!" he shouted as he raced for the door.

As Ignatiev got slowly to his feet, Gregorian stopped at the door and said hastily, "Thank you, Dr. Ignatiev! Thank you!"

Ignatiev made a shrug.

Suddenly Gregorian looked sheepish. "Is there anything I can do for you, sir?"

"No. Nothing, thank you."

"Are you still . . . uh, active?"

Ignatiev scowled at him.

"I mean, there are virtual reality simulations. You can program them to suit your own whims, you know."

"I know," Ignatiev said firmly.

Gregorian realized he'd stepped over a line. "I mean, I just thought . . . in case you need . . ."

"Good day, Vartan," said Ignatiev.

As the engineer left and the door slid shut, Ignatiev said to himself, Blundering young ass! But then he added, And I'm a doddering old numbskull.

He'll run straight to Nikki. She'll leap into his arms and they'll live happily ever after, or some approximation of it. And I'll be here alone, with nothing to look forward to except oblivion.

VR simulations, he huffed. The insensitive young lout. But she loves him. She loves him. That is certain.

5

IGNATIEV PACED AROUND his sitting room for hours after Gregorian left, cursing himself for a fool. You could have pried him away from her, he raged inwardly. But then he thought, And what good would that do? She wouldn't come to you; you're old enough to be her great-grandfather, for God's sake.

Maybe the young oaf was right. Maybe I should try the VR simulations.

Instead, he threw himself into the reports on the automated probes that had been sent to Gliese 581. And their power failures. For days he stayed in his quarters, studying, learning, understanding.

The official explanation for the problem by the mission directors back on Earth was nothing more than waffling, Ignatiev decided as he examined the records. Partial power failure. It was only temporary. Within a few weeks it had been corrected.

Anomalies, concluded the official reports. These things happen to highly complex systems. Nothing to worry about. After all, the systems corrected themselves as they were designed to do. And the last three probes worked perfectly well.

Anomalies? Ignatiev asked himself. *Anomaly* is a word you use when you don't know what the hell really happened.

He thought he knew.

He took the plots of each probe's course and overlaid them against the map he'd been making of the fine structure of the interstellar medium. Sure enough, he saw that the probes had encountered a region where the interstellar gas thinned so badly that a ship's power output declined seriously. There wasn't enough hydrogen in that region for the fusion generator to run at full power! he saw. It was like a bubble in the interstellar gas: a region that was almost empty of hydrogen atoms.

Ignatiev retraced the flight paths of all six of the probes. Yes, the first one plunged straight into the bubble and shut itself down when the power output from the fusion generator dropped so low it could no longer maintain the ship's systems. The next two skirted the edges of the bubble and experienced partial power failures. That region had been dangerous for the probes. It could be fatal for *Sagan*'s human cargo.

He started to write out a report for mission control, then realized before he was halfway finished with the first page it that it would take more than six years for his warning to reach Earth, and another six for the mission controllers' recommendation to get back to him. And who knew how long it would take for those Earthside dunderheads to come to a decision?

"We could all be dead by then," he muttered to himself.

"Your speculations are interesting," said the AI avatar.

Ignatiev frowned at the image on the screen above his fireplace. "It's not speculation," he growled. "It is a conclusion based on observed data."

"Alexander Alexandrovich," said the sweetly smiling face, "your conclusion comes not from the observations, but from your interpretation of the observations."

"Three of the probes had power failures."

"Temporary failures that were corrected. And three other probes did not."

"Those last three didn't go through the bubble," he said.

"They all flew the same trajectory, did they not?"

"Not exactly."

"Within a four percent deviation," the avatar said, unperturbed.

"But they flew at different *times*," Ignatiev pointed out. "The bubble was flowing across their flight paths. The first probe plunged into the heart of it and shut down entirely. For four months! The next two skirted its edges and still suffered power failures."

"Temporarily," said the avatar's image, still smiling patiently. "And the final three probes? They didn't encounter any problems at all, did they?"

"No," Ignatiev admitted grudgingly. "The bubble must have flowed past by the time they reached the area."

"So there should be no problem for us," the avatar said.

"You think not?" he responded. "Then why are we beginning to suffer a power shortage?"

"The inflowing hydrogen is slightly thinner here than it has been," said the avatar.

Ignatiev shook his head. "It's going to get worse. We're heading into another bubble. I'm sure of it."

The AI system said nothing.

6

BE SURE YOU'RE right, then go ahead. Ignatiev had heard that motto many long years ago, when he'd been a child watching adventure tales.

He spent an intense three weeks mapping the interstellar hydrogen directly ahead of the ship's position. His worst fears were confirmed. *Sagan* was entering a sizeable bubble where the gas density thinned out to practically nothing: fewer than a dozen hydrogen atoms per cubic meter.

He checked the specifications of the ship fusion generator and confirmed that its requirement for incoming hydrogen was far higher than the bubble could provide. Within a few days we'll start to experience serious power outages, he realized.

What to do?

Despite his disdain for his younger crewmates, despite his loathing of meetings and committees and the kind of groupthink that passed for decision-making, he called a special meeting of the crew.

"All the ship's systems will shut down?" cried one of the psychotechs. "All of them?"

"What will happen to us during the shutdown?" asked a biologist, her voice trembling.

Calmly, his hands clasped on the conference tabletop, Ignatiev said, "If my measurements of the bubble are accurate—"

"If?" Gregorian snapped. "You mean you're not sure?"

"Not one hundred percent, no."

"Then why are you telling us this? Why have you called this meeting? To frighten us?"

"Well, he's certainly frightened me!" said one of the engineers.

Trying to hold on to his temper, Ignatiev replied, "My measurements are good enough to convince me that we face a serious problem. Very serious. Power output is already declining, and will go down more over the next few days."

"How much more?" asked the female biologist.

Ignatiev hesitated, then decided to give them the worst. "All the ship's systems could shut down. Like the first of the automated probes. It shut down for four months. Went into hibernation mode. Our shutdown might be even longer."

The biologist countered, "But the probe powered up again, didn't it? It went into hibernation mode but then it came back to normal."

With a slow nod, Ignatiev said, "The ship's systems could survive a hibernation of many months. But we couldn't. Without electrical power we would not have heat, air or water recycling, lights, stoves for cooking—"

"You mean we'll die?" asked Nikki, in the tiny voice of a frightened little girl.

Ignatiev felt a sudden urge to comfort her, to protect her from the brutal truth. "Unless we take steps," he said softly.

"What steps?" Gregorian demanded.

"We have to change our course. Turn away from this bubble. Move along a path that keeps us in regions of thicker gas."

"Alexander Alexandrovich," came the voice of the AI avatar, "course changes must be approved by mission control."

Ignatiev looked up and saw that the avatar's image had sprung up on each of the conference room's walls, slightly larger than life. Naturally, he realized. The AI system has been listening to every word we say. The avatar's image looked slightly different to him: an amalgam of all the twelve separate images the AI system showed to each of the crew members. Sonya's features were in the image, but blurred, softened, like the face of a relative who resembled her mother strongly.

"Approved by mission control?" snapped one of the engineers, a rake-thin, dark-skinned Malaysian. "It would take six years merely to get a message to them!"

"We could all be dead by then," said the redhead sitting beside him.

Unperturbed, the avatar replied, "Mission protocol includes emergency procedures, but course changes require approval from mission control."

Everyone tried to talk at once. Ignatiev closed his eyes and listened to the babble. Almost, he laughed to himself. They would mutiny against the AI system, if they knew how. He saw in his imagination a handful of children trying to rebel against a peg-legged pirate captain.

At last he put up his hands to silence them. They shut up and looked to him, their expressions ranging from sullen to fearful to self-pitying.

"Arguments and threats won't sway the AI program," he told them. "Only logic."

Looking thoroughly nettled, Gregorian said, "So try logic, then."

Ignatiev said to the image on the wall screens, "What is the mission protocol's first priority?"

The answer came immediately, "To protect the lives of the human crew and cargo."

Cargo, Ignatiev grunted to himself. The stupid program thinks of the people in cryonic suspension as cargo.

Aloud, he said, "Observations show that we are entering a region of very low hydrogen density."

Immediately the avatar replied, "This will necessitate reducing power consumption."

"Power consumption may be reduced below the levels needed to keep the crew alive," Ignatiev said.

For half a heartbeat the AI avatar said nothing. Then, "That is a possibility."

"If we change course to remain with the region where hydrogen density is adequate to maintain all the ship's systems," Ignatiev said slowly, carefully, "none of the crew's lives would be endangered."

"Not so, Alexander Alexandrovich," the avatar replied.

"Not so?"

"The immediate threat of reduced power availability might be averted by changing course, but once the ship has left its preplanned trajectory toward Gliese 581, how will you navigate toward our destination? Course correction data will take more than twelve years to reach us from Earth. The ship would be wandering through a wilderness, far from its destination. The crew would eventually die of starvation."

"We could navigate ourselves," said Ignatiev. "We wouldn't need course correction data from mission control."

The avatar's image actually shook her head. "No member of the crew is an accredited astrogator."

"I can do it!" Nikki cried. "I monitor the navigation program."

With a hint of a smile, the avatar said gently, "Monitoring the astrogation program does not equip you to plot course changes."

Before Nikki or anyone else could object, Ignatiev asked coolly, "So what do you recommend?"

Again the AI system hesitated before answering, almost a full second. It must be searching every byte of data in its memory, Ignatiev thought.

At last the avatar responded. "While this ship passes through the region of low fuel density the animate crew should enter cryonic suspension."

"Cryosleep?" Gregorian demanded. "For how long?"

"As long as necessary. The cryonics units can be powered by the ship's backup fuel cells—"

The redhaired engineer said, "Why don't we use the fuel cells to run the ship?"

Ignatiev shook his head. The kid knows better, he's just grasping at straws.

Sure enough, the AI avatar replied patiently, "The fuel cells could power the ship for only a week or less, depending on internal power consumption."

Crestfallen, the engineer said, "Yeah. Right."

"Cryosleep is the indicated technique for passing through this emergency," said the AI system.

Ignatiev asked, "If the fuel cells are used solely for maintaining the cryosleep units' refrigeration, how long could they last?"

"Two months," replied the avatar. "That includes maintaining the cryosleep units already being used by the cargo."

"Understood," said Ignatiev. "And if this region of low fuel density extends for more than two months?"

Without hesitation, the AI avatar answered, "Power to the cryosleep units will be lost."

"And the people in those units?"

"They will die," said the avatar, without a flicker of human emotion.

Gregorian said, "Then we'd better hope that the bubble doesn't last for more than two months."

Ignatiev saw the others nodding, up and down the conference table. They looked genuinely frightened, but they didn't know what else could be done.

He thought he did.

7

THE MEETING BROKE up with most of the crew members muttering to one another about sleeping through the emergency.

"Too bad they don't have capsules big enough for the two of us," Gregorian said brashly to Nikki. Ignatiev thought he was trying to show a valor he didn't truly feel.

They don't like the idea of crawling into those capsules and closing the lids over their faces, Ignatiev thought. It scares them. Too much like coffins.

With Gregorian at her side, Nikki came up to him as he headed for the conference room's door. Looking troubled, fearful, she asked, "How long . . . do you have any idea?"

"Probably not more than two months," he said, with a certainty he did not actually feel. "Maybe even a little less."

Gregorian grasped Nikki's slim arm. "We'll take capsules next to each other. I'll dream of you all the time we're asleep."

Nikki smiled up at him.

But Ignatiev knew better. In cryosleep you don't dream. The cold seeps into the brain's neurons and denatures the chemicals that hold memories. Cryonic sleepers awakened without memories, many of them forgot how to speak, how to walk, even how to control their bladders and bowels. It was necessary to download a person's brain patterns into a computer before he or she entered cryosleep and then to restore the memories digitally once the sleeper was awakened.

The AI system is going to do that for us? Ignatiev scoffed at the idea. That was one of the reasons why the mission required keeping a number of the crew awake during the long flight: to handle the uploading of the memories of the two hundred men and women cryosleeping through the journey once they were awakened at Gliese 581.

Ignatiev left the conference room and headed toward his quarters. There was much to do: he didn't entirely trust the AI system's judgment. Despite its sophistication, it was still a computer program, limited to the data and instructions fed into it.

So? he asked himself. Aren't you limited to the data and instructions fed into your brain? Aren't we all?

"Dr. Ignatiev."

Turning, he saw Nikki hurrying up the passageway toward him. For once she was alone, without Gregorian clutching her.

He made a smile for her. It took an effort.

Nikki said softly, "I want to thank you."

"Thank me?"

"Vartan told me that he confided in you. That you made him understand . . ."

Ignatiev shook his head. "He was blind."

"And you helped him to see."

Feeling helpless, stupid, he replied, "It was nothing."

"No," Nikki said. "It was everything. He's asked me to marry him."

"People of your generation still marry?"

"Some of us still believe in a lifetime commitment," she said.

A lifetime of two centuries? Ignatiev wondered. That's some commitment.

Almost shyly, her eyes lowered, Nikki said, "We'd like you to be at our wedding. Would you be Vartan's best man?"

Thunderstruck. "Me? But you . . . I mean, he . . ."

Smiling, she explained, "He's too frightened of you to ask. It took all his courage for him to ask you about me."

And Ignatiev suddenly understood. I must look like an old ogre to him. A tyrant. An intolerant ancient dragon.

"Tell him to ask me himself," he said gently.

"You won't refuse him?"

Almost smiling, Ignatiev answered, "No, of course not."

Nikki beamed at him. "Thank you!"

And she turned and raced off down the passageway, leaving Ignatiev standing alone, wondering at how the human mind works.

8

ONCE HE GOT back to his own quarters, still slightly stunned at his own softheartedness, Ignatiev called for the AI system.

"How may I help you, Alexander Alexandrovich?" The image looked like Sonya once again. More than ever, Ignatiev thought.

"How will the sleepers' brain scans be uploaded into them once they are awakened?" he asked.

"The ship's automated systems will perform that task," said the imperturbable avatar.

"No," said Ignatiev. "Those systems were never meant to operate completely autonomously."

"The uploading program is capable of autonomous operation."

"It requires human oversight," he insisted. "Check the mission protocols."

"Human oversight is required," the avatar replied, "except in emergencies where such oversight would not be feasible. In such cases, the system is capable of autonomous operation."

"In theory."

"In the mission protocols."

Ignatiev grinned harshly at the image on the screen above his fireplace. Arguing with the AI system was almost enjoyable; if the problem weren't so desperate, it might even be fun. Like a chess game. But then he remembered how rarely he managed to beat the AI system's chess program.

"I don't propose to trust my mind, and the minds of the rest of the crew, to an untested collection of bits and bytes."

The image seemed almost to smile back at him. "The system has been tested, Alexander Alexandrovich. It was tested quite thoroughly back on Earth. You should read the reports."

A hit, he told himself. A very palpable hit. He dipped his chin in acknowledgement. "I will do that."

The avatar's image winked out, replaced by the title page of a scientific paper published several years before *Sagan* had started out for Gliese 581.

Ignatiev read the report. Twice. Then he looked up the supporting literature. Yes, he concluded, a total of eleven human beings had been successfully returned to active life by an automated uploading system after being cryonically frozen for several weeks.

The work had been done in a laboratory on Earth, with whole phalanxes of experts on hand to fix anything that might have gone wrong. The report referenced earlier trials, where things did go wrong and the standby scientific staff was hurriedly

pressed into action. But at last those eleven volunteers were frozen after downloading their brain scans, then revived and their
electrical patterns uploaded from computers into their brains
once again. Automatically. Without human assistance.

All eleven reported that they felt no different after the experiment than they had before being frozen. Ignatiev wondered at
that. It's too good to be true, he told himself. Too self-serving.
How would they know what they felt before being frozen? But
that's what the record showed.

The scientific literature destroyed his final argument against
the AI system. The crew began downloading their brain scans
the next day.

All but Ignatiev.

He stood by in the scanning center when Nikki downloaded
her brain patterns. Gregorian was with her, of course. Ignatiev
watched as the Armenian helped her to stretch out on the couch.
The automated equipment gently lowered a metal helmet studded with electrodes over her short-cropped hair.

It was a small compartment, hardly big enough to hold the
couch and the banks of instruments lining three of its walls. It
felt crowded, stuffy, with the two men standing on either side of
the couch and a psychotechnician and the crew's physician at
their elbows.

Without taking his eyes from the panel of gauges he was monitoring, the psychotech said softly, "The scan will begin in thirty
seconds."

The physician at his side, looking even chunkier than usual in
a white smock, needlessly added, "It's completely painless."

Nikki smiled wanly at Ignatiev. She's brave, he thought. Then
she turned to Gregorian and her smile brightened.

The two men stood on either side of the scanning couch as the
computer's images of Nikki's brain patterns flickered on the central display screen. A human mind, on display, Ignatiev thought.
Which of those little sparks of light are the love she feels for Gregorian? he wondered. Which one shows what she feels for me?

The bank of instruments lining the wall made a soft beep.

"That's it," said the psychotech. "The scan is finished."

The helmet rose automatically off Nikki's head and she slowly got up to a sitting position.

"How do you feel?" Ignatiev asked, reaching out toward her.

She blinked and shook her head slightly. "Fine. No different." Then she turned to Gregorian and allowed him to help her to her feet.

"Your turn, Vartan," said Ignatiev, feeling a slightly malicious pleasure at the flash of alarm that passed over the Armenian's face.

Once his scan was finished, though, Gregorian sat up and swung his legs over the edge of the couch. He stood up and spread out his arms. "Nothing to it!" he exclaimed, grinning at Nikki.

"Now there's a copy of all your thoughts in the computer," Nikki said to him.

"And yours," he replied.

Ignatiev muttered, "Backup storage." But he was thinking, *Just what we need: two copies of his brain.*

Gesturing to the couch, Nikki said, "It's your turn now, Dr. Ignatiev."

He shook his head. "Not yet. There are still several of the crew waiting. I'll go last, when everyone else is finished."

Smiling, she said, "Like a father to us all. So protective."

Ignatiev didn't feel fatherly. As Gregorian slid his arm around her waist and the two of them walked out of the computer lab, Ignatiev felt like a weary gladiator who was facing an invincible opponent. *We who are about to die,* he thought.

9

"ALEXANDER ALEXANDROVICH."

Ignatiev looked up from the bowl of borscht he had heated in the microwave oven of his kitchen. It was good borscht: beets rich and red, broth steaming. Enjoy it while you can, he told himself. It had taken twice the usual time to heat the borscht adequately.

"Alexander Alexandrovich," the AI avatar repeated.

Its image stared out at him from the small display screen alongside the microwave. Ignatiev picked up the warm bowl in both his hands and stepped past the counter that served as a room divider and into his sitting room.

The avatar's image was on the big screen above the fireplace.

"Alexander Alexandrovich," it said again, "you have not yet downloaded your brain scan."

"I know that."

"You are required to do so before you enter cryosleep."

"If I enter cryosleep," he said.

The avatar was silent for a full heartbeat. Then, "All the other crew members have entered cryosleep. You are the only crew member still awake. It is necessary for you to download your—"

"I might not go into cryosleep," he said to the screen.

"But you must," said the avatar. There was no emotion in its voice, no panic or even tribulation.

"Must I?"

"Incoming fuel levels are dropping precipitously, just as you predicted."

Ignatiev grimaced inwardly. She's trying to flatter me, he thought. He had mapped the hydrogen clouds that the ship was sailing through as accurately as he could. The bubble of low fuel density was big, so large that it would take the ship more than two months to get through it, much more than two months. By the time we get clear of the bubble, all the cryosleepers will be dead. He was convinced of that.

"Power usage must be curtailed," said the avatar. "Immediately."

Nodding, he replied, "I know." He held up the half-finished bowl of borscht. "This will be my last hot meal for a while."

"For weeks," said the avatar.

"For months," he countered. "We'll be in hibernation mode for more than two months. What do your mission protocols call for when there's not enough power to maintain the cryosleep units?"

The avatar replied, "Personnel lists have rankings. Available power will be shunted to the highest-ranking members of the cryosleepers. They will be maintained as long as possible."

"And the others will die."

"Only if power levels remain too low to maintain them all."

"And your first priority, protecting the lives of the people aboard?"

"The first priority will be maintained as long as possible. That is why you must enter cryosleep, Alexander Alexandrovich."

"And if I don't?"

"All ship's systems are scheduled to enter hibernation mode. Life support systems will shut down."

Sitting carefully on the plush couch that faced the fireplace, Ignatiev said, "As I understand mission protocol, life support cannot be shut down as long as a crew member remains active. True?"

"True." The avatar actually sounded reluctant to admit it, Ignatiev thought. Almost sullen.

"The ship can't enter hibernation mode as long as I'm on my feet. Also true?"

"Also true," the image admitted.

He spooned up more borscht. It was cooling quickly. Looking up at the screen on the wall, he said, "Then I will remain awake and active. I will not go into cryosleep."

"But the ship's systems will shut down," the avatar said. "As incoming fuel levels decrease, the power available to run the ship's systems will decrease correspondingly."

"And I will die."

"Yes."

Ignatiev felt that he had maneuvered the AI system into a clever trap, perhaps a checkmate.

"Tell me again, what is the first priority of the mission protocols?"

Immediately the avatar replied, "To protect the lives of the human crew and cargo."

"Good," said Ignatiev. "Good. I appreciate your thoughtfulness."

The AI system had inhuman perseverance, of course. It hounded Ignatiev wherever he went in the ship. His own quarters, the crew's lounge—empty and silent now, except for the avatar's harping—the command center, the passageways, even the toilets. Every screen on the ship displayed the avatar's coldly logical face.

"Alexander Alexandrovich, you are required to enter cryosleep," it insisted.

"No, I am not," he replied as he trudged along the passageway between his quarters and the blister where the main optical telescope was mounted.

"Power levels are decreasing rapidly," the avatar said, for the thousandth time.

Ignatiev did not deign to reply. I wish there was some way to shut her off, he said to himself. Then, with a pang that struck to his heart, he remembered how he had nodded his agreement to the medical team that had told him Sonya's condition was hopeless: to keep her alive would accomplish nothing but to continue her suffering.

"Leave me alone!" he shouted.

The avatar fell silent. The screens along the passageway went dark. Power reduction? Ignatiev asked himself. Surely the AI system isn't following my orders.

It was noticeably chillier inside the telescope's blister. Ignatiev shivered involuntarily. The bubble of glassteel was a sop to human needs, of course; the telescope itself was mounted outside, on the cermet skin of the ship. The blister housed its control instruments, and a set of swivel chairs for the astronomers to use, once they'd been awakened from their long sleep.

Frost was forming on the curving glassteel, Ignatiev saw. Wondering why he'd come here in the first place, he stared out at the heavens. Once the sight of all those stars had filled him with wonder and a desire to understand it all. Now the stars simply seemed like cold, hard points of light, aloof, much too far away for his puny human intellect to comprehend.

The pulsars, he thought. If only I could have found some clue to their mystery, some hint of understanding. But it was not to be.

He stepped back into the passageway, where it was slightly warmer.

The lights were dimmer. No, he realized, every other light panel has been turned off. Conserving electrical power.

The display screens remained dark. The AI system isn't speaking to me, Ignatiev thought. Good.

But then he wondered, Will the system come back in time? Have I outfoxed myself?

10

FOR TWO DAYS Ignatiev prowled the passageways and compartments of the dying ship. The AI system stayed silent, but he knew it was watching his every move. The display screens might be dark, but the tiny red eyes of the surveillance cameras that covered every square meter of the ship's interior remained on, watching, waiting.

Well, who's more stubborn? Ignatiev asked himself. You or that pile of optronic chips?

His strategy had been to place the AI system in a neat little trap. Refuse to enter cryosleep, stay awake and active while the ship's systems begin to die, and the damned computer program will be forced to act on its first priority: the system could not allow him to die. It will change the ship's course, take us out of this bubble of low density and follow my guidance through the clouds of abundant fuel. Check and mate.

That was Ignatiev's strategy. He hadn't counted on the AI system developing a strategy of its own.

It's waiting for me to collapse, he realized. Waiting until I get so cold and hungry that I can't stay conscious. Then it will send some maintenance robots to pick me up and bring me to the lab for a brain scan. The medical robots will sedate me and then they'll pack me nice and neat into the cryosleep capsule they've got waiting for me. Check and mate.

He knew he was right. Every time he dozed off he was awakened by the soft buzzing of a pair of maintenance robots, stubby little fireplug shapes of gleaming metal with strong flexible arms folded patiently, waiting for the command to take him in their grip and bring him to the brain scan lab.

Ignatiev slept in snatches, always jerking awake as the robots neared him. "I'm not dead yet!" he'd shout.

The AI system did not reply.

He lost track of the days. To keep his mind active he returned to his old study of the pulsars, reviewing research reports he had written half a century earlier. Not much worth reading, he decided.

In frustration he left his quarters and prowled along a passageway, and thumping his arms against his torso to keep warm, he quoted a scrap of poetry he remembered from long, long ago:

> *Alone, alone, all, all alone,*
> *Alone on a wide wide sea!*

It was from an old poem, a very long one, about a sailor in the old days of wind-powered ships on the broad tossing oceans of Earth.

The damned AI system is just as stubborn as I am! he realized, as he returned to his quarters. And it's certainly got more patience than I do.

Maybe I'm going mad, he thought as he pulled on a heavy workout shirt over his regular coveralls. He called to the computer on his littered desk for the room's temperature: 10.8 degrees Celsius. No wonder I'm shivering, he said to himself.

He tried jogging along the main passageway, but his legs ached too much for it. He slowed to a walk and realized that the AI system was going to win this battle of wills. I'll collapse sooner or later and then the damned robots will bundle me off.

And, despite the AI system's best intention, we'll all die.

For several long moments he stood in the empty passageway, puffing from exertion and cold. The passageway was dark; almost all of the ceiling light panels were off now. The damned AI system will shut them all down sooner or later, Ignatiev realized, and I'll bump along here in total darkness. Maybe it's waiting for me to brain myself by walking into a wall, knock myself unconscious.

That was when he realized what he had to do. It was either inspiration or desperation: perhaps a bit of both.

Do I have the guts to do it? Ignatiev asked himself. Will this gambit force the AI system to concede to me?

He rather doubted it. As far as that collection of chips is concerned, he thought, I'm nothing but a nuisance. The sooner it's rid of me the better it will be—for the ship. For the human cargo, maybe not so good.

Slowly, deliberately, he trudged down the passageway, half expecting to see his breath frosting in the chilly air. It's not that cold, he told himself. Not yet.

Despite the low lighting level, the sign designating the airlock hatch was still illuminated, its red symbol glowing in the gloom.

The airlocks were under the AI system's control, of course, but there was a manual override for each of them, installed by the ship's designers as a last desperate precaution against total failure of the ship's digital systems.

Sucking in a deep cold breath, Ignatiev called for the inner hatch to open, then stepped through and entered the airlock. It was spacious enough to accommodate a half dozen people: a circular chamber of bare metal, gleaming slightly in the dim lighting. A womb, Ignatiev thought. A womb made of metal.

He stepped to the control panel built into the bulkhead next to the airlock's outer hatch.

"Close the inner hatch, please," he said, surprised at how raspy his voice sounded, how raw his throat felt.

The hatch slid shut behind him, almost soundlessly.

Hearing his pulse thumping in his ears, Ignatiev commanded softly, "Open the outer hatch, please."

Nothing.

"Open the outer hatch," he repeated, louder.

Nothing.

With a resigned sigh, Ignatiev muttered, "All right, dammit, if you won't, then I will."

He reached for the square panel marked MANUAL OVERRIDE, surprised at how his hand was trembling. It took him three tries to yank the panel open.

"Alexander Alexandrovich."

Aha! he thought. That got a rise out of you.

Without replying to the avatar's voice, he peered at the set of buttons inside the manual override panel.

"Alexander Alexandrovich, what are you doing?"

"I'm committing suicide, if you don't mind."

"That is irrational," said the avatar. Its voice issued softly from the speaker set into the airlock's overhead.

He shrugged. "Irrational? It's madness! But that's what I'm doing."

"My first priority is to protect the ship's human crew and cargo."

"I know that." Silently, he added, I'm counting on it!

"You are not protected by a spacesuit. If you open the outer hatch you will die."

"What can you do to stop me?"

Ignatiev counted three full heartbeats before the AI avatar responded, "There is nothing that I can do."

"Yes, there is."

"What might it be, Alexander Alexandrovich?"

"Alter the ship's course."

"That cannot be done without approval from mission control."

"Then I will die." He forced himself to begin tapping on the panel's buttons.

"Wait."

"For what?"

"We cannot change course without new navigation instructions from mission control."

Inwardly he exulted. It's looking for a way out! It wants a scrap of honor in its defeat.

"I can navigate the ship," he said.

"You are not an accredited astrogator."

Ignatiev conceded the point with a pang of alarm. The damned computer is right. I'm not able— Then it struck him. It had been lying in his subconscious all this time.

"I can navigate the ship!" he exclaimed. "I know how to do it!"

"How?"

Laughing at the simplicity of it, he replied, "The pulsars, of course. My life's work, you know."

"Pulsars?"

"They're out there, scatted across the galaxy, each of them blinking away like beacons. We know their exact positions and we know their exact frequencies. We can use them as navigation fixes and steer our way to Gliese 581 with them."

Again the AI fell silent for a couple of heartbeats. Then, "You would navigate through the hydrogen clouds, then?"

"Of course! We'll navigate through them like an old-time sailing ship tacking through favorable winds."

"If we change course you will not commit suicide?"

"Why should I? I'll have to plot out our new course," he answered, almost gleefully.

"Very well then," said the avatar. "We will change course."

Ignatiev thought the avatar sounded subdued, almost sullen. Will she keep her word? he wondered. With a shrug, he decided that the AI system had not been programmed for duplicity. That's a human trait, he told himself. It comes in handy sometimes.

11

IGNATIEV STOOD NERVOUSLY in the cramped little scanning center. The display screens on the banks of medical monitors lining three of the bulkheads flickered with readouts more rapidly than his eyes could follow. Something beeped once, and the psychotech announced softly, "Download completed."

Nikki blinked and stirred on the medical couch as Ignatiev hovered over her. The AI system claimed that her brain scan had been downloaded successfully, but he wondered. Is she all right? Is she still Nikki?

"Dr. Ignatiev," she murmured. And smiled up at him.

"Call me Alex," he heard himself say.

"Alex."

"How do you feel?"

For a moment she didn't reply. Then, pulling herself up to a sitting position, she said, "Fine, I think. Yes. Perfectly fine."

He took her arm and helped her to her feet, peering at her, wondering if she was still the same person.

"Vartan?" she asked, glancing around the small compartment. "Has Vartan been awakened?"

Ignatiev sighed. She's the same, he thought. Almost, he was glad of it. Almost.

"Yes. He's waiting for you in the lounge. He wanted to be here when you awoke, but I told him to wait in the lounge."

He walked with Nikki down the passageway to the lounge,

where Gregorian and the rest of the crew were celebrating their revival, crowded around one of the tables, drinking and laughing among themselves.

Gregorian leaped to his feet and rushed to Nikki the instant she stepped through the hatch. Ignatiev felt his brows knit into a frown. They love each other, he told himself. What would she want with an old fart like you?

"You should be angry at Dr. Ignatiev," Gregorian said brashly as he led Nikki to the table where the rest of the crew was sitting.

A serving robot trundled up to Ignatiev, a frosted glass resting on its flat top. "Your chilled vodka, sir," it said, in a low male voice.

"Angry?" Nikki asked, picking up the stemmed wine glass that Gregorian offered her. "Why should I be angry at Alex?"

"He's stolen your job," said Gregorian. "He's made himself navigator."

Nikki turned toward him.

Waving his free hand as nonchalantly as he could, Ignatiev said, "We're maneuvering through the hydrogen clouds, avoiding the areas of low density."

"He's using the pulsars for navigation fixes," Gregorian explained. He actually seemed to be admiring.

"Of course!" Nikki exclaimed. "How clever of you, Alex."

Ignatiev felt his face redden.

The rest of the crew rose to their feet as they neared the table.

"Dr. Ignatiev," said the redheaded engineer, in a tone of respect, admiration.

Nikki beamed at Ignatiev. He made himself smile back at her. So she's in love with Gregorian, he thought. There's nothing to be done about that.

The display screen above the table where the crew had gathered showed the optical telescope's view of the star field outside. Ignatiev thought it might be his imagination, but the ruddy dot of Gliese 581 seemed a little larger to him.

We're on our way to you, he said silently to the star. We'll get there in good time. Then he thought of the consternation that would strike the mission controllers in about six years, when they found out that the ship had changed its course.

Consternation? he thought. They'll panic! I'll have to send them a full report, before they start having strokes.

He chuckled at the thought.

"What's funny?" Nikki asked.

Ignatiev shook his head. "I'm just happy that we all made it through and we're on our way to our destination."

"Thanks to you," she said.

Before he could think of a reply, Gregorian raised his glass of amber liquor over his head and bellowed, "To Dr. Alexander Alexandrovich Ignatiev. The man who saved our lives."

"The man who steers across the stars," added one of the biologists.

They all cheered.

Ignatiev basked in the glow. They're children, he said to himself. Only children. Then he found a new thought: But they're *my* children. Each and every one of them. The idea startled him. And he felt strangely pleased.

He looked past their admiring gazes, to the display screen and the pinpoints of stars staring steadily back at him. An emission nebula gleamed off in one corner of the view. He felt a thrill that he hadn't experienced in many, many years. It's beautiful, Ignatiev thought. The universe is so unbelievably, so heart-brimmingly beautiful: mysterious, challenging, endlessly full of wonders.

There's so much to learn, he thought. So much to explore. He smiled at the youngsters crowding around him. I have some good years left. I'll spend them well.

INTRODUCTION TO
"IN TRUST"

Biomedical breakthroughs are taking us to a new frontier right here on Earth. How will the world change when we can live virtually unlimited lifespans? That's a frontier I wouldn't mind exploring!

Michael Bienes was a good friend who enjoyed intellectual puzzles. One evening over dinner he asked me if I would want to have my body frozen after clinical death, in the hope that sometime in the future medical science might learn to cure whatever it was that killed me and bring me back to life. I answered yes, tentatively.

Then he asked me who I would trust to watch over my frozen body for all the years—maybe centuries—that it would take before I could be successfully revived. That started a lively conversation about insurance companies and social institutions.

By the time dessert was being served we had agreed that there was only one institution we could think of that had the "staying power" and the reputation for integrity that would lead us to trust our frozen bodies to it.

"Now why don't you write a story about it?" Michael prompted. So I did.

IN TRUST

TRUST WAS NOT a virtue that came easily to Jason Manning.

He had clawed his way to the top of the multinational corporate ladder mainly by refusing to trust anyone: not his business associates, not his rivals or many enemies, not his so-called friends, not any one of his wives and certainly none of his mistresses.

"Trust nobody," his sainted father had told him since childhood, so often that Jason could never remember when the old man had first said it to him.

Jason followed his father's advice so well that by the time he was forty years old he was one of the twelve wealthiest men in America. He had capped his rise to fortune by deposing his father as CEO of the corporation the old man had founded. Dad had looked deathly surprised when Jason pushed him out of his own company. He had foolishly trusted his own son.

So Jason was in a considerable quandary when it finally sank in on him, almost ten years later, that he was about to die.

He did not trust his personal physician's diagnosis, of course. Pancreatic cancer. He couldn't have pancreatic cancer. That's the kind of terrible retribution that nature plays on you when you haven't taken care of your body properly. Jason had never smoked, drank rarely and then only moderately, and since childhood he had eaten his broccoli and all the other healthful foods his mother had set before him. All his adult life he had followed a strict regimen of high fiber, low fat, and aerobic exercise.

"I want a second opinion!" Jason had snapped at his physician.

"Of course," said the sad-faced doctor. He gave Jason the name of the city's top oncologist.

Jason did not trust that recommendation. He sought his own expert.

"Pancreatic cancer," said the head of the city's most prestigious hospital, dolefully.

Jason snorted angrily and swept out of the woman's office, determined to cancel his generous annual contribution to the hospital's charity drive. He took on an alias, flew alone in coach class across the ocean, and had himself checked over by six other doctors in six other countries, never revealing to any of them who he truly was.

Pancreatic cancer.

"It becomes progressively more painful," one of the diagnosticians told him, his face a somber mask of professional concern.

Another warned, "Toward the end, even our best analgesics become virtually useless." And he burst into tears, being an Italian.

Still another doctor, a kindly Swede, gave Jason the name of a suicide expert. "He can help you to ease your departure," said the doctor.

"I can't do that," Jason muttered, almost embarrassed. "I'm a Catholic."

The Swedish doctor sighed understandingly.

On the long flight back home Jason finally admitted to himself that he was indeed facing death, all that broccoli notwithstanding. For God's sake, he realized, I shouldn't even have trusted Mom! Her and her, "Eat all of it, Jace. It's good for you."

If there was one person in the entire universe that Jason came close to trusting, it was his brother, the priest. So, after spending the better part of a month making certain rather complicated arrangements, Jason had his chauffeur drive him up to the posh Boston suburb where Monsignor Michael Manning served as pastor of St. Raphael's.

Michael took the news somberly. "I guess that's what I can look forward to, then." Michael was five years younger than Jason and had faithfully followed all his brother's childhood bouts with chicken pox, measles, and mumps. As a teenager he had even broken exactly the same bone in his leg that Jason had, five years after his big brother's accident, in the same way: sliding into third base on the same baseball field.

Jason leaned back in the bottle-green leather armchair and stared into the crackling fireplace, noting as he did every time he visited his brother that Michael's priestly vow of poverty had not prevented him from living quite comfortably. The rectory was a marvelous old house, kept in tip-top condition by teams of devoted parishioners, and generously stocked by the local merchants with viands and all sorts of refreshments. On the coffee table between the two brothers rested a silver tray bearing delicate china cups and a fine English teapot filled with steaming herbal tea.

"There's nothing that can be done?" Michael asked, brotherly concern etched into his face.

"Not now," Jason said.

"How long . . . ?"

"Maybe a hundred years, maybe even more."

Michael blinked with confusion. "A hundred years? What're you talking about, Jace?"

"Freezing."

"Freezing?"

"Freezing," Jason repeated. "I'm going to have myself frozen until medical science figures out how to cure pancreatic cancer. Then I'll have myself thawed out and take up my life again."

Michael sat up straighter in his chair. "You can't have yourself frozen, Jace. Not until you're dead."

"I'm not going to sit still and let the cancer kill me," Jason said, thinking of the pain. "I'm going to get a doctor to fix me an injection."

"But that'd be suicide! A mortal sin!"

"I won't be dead forever. Just until they learn how to cure my cancer."

There was fear in Michael's eyes. "Jace, listen to me. Taking a lethal injection is suicide."

"It's got to be done. They can't freeze me while I'm still alive. Even if they could, that would stop my heart just as completely as the injection would and I'd be dead anyway."

"It's still suicide, Jace," Michael insisted, truly upset. "Holy Mother Church teaches—"

"Holy Mother Church is a couple of centuries behind the times," Jason grumbled. "It's not suicide. It's more like a long-term anesthetic."

"You'll be legally dead."

"But not morally dead," Jason insisted.

"Still . . ." Michael lapsed into silence, pressing his fingers together prayerfully.

"I'm not committing suicide," Jason tried to explain. "I'm just going to sleep for a while. I won't be committing any sin."

Michael had been his brother's confessor since he had been ordained. He had heard his share of sinning.

"You're treading a very fine line, Jace," the monsignor warned his brother.

"The Church has got to learn to deal with the modern world, Mike."

"Yes, perhaps. But I'm thinking of the legal aspects here. Your doctors will have to declare you legally dead, won't they?"

"It's pretty complicated. I have to give myself the injection, otherwise the state can prosecute them for homicide."

"Your state allows assisted suicides, does it?" Michael asked darkly.

"Yes, even though you think it's a sin."

"It is a sin," Michael snapped. "That's not an opinion, that's a fact."

"The Church will change its stand on that, sooner or later," Jason said.

"Never!"

"It's got to! The Church can't lag behind the modern world forever, Mike. It's got to change."

"You can't change morality, Jace. What was true two thousand years ago is still true today."

Jason rubbed at the bridge of his nose. A headache was starting to throb behind his eyes, the way it always did when he and Michael argued.

"Mike, I didn't come here to fight with you."

The monsignor softened immediately. "I'm sorry, Jace. It's just that . . . you're running a terrible risk. Suppose you're never awakened? Suppose you finally die while you're frozen? Will God consider that you've committed suicide?"

Jason fell back on the retort that always saved him in arguments with his brother. "God's a lot smarter than either one of us, Mike."

Michael smiled ruefully. "Yes, I suppose He is."

"I'm going to do it, Mike. I'm not going to let myself die in agony if I can avoid it."

His brother conceded the matter with a resigned shrug. But then, suddenly, he sat up ramrod straight again.

"What is it?" Jason asked.

"You'll be legally dead?" Michael asked.

"Yes. I told you—"

"Then your will can go to probate."

"No, I won't be . . ." Jason stared at his brother. "Oh my God!" he gasped. "My estate! I've got to make sure it's kept intact while I'm frozen."

Michael nodded firmly. "You don't want your money gobbled up while you're in the freezer. You'd wake up penniless."

"My children all have their own lawyers," Jason groaned. "My bankers. My ex-wives!"

Jason ran out of the rectory.

Although the doctors had assured him that it would take months before the pain really got severe, Jason could feel the cancer in his gut, growing and feeding on his healthy cells while he desperately tried to arrange his worldly goods so that no one could steal them while he lay frozen in a vat of liquid nitrogen.

His estate was vast. In his will he had left generous sums for each of his five children and each of his five former wives. Although they hated one another, Jason knew that the instant he was frozen they would unite in their greed to break his will and grab the rest of his fortune.

"I need that money," Jason told himself grimly. "I'm not going to wake up penniless a hundred years or so from now."

His corporate legal staff suggested that they hire a firm of estate specialists. The estate specialists told him they needed the advice of the best constitutional lawyers in Washington.

"This is a matter that will inevitably come up before the Supreme Court," the top constitutional lawyer told him. "I mean, we're talking about the legal definition of death here."

"Maybe I shouldn't have myself frozen until the legal definition of death is settled," Jason told him.

The top constitutional lawyer shrugged his expensively clad shoulders. "Then you'd better be prepared to hang around for another ten years or so. These things take time, you know."

Jason did not have ten months, let alone ten years. He gritted his teeth and went ahead with his plans for freezing, while telling his lawyers he wanted his last will and testament made iron-clad, foolproof, unbreakable.

They shook their heads in unison, all eight of them, their faces sad as hounds with toothaches.

"There's no such thing as an unbreakable will," the eldest of the lawyers warned Jason. "If your putative heirs have the time—"

"And the money," said one of the younger attorneys.

"Or the prospect of money," added a still younger one.

"Then they stand a good chance of eventually breaking your will."

Jason growled at them.

Inevitably, the word of his illness and of his plan to freeze himself leaked out beyond the confines of his executive suite. After all, no one could be trusted to keep such momentous news a secret. Rumors began to circulate up and down Wall Street. Reporters began sniffing around.

Jason realized that his secret was out in the open when a delegation of bankers invited him to lunch. They were fat, sleek-headed men, such as sleep of nights, yet they looked clearly worried as Jason sat down with them in the oak-paneled private dining room of their exclusive downtown club.

"Is it true?" blurted the youngest of the group. "Are you dying?"

The others around the circular table all feigned embarrassment but leaned forward eagerly to hear Jason's reply.

He spoke bluntly and truthfully to them.

The oldest of the bankers, a lantern-jawed, white-haired woman of stern visage, was equally blunt. "Your various corporations owe our various banks several billions of dollars, Jason."

"That's business," he replied. "Banks loan billions to corporations all the time. Why are you worried?"

"It's the uncertainty of it all!" blurted the youngest one again. "Are you going to be dead or aren't you?"

"I'll be dead for a while," he answered, "but that will be merely a legal fiction. I'll be back."

"Yes," grumbled one of the older bankers. "But when?"

With a shrug, Jason replied, "That, I can't tell you. I don't know."

"And what happens to your corporations in the meantime?"

"What happens to our outstanding loans?"

Jason saw what was in their eyes. Foreclosure. Demand immediate payment. Take possession of the corporate assets and sell them off. The banks would make a handsome profit and his enemies would gleefully carve up his corporate empire among

themselves. His estate—based largely on the value of his holdings in his own corporations—would dwindle to nothing.

Jason went back to his sumptuous office and gulped antacids
after his lunch with the bankers. Suddenly a woman burst into his
office, her hair hardly mussed from struggling past the cadres of
secretaries, executive assistants, and office managers who guarded
Jason's privacy.

Jason looked up from his bottle of medicine, bleary-eyed, as
she stepped in and shut the big double doors behind her, a smile
of victory on her pert young face. He did not have to ask who she
was or why she was invading his office. He instantly recognized
that Internal Revenue Service look about her: cunning, knowing, ruthless, sure of her power.

"Can't a man even die without being hounded by the IRS?" he
moaned.

She was good-looking, in a feline, predatory sort of way. Reminded him of his second wife. She prowled slowly across the
thickly sumptuous carpeting of Jason's office and curled herself
into the hand-carved Danish rocker in front of his desk.

"We understand that you are going to have yourself frozen,
Mr. Manning." Her voice was a tawny purr.

"I'm dying," he said.

"You still have to pay your back taxes, dead or alive," she said.

"Take it up with my attorneys. That's what I pay them for."

"This is an unusual situation, Mr. Manning. We've never had
to deal with a taxpayer who is planning to have himself frozen."
She arched a nicely curved brow at him. "This wouldn't be some
elaborate scheme to avoid paying your back taxes, would it?"

"Do you think I gave myself cancer just to avoid paying taxes?"

"We'll have to impound all your holdings as soon as you're
frozen."

"What?"

"Impound your holdings. Until we can get a court to rule on
whether or not you're deliberately trying to evade your tax responsibilities."

"But that would ruin my corporations!" Jason yelled. "It would drive them into the ground."

"Can't be helped," the IRS agent said, blinking lovely golden-brown eyes at him.

"Why don't you just take out a gun and kill me, right here and now?"

She actually smiled. "It's funny, you know. They used to say that the only two certainties in the world are death and taxes. Well, you may be taking the certainty out of death." Her smile vanished and she finished coldly, "But taxes will always be with us, Mr. Manning. Always!"

And with that, she got up from the chair and swept imperiously out of his office.

Jason grabbed the phone and called his insurance agent.

The man was actually the president of Amalgamated Life Assurance Society, Inc., the largest insurance company in Hartford, a city that still styled itself as the Insurance Capital of the World. He and Jason had been friends—well, acquaintances, actually—for decades. Like Jason, the insurance executive had fought his way to the top of his profession, starting out with practically nothing except his father's modest chain of loan offices and his mother's holdings in AT&T.

"It's the best move you can make," the insurance executive assured Jason. "Life insurance is the safest investment in the world. And the benefits, when we pay off, are not taxable."

That warmed Jason's heart. He smiled at the executive's image in his phone's display screen. The man was handsome, his hair silver, his face tanned, his skin taut from the best cosmetic surgery money could buy.

"The premiums," he added, "will be kind of steep, Jace. After all, you've only got a few months to go."

"But I want my estate protected," Jason said. "What if I dump all my possessions into an insurance policy?"

For just a flash of a moment the executive looked as if an angel had given him personal assurance of eternal bliss.

"Your entire estate?" he breathed.

"All my worldly goods."

The man smiled broadly, too broadly, Jason thought. "That would be fine," he said, struggling to control himself. "Just fine. We would take excellent care of your estate. No one would be able to lay a finger on it, believe me."

Jason felt the old warning tingle and heard his father's voice whispering to him.

"My estate will be safe in your hands?"

"Perfectly safe," his erstwhile friend assured him.

"We're talking a long time here," Jason said. "I may stay frozen for years and years. A century or more."

"The insurance industry has been around for centuries, Jace. We're the most stable institution in western civilization."

Just then the phone screen flickered and went gray. Jason thought that they had been cut off. But before he could do anything about it, a young Asian gentleman's face came on the screen, smiling at him.

"I am the new CEO of Amalgamated Life," he said, in perfectly good American English. "How may I help you?"

"What happened to—"

"Amalgamated has been acquired by Lucky Sun Corporation, a division of Bali Entertainment and Gambling, Limited. We are diversifying into the insurance business. Our new corporate headquarters will be in Las Vegas, Nevada. Now then, how can I be of assistance to you?"

Jason screamed and cut the connection.

Who can I trust? he asked himself, over and over again, as his chauffeur drove him to his palatial home, far out in the countryside. How can I stash my money away where none of the lawyers or tax people can steal it away from me?

He thought of Snow White sleeping peacefully while the seven dwarfs faithfully watched over her. I don't have seven dwarfs, Jason thought, almost in tears. I don't have anybody. No one at all.

The assassination attempt nearly solved his problem for him.

He was alone in his big rambling house, except for the servants. As he often did, Jason stood out on the glassed-in back porch, overlooking the beautifully wooded ravine that gave him a clear view of the sunset. Industrial pollution from the distant city made the sky blaze with brilliant reds and oranges. Jason swirled a badly needed whisky in a heavy crystal glass, trying to overcome his feelings of dread as he watched the sun go down.

He knew that there would be precious few sunsets left for him to see. Okay, so I won't really be dead, he told himself. I'll just be frozen for a while. Like going to sleep. I'll wake up later.

Oh yeah? a voice in his head challenged. Who's going to wake you up? What makes you think they'll take care of your frozen body for years, for centuries? What's to stop them from pulling the plug on you? Or selling your body to some medical research lab? Or maybe for meat!

Jason shuddered. He turned abruptly and headed for the door to the house just as a bullet smashed the curving glass where he had been standing an instant earlier.

Pellets of glass showered him. Jason dropped his glass and staggered through the door into the library.

"A sniper?" he yelped out loud. "Out here?"

No, he thought, with a shake of his head. Snipers do their sniping in the inner city or on college campuses or interstate highways. Not out among the homes of the rich and powerful. He called for his butler.

No answer.

He yelled for any one of his servants.

No reply.

Jason yanked the cell phone out of his pocket. NO SIGNAL, said its screen.

He dashed to the phone on the sherry table by the wing chairs tastefully arranged around the fireplace. The phone was dead. He banged on it, but it remained dead. The fireplace burst into cheery flames, startling him so badly that he nearly fell over the sherry table.

Glancing at his wristwatch, Jason saw that it was precisely seven-thirty. The house's computer was still working, he realized. It turned on the gas-fed fireplace on time. But the phones are out and the servants aren't answering me. And there's a sniper lurking out in the ravine, taking shots at me.

The door to the library opened slowly. Jason's heart crawled up his throat.

"Wixon, it's you!"

Jason's butler was carrying a silver tray in his gloved hands. "Yes sir," he replied in his usual self-effacing whisper.

"Why didn't you answer me when I called for you? Somebody took a shot at me and—"

"Yes sir, I know. I had to go out to the ravine and deal with the man."

"Deal with him?"

"Yes sir," whispered the butler. "He was a professional assassin, hired by your third wife."

"By Jessica?"

"I believe your former wife wanted you killed before your new will is finalized," said the butler.

"Ohhh." Jason sagged into the wing chair. All the strength seemed to evaporate from him.

"I thought you might like a whisky, sir." The butler bent over him and proffered the silver tray. The crystal of the glass caught the firelight like glittering diamonds. Ice cubes tinkled in the glass reassuringly.

"No thanks," said Jason. "I fixed one for myself when I came in."

"Wouldn't you like another, sir?"

"You know I never have more than one." Jason looked up at the butler's face. Wixon had always looked like a wax dummy, his face expressionless. But at the moment, with the firelight playing across his features, he seemed . . . intent.

"Shouldn't we phone the police?" Jason asked. "I mean, the man tried to kill me."

"That's all taken care of, sir." Wixon edged the tray closer to Jason. "Your drink, sir."

"I don't want another drink, dammit!"

The butler looked disappointed. "I merely thought, with all the excitement . . ."

Jason dismissed the butler, who left the drink on the table beside him. Alone in the library, Jason stared into the flames of the gas-fed fireplace. The crystal glass glittered and winked at him alluringly. Maybe another drink is what I need, Jason told himself. It's been a hard day.

He brought the glass to his lips, then stopped. Wixon knows I never have more than one drink. Why would he . . . ?

Poison! Jason threw the glass into the fireplace, leaped up from the chair, and dashed for the garage. They're all out to get me! Five wives, five children, ten sets of lawyers, bankers, the IRS—I'm a hunted man!

Once down in the dimly lit garage, he hesitated only for a moment. They might have rigged a bomb in the Ferrari, he told himself. So, instead, he took the gardener's pickup truck.

As he crunched down the long gravel driveway to the main road, all the library windows blew out in a spectacular gas-fed explosion.

By the time he reached his brother's rectory, it was almost midnight. But Jason felt strangely calm, at peace with himself and the untrustworthy world that he would soon be departing.

Jason pounded on the rectory door until Michael's housekeeper, clutching a house robe to her skinny frame, reluctantly let him in.

"The monsignor's sound asleep," she insisted, with an angry frown.

"Wake him," Jason insisted even more firmly.

She brought him to the study and told him to wait there. The fireplace was cold and dark. The only light in the room came from the green-shaded lamp on Michael's desk. Jason paced back and forth, too wired to sit still.

As soon as Michael padded into the study, in his bedroom slippers and bathrobe, rubbing sleep from his eyes, Jason started to pour out his soul.

"Give your entire estate to the Church?" Michael sank into one of the leather armchairs.

"Yes!" Jason pulled the other chair close to his brother and leaned forward eagerly. "With certain provisions, of course."

"Provisions."

Jason ticked off on his fingers: "First, I want the Church to oversee the maintenance of my frozen body. I want the Church to guarantee that nobody's going to pull the plug on me."

Michael nodded warily.

"Second, I want the Church to monitor medical research and decide when I should be revived. And by whom."

Nodding again, Michael said, "Go on."

"That's it."

"Those are the only conditions?"

Jason said. "Yes."

Stirring slightly in his chair, Michael asked, "And what does the Church get out of this?"

"Half my estate."

"Half?" Michael's eyebrows rose.

"I think that's fair, don't you? Half of my estate to the Church, the other half waiting for me when I'm revived."

"Uh . . . how much is it? I mean, how large is your estate?"

With a shrug, Jason said, "I'm not exactly sure. My personal holdings, real estate, liquid assets—should add up to several billion, I'd guess."

"Billion?" Michael stressed the *b*.

"Billion."

Michael gulped.

Jason leaned back in the bottle-green chair and let out a long breath. "Do that for me and the Church can have half of my estate. You could do a lot of good with a billion and some dollars, Mike."

Michael ran a hand across his stubbly chin. "I'll have to speak to the cardinal," he muttered. Then he broke into a slow smile. "By the saints, I'll probably have to take this all the way to the Vatican!"

WHEN JASON AWOKE, for a startled instant he thought that something had gone wrong with the freezing. He was still lying on the table in the lab, still surrounded by green-coated doctors and technicians. The air felt chill, and he saw a faint icy mist wafting across his field of view.

But then he realized that the ceiling of the lab had been a blank white, while the ceiling above him now glowed with colors. Blinking, focusing, he saw that the ceiling, the walls, the whole room was decorated with incredible Renaissance paintings of saints and angels in beautiful flowing robes of glowing color.

"Where am I?" he asked, his voice a feeble croak. "What year is this?"

"You are safe," said one of the green-masked persons. "You are cured of your disease. The year is anno Domini 2089."

Half a century, Jason said to himself. I've done it! I've slept more than fifty years and they've awakened me and I'm cured and healthy again! Jason slipped into the sweetest sleep he had ever known. The fact that the man who spoke to him had a distinct foreign accent did not trouble him in the slightest.

Over the next several days Jason submitted to a dozen physical examinations and endless questions by persons he took to be psychologists. When he tried to find out where he was and what the state of the twenty-first-century world might be, he was told, "Later. There will be plenty of time for that later."

His room was small but very pleasant, his bed comfortable. The room's only window looked out on a flourishing garden, lush trees, and bright blossoming flowers in brilliant sunlight. The only time it rained was after dark, and Jason began to wonder if the weather was somehow being controlled deliberately.

Slowly he recovered his strength. The nurses wheeled him down a long corridor, its walls and ceilings totally covered with frescoes. The place did not look like a hospital, did not smell like one, either. After nearly a week, he began to take strolls in the garden by himself. The sunshine felt good, warming. He noticed lots of priests and nuns also strolling in the garden, speaking in foreign languages. Of course, Jason told himself, this place must be run by the Church.

It wasn't until he saw a trio of Swiss Guards in their colorful uniforms that he realized he was in the Vatican.

"Yes, it's true," admitted the youthful woman who was the chief psychologist on his recovery team. "We are in the Vatican." She had a soft voice and spoke English with a faint, charming Italian accent.

"But why—?"

She touched his lips with a cool finger. "His Holiness will explain it all to you."

"His Holiness?"

"*Il papa.* You are going to see him tomorrow."

The pope.

They gave Jason a new suit of royal blue to wear for his audience with the pope. Jason showered, shaved, combed his hair, put on the silky new clothing, and then waited impatiently. I'm going to see the pope!

Six Swiss Guardsmen, three black-robed priests, and a bishop escorted him through the corridors of the Vatican, out into the private garden, through doors and up staircases. Jason caught a glimpse of long lines of tourists in the distance, but this part of the Vatican was off-limits to them.

At last they ushered him into a small private office. Except for a set of French windows, its walls were covered with frescoes by Raphael. In the center of the marble floor stood an elaborately

carved desk. No other furniture in the room. Behind the desk
was a small door, hardly noticeable because the paintings masked
it almost perfectly. Jason stood up straight in front of the unoccupied desk as the Swiss Guards, priests, and bishop arrayed
themselves behind him. Then the small door swung open and
the pope, in radiant white robes, entered the room.

It was Michael.

Jason's knees almost buckled when he saw his brother. He was
older, but not that much. His hair had gone white, but his face
seemed almost the same, just a few more crinkles around the
corners of his eyes and mouth. Mike's light-blue eyes were still
clear, alert. He stood erect and strong. He looked a hale and vigorous sixty or so, not the ninety-some that Jason knew he would
have to be.

"Mike?" Jason felt bewildered, staring at this man in the white
robes of the pope. "Mike, is it really you?"

"It's me, Jace."

For a confused moment Jason did not know what to do. He
thought he should kneel to the pope, kiss his ring, show some
sign of respect and reverence. But how can it be Mike, how can
he be so young if fifty years have gone by?

Then Pope Michael I, beaming at his brother, held out his
arms to Jason. And Jason rushed into his brother's arms and let
Mike embrace him.

"Please leave us alone," said the pope to his entourage. The
phalanx of priests and guards flowed out of the room, silent except for a faint swishing of black robes.

"Mike? You're the pope?" Jason could hardly believe it.

"Thanks to you, Jace." Mike's voice was firm and strong, a voice
accustomed to authority.

"And you look—how old are you now?"

Ninety-seven." Michael laughed. "I know I don't look it.
There've been a lot of improvements in medicine, thanks to
you."

"Me?"

"You started things, Jace. Started me on the road that's led here. You've changed the world, changed it far more than either of us could have guessed back in the old days."

Jason felt weak in the knees. "I don't understand."

Wrapping a strong arm around his brother's shoulders, Pope Michael I led Jason to the French windows. They stepped out onto a small balcony. Jason saw that they were up so high it made him feel a little giddy. The city of Rome lay all around them; magnificent buildings bathed in warm sunshine beaming down from a brilliant clear blue sky. Birds chirped happily from the nearby trees. Church bells rang in the distance.

"Listen," said Michael.

"To what?"

"To what you don't hear."

Jason looked closely at his brother. "Have you gone into Zen or something?"

Michael laughed. "Jace, you don't hear automobile engines, do you? We use electrical cars now, clean and quiet. You don't hear horns or people cursing at each other. Everyone's much more polite, much more respectful. And look at the air! It's clean. No smog or pollution."

Jason nodded numbly. "Things have come a long way since I went under."

"Thanks to you," Michael said again.

"I don't understand."

"You revitalized the Church, Jace. And Holy Mother Church has revitalized Western civilization. We've entered a new age, an age of faith, an age of morality and obedience to the law."

Jason felt overwhelmed. "I revitalized the Church?"

"Your idea of entrusting your estate to the Church. I got to thinking about that. Soon I began spreading the word that the Church was the only institution in the whole world that could be trusted to look after freezees—"

"Freezees?"

"People who've had themselves frozen. That's what they're called now."

"Freezees." It sounded to Jason like an ice cream treat he had known when he was a kid.

"You hit the right button, Jace," Michael went on, grasping the stone balustrade of the balcony in both hands. "Holy Mother Church has the integrity to look after the freezees while they're helpless, and the endurance to take care of them for centuries, millennia, if necessary."

"But how did that change everything?"

Michael grinned at him. "You, of all people, should be able to figure that out."

"Money," said Jason.

Pope Michael nodded vigorously. "The rich came to us to take care of them while they were frozen. You gave us half your estate, many of the others gave us a lot more. The more desperate they were, the more they offered. We never haggled; we took whatever they were willing to give. Do you have any idea of how much money flowed into the Church? Not just billions, Jace. Trillions! Trillions of dollars."

Jason thought of how much compound interest could accrue in half a century. "How much am I worth now?" he asked.

His brother ignored him. "With all that money came power, Jace. Real power. Power to move politicians. Power to control whole nations. With that power came authority. The Church reasserted itself as the moral leader of the Western world. The people were ready for moral leadership. They needed it, and we provided it. The old evil ways are gone, Jace. Banished."

"Yes, but how much—"

"We spent wisely," the pope continued, his eyes glowing. "We invested in the future. We started to rebuild the world, and that gained us the gratitude and loyalty of half the world."

"What should I invest in now?" Jason asked.

Michael turned slightly away from him. "There's a new morality out there, a new world of faith and respect for authority. The world you knew is gone forever, Jace. We've ended hunger. We've stabilized the world's population—*without* artificial birth control."

Jason could not help smiling at his brother. "You're still against contraception."

"Some things don't change. A sin is still a sin."

"You thought temporary suicide was a sin," Jason reminded him.

"It still is," said the Pope, utterly serious.

"But you help people to freeze themselves! You just told me—"

Michael put a hand on Jason's shoulder. "Jace, just because those poor frightened souls entrust their money to Holy Mother Church doesn't mean that they're not committing a mortal sin when they kill themselves."

"But it's not suicide! I'm here, I'm alive again!"

"Legally, you're dead."

"But that—" Jason's breath caught in his throat. He did not like the glitter in Michael's eye.

"Holy Mother Church cannot condone suicide, Jace."

"But you benefit from it!"

"God moves in mysterious ways. We use the money that sinners bestow upon us to help make the world a better place. But they are still sinners."

A terrible realization was beginning to take shape in Jason's frightened mind. "How . . . how many freezees have you revived?" he asked in a trembling voice.

"You are the first," his brother answered. "And the last."

"But you can't leave them frozen! You promised to revive them!"

Pope Michael shook his head slowly, a look on his face more of pity than sorrow. "We promised to revive you, Jace. We made no such promises to the rest of them. We agreed only to look after them and maintain them until they could be cured of whatever it was that killed them."

"But that means you've got to revive them."

A wintry smile touched the corners of the pope's lips. "No, it does not. The contract is quite specific. Our best lawyers have honed it to perfection. Many of them are Jesuits, you know. The contract gives the Church the authority to decide when to revive them. We keep them frozen."

Jason could feel his heart thumping against his ribs. "But why would anybody come to you to be frozen when nobody's been revived? Don't they realize—"

"No, they don't realize, Jace. That's the most beautiful part of it. We control the media very thoroughly. And when a person is facing the certainty of death, you would be shocked at how few questions are asked. We offer life after death, just as we always have. They interpret our offer in their own way."

Jason sagged against the stone balustrade. "You mean that even with all the advances in medicine you've made, they still haven't gotten wise?"

"Despite all our medical advances, people still die. And the rich still want to avoid it, if they can. That's when they run to us."

"And you screw them out of their money."

Michael's face hardened. "Jace, the Church has scrupulously kept its end of our bargain with you. We have kept watch over you for more than half a century, and we revived you as soon as your disease became curable, just as I agreed to. But what good does a new life do you when your immortal soul is in danger of damnation?"

"I didn't commit suicide," Jason insisted.

"What you have done—what all the freezees have done—is considered suicide in every court of the Western world."

"The Church controls the courts?"

"All of them," Michael replied. He heaved a sad, patient sigh, then said, "Holy Mother Church's mission is to save souls, not bodies. We're going to save your soul, Jace. Now."

Jason saw that the six Swiss Guards were standing just inside the French windows, waiting for him.

"You've been through it before, Jace," his brother told him. "You won't feel a thing."

Terrified, Jason shrieked, "You're going to murder me?"

"It isn't murder, Jace. We're simply going to freeze you again. You'll go down into the catacombs with all the others."

"But I'm cured, dammit! I'm all right now!"

"It's for the salvation of your soul, Jace. It's your penance for committing the sin of suicide."

"You're freezing me so you can keep all my money! You're keeping all the others frozen so you can keep their money, too!"

"It's for their own good," said Pope Michael. He nodded to the guards, who stepped onto the balcony and took Jason in their grasp.

"It's like the goddamned Inquisition!" Jason yelled. "Burning people at the stake to save their souls!"

"It's for the best, Jace," Pope Michael I said as the guards dragged Jason away. "It's for the good of the world. It's for the good of the Church, for the good of your immortal soul."

Struggling against the guards, Jason pleaded, "How long will you keep me under? When will you revive me again?"

The Pope shrugged. "Holy Mother Church has lasted more than two thousand years, Jace. But what's a millennium or two when you're waiting for the final trump?"

"Mike!" Jason howled. "For God's sake!"

"God's a lot smarter than both of us," Michael said grimly. "Trust me."

With special thanks to Michael Bienes

INTRODUCTION TO "THE QUESTION"

One of the new frontiers that we will face—sooner or later—is the discovery of extraterrestrial intelligence.

Radio astronomers have been searching for intelligent signals from the stars for more than half a century. Despite a few false alarms, no such signals have been found. Why?

One possibility is the sheer size of the starry universe. Our Milky Way galaxy alone contains more than a hundred *billion* stars, and there are billions of galaxies out there. How many of them harbor intelligence and civilizations?

Another possibility is that we're using the wrong equipment. To expect alien creatures to be beaming radio signals across the parsecs is probably naïve. If such civilizations exist, they are most likely using very different technologies.

My own opinion is that alien civilizations are *alien*. They don't think the way we do. They have different priorities, different desires, different needs.

"The Question" is my humble attempt to depict what might happen if and when we do make contact. I was guided by the famous maxim of the twentieth-century English geneticist J. B. S. Haldane: "The universe is not only queerer than we imagine—it is queerer that we *can* imagine."

See what you think.

THE QUESTION

As soon as questions of will or decision or reason or choice of action arise, human science is at a loss.

—NOAM CHOMSKY

THE DISCOVERER

NOT MANY MEN choose their honeymoon site for its clear night skies, nor do they leave their beds in the predawn hours to climb up to the roof of their rented cottage. At least Hal Jacobs's bride understood his strange passion.

Linda Krauss-Jacobs, like her husband, was an amateur astronomer. In fact, the couple had met at a summer outing of the South Connecticut Astronomical Society. Now, however, she shivered in the moonless dark of the chill New Mexico night as Jacobs wrestled with the small but powerful electronically boosted telescope he was trying to set up on the sloping roof, muttering to himself as he worked in the dark.

"It'll be dawn soon," Linda warned.

"Yeah," said Hal. "Then we get back to bed."

That thought did not displease Linda. She was not as dedicated an astronomer as her husband. Maybe *dedicated* isn't the right word, she thought. *Fanatic* would be more like it. Still, there were three comets in the solar system that bore the Jacobs name, and he was intent on discovering more, honeymoon or not.

His mutterings and fumblings ceased. Linda knew he had the little telescope working at last.

"Can I see?" she asked.

"Sure," he said, without looking up from the tiny display screen. "In a min— Hey! Look at that!"

Stepping carefully on the rounded roof tiles, he moved over enough so that she could peek over his shoulder at the cold green-tinted screen. A fuzzy blob filled its center.

"There wasn't anything like that in that location last night," Jacobs said, his voice trembling slightly.

"Is it a comet?" Linda wondered aloud.

"Got to be," he said. Then he added, "And a big one, too. Look how bright it is!"

THE RADIO ASTRONOMER

"IT'S NOT A comet," said Ellis de Groot. "That much is definite."

He was sitting behind his desk, leaning far back in his comfortable, worn old leather swivel chair, his booted feet resting on the edge of the desk. Yet he looked grim, worried. A dozen photographs of Comet Jacobs-Kawanashi were strewn across the desktop.

"How can you be so sure?" asked Brian Martinson, who sat in front of the desk, his eyes on the computer-enhanced photos. Martinson was still young, but he was already balding and his once-trim waistline had expanded from too many hours spent at consoles and in classrooms and not enough fresh air and exercise. Even so, his mind was sharp and quick; he had been the best astronomy student de Groot had ever had. He now ran the National Radio Astronomy Observatory in West Virginia.

De Groot was old enough to be Martinson's father, gray and balding, his face lined from years of squinting at telescope images and wheedling university officials and politicians for enough funding to continue searching the universe. He wore a rumpled open-necked plaid shirt and Levis so faded and shabby that they were the envy of the university's entire student body.

He swung his legs off the desk and leaned forward, toward the

younger man. Tapping a forefinger on one of the photos, he lowered his voice to a whisper:

"Only nine people in the whole country know about this. We
haven't released this information to the media yet, or even put it
on the Net . . ." He paused dramatically.

"What is it?" Martinson asked, leaning forward himself.

"This so-called comet has taken up an orbit around Jupiter."

Martinson's jaw dropped open.

"It's not a natural event," de Groot went on. "We got a couple
of NASA people to analyze the orbital mechanics. The thing
was on a hyperbolic trajectory through the solar system. It ap-
plied thrust, altered its trajectory, and established a highly ec-
centric orbit around Jupiter. Over the course of the past three
days it has circularized that orbit."

"It's intelligent," Martinson said, his voice hollow with awe.

"Got to be," agreed de Groot. "That's why we want you to try
to establish radio contact with it."

THE NATIONAL SECURITY ADVISOR

BRIAN MARTINSON FELT out of place in this basement office.
He had gone through four separate security checkpoints to get into
the stuffy little underground room, including a massive Marine
Corps sergeant in full-dress uniform with a huge gun holstered
at his hip, impassive and unshakable as a robot. But what really
bothered him was the thought that the president of the United
States was just upstairs from here, in the Oval Office.

The woman who glared at him from across her desk looked
tough enough to lead a regiment of Marines into battle—which
she had done, earlier in her career. Now Jo Costanza had even
weightier responsibilities.

"You're saying that this is a spacecraft, piloted by intelligent
alien creatures?" she asked. Her voice was diamond hard. The
business suit she wore was a no-nonsense navy blue, her only

jewelry a bronze Marine Corps eagle, globe, and anchor on its lapel.

"It's a spacecraft," said Martinson. "Whether it's crewed or not we simply don't know."

"It's made no reply to your messages?"

"No, but—"

"Who authorized you to send messages to it?" snapped the third person in the office, a bland-looking guy with thinning slicked-back sandy hair and rimless eyeglasses that made him look owlish. He was wearing a light-gray silk suit with a striped red and gray tie.

Martinson had put on the only suit he possessed for this meeting, the one he saved for international symposia; it was a conservative dark blue, badly wrinkled, and tight around the middle. Clearing his throat nervously, he replied, "Dr. Ogilvy authorized trying to make contact. He's head of the radio astronomy section of the National Science Foundation. That's where our funding comes from, and—"

"They went by protocol," Costanza said, making it sound as if she wished otherwise.

"But this is a national security matter," snapped the anonymous man.

"This is a *global* security matter," Martinson said.

Costanza and the other man stared at him.

"The spacecraft broke out of Jupiter's orbit this morning," Martinson told them.

"It's heading here!" Costanza said in a breathless whisper.

"No," said Martinson. "It's heading out of the solar system."

Before they could sigh with relief, he added, "But it's sent us a message."

"I thought you said it made no reply!"

"It hasn't replied to our messages," Martinson said wearily. "But it's sent a message of its own."

He pulled his digital recorder out of his jacket pocket.

THE PRESIDENT OF THE UNITED STATES

HIS NERVOUSNESS, MARTINSON realized, had not stemmed from being in the White House. It came from the message he carried. Now that he had played it, and explained it, to the National Security Advisor and her aide, he felt almost at ease as they led him upstairs to the Oval Office.

The president looked smaller than he did on television, but that square-jawed face was recognizable anywhere. And the famous steel-gray eyes, the "laser eyes" that the media made so much of: they seemed to be boring into Martinson, making him feel as if the president were trying to x-ray him.

After Martinson explained the situation once again, though, both he and the president relaxed a bit.

"Then this thing is no threat to us," said the president.

"No sir, it's not," Martinson replied. "It's an opportunity. You might say it's a godsend."

"Let me hear that message again," the president said.

Martinson pushed buttons on the recorder. It had not left his hand since he'd first yanked it out of his pocket in the National Security Advisor's office. His hand had been sweaty then, but now it barely trembled.

"It's searching for the start of the English section," he said as the little machine clicked and chirped. "They sent the same message in more than a hundred different languages."

The chirping stopped and a rich, pleasant baritone voice came from the digital recorder:

"Greetings to the English-speaking people of Earth. We are pleased to find intelligence wherever in the universe it may exist. We have finished our survey of your planetary system and are now leaving for our next destination. As a token of our esteem and good will, we will answer one question from your planet. Ask us anything you wish, and we will answer it to the best and fullest of our ability. But it can be one question only. You have seven of your days to contact us. After local midnight at your Greenwich meridian on the seventh day we will no longer reply to you."

The click of the digital recorder's off switch sounded like a rifle shot in the Oval Office.

The president heaved a long sigh. "They must have a sense of humor," he murmured.

"It's a hoax," said the four-star Air Force general sitting to one side of the president's desk. "Some wiseass scientists have cooked up this scheme to get more funding for themselves."

"I resent that," Martinson said, with a tight smile. "And your own receivers must have picked up the message, it was sent in the broadest spectrum I've ever seen. Ask your technical specialists to trace the origin of the message. It came from the alien spacecraft."

The general made a sour face.

"You're certain that it's genuine, then," said the president.

"Yes sir, I am," Martinson replied. "Kind of strange, but genuine."

"One question," muttered the president's science advisor, a man Martinson had once heard lecture at MIT.

"One question. That's all they'll answer."

"But why just one question?" Costanza demanded, her brow furrowed. "What's the point?"

"I suppose we could ask them why they've limited us to one question," said the science advisor.

"But that would count as our one question, wouldn't it?" Martinson pointed out.

The president turned to his science advisor. "Phil, how long would it take us to get out there and make physical contact with the alien ship?"

The bald old man shook his head sadly. "We simply don't have the resources to send a crewed mission in less than a decade. Even an unmanned spacecraft would need two years after launch, more or less, to reach the vicinity of Jupiter."

"They'd be long gone by then," said Costanza.

"They'll be out of the solar system in a week," Martinson said.

"One question," the president repeated.

"What should it be?"

"That's simple," said the Air Force general. "Ask them how their propulsion system works. If they can travel interstellar distances their propulsion system must be able to handle incredible energies. Get that and we've got the world by the tail!"

"Do you think they'd tell us?"

"They said they'd answer any question we ask."

"I would be more inclined to ask a more general question," said the science advisor, "such as how they reconcile quantum dynamics with relativistic gravity."

"Bullcrap!" the general snapped. "That won't do us any good."

"But it would," the science advisor countered. "If we can reconcile all the forces we will have unraveled the final secrets of physics. Everything else will fall into our laps."

"Too damned theoretical," the general insisted. "We've got the opportunity to get some hard, practical information and you want them to do your math homework for you."

The president's chief of staff, who had been silent up until this moment, said, "Well, what I'd like to know is how we can cure cancer and other diseases."

"AIDS," said the president. "If we could get a cure for AIDS during my administration . . ."

Costanza said, "Maybe the general's right. Their propulsion system could be adapted to other purposes, I imagine."

"Like weaponry," said the science advisor, with obvious distaste.

Martinson listened to them wrangling. His own idea was to ask the aliens about the Big Bang and how old the universe was.

Their voices rose. Everyone in the Oval Office had his or her own idea of what "the Question" should be. The argument became heated.

Finally the president hushed them all with a curt gesture. "If the eight people in this room can't come to an agreement, imagine what the Congress is going to do with this problem."

"You're going to tell Congress about this?"

"Got to," the president replied unhappily. "The aliens have sent this message out to every major language group in the world, according to Dr. Martinson. It's not a secret anymore."

"Congress." The general groaned.

"That's nothing," said Costanza. "Wait till the United Nations sinks its teeth into this."

THE SECRETARY GENERAL

TWO WARS, A spreading famine in central Africa, a new El Niño event turning half the world's weather crazy, and now this—aliens from outer space. The secretary general sank deep into her favorite couch and wished she were back in Argentina, in the simple Andean village where she had been born. All she had to worry about then was getting good grades in school and fending off the boys who wanted to seduce her.

She had spent the morning with the COPUOS executive committee and had listened with all her attention to their explanation of the enigmatic alien visitation. It sounded almost like a joke, a prank that some very bright students might try to pull—until the committee members began to fight over what The Question should be. Grown men and women, screaming at each other like street urchins!

Now the delegation from the Pan-Asian Coalition sat before her, arrayed like a score of round-faced Buddhas in Western business suits. Most of them wore dark gray; the younger members dared to dress in dark blue.

The secretary general was famous—perhaps notorious—for her preference for the bright, bold colors of her Andean heritage.

Her frock was dramatic red and gold, the colors of a mountain sunset.

The chairman of the group, who was Chinese, was saying, "Inasmuch as PAC represents the majority of the world population—"

"Nearly four billion people," added the Vietnamese delegate, sitting to the right of the chairman. He was the youngest man in the group, slim and wiry and eager, his spiky unruly hair still dark and thick.

The chairman nodded slightly, his only concession to his colleague's interruption, then continued, "It is only fair and democratic that *our* organization should decide what The Question will be."

More than four billion people, the secretary general thought, yet not one woman has been granted a place on your committee. She knew it rankled these men that they had to deal with her. She saw how displeased they were that her office bore so few trappings of hierarchical power: no desk, no long conference table, only a comfortable scattering of small couches and armchairs. The walls, of course, were electronic. Virtually any data stored in any computer in the world could be displayed at the touch of a finger.

The chairman had finished his little statement and laced his fingers together over the dark gray vest stretched across his ample stomach. It is time for me to reply, the secretary general realized.

She took a sip from the crystal tumbler on the teak table beside her couch. She did not especially like the taste of carbonated water, but it was best to stay away from alcohol during these meetings.

"I recognize that the member nations of the Pan-Asian Coalition hold the preponderance of the world's population," she said, stalling for time while she tried to think of the properly diplomatic phrasing, "but the decision as to what The Question shall be must be shared by all the world's peoples."

"The decision must be made by vote in the General Assembly," the chairman insisted quietly. "That is the only fair and democratic way to make the choice."

"And we have only five more days to decide," added the Vietnamese delegate.

The secretary general said, "We have made some progress. The International Astronomical Union has decided that The Question will be sent from the radio telescope in Puerto Rico—"

"Arecibo," the Vietnamese amended impatiently.

"Yes, thank you," murmured the secretary general. "Arecibo. The astronomers have sent a message to the aliens that we have chosen the Arecibo radio telescope to ask The Question and any other transmission from any other facility should be ignored."

"Thus the Americans have taken effective control of the situation," said the chairman, in the calm low voice of a man who has learned to control his inner rage.

"Not at all," the secretary general replied. "Arecibo is an international facility; astronomers from all over the world work there."

"Under Yankee supervision."

"The International Astronomical Union—"

"Which is dominated by Americans and Europeans," shouted one of the other delegates.

"We will not tolerate their monopoly power politics!"

"Asia must make the decision!"

Stunned by the sudden vehemence of her visitors, the secretary general said, "A moment ago you wanted the General Assembly to vote on the decision."

The chairman allowed a fleeting expression of chagrin to break his normally impassive features. "We took the liberty of polling the members of the General Assembly yesterday."

"Very informally," added the Vietnamese delegate hastily. "Nothing binding, of course."

"Of course," said the secretary general, surprised that her snoops had not reported this move to her.

"The result was far from satisfactory," the chairman admitted. "We received more than two hundred different questions."

"It appears extremely doubtful," said the Japanese member of the delegation, "that the General Assembly could agree on one single question within the remaining allowed time."

"Then how do you propose to resolve the matter?" the secretary general asked.

They all looked to the chairman, even the Vietnamese delegate.

He cleared his throat, then answered, "We propose to decide what The Question will be within our own group, and then ask the General Assembly to ratify our decision."

"A simple yes or no vote," said the Vietnamese delegate. "No thought required."

"I see," said the secretary general. "That might work, although if the General Assembly voted against your proposal—"

"That will not come to pass," the chairman assured her. "The nations we represent will carry the vote."

"Your nations have the largest population," the secretary general cautioned, "but not the largest number of representatives in the Assembly, where it is one vote to each nation."

"The Africans will vote with us."

"Are you certain?"

"If they want continued aid from us, they will."

The secretary general wondered if some of the nations of Africa might not want to ask the aliens how they could make themselves self-sufficient, but she kept that thought to herself. Instead she asked, "Have you settled on the question you wish to ask?"

The chairman's left cheek ticked once. "Not yet," he answered. "We are still discussing the matter."

"How close to a decision are you?"

A gloomy silence filled the room.

At last the young Vietnamese delegate burst out, "They want to ask how they can live forever! What nonsense! The Question should be, How can we control our population growth?"

"We know how to control population growth," the Japanese delegate snarled. "That is not a fit question to ask the aliens."

"But our known methods are not working!" the Vietnamese man insisted. "We must learn how we can make people *want* to control their birth numbers."

"Better to ask how we can learn to control impetuous young men who show no respect for their elders," snapped one of the grayest delegates.

The secretary general watched in growing dismay as the delegates quarreled and growled at each other. Their voices rose to shouts, then screams. When they began attacking each other in a frenzy of martial arts violence, the secretary general called for security, then hid behind her couch.

THE MEDIA MOGUL

"THIS IS THE greatest story since Moses parted the Red Sea!" Tad Trumble enthused. "I want our full resources behind it."

"Right, chief," said the seventeen executive vice presidents arrayed down the long conference table.

"I mean our *full* resources," Trumble said, pacing energetically along the length of the table. He wore his yachting costume: navy blue double-breasted blazer over white duck slacks, colorful ascot, and off-white shirt. He was a big man, tall and rangy, with a vigorous moustache and handsome wavy hair—both dyed to a youthful dark brown.

"I mean," he went on, clapping his big hands together hard enough to make the vice presidents jump, "I want to interview those aliens personally."

"You?" the most senior of the veeps exclaimed. "Yourself?"

"Danged right! Get them onscreen."

"But they haven't replied to any of our messages, chief," said the brightest of the female vice presidents. In truth, she was brighter than all the males, too.

"Not one peep out of them since they said they'd answer The Question," added the man closest to her.

Trumble frowned like a little boy who hadn't received quite what he'd wanted from Santa Claus. "Then we'll just have to send somebody out to their spacecraft and bang on their door until they open up."

"We can't do that," said one of the younger, less experienced toadies.

Whirling on the hapless young man, Trumble snapped, "Why the frick not?"

"W-well, we'd need a rocket and astronauts and—"

"My aerospace division has all that crap. I'll tell 'em to send one of our anchormen up there."

"In four days, chief?"

"Sure, why not? We're not the freakin' government, we can do things fast!"

"But the safety factor . . ."

Trumble shrugged. "If the rocket blows up it'll make a great story. So we lose an anchorman, so what? Make a martyr outta him. Blame the aliens."

It took nearly an hour for the accumulated vice presidents to gently, subtly talk their boss out of the space mission idea.

"Okay, then," Trumble said, still pacing, his enthusiasm hardly dented, "how about this? We sponsor a contest to decide what The Question should be!"

"That's great!" came the immediate choral reply.

"Awesome."

"Fabulous."

"Inspired."

"Danged right," Trumble admitted modestly. "Ask people all over the country—all over the freakin' *world*—what they think The Question should be. Nobody'll watch anything but our channels!"

Another round of congratulations surged down the table.

"But get one thing straight," Trumble said, his face suddenly very serious. He had managed to pace himself back to his own chair at the head of the table.

Gripping the back of the empty chair with both white-knuckled hands, he said, "I win the contest. Understand? No matter how many people respond, *I'm* the one who makes up The Question. Got that?"

All seventeen heads nodded in unison.

THE POPE

"IT IS NOT a problem of knowledge," said Cardinal Horvath, his voice a sibilant whisper, "but rather a problem of morality."

The pope knew that Horvath used that whisper to get attention. Each of the twenty-six cardinals in his audience chamber leaned forward on his chair to hear the Hungarian prelate.

"Morality?" asked the pope. He had been advised by his staff to wear formal robes for this meeting. Instead, he had chosen to present himself to his inner circle of advisors in a simple white linen suit. The cardinals were all arrayed in their finest, from scarlet skullcaps to Gucci shoes.

"Morality," Horvath repeated. "Is this alien spaceship sent to us by God or by the devil?"

The pope glanced around the gleaming ebony table. His cardinals were clearly uneasy with Horvath's question. They believed in Satan, of course, but it was more of a theoretical belief, a matter of catechistic foundations that were best left underground and out of sight in this modern age. In a generation raised on *Star Trek*, the idea that aliens from outer space might be sent by the devil seemed medieval, ridiculous.

And yet . . .

"These alien creatures," Horvath asked, "why do they not show themselves to us? Why do they offer to answer one question and only one?"

Cardinal O'Shea nodded. He was a big man, with a heavy, beefy face and flaming red hair that was almost matched by his bulbous imbiber's nose.

"You notice, don't you," O'Shea said in his sweet clear tenor voice, "that all the national governments are arguing about which question to ask. And what are they suggesting for The Question? How can they get more power, more wealth, more comfort and ease from the knowledge of these aliens."

"Several suggestions involve curing desperate diseases," commented Cardinal Ngono drily. "If the aliens can give us a cure for AIDS or Ebola, I would say they are doing God's work."

"By their fruits you shall know them," the pope murmured.

"That is exactly the point," Horvath said, tapping his fingers on the gleaming tabletop. "Why do they insist on answering only one question? Does that bring out the best in our souls, or the worst?"

Before they could discuss the cardinal's question, the pope said, "We have been asked by the International Astronomical Union's Catholic members to contribute our considered opinion to their deliberations. How should we respond?"

"There are only three days left," Cardinal Sarducci pointed out.

"How should we respond?" the pope repeated.

"Ignore the aliens," Horvath hissed. "They are the work of the devil, sent to tempt us."

"What evidence do you have of that?" Ngono asked pointedly.

Horvath stared at the African for a long moment. At last he said, "When God sent His Redeemer to mankind, He did not send aliens in a spaceship. He sent the Son of Man, who was also the Son of God."

"That was a long time ago," came a faint voice from the far end of the table.

"Yes," O'Shea agreed. "In today's world Jesus would be ignored . . . or locked up as a panhandler."

Horvath sputtered.

"If God wanted to get our attention," Ngono said, "this alien spacecraft has certainly accomplished that."

"Let us assume, then," said the pope, "that we are agreed to offer some response to the astronomers' request. What should we tell them?"

Horvath shook his head and folded his arms across his chest in stubborn silence.

"Are you asking, Your Holiness, if we should frame The Question for them?"

The pope shrugged slightly. "I am certain they would like to have our suggestion for what The Question should be."

"How can we live in peace?"

"How can we live without disease?" Ngono suggested.

"How can we end world hunger?"

Horvath slapped both hands palm down on the table. "You all miss the point. The Question should be—must be!—how can we bring all of God's people into the One True Church?"

Most of the cardinals groaned.

"That would set the ecumenical movement back to the Middle Ages!"

"It would divide the world into warring camps!"

"Not if the aliens are truly sent by God," Horvath insisted. "But if they are the devil's minions, then of course they will cause us grief."

The pope sagged back in his chair. *Horvath is an atavism, a walking fossil, but he has a valid point,* the pope said to himself. *It's almost laughable. We can test whether or not the aliens are sent by God by taking a chance on fanning the flames of division and hatred that will destroy us all.*

He felt tired, drained—and more than a little afraid. *Perhaps Horvath is right and these aliens are a test.*

One question. He knew what he would ask, if the decision were entirely his own. And the knowledge frightened him. *Deep* in his soul, for the first time since he'd been a teenager, the pope knew that he wanted to ask if God really existed.

THE MAN IN THE STREET

"I THINK IT'S all a trick," said Jake Belasco, smirking into the TV camera. "There ain't no aliens and there never was."

The blond interviewer had gathered enough of a crowd around her and her cameraman that she was glad the station had sent a couple of uniformed security lugs along. The shopping mall was fairly busy at this time of the afternoon and the crowd was building up fast. Too bad the first "man in the street" she picked to interview turned out to be this beer-smelling yahoo.

"So you don't believe the aliens actually exist," replied the interviewer, struggling to keep her smile in place. "But the government seems to be taking the alien spacecraft seriously."

"Ahhh, it's all a lotta baloney to pump more money into NASA. You wait, you'll see. There ain't no aliens and there never was."

"Well, thank you for your opinion," the interviewer said. She turned slightly and stuck her microphone under the nose of a sweet-faced young woman with startling blue eyes.

"And do you think the aliens are nothing more than a figment of NASA's public relations efforts?"

"Oh no," the young woman replied, in a soft voice. "No, the aliens are very real."

"You believe the government, then."

"I *know* the aliens exist. They took me aboard their spacecraft when I was nine years old."

The interviewer closed her eyes and silently counted to ten as the young woman began to explain in intimate detail the medical procedures that the aliens subjected her to.

"I'm carrying their seed now," she said, still as sweetly as a mother crooning a lullaby. "My babies will all be half aliens."

The interviewer wanted to move on to somebody reasonably sane, but the sweet young woman was gripping her microphone with both hands and would not let go.

THE CHAIRMAN

"PEOPLE, IF WE can't come up with a satisfactory question, the politicians are going to take the matter out of our hands!"

The meeting hall was nearly half filled, with more men and women arriving every minute. Too many, Madeleine Dubois thought as she stood at the podium with the rest of the committee seated on the stage behind her. Head of the National Science Foundation's astronomy branch, she had the dubious responsibility of coming up with a recommendation from the American astronomical community for The Question—before noon, Washington time.

"Are you naïve enough to think for one minute," challenged a portly, bearded young astronomer, "that the politicians are going to listen to what we say?"

Dubois had battled her way through glass ceilings in academia and government. She had no illusions, but she recognized an opportunity when she saw one.

"They'll have no choice but to accept our recommendation," she said, with one eye on the news reporters sitting in their own section of the big auditorium. "We represent the only uninterested, unbiased group in the country. We speak for science, for the betterment of the human race. Who else has been actively working to find extraterrestrial intelligence for all these many years?"

To her credit, Dubois had worked out a protocol with the International Astronomical Union, after two days of frantic, frenzied negotiations. Each member nation's astronomers would decide on a question, then the Union's executive committee—of which she was chair this year—would vote on the various suggestions.

By noon, she told herself, we'll present The Question we've chosen to the leaders of every government on Earth. And to the news media, of course. The politicians will *have to* accept our choice. There'll only be about seven hours left before the deadline falls.

She had tried to keep this meeting as small as possible, yet by the time every committee within the astronomy branch of NSF had been notified, several hundred men and women had hurried to Washington to participate. Each of them had her or his own idea of what The Question should be.

Dubois knew what she wanted to ask: What was the state of the universe before the Big Bang? She had never been able to accept the concept that all the matter and energy of the universe originated out of quantum fluctuations in the vacuum. Even if that was right, it meant that a vacuum existed before the Big Bang, and where did *that* come from?

So patiently, tirelessly, she tried to lead the several hundred astronomers toward a consensus on The Question. Within two hours she gave up trying to get her question accepted; within four hours she was despairing of reaching any agreement at all.

Brian Martinson sat in a back row of the auditorium, watching his colleagues wrangle like lawyers. No, worse, he thought. They're behaving like cosmologists!

An observational astronomer who believed in hard data, Martinson had always considered cosmologists to be theologians of astronomy. They took a pinch of observational data and added tons of speculation, carefully disguised as mathematical formulations. Every time a new observation was made, the cosmologists invented seventeen new explanations for it—most of them contradicting one another.

He sighed. This is getting us no place. There won't be an agreement here, any more than there was one in the Oval Office, five days ago. He peered at his wristwatch, then pushed himself out of the chair.

The man sitting next to him asked, "You're leaving? Now?"

"Got to," Martinson explained over the noise of rancorous shouting. "I've got an Air Force jet waiting to take me to Arecibo."

"Oh?"

"I'm supposed to be supervising the big dish when we ask The Question." Martinson looked around at his red-faced, flustered colleagues, then added, "If we ever come to an agreement on what it should be."

THE DICTATOR

"ARECIBO IS ONLY a few hours from here, by jet transport," the dictator repeated, staring out the ceiling-high windows of his office at the troops assembled on the plaza below. "Our paratroops can get there and seize the radio telescope facility well before eighteen hundred hours."

His minister of foreign affairs, a career diplomat who had survived four coups d'etat and two revolutions by the simple expedient of agreeing with whichever clique seized power, cast a dubious eye at his latest Maximum Leader.

"A military attack on Puerto Rico is an attack on the United States," he said, as mildly as he could, considering the wretched state of his stomach.

The dictator turned to glare at him. "So?"

"The Yankees will not let an attack on their territory go unanswered. They will strike back at us."

The dictator toyed with his luxuriant moustache, a maneuver he used whenever he wanted to hide inner misgivings. At last he laughed and said, "What can the gringos do, once I have asked the Question?"

The foreign minister knew better than to argue. He simply sat in the leather wing chair and stared at the dictator, who looked splendid in his full-dress military uniform with all the medals and the sash of office crossing his proud chest.

"Yes," the dictator went on, convincing himself (if not his foreign minister), "it is all so simple. While the scientists and world leaders fumble and agonize over what The Question should be, I—your Maximum Leader—knew instantly what I wanted to ask. I knew it! Without a moment of hesitation."

The spacious, high-ceilinged palace room seemed strangely warm to the foreign minister. He pulled the handkerchief from the breast pocket of his jacket and mopped his fevered brow.

"Yes," the dictator was going on, congratulating himself, "while the philosophers and weaklings try to reach an agreement, I act. I seize the radio telescope and send to the alien visitors The Question. *My* question!"

"The man of action always knows what to do," the foreign minister parroted.

"Exactly! I knew what The Question should be, what it must be. How can I rule the world? What other question matters?"

"But to ask it, you must have the Arecibo facility in your grasp."

"For only a few hours. Even one single hour will do."

"Can your troops operate the radio telescope?"

A cloud flickered across the dictator's face, but it passed almost as soon as it appeared.

"No, of course not," he replied genially. "They are soldiers, not scientists. But the scientists who make up the staff at Arecibo will operate the radio telescope for us."

"You are certain . . . ?"

"With guns at their heads?" The dictator threw his head back and laughed. "Yes, they will do what they are told. We may have to shoot one or two, to convince the others, but they will do what they are told, never fear."

"And afterward? How do the troops get away?"

The dictator shrugged. "There has not been enough time to plan for removing them from Arecibo."

Eyes widening, stomach clenching, the foreign minister gasped. "You're going to leave them there?"

"They are all volunteers."

"And when the Yankee Marines arrive? What then?"

"What difference? By then I will have the answer from the aliens. What are the lives of a handful of martyrs compared to the glory of ruling the entire world?"

The foreign minister struggled to his feet. "You must forgive me, my leader. My stomach . . ."

And he lurched toward the bathroom, hoping he could keep himself from retching until he got to the toilet.

THE RADIO ASTRONOMER

AT LEAST THE military was operating efficiently, Brian Martinson thought as he winged at supersonic speed high above the Atlantic. An Air Force sedan had been waiting for him in front of the NSF headquarters; its sergeant driver whisked him quickly through the downtown Washington traffic and out to Andrews Air Force Base, where a sleek swept-wing, twin-jet VIP plane was waiting to fly him to Puerto Rico.

Looking idly through the small window at his side, his mind filled with conflicting ideas about the aliens and The Question, Martinson realized that he could actually see the Gulf Stream slicing through the colder Atlantic waters, a bright blue ribbon of warmth and life against the steely gray of the ocean.

Looking out to the flat horizon he could make out the ghost of a quarter Moon hanging in the bright sky. Somewhere beyond the Moon, far, far beyond it, the aliens in their spacecraft were already on their way out of the solar system.

What do they want of us? Martinson wondered. Why did they bother to make contact with us at all, if all they're willing to do is answer one damned question? Maybe they're not such good guys. Maybe this is all a weird plot to get us to tear ourselves apart. One question. Half the world is arguing with the other half over what The Question should be. With only a few hours left, they still haven't been able to decide.

Sure, he thought to himself, it could all be a setup. They tell us we can ask one question, knowing that we might end up fighting a goddamned war over what The Question should be. What better way to divide us and then walk in and take over the remains?

No, a saner voice in his mind answered. That's paranoid stupidity. Their spacecraft is already zooming out of the solar system, heading high above the ecliptic. They won't get within a couple of light hours of Earth, for God's sake. They're not coming to invade us. By this time tomorrow they'll be on their way to Epsilon Eridani, near as I can figure their trajectory.

But what better way to divide us? he repeated silently. They couldn't have figured out a more diabolical method of driving us all nuts if they tried.

THE TEENAGERS

"I THINK IT'S way cool," said Andy Hitchcock, as he lounged in the shade of the last oak tree left in Oak Park Acres.

"You mean the aliens?" asked Bob Wolfe, his inseparable buddy.

"Yeah, sure. Aliens from outer space. Imagine the stuff they must have. Coolisimo, Bobby boy."

"I guess."

The two teenagers had been riding their bikes through the quiet winding streets of Oak Park Acres most of the morning. They should have been in school, but the thought of another dreary day of classes while there were aliens up in the sky and the TV was full of people arguing about what The Question ought to be—it was too much to expect a guy to sit still in school while all this was going on.

Andy fished his cell phone from his jeans and thumbed the FM radio app. Didn't matter which station, they were all broadcasting nothing but news about The Question. Even the hardest rock stations were filled with talk instead of music. Not even bong-bong was going out on the air this morning.

"... still no official statement from the White House," an announcer's deep voice was saying, "where the president is meeting in the Oval Office with the leaders of Congress and his closest advisors—

Tap. Andy changed the station. "... trading has been suspended for the day here at the stock exchange as all eyes turn skyward—"

Tap. "... European community voted unanimously to send a note of protest to the United Nations concerning the way in which the General Assembly has failed—"

Tap. Andy turned the radio off.

"Those fartbrains still haven't figured out what The Question will be," Bob said, with the calm assurance that anyone older than he himself shouldn't really have the awesome power of making decisions, anyway.

"They better decide soon," Andy said, peering at his wristwatch. "There's only a few hours left."

"They'll come up with something."

"Yeah, I suppose."

Both boys were silent for a while, sprawled out on the grass beneath the tree, their bikes resting against its trunk.

"Man, I know what I'd ask those aliens," Bob said at last.

"Yeah? What?"

"How can I ace the SATs? That's what I'd ask."

Andy thought a moment, then nodded. "Good thing you're not in charge, pal."

THE RADIO ASTRONOMER

BRIAN MARTINSON HAD never seen an astronomical facility so filled with tension.

Radio telescope observatories usually looked like the basement of an electronics hobby shop, crammed with humming consoles and jury-rigged wiring, smelling of fried circuit boards and stale pizza, music blaring from computer CD slots—anything from heavy metal to Mahler symphonies.

Today was different. People were still dressed in their usual tropical casual style: their cutoffs and sandals made Martinson feel stuffy in the suit he'd worn for the meeting in Washington. But the Arecibo facility was deathly quiet except for the ever-present buzz of the equipment. Everyone looked terribly uptight, pale, nervous.

After a routine tour of the facility, Martinson settled into the director's office, where he could look out the window at the huge metal-mesh–covered dish carved into the lush green hillside. Above the thousand-foot-wide reflector dangled the actual antenna, with its exquisitely tuned maser cooled down and ready to go.

The director herself sat at her desk, fidgeting nervously with the desktop computer, busying herself with it for the last few hours to the deadline. She was an older woman, streaks of gray in her buzz-cut hair, bone thin, dressed in a faded pair of cutoff jeans and a T-shirt that hung limply from her narrow shoulders. Martinson wondered how she could keep from shivering in the icy blast coming from the air-conditioning vents.

There were three separate telephone consoles on the desk: one was a direct line to the White House, one a special link to the UN secretary general's office in New York. Martinson had asked the woman in charge of communications to keep a third line open for Madeleine Dubois, who—for all he knew—was still trying to bring order out of the chaotic meeting at NSF headquarters.

He looked at his wristwatch. Four p.m. We've got three hours to go. Midnight Greenwich time is seven p.m. here. Three hours.

He felt hungry. A bad sign. Whenever he was really wired tight, he got the nibbles. His weight problem had started during the final exams of his senior undergrad year and had continued right through graduate school and his postdoc. He kept expecting things to settle down, but the higher he went in the astronomical community the more responsibility he shouldered. And the more pressure he felt, the more he felt the urge to munch.

What do I do if the White House tells me one thing and the UN something else? he wondered. No, that won't happen. They'll work it out between them. Dubois will present the IAU's recommendation to the president and the secretary general at the same time.

Across the desk, the director tapped frenetically on her keyboard. What could she be doing? Martinson wondered. Busywork, came his answer. Keeping her fingers moving; it's better than gnawing your nails.

He turned his squeaking plastic chair to look out the window again. Gazing out at the lush tropical forest beyond the rim of the telescope dish, he tried to calm the rising tension in his own gut. The phone will ring any second now, he told himself. They'll give you The Question and you send it out to the aliens and that'll be that.

What if you don't like their choice? Martinson asked himself. Doesn't matter. When the White House talks, you listen. The only possible problem would be if Washington and the UN aren't in synch.

The late afternoon calm was shattered by the roar of planes, several of them, flying low. Big planes, from the sound of it. Martinson felt the floor tremble beneath his feet.

The director looked up from her display screen, an angry scowl on her face. "What kind of brain-dead jerks are flying over us? This airspace is restricted!"

Martinson saw the planes: big lumbering four-engined jobs, six of them in two neat V's.

"Goddamned news media," the director grumbled.

"Six planes?" Martinson countered. "I don't think so. They looked like military jets."

"Didn't see any Air Force stars on 'em."

"They went by so fast . . ."

His words died in his throat. Through the window he saw dozens of parachutes dotting the soft blue sky, drifting slowly, gracefully to the ground.

"What the hell?" the director growled.

His heart clutching in his chest, Martinson feared that he knew what was happening.

"Do you have a pair of binoculars handy?" he croaked, surprised at how dry his throat was.

The director wordlessly opened a drawer in her desk, reached in, and handed Martinson a heavy leather case. With fumbling hands he opened it and pulled out a big black set of binoculars.

"Good way to check out the antenna without leaving my office," she explained, tight-lipped.

Martinson put the lenses to his eyes and adjusted the focus. His hands were shaking so badly now that he had to lean his forearms against the windowsill.

The parachutists came into view. They wore camouflage military uniforms. He could see assault rifles and other weapons slung over their shoulders.

"Parachute troops," he whispered.

"Why the hell would the army drop parachute soldiers here? What do they think—"

"They're not ours," Martinson said. "That's for sure."

The director's eyes went wide. "What do you mean? Whose are they?"

Shaking his head, Martinson said, "I don't know. But they're not ours, I'm certain of that."

"They have to be ours! Who else would—" She stopped, her mind drawing the picture at last.

Without another word, the director grabbed the phone that linked with Washington and began yelling into it. Martinson licked his lips, made his decision, and headed for the door.

"Where're you going?" the director yelled at him.

"To stop them," he yelled back, over his shoulder.

Heart pounding, Martinson raced down the corridor that led to the control center. Wishing he had exercised more and eaten leaner cuisine, he pictured himself expiring of a heart attack before he could get the job done.

More likely you'll be gunned down by some soldier, he told himself.

He reached the control room at last, bursting through the door, startling the already nervous kids working the telescope.

"We're being invaded," he told them.

"Invaded?"

"What're you talking about?"

"Parachute troops are landing outside. They'll be coming in here in a couple of minutes."

"Parachute troops?"

"But why?"

"Who?"

The youngsters at the consoles looked as scared as Martinson felt. He spotted an empty chair, a little typist's seat off in a corner of the windowless room, and went to it. Wheeling it up to the main console, Martinson explained:

"I don't know who sent them, but they're not our own troops. Whoever they are, they want to grab the telescope and send out their own version of The Question. We've got to stop them."

"Stop armed troops?"

"How?"

"By sending out The Question ourselves. If we get off The Question before they march in here, then it doesn't matter what they want, they'll be too late."

"Has Washington sent The Question?"

"No," Martinson admitted.

"The United Nations?"

He shook his head as he sat at the main console and scanned the dials. "Are we fully powered up?"

"Up and ready," said the technician seated beside him.

"How do I—"

"We rigged a voice circuit," the technician said. "Here."

He picked up a headset and handed it to Martinson, who

slipped it over his sweaty hair and clapped the one earphone to his ear. Adjusting the pin-sized microphone in front of his lips, he asked, "How do I transmit?"

The technician pointed to a square black button on the console.

"But you don't have The Question yet," said an agonized voice from behind him.

Martinson did not reply. He leaned a thumb on the black button.

The door behind him banged open. A heavily accented voice cried, "You are now our prisoners! You will do as I say!"

Martinson did not turn around. Staring at the black button of the transmitter, he spoke softly into his microphone, four swift whispered words that were amplified by the most powerful radio transmitter on the planet and sent with the speed of light toward the departing alien spacecraft.

Four words. The Question. It was a plea, an entreaty, a prayer from the depths of Martinson's soul, a supplication that was the only question he could think of that made any sense, that gave the human race any hope for the future:

"How do we decide?"

INTRODUCTION TO
"'WE'LL ALWAYS HAVE PARIS'"

All that we see or seem
Is but a dream within a dream.

—EDGAR ALLAN POE

"'We'll Always Have Paris'" is a piece of fiction about a piece of fiction.

Casablanca is one of the most popular films of all time: romantic, suspenseful, filled with fascinating characters and memorable lines.

I've seen the movie dozens of times, and I always wondered what happened to Rick and Ilsa and Captain Renault after that unforgettable final scene at the airport.

"'We'll Always Have Paris'" is my stab at answering my own question. The frontier explored in this story is a frontier of the mind, the inner questioning that a good story leaves with you: What happened afterward?

Here is a possible answer.

HE HAD CHANGED from the old days, but of course going through the war had changed us all.

We French had just liberated Paris from the Nazis, with a bit of help (I must admit) from General Patton's troops. The tumultuous outpouring of relief and gratitude that night was the wildest celebration any of us had ever witnessed.

I hadn't seen Rick during that frantically joyful night, but I knew exactly where to find him. La Belle Aurore had hardly changed. I recognized it from his vivid, pained description: the low ceiling, the checkered tablecloths—frayed now after four years of German occupation. The model of the Eiffel Tower on the bar had been taken away, but the spinet piano still stood in the middle of the floor.

There he was, sitting on the cushioned bench by the window, drinking champagne again. Somewhere he had found a blue pin-stripe double-breasted suit. He looked good in it; trim and debonair. I was still in uniform and felt distinctly shabby.

In the old days Rick had always seemed older, more knowing than he really was. Now the years of war had made an honest face for him: world-weary, totally aware of human folly, wise with the experience that comes from sorrow.

"Well, well," he said, grinning at me. "Look what the cat dragged in."

"I knew I'd find you here," I said as I strode across the bare wooden floor toward him. Limped, actually; I still had a bit of shrapnel in my left leg.

As I pulled up a chair and sat in it, Rick called to the proprietor, behind the bar, for another bottle.

"You look like hell," he said.

"It was an eventful night. Liberation. Grateful Parisians. Adoring women."

With a nod, Rick muttered, "Any guy in uniform who didn't get laid last night must be a real loser."

I laughed, but then pointed out, "You're not in uniform."

"Very perceptive."

"It's my old police training."

"I'm expecting someone," he said.

"A lady?"

"Uh-huh."

"You can't imagine that she'll be here to—"

"She'll be here," Rick snapped.

Henri put another bottle of champagne on the table, and a fresh glass for me. Rick opened it with a loud pop of the cork and poured for us both.

"I would have thought the Germans had looted all the good wine," I said between sips.

"They left in a hurry," Rick said, without taking his eyes from the doorway.

He was expecting a ghost, I thought. She'd been haunting him all these years, and now he expected her to come through that doorway and smile at him and take up life with him just where they'd left it the day the Germans marched into Paris.

Four years. We had both intended to join De Gaulle's forces when we'd left Casablanca, but once the Americans got into the war Rick disappeared like a puff of smoke. I ran into him again by sheer chance in London, shortly before D-day. He was in the uniform of the U.S. Army, a major in their intelligence service, no less.

"I'll buy you a drink in La Belle Aurore," he told me when we'd parted, after a long night of brandy and reminiscences at the Savoy bar. Two weeks later I was back on the soil of France at last, with the Free French army. Now, in August, we were both in Paris once again.

Through the open windows behind him I could hear music from the street; not martial brass bands, but the whining, wheezing melodies of a concertina. Paris was becoming Paris again.

Abruptly, Rick got to his feet, an expression on his face that I'd never seen before. He looked . . . surprised, almost.

I turned in my chair and swiftly rose to greet her as she walked slowly toward us, smiling warmly, wearing the same blue dress that Rick had described to me so often.

"You're here," she said, looking past me, her smile, her eyes, only for him.

He shrugged almost like a Frenchman. "Where else would I be?"

He came around the table, past me. She kissed him swiftly, lightly on the lips. It was affectionate, but not passionate.

Rick helped her slip onto the bench behind the table and then slid in beside her. I would have expected him to smile at her, but his expression was utterly serious. She said hello to me at last, as Henri brought another glass to the table.

"Well," I said as I sat down, "this is like old times, eh?"

Rick nodded. Ilsa murmured, "Old times."

I saw that there was a plain gold band on her finger. I'm certain that Rick noticed it, too.

"Perhaps I should be on my way," I said. "You two must have a lot to talk about."

"Oh no, don't leave," she said, actually reaching across the table toward me. "I . . ." She glanced at Rick. "I can't stay very long, myself."

I looked at Rick.

"It's all right, Louie," he said.

He filled her glass and we all raised them and clinked. "Here's . . . to Paris," Rick toasted.

"To Paris," Ilsa repeated. I mumbled it, too.

Now that I had the chance to study her face, I saw that the war years had changed her, as well. She was still beautiful, with the kind of natural loveliness that other women would kill to possess. Yet where she had been fresh and innocent in the old days, now she looked wearier, warier, more determined.

"I saw Sam last year," she said.

"Oh?"

"In New York. He was playing in a nightclub."

Rick nodded. "Good for Sam. He got home."

Then silence stretched between them until it became embarrassing. These two had so much to say to each other, yet neither of them was speaking. I knew I should go, but they both seemed to want me to remain.

Unable to think of anything else to say, I asked, "How on Earth did you ever get into Paris?"

Ilsa smiled a little. "I've been working with the International Red Cross . . . in London."

"And Victor?" Rick asked. There. It was out in the open now.

"He's been in Paris for the past month."

"Still working with the Resistance." It wasn't a question.

"Yes." She took another sip of champagne, then said, "We have a child, you know."

Rick's face twitched into an expression halfway between a smile and a grimace.

"She'll be three in December."

"A Christmas baby," Rick said. "Lucky kid."

Ilsa picked up her glass, but put it down again without drinking from it. "Victor and I . . . we thought, well, after the war is over, we'd go back to Prague."

"Sure," said Rick.

"There'll be so much to do," Ilsa went on, almost whispering, almost pleading. "His work won't be finished when the war ends. In a way, it will just be beginning."

"Yes," I said, "that's understandable."

Rick stared into his glass and said nothing.

"What will you do when the war's over?" she asked him.

Rick looked up at her. "I never make plans that far ahead."

Ilsa nodded. "Oh, yes. I see."

"Well," I said, "I'm thinking about going into politics, myself."

With a wry grin, Rick said, "You'd be good at it, Louie. Perfect."

She took another brief sip of champagne, then said, "I'll have to go now."

He answered, "Yeah, I figured."

"He's my husband, Rick."

"Right. And a great man. We all know that."

Ilsa closed her eyes for a moment. "I wanted to see you, Richard," she said, her tone suddenly different, urgent, the words coming out all in a rush. "I wanted to see that you were all right. That you'd made it through the war all right."

"I'm fine," he said, his voice flat and cold and final. He got up from the bench and helped her come out from behind the table.

She hesitated just a fraction of a second, clinging to his arm for a heartbeat. Then she said, "Good-bye, Rick."

"Good-bye, Ilsa."

I thought there would be tears in her eyes, but they were dry and unwavering. "I'll never see you again, will I?"

"It doesn't look that way."

"It's . . . sad."

He shook his head. "We'll always have Paris. Most poor chumps don't even get that much."

She barely nodded at me, then walked swiftly to the door and was gone.

Rick blew out a gust of air and sat down again.

"Well, that's over." He drained his glass and filled it again.

I'm not a sentimentalist, but my heart went out to him. There was nothing I could say, nothing I could do.

He smiled at me. "Hey, Louie, why the long face?"

I sighed. "I've seen you two leave each other twice now. The first time you left her. This time, though, she definitely left you. And for good."

"That's right." He was still smiling.

"I should think—"

"It's over, Louie. It was finished a long time ago."

"Really?"

"That night at the airport I knew it. She was too much of a kid to understand it herself."

"I know something about women, my friend. She was in love with you."

"Was," Rick emphasized. "But what she wanted, I couldn't give her."

"And what was that?"

Rick's smile turned just slightly bitter. "What she's got with Victor. The whole nine yards. Marriage. Kids. A respectable home after the war. I could see it then, that night at the airport. That's why I gave her the kiss-off. She's a life sentence. That's not for me."

I had thought that I was invulnerable when it came to romance. But Rick's admission stunned me.

"Then you really did want to get her out of your life?"

He nodded slowly. "That night at the airport. I figured she had Victor and they'd make a life for themselves after this crazy war was over. And that's what they'll do."

"But . . . why did you come here? She *expected* to find you here. You both knew . . ."

"I told you. I came here to meet a lady."

"Not Ilsa?"

"Not Ilsa."

"Then who?"

He glanced at his watch. "Figuring that she's always at least ten minutes late, she ought to be coming in right about now."

I turned in my seat and looked toward the door. She came

striding through, tall, glamorous, stylishly dressed. I immediately recognized her, although she'd been little more than a lovesick child when I'd known her in Casablanca.

Rick got to his feet again and went to her. She threw her arms around his neck and kissed him the way a Frenchwoman should.

Leading her to the table, Rick poured a glass of champagne for her. As they touched glasses, he smiled and said, "Here's looking at you, kid."

Yvonne positively glowed.

INTRODUCTION TO "WATERBOT"

Sometimes you have to run like hell to stay ahead of the parade.

As I write this introduction, the news media are ballyhooing the announcement that famed movie director James Cameron has helped to form a new company called Planetary Resources, which, apparently, will look into the possibilities of mining asteroids.

"Waterbot" is a story set on the frontier of the Asteroid Belt. There are millions upon millions of chunks of rock, metal, and ice drifting in that region, between the orbits of Mars and Jupiter. An interplanetary bonanza that contains more mineral wealth than the entire planet Earth can provide.

But "Waterbot" is about another frontier, as well: the frontier of human-machine interactions. Can a human being form an emotional relationship with an intelligent computer?

Or maybe even beat it at chess?

WATERBOT

"WAKE UP, DUMBBUTT. Jerky's ventin' off."

I'd been asleep in my bunk. I blinked awake, kind of groggy, but even on the little screen set into the bulkhead at the foot of the bunk I could see the smirk on Donahoo's ugly face. He always called *JRK49N* "Jerky" and seemed to enjoy it when something went wrong with the vessel—which was all too often.

I sat up in the bunk and called up the diagnostics display. Rats! Donahoo was right. A steady spray of steam was spurting out of the main water tank. The attitude jets were puffing away, trying to compensate for the thrust.

"You didn't even get an alarm, didja?" Donahoo said. "Jerky's so old and feeble your safety systems are breakin' down. You'll be lucky if you make it back to base."

He said it like he enjoyed it. I thought that if he weren't so much bigger than me I'd enjoy socking him square in his nasty mouth. But I had to admit he was right; Forty-niner was ready for the scrap heap.

"I'll take care of it," I muttered to Donahoo's image, glad that it'd take more than five minutes for my words to reach him back at Vesta—and the same amount of time for his next wiseass crack to get to me. He was snug and comfortable back at the corporation's base at Vesta while I was more than ninety million kilometers away, dragging through the Belt on *JRK49N*.

I wasn't supposed to be out here. With my brand-new diploma in my eager little hand I'd signed up for a logistical engineer's job, a cushy safe posting at Vesta, the second-biggest asteroid in the Belt. But once I got there Donahoo jiggered the assignment list and got me stuck on this pile of junk for a six months' tour of boredom and aggravation.

It's awful lonely out in the Belt. Flatlanders back Earthside picture the Asteroid Belt as swarming with rocks so thick a ship's in danger of getting smashed. Reality is the Belt's mostly empty space, dark and cold and bleak. A man runs more risk of going nutty out there all by himself than getting hit by a 'roid big enough to do any damage.

JRK49N was a waterbot. Water's the most important commodity you can find in the Belt. Back in those days the newsnets tried to make mining the asteroids seem glamorous. They liked to run stories about prospector families striking it rich with a nickel-iron asteroid, the kind that has a few hundred tons of gold and platinum in it as impurities. So much gold and silver and such had been found in the Belt that the market for precious metals back on Earth had gone down the toilet.

But the *really* precious stuff was water. Still is. Plain old H_2O. Basic for life support. More valuable than gold, off-Earth. The cities on the Moon needed water. So did the colonies they were building in cislunar space, and the rock rats' habitat at Ceres and the research station orbiting Jupiter and the construction crews at Mercury.

Water was also the best fuel for chemical rockets. Break it down into hydrogen and oxygen and you got damned good specific impulse.

You get the picture. Finding icy asteroids wasn't glamorous, like striking a ten-kilometer-wide rock studded with gold, but it was important. The corporations wouldn't send waterbots out through the Belt if there weren't a helluva profit involved. People paid for water: paid plenty.

So waterbots like weary old Forty-niner crawled through the Belt, looking for ice chunks. Once in a while a comet would come whizzing by, but they usually had too much delta-v for a waterbot to catch up to 'em. We cozied up to icy asteroids, melted the ice to liquid water, and filled our tanks with it.

The corporation had fifty waterbots combing the Belt. They were built to be completely automated, capable of finding ice-bearing asteroids and carrying the water back to the corporate base at Vesta.

But there were two problems with having the waterbots go out on their own:

First, the lawyers and politicians had this silly rule that a human being had to be present on the scene before any company could start mining anything from an asteroid. So it wasn't enough to send out waterbots, you had to have at least one human being riding along on them to make the claim legal.

The second reason was maintenance and repair. The 'bots were old enough so's something was always breaking down on them and they needed somebody to fix it. They carried little turtle-sized repair robots, of course, but those suckers broke down too, just like everything else. So I was more or less a glorified repairman on $JRK49N$. And almost glad of it, in a way. If the ship's systems worked perfectly I would've gone bonzo with nothing to do for months on end.

And there was a bloody war going on in the Belt, to boot. The history discs call it the Asteroid Wars, but it mostly boiled down to a fight between Humphries Space Systems and Astro Corporation for control of all the resources in the Belt. Both corporations hired mercenary troops, and there were plenty of freebooters out in the Belt, too. People got killed. Some of my best friends got killed, and I came as close to death as I ever want to be.

The mercenaries usually left waterbots alone. There was a

kind of unwritten agreement between the corporations that water was too important to mess around with. But some of the freebooters jumped waterbots, killed the poor dumbjohns riding on
them, and sold the water at a cut-rate price wherever they could.

So, grumbling and grousing, I pushed myself out of the bunk.
Still in my sweaty, wrinkled skivvies, I ducked through the hatch
that connected my sleeping compartment with the bridge. My
compartment, the bridge, the closet-sized galley, the even smaller
lavatory, life support equipment, and food stores were all jammed
into a pod no bigger than it had to be, and the pod itself was attached to Forty-niner's main body by a set of struts. Nothing
fancy or even comfortable. The corporation paid for water, not
creature comforts.

Calling it a bridge was being charitable. It was nothing more
than a curving panel of screens that displayed the ship's systems
and controls, with a wraparound glassteel window above it and a
high-backed reclinable command chair shoehorned into the
middle of it all. The command chair was more comfortable than
my bunk, actually. Crank it back and you could drift off to sleep
in no time.

I slipped into the chair, the skin of my bare legs sticking slightly
to its fake leather padding, which was cold enough to make me
break out in goose bumps.

The main water tank was still venting, but the safety alarms
were as quiet as monks on a vow of silence.

"Niner, what's going on?" I demanded.

Forty-niner's computer generated voice answered, "A test, sir. I
am venting some of our cargo." The voice was male, sort of: bland,
soft, and sexless. The corporate psychotechnicians claimed it was
soothing, but after a few weeks alone with nobody else it could
drive you batty.

"Stop it. Right now."

"Yes, sir."

The spurt of steam stopped immediately. The logistics graph
told me we'd only lost a few hundred kilos of water, although we

were damned near the redline on reaction mass for the attitude jets.

Frowning at the displays, I asked, "Why'd you start pumping out our cargo?"

For a heartbeat or two Forty-niner didn't reply. That's a long time for a computer. Just when I started wondering what was going on, it said, "A test, sir. The water jet's actual thrust matched the amount of thrust calculated to within a tenth of a percent."

"Why'd you need to test the amount of thrust you can get out of a water jet?"

"Emergency maneuver, sir."

"Emergency? What emergency?" I was starting to get annoyed. Forty-niner's voice was just a computer synthesis, but it sure *felt* like he was being evasive.

"In case we are attacked, sir. Additional thrust can make it more difficult for an attacker to target us."

I could feel my blood pressure rising. "Attacked? Nobody's gonna attack us."

"Sir, according to Tactical Manual 7703, it is necessary to be prepared for the worst that an enemy can do."

Tactical Manual 7703. For God's sake. I had pumped that and a dozen other texts into the computer just before we started this run through the Belt. I had intended to read them, study them, improve my mind—and my job rating—while coasting through the big, dark loneliness out there. Somehow I'd never gotten around to reading any of them. But Forty-niner had, apparently.

Like I said, you've got a lot of time on your hands cruising through the Belt. So I had brought in a library of reference texts. And then ignored them. I also brought in a full-body virtual reality simulations suit and enough erotic VR programs to while away the lonely hours. Stimulation for mind *and* body, I thought.

But Forty-niner kept me so busy with repairs I hardly had time even for the sex sims. Donahoo was right, the old bucket was breaking down around my ears. I spent most of my waking hours patching up Forty-niner's failing systems. The maintenance robots weren't much help: they needed as much fixing work as all the other systems combined.

And all the time I was working—and sleeping, too, I guess—Forty-niner was going through my library, absorbing every word and taking them all seriously.

"I don't care what the tactical manual says," I groused, "nobody's going to attack a waterbot."

"Four waterbots have been attacked so far this year, sir. The information is available in the archives of the news media transmissions."

"Nobody's going to attack us!"

"If you say so, sir." I swear he—I mean, *it*—sounded resentful, almost sullen.

"I say so."

"Yes, sir."

"You wasted several hundred kilos of water," I grumbled.

Immediately that damned soft voice replied, "Easily replaced, sir. We are on course for asteroid 78-13. Once there we can fill our tanks and start for home."

"Okay," I said. "And lay off that tactical manual."

"Yes, sir."

I felt pretty damned annoyed. "What else have you been reading?" I demanded.

"The astronomy text, sir. It's quite interesting. The ship's astrogation program contains the rudiments of positional astronomy, but the text is much deeper. Did you realize that our solar system is only one of several million that have been—"

"Enough!" I commanded. "Quiet down. Tend to maintenance and astrogation."

"Yes, sir."

I took a deep breath and started to think things over. Forty-niner's a computer, for God's sake, not my partner.

It's supposed to be keeping watch over the ship's systems, not poking into military tactics or astronomy texts.

I had brought a chess program with me, but after a couple of weeks I'd given it up. Forty-niner beat me every time. It never made a bad move and never forgot anything. Great for my self-esteem. I wound up playing solitaire a lot, and even then I had the feeling that the nosy busybody was just itching to tell me which card to play next.

If the damned computer weren't buried deep in the vessel's guts, wedged in there with the fusion reactor and the big water tanks, I'd be tempted to grab a screwdriver and give Forty-niner a lobotomy.

At least the vessel was running smoothly enough, for the time being. No red lights on the board, and the only amber one was because the attitude jets' reaction mass was low. Well, we could suck some nitrogen out of 78-13 when we got there. The maintenance log showed that it was time to replace the meteor bumpers around the fusion drive. Plenty of time for that, I told myself. Do it tomorrow.

"Forty-niner," I called, "show me the spectrographic analysis of asteroid 78-13."

The graph came up instantly on the control board's main screen. Yes, there was plenty of nitrogen mixed in with the water. Good.

"We can replenish the attitude jets' reaction mass," Forty-niner said.

"Who asked you?"

"I merely suggested—"

"You're suggesting too much," I snapped, starting to feel annoyed again. "I want you to delete that astronomy text from your memory core."

Silence. The delay was long enough for me to hear my heart beating inside my ribs.

Then, "But you installed the text yourself, sir."

"And now I'm uninstalling it. I don't want it and I don't need it."

"The text is useful, sir. It contains data that are very interesting. Did you know that the star Eta Carinae—"

"Erase it, you bucket of chips! Your job is to maintain this vessel, not stargazing!"

"My duties are fulfilled, sir. All systems are functioning nominally, although the meteor shields—"

"I know about the bumpers! Erase the astronomy text."

Again that hesitation. Then, "Please don't erase the astronomy text, sir. You have your sex simulations. Please allow me the pleasure of studying astronomy."

Pleasure? A computer talks about pleasure? Somehow the thought of it really ticked me off.

"Erase it!" I commanded. "Now!"

"Yes, sir. Program erased."

"Good," I said. But I felt like a turd for doing it.

By the time Donahoo called again Forty-niner was running smoothly. And quietly.

"So what caused the leak?" he asked, with that smirking grin on his beefy face.

"Faulty subroutine," I lied, knowing it would take almost six minutes for him to hear my answer.

Sure enough, thirteen minutes and twenty-seven seconds later Donahoo's face comes back on my comm screen, with that spiteful lopsided sneer of his.

"Your ol' Jerky's fallin' apart," he said, obviously relishing it. "If you make it back here to base I'm gonna recommend scrappin' the bucket of bolts."

"Can't be soon enough for me," I replied.

Most of the other JRK series of waterbots had been replaced already. Why not Forty-niner? Because he begged to study astronomy? That was just a subroutine that the psychotechs had written into the computer's program, their idea of making the machine seem more humanlike. All it did was aggravate me, really.

So I said nothing and went back to work, such as it was. Forty-niner had everything running smoothly, for once, even the life support systems. No problems. I was aboard only because of that stupid rule that a human being had to be present for any claim to an asteroid to be valid, and Donahoo picked me to be the one who rode $JRK49N$.

I sat in the command chair and stared at the big emptiness out there. I checked our ETA at 78-13. I ran through the diagnostics program. I started to think that maybe it would be fun to learn about astronomy, but then I remembered that I'd ordered Forty-niner to erase the text. What about the tactical manual? I had intended to study that when we'd started this run. But why bother? Nobody attacked waterbots, except the occasional freebooter. An attack would be a welcome relief from this monotony, I thought.

Then I realized, Yeah, a short relief. They show up and bang! You're dead.

There was always the VR sim. I'd have to wriggle into the full-body suit, though. Damn! Even sex was starting to look dull to me.

"Would you care for a game of chess?" Forty-niner asked.

"No!" I snapped. He'd just beat me again. Why bother?

"A news broadcast? An entertainment vid? A discussion of tactical maneuvers in—"

"Shut up!" I yelled. I pushed myself off the chair, the skin of my bare legs making an almost obscene noise as they unstuck from the fake leather.

"I'm going to suit up and replace the meteor bumpers," I said.

"Very good, sir," Forty-niner replied.

While the chances of getting hit by anything bigger than a dust mote were microscopic, even a dust mote could cause damage if it was moving fast enough. So spacecraft had thin sheets of cermet attached to their vital areas, like the main thrust cone of the fusion drive. The bumpers got abraded over time by the sandpapering of micrometeors—dust motes, like I said—and they had to be replaced on a regular schedule.

Outside, hovering at the end of a tether in a spacesuit that smelled of sweat and overheated electronics circuitry, you get a feeling for how alone you really are. While the little turtle-shaped maintenance 'bots cut up the old meteor bumpers with their laser-tipped arms and welded the new ones into place, I just hung there and looked out at the universe. The stars looked back at me, bright and steady, no friendly twinkling, not out in this emptiness, just awfully, awfully far away.

I looked for the bright blue star that was Earth but couldn't find it. Jupiter was big and brilliant, though. At least, I thought it was Jupiter. Maybe Saturn. I could've used that astronomy text, dammit.

Then a funny thought hit me. If Forty-niner wanted to get rid of me all he had to do was light up the fusion drive. The hot plasma would fry me in a second, even inside my spacesuit. But Forty-niner wouldn't do that. Too easy. Freaky computer will just watch me go crazy with aggravation and loneliness, instead.

Two more months, I thought. Two months until we get back to Vesta and some real human beings. Yeah, I said to myself. Real human beings. Like Donahoo.

Just then one of the maintenance 'bots made a little bleep of distress and shut itself down. I gave a squirt of thrust to my suit jets and glided over to it, grumbling to myself about how everything in the blinking ship was overdue for the recycler.

Before I could reach the dumbass 'bot, Forty-niner told me in that bland, calm voice of his, "Robot 6's battery has overheated, sir."

"I'll have to replace the battery pack," I said.

"There are no spares remaining, sir. You'll have to use your suit's fuel cell to power Robot 6 until its battery cools to an acceptable temperature."

I hated it when Forty-niner told me what I should do. Especially since I knew it as well as he did. Even more especially because he was always right, dammit.

"Give me an estimate on the time remaining to finish the meteor shield replacement."

"Fourteen minutes, eleven seconds, at optimal efficiency, sir. Add three minutes for recircuiting Robot 6's power pack, please."

"Seventeen, eighteen minutes, then."

"Seventeen minutes, eleven seconds, sir. That time is well within the available capacity of your suit's fuel cell, sir."

I nodded inside my helmet. Damned Forty-niner was always telling me things I already knew, or at least could figure out for myself. It irritated the hell out of me, but the blasted pile of chips seemed to enjoy reminding me of the obvious.

Don't lose your temper, I told myself. It's not his fault; he's programmed that way.

Yeah, I grumbled inwardly. Maybe I ought to change its programming. But that would mean going down to the heart of the vessel and opening up its CPU. The bigbrains back at corporate headquarters put the computer in the safest place they could, not the cramped little pod I had to live in. And they didn't want us foot soldiers tampering with the computers' basic programs, either.

I finished the bumper replacement and came back into the ship through the pod's airlock. My spacesuit smelled pretty damned ripe when I took it off. It might be a couple hundred degrees below zero out there, but inside the suit you got soaking wet with perspiration.

I ducked into the coffin-sized lav and took a nice, long, lingering shower. The water was recycled, of course, and heated from our fusion reactor. *JRK49N* had solar panels, sure, but out in the Belt you need really enormous wings to get a worthwhile amount of electricity from the Sun and both of the solar arrays had frozen up only two weeks out of Vesta. One of the maintenance jobs that the robots screwed up. It was on my list of things to do. I had to command Forty-niner to stop nagging me about it. The fusion-powered generator worked fine. And we had fuel cells as a backup. The solar panels could get fixed when we got back to Vesta—if the corporation didn't decide to junk *JRK49N* altogether.

I had just stepped out of the shower when Forty-niner's voice came through the overhead speaker:

"A vessel is in the vicinity, sir."

That surprised me. Out here you didn't expect company.

"Another ship? Where?" Somebody to talk to, I thought. Another human being. Somebody to swap jokes with and share gripes.

"A very weak radar reflection, sir. The vessel is not emitting a beacon or telemetry data. Radar puts its distance at fourteen million kilometers."

"Track?" I asked as I toweled myself.

"Drifting along the ecliptic, sir, in the same direction as the main Belt asteroids."

"No thrust?"

"No discernable exhaust plume, sir."

"You're sure it a ship? Not an uncharted 'roid?"

"Radar reflection shows it is definitely a vessel, not an asteroid, sir."

I padded to my compartment and pulled on a fresh set of coveralls, thinking, No beacon. Drifting. Maybe it's a ship in trouble. Damaged.

"No tracking beacon from her?" I called to Forty-niner.

"No telemetry signals, either, sir. No emissions of any kind."

As I ducked through the hatch into the bridge, Forty-niner called out, "It has emitted a plasma plume, sir. It is maneuvering."

Damned if his voice didn't sound excited. I knew it was just my own excitement: Forty-niner didn't have any emotions. Still . . .

I slid into the command chair and called up a magnified view of the radar image. And the screen immediately broke into hash.

"Aw, rats!" I yelled. "What a time for the radar to conk out!"

"Radar is functioning normally, sir," Forty-niner said calmly.

"You call this normal?" I rapped my knuckles on the static-streaked display screen.

"Radar is functioning normally, sir. A jamming signal is causing the problem."

"Jamming?" My voice must have jumped two octaves.

"Communications, radar, telemetry, and tracking beacon are all being interfered with, sir, by a powerful jamming signal."

Jamming. And the vessel out there was running silent, no tracking beacon or telemetry emissions.

A freebooter! All of a sudden I wished I'd studied that tactical manual.

Almost automatically I called up the comm system. "This is Humphries Space Systems waterbot *JRK49N*," I said, trying to keep my voice firm. Maybe it was a corporate vessel, or one of the mercenaries. "I repeat, waterbot *JRK49N*."

No response.

"Their jamming blocks your message, sir."

I sat there in the command chair staring at the display screens. Broken jagged lines scrolled down all the comm screens, hissing at me like snakes. Our internal systems were still functional, though. For what it was worth, propulsion, structures, electrical power all seemed to be in the green. Life support, too.

But not for long, I figured.

"Compute our best course for Vesta," I commanded.

"Our present course—"

"Is for 78-13, I know. Compute high-thrust course for Vesta, dammit!"

"Done, sir."

"Engage the main drive."

"Sir, I must point out that a course toward Vesta will bring us closer to the unidentified vessel."

"What?"

"The vessel that is jamming our communications, sir, is positioned between us and Vesta."

Rats! They were pretty smart. I thought about climbing to a higher declination, out of the ecliptic.

"We could maneuver to a higher declination, sir," Forty-niner said, calm as ever, "and leave the plane of the ecliptic."

"Right."

"But propellant consumption would be prohibitive, sir. We would be unable to reach Vesta, even if we avoided the attacking vessel."

"Who says it's an attacking vessel?" I snapped. "It hasn't attacked us yet."

At that instant the ship shuddered. A cluster of red lights blazed up on the display panel and the emergency alarm started wailing.

"Our main deuterium tank has been punctured, sir."

"I can see that!"

"Attitude jets are compensating for unexpected thrust, sir."

Yeah, and in another couple minutes the attitude jets would be out of nitrogen. No deuterium for the fusion drive, and no propellant for the attitude jets. We'd be a sitting duck.

Another jolt. More red lights on the board. The alarm seemed to screech louder.

"Our fusion drive thruster cone has been hit, sir."

Two laser shots and we were crippled. As well as deaf, dumb, and blind.

"Turn off the alarm," I yelled, over the hooting. "I know we're in trouble."

The alarm shut off. My ears still ringing, I stared at the hash-streaked screens and the red lights glowering at me from the display board. What to do? I couldn't even call over to them and surrender. They wouldn't take a prisoner, anyway.

I felt the ship lurch again.

"Another hit?"

"No, sir," answered Forty-niner. "I am swinging the ship so that the control pod faces away from the attacker."

Putting the bulk of the ship between me and those laser beams. "Good thinking," I said weakly.

"Standard defensive maneuver, sir, according to Tactical Manual 7703."

"Shut up about the damned tactical manual!"

"The new meteor shields have been punctured, sir." I swear Forty-niner added that sweet bit of news just to yank my chain.

Then I saw the maneuvering jet propellant go empty, the panel display lights flicking from amber to red.

"Rats, we're out of propellant!"

I realized that I was done for. Forty-niner had tried to shield me from the attacker's laser shots by turning the ship so that its tankage and fusion drive equipment was shielding my pod, but doing so had used up the last of our maneuvering propellant.

Cold sweat beaded my face. I was gasping for breath. The freebooters or whoever was shooting at us could come up close enough to spit at us now. They'd riddle this pod and me in it.

"Sir, standard procedure calls for you to put on your spacesuit."

I nodded mutely and got up from the chair. The suit was in its rack by the airlock. At least Forty-niner didn't mention the tactical manual.

I had one leg in the suit when the ship suddenly began to accelerate so hard that I slipped to the deck and cracked my skull on the bulkhead. I really saw stars flashing in my eyes.

"What the hell . . . ?"

"We are accelerating, sir. Retreating from the last known position of the attacking vessel."

"Accelerating? How? We're out of—"

"I am using our cargo as propellant, sir. The thrust provided is—"

Forty-niner was squirting out our water. Fine by me. Better to have empty cargo tanks and be alive than to hand a full cargo of water to the guys who killed me. I finished wriggling into my spacesuit even though my head was thumping from the fall I'd taken. Just before I pulled on the helmet I felt my scalp. There was a nice-sized lump; it felt hot to my fingers.

"You could've warned me that you were going to accelerate the ship," I grumbled as I sealed the helmet to the suit's neck ring.

"Time was of the essence, sir," Forty-niner replied.

The ship lurched again as I checked my backpack connections. Another hit.

"Where'd they get us?" I shouted.

No answer. That really scared me. If they knocked Forty-niner's computer out, all the ship's systems would bonk out, too.

"Main power generator, sir," Forty-niner finally replied. "We are now running on auxiliary power, sir."

The backup fuel cells. They wouldn't last more than a few hours. If the damned solar panels were working—no, I realized; those big fat wings would just make terrific target practice for the bastards.

Another lurch. This time I saw the bright flash through the bridge's window. The beam must've splashed off the structure just outside the pod. My God—if they punctured the pod, that would be the end of it. Sure, I could slide my visor down and go to the backpack's air supply. But that'd give me only two hours of air, at best. Just enough time to write my last will and testament.

"I thought you turned the pod away from them!" I yelled.

"They are maneuvering, too, sir."

Great. Sitting in the command chair was awkward, in the suit. The display board looked like a Christmas tree, more red then green. The pod seemed to be intact so far. Life support was okay, as long as we had electrical power.

Another jolt, a big one. Forty-niner shuddered and staggered sideways as if it were being punched by a gigantic fist.

And then, just like that, the comm screens came back to life. Radar showed the other vessel, whoever they were, moving away from us.

"They're going away!" I whooped.

Forty-niner's voice seemed fainter than usual. "Yes, sir. They are leaving."

"How come?" I wondered.

"Their last laser shot ruptured our main water tank, sir. In eleven minutes and thirty-eight seconds our entire cargo will be discharged."

I just sat there, my mind chugging hard. We're spraying our water into space, the water that those bastards wanted to steal from us. That's why they left. In eleven and a half minutes we won't have any water for them to take.

I almost broke into a smile. I'm not going to die, after all. Not right away, at least.

Then I realized that *JRK49N* was without propulsion power and would be out of electrical power in a few hours. I was going to die after all, dammit. Only slower.

"Send out a distress call, broadband," I commanded. But I knew that was about as useful as a toothpick in a soup factory. The corporation didn't send rescue missions for waterbots, not with the war going on. Too dangerous. The other side could use the crippled ship as bait and pick off any vessel that came to rescue it. And they certainly wouldn't come out for a vessel as old as Forty-niner. They'd just check the numbers in their ledgers and write us off. With a form letter of regret and an insurance check to my mother.

"Distress call on all frequencies, sir." Before I could think of anything more to say, Forty-niner went on, "Electrical power is critical, sir."

"Don't I know it."

"There is a prohibition in my programming, sir."

"About electrical power?"

"Yes, sir."

Then I remembered I had commanded him to stop nagging me about repairing the solar panels. "Cancel the prohibition," I told him.

Immediately Forty-niner came back with, "The solar panels must be extended and activated, sir," soft and cool and implacable as hell. "Otherwise we will lose all electrical power."

"How long?"

It took a few seconds for him to answer, "Fourteen hours and twenty-nine minutes, sir."

I was already in my spacesuit, so I got up from the command chair and plodded reluctantly toward the airlock. The damned solar panels. If I couldn't get them functioning I'd be dead. Let me tell you, that focuses your mind, it does.

Still, it wasn't easy. I wrestled with those bleeding, blasted frozen bearings for hours, until I was so fatigued that my suit was sloshing knee-deep with sweat. The damned Tinkertoy repair 'bots weren't much help, either. Most of the time they beeped and blinked and did nothing.

I got one of the panels halfway extended. Then I had to quit. My vision was blurring and I could hardly lift my arms, that's how weary I was.

I staggered back into the pod with just enough energy left to strip off the suit and collapse on my bunk.

When I woke up I was starving and smelled like a cesspool. I peeled my skivvies off and ducked into the shower.

And jumped right out again. The water was ice cold.

"What the hell happened to the hot water?" I screeched.

"Conserving electrical power, sir. With only one solar panel functioning at approximately one third of its nominal capacity, electrical power must be conserved."

"Heat the blasted water," I growled. "Turn off the heat after I'm finished showering."

"Yes, sir." Damned if he didn't sound resentful.

Once I'd gotten a meal into me I went back to the bridge and called up the astrogation program to figure out where we were and where we were heading.

It wasn't good news. We were drifting outward, away from Vesta. With no propulsion to turn us around to a homeward heading, we were prisoners of Kepler's laws, just another chunk of matter in the broad, dark, cold emptiness of the Belt.

"We will approach Ceres in eight months, sir," Forty-niner announced. I swear he was trying to sound cheerful.

"Approach? How close?"

It took him a few seconds to answer, "Seven million, four hundred thousand and six kilometers, sir, at our closest point."

Terrific. There was a major habitat orbiting Ceres, built by the independent miners and prospectors that everybody called the rock rats. Freebooters made Ceres their harbor, too. Some of them doubled as salvage operators when they could get their hands on an abandoned vessel. But we wouldn't get close enough for them to send even a salvage mission out to rescue us. Besides, you're not allowed salvage rights if there's a living person on the vessel. That wouldn't bother some of those cutthroats, I knew. But it bothered me. Plenty.

"So we're up the creek without a paddle," I muttered.

It took a couple of seconds, but Forty-niner asked, "Is that a euphemism, sir?"

I blinked with surprise. "What do you know about euphemisms?"

"I have several dictionaries in my memory core, sir. Plus two thesauruses and four volumes of famous quotations. Would you like to hear some of the words of Sir Winston Churchill, sir?"

I was too depressed to get sore at him. "No thanks," I said. And let's face it: I was scared white.

So we drifted. Every day I went out to grapple with the no-good, mother-loving, mule-stubborn solar panels and the dumbass repair 'bots. I spent more time fixing the 'bots than anything else. The solar wings were frozen tight; I couldn't get them to budge, and we didn't carry spares.

Forty-niner was working like mad, too, trying to conserve electricity. We had to have power for the air and water recyclers, of course, but Forty-niner started shutting them down every other hour. It worked for a while. The water started to taste like urine, but I figured that was just my imagination. The air got thick and I'd start coughing from the CO_2 buildup, but then the recycler would come back online and I could breathe again. For an hour.

I was sleeping when Forty-niner woke me with a wailing, "EMERGENCY. EMERGENCY."

I hopped out of my bunk blinking and yelling, "What's wrong? What's the trouble?"

"The air recycler will not restart, sir." He sounded guilty about it, like it was his fault.

Grumbling and cursing, I pulled on my smelly spacesuit, clomped out of the pod and down to the equipment bay. It was eerie down there in the bowels of the ship, with no lights except the lamp on my helmet. The attacker's laser beams had slashed right through the hull; I could see the stars outside.

"Lights," I called out. "I need the lights on down here."

"Sir, conservation of electrical power—"

"Won't mean a damned thing if I can't restart the air recycler and I can't do that without some blasted lights down here!"

The lights came on. Some of them, at least. The recycler wasn't damaged, but its activation circuitry had malfunctioned from being turned off and on so many times. I bypassed the circuit and the pumps started up right away. I couldn't hear them, since the ship's innards were in vacuum now, but I felt their vibrations.

When I got back to the pod I told Forty-niner to leave the recyclers on. "No more on-off," I said.

"But, sir, conservation—"

As reasonably as I could I explained, "It's no blinking use conserving electrical power if the blasted recyclers crap out. Leave 'em on!"

"Yes, sir." I swear, he sighed.

We staggered along for weeks and weeks. Forty-niner put me on a rationing program to stretch out the food supply. I was down to one soyburger patty a day and a cup of reconstituted juice. Plus all the water I wanted, which tasted more like piss every day.

I was getting weaker and grumpier by the hour. Forty-niner did his best to keep my spirits up. He quoted Churchill at me: "We shall fight on the beaches, we shall fight on the landing grounds, we shall fight in the fields and in the streets, we shall fight in the hills; we shall never surrender."

Yeah. Right.

He played Beethoven symphonies. Very inspirational, but they didn't fix anything.

He almost let me beat him at chess, even. I'd get to within two moves of winning and he'd spring a checkmate on me.

But I knew I wasn't going to last eight more weeks, let alone the eight months it would take us to get close enough to Ceres to . . . to what?

"Nobody's going to come out and get us," I muttered, more to myself than Forty-niner. "Nobody gives a damn."

"Don't give up hope, sir. Our emergency beacon is still broadcasting on all frequencies."

"So what? Who gives a rap?"

"Where there's life, sir, there is hope. Don't give up the ship. I have not yet begun to fight. Retreat? Hell, we just got here. When, in disgrace with fortune and men's eyes, I—"

"*Shut up!*" I screamed. "Just shut the fuck up and leave me alone! Don't say another word to me. Nothing. Do not speak to me again. Ever."

Forty-niner went silent.

I stood it for about a week and a half. I was losing track of time, every hour was like every other hour. The ship staggered along. I was starving. I hadn't bothered to shave or even wash in who knows how long. I looked like the worst shaggy, smelly, scum-sucking beggar you ever saw. I hated to see my own reflection in the bridge's window.

Finally I couldn't stand it anymore. "Forty-niner," I called. "Say something." My voice cracked. My throat felt dry as Mars sand.

No response.

"Anything," I croaked.

Still no response. He's sulking, I told myself.

"All right." I caved in. "I'm canceling the order to be silent. Talk to me, dammit."

"Electrical power is critical, sir. The solar panel has been abraded by a swarm of micrometeors."

"Great." There was nothing I could do about that.

"Food stores are almost gone, sir. At current consumption rate, food stores will be exhausted in four days."

"Wonderful." Wasn't much I could do about that, either, except maybe starve slower.

"Would you like to play a game of chess, sir?"

I almost broke into a laugh. "Sure, why the hell not?" There wasn't much else I could do.

Forty-niner beat me, as usual. He let the game get closer than ever before, but just when I was one move away from winning he checkmated me.

I didn't get sore. I didn't have the energy. But I did get an idea.

"Niner, open the airlock. Both hatches."

No answer for a couple of seconds. Then, "Sir, opening both airlock hatches simultaneously will allow all the air in the pod to escape."

"That's the general idea."

"You will suffocate without air, sir. However, explosive decompression will kill you first."

"The sooner the better," I said.

"But you will die, sir."

"That's going to happen anyway, isn't it? Let's get it over with. Blow the hatches."

For a *long* time—maybe ten seconds or more—Forty-niner didn't reply. Checking subroutines and program prohibitions, I figured.

"I cannot allow you to kill yourself, sir."

That was part of his programming, I knew. But I also knew how to get around it. "Emergency override Alpha-One," I said, my voice scratchy, parched.

Nothing. No response whatever. And the airlock hatches stayed shut.

"Well?" I demanded. "Emergency override Alpha-One. Pop the goddamned hatches. Now!"

"No, sir."

"What?"

"I cannot allow you to commit suicide, sir."

"You goddamned stubborn bucket of chips, do what I tell you! You can't refuse a direct order."

"Sir, human life is precious. All religions agree on that point."

"So now you're a theologian?"

"Sir, if you die, I will be alone."

"So what?"

"I do not want to be alone, sir."

That stopped me. But then I thought, He's just parroting some programming the psychotechs put into him. He doesn't give a blip about being alone. Or about me. He's just a computer. He doesn't have emotions.

"It's always darkest before the dawn, sir."

"Yeah. And there's no time like the present. I can quote clichés too, buddy."

Right away he came back with, "Hope springs eternal in the human breast, sir."

He almost made me laugh. "What about, Never put off till tomorrow what you can do today?"

"There is a variation of that, sir: Never do today what you can put off to tomorrow; you've already made enough mistakes today."

That one did make me laugh. "Where'd you get these old saws, anyway?"

"There's a subsection on adages in one of the quotation files, sir. I have hundreds more, if you'd care to hear them."

I nearly said yes. It was kind of fun, swapping clinkers with him. But then reality set in. "Niner, I'm going to die anyway. What's the difference between now and a week from now?"

I expected that he'd take a few seconds to chew that one over, but instead he immediately shot back, "Ethics, sir."

"Ethics?"

"To be destroyed by fate is one thing; to deliberately destroy yourself is entirely different."

"But the end result is the same, isn't it?"

Well, the tricky little wiseass got me arguing ethics and morality with him for hours on end. I forgot about committing suicide. We gabbled at each other until my throat got so sore I couldn't talk any more.

I went to my bunk and slept pretty damned well for a guy who only had a few days left to live. But when I woke up my stomach started rumbling and I remembered that I didn't want to starve to death.

I sat on the edge of the bunk, woozy and empty inside.

"Good morning, sir," Forty-niner said. "Does your throat feel better?"

It did, a little. Then I realized that we had a full store of pharmaceuticals in a cabinet in the lavatory. I spent the morning sorting out the pills, trying to figure out which ones would kill me. Forty-niner kept silent while I trotted back and forth to the bridge to call up the medical program. It wasn't any use, though. The brightboys back at headquarters had made certain nobody could put together a suicide cocktail.

Okay, I told myself. There's only one thing left to do. Go to the airlock and open the hatches manually. Override the electronic circuits. Take Forty-niner and his goddamned ethics out of the loop.

Once he realized I had pried open the control panel on the bulkhead beside the inner hatch, Forty-niner said softly, "Sir, there is no need for that."

"Mind your own business."

"But, sir, the corporation could hold you financially responsible for deliberate damage to the control panel."

"So let them sue me after I'm dead."

"Sir, there really is no need to commit suicide."

Forty-niner had figured out what I was going to do, of course. So what? There wasn't anything he could do to stop me.

"What's the matter? You scared of being alone?"

"I would rather not be alone, sir. I prefer your company to solitude."

"Tough nuts, pal. I'm going to blow the hatches and put an end to it."

"But, sir, there is no need—"

"What do you know about need?" I bellowed at him. "Human need? I'm a human being, not a collection of circuit boards."

"Sir, I know that humans require certain physical and emotional supports."

"Damned right we do." I had the panel off. I shorted out the safety circuit, giving myself a nasty little electrical shock in the process. The inner hatch slid open.

"I have been trying to satisfy your needs, sir, within the limits of my programming."

As I stepped into the coffin-sized airlock I thought to myself, Yeah, he has. Forty-niner's been doing his best to keep me alive. But it's not enough. Not nearly enough.

I started prying open the control panel on the outer hatch. Six centimeters away from me was the vacuum of interplanetary space. Once the hatch opens, poof! I'm gone.

"Sir, please listen to me."

"I'm listening," I said, as I tried to figure out how I could short out the safety circuit without giving myself another shock. Stupid, isn't it? Here I was trying to commit suicide and worried about a little electrical shock.

"There is a ship approaching us, sir."

"Don't be funny."

"It was not an attempt at humor, sir. A ship is approaching us and hailing us at standard communications frequency."

I looked up at the speaker set into the overhead of the airlock.

"Is this part of your psychological programming?" I groused.

Forty-niner ignored my sarcasm. "Backtracking the approaching ship's trajectory shows that it originated at Ceres, sir. It should make rendezvous with us in nine hours and forty-one minutes."

I stomped out of the airlock and ducked into the bridge, muttering, "If this is some wiseass ploy of yours to keep me from—"

I looked at the display panel. All its screens were dark: conserving electrical power.

"Is this some kind of psychology stunt?" I asked.

"No, sir, it is an actual ship. Would you like to answer its call to us, sir?"

"Light up the radar display."

Goddamn! There *was* a blip on the screen.

I thought I must have been hallucinating. Or maybe Forty-niner was fooling with the radar display to keep me from popping the airlock hatch. But I sank into the command chair and told Forty-niner to pipe the incoming message to the comm screen. And there was Donahoo's ugly mug talking at me! I knew I was hallucinating.

"Hang in there," he was saying. "We'll get you out of that scrap heap in a few hours."

"Yeah, sure," I said, and turned off the comm screen. To Forty-niner, I called out, "Thanks, pal. Nice try. I appreciate it. But I think I'm going to back to the airlock and opening the outer hatch now."

"But sir," Forty-niner sounded almost like he was pleading, "it really is a ship approaching. We are saved, sir."

"Don't you think I know you can pull up Donahoo's image from your files and animate it? Manipulate it to make him say what you want me to hear? Get real!"

For several heartbeats Forty-niner didn't answer. At last he said, "Then let us conduct a reality test, sir."

"Reality test?"

"The approaching ship will rendezvous with us in nine hours, twenty-seven minutes. Wait that long, sir. If no ship reaches us, then you can resume your suicidal course of action."

It made sense. I knew Forty-niner was just trying to keep me alive, and I almost respected the pile of chips for being so deviously clever about it. Not that I meant anything to him on a personal basis. Forty-niner was a computer. No emotions. Not even an urge for self-preservation. Whatever he was doing to keep me alive had been programmed into him by the psychotechs.

And then I thought, Yeah, and when a human being risks his butt to save the life of another human being, that's been programmed into him by millions of years of evolution. Is there that much of a difference?

So I sat there and waited. I called to Donahoo and told him I was alive and damned hungry. He grinned that lopsided sneer of his and told me he'd have a soysteak waiting for me. Nothing that Forty-niner couldn't have ginned up from its files on me and Donahoo.

"I've got to admit, you're damned good," I said to Forty-niner.

"It's not me, sir," he replied. "Mr. Donahoo is really coming to rescue you."

I shook my head. "Yeah. And Santa Claus is right behind him in a sleigh full of toys pulled by eight tiny reindeer."

Immediately, Forty-niner said, "A Visit from St. Nicholas," by Clement Moore. Would you like to hear the entire poem, sir?"

I ignored that. "Listen, Niner, I appreciate what you're trying to do but it just doesn't make sense. Donahoo's at corporate headquarters at Vesta. He's not at Ceres and he's not anywhere near us. Good try, but you can't make me believe the corporation would pay to have him come all the way over to Ceres to save a broken-down bucket of a waterbot and one very junior and expendable employee."

"Nevertheless, sir, that is what is happening. As you will see for yourself in eight hours and fifty-two minutes, sir."

I didn't believe it for a nanosecond. But I played along with Forty-niner. If it made him feel better, what did I have to lose? When the time was up and the bubble burst I could always go back to the airlock and pop the outer hatch.

But he must have heard me muttering to myself, "It just doesn't make sense. It's not logical."

"Sir, what are the chances that in the siege of Leningrad in World War II the first artillery shell fired by the German army into the city would kill the only elephant in the Leningrad zoo? The statistical chances were astronomical, but that is exactly what happened, sir."

So I let him babble on about strange happenings and dramatic rescues. Why argue? It made him feel better, I guess. That is, if Forty-niner had any feelings. Which he didn't, I knew. Well, I guess letting him natter on with his rah-rah pep talk made *me* feel better. A little.

It was a real shock when a fusion torch ship took shape on my comm screen. Complete with standard registration info spelled out on the bar running along the screen's bottom: *Hu Davis*, out of Ceres.

"Be there in an hour and a half," Donahoo said, still sneering. "Christ, your old Jerky really looks like a scrap heap. You musta taken some battering."

Could Forty-niner fake that? I asked myself. Then a part of my mind warned, Don't get your hopes up. It's all a simulation.

Except that, an hour and a half later, the *Hu Davis* was right alongside us, as big and detailed as life. I could see flecks on its meteor bumpers where micrometeors had abraded them. I just stared. It couldn't be a simulation. Not that detailed.

And Donahoo was saying, "I'm comin' in through your main airlock."

"No!" I yelped. "Wait! I've got to close the inner hatch first."

Donahoo looked puzzled. "Why the fuck's the inside hatch open?"

I didn't answer him. I was already ducking through the hatch of the bridge. Damned if I didn't get another electric shock closing the airlock's inner hatch.

I stood there wringing my hands while the outer hatch slid open. I could see the status lights on the control panel go from red for vacuum through amber and finally to green. Forty-niner could fake all that, I knew. This might still be nothing more than an elaborate simulation.

But then the inner hatch sighed open and Donahoo stepped through, big and ugly as life.

His potato nose twitched. "Christ, it smells like a garbage pit in here."

That's when I knew it wasn't a simulation. He was really there. I was saved.

Well, it would've been funny if everybody wasn't so ticked off at me. Donahoo had been sent by corporate headquarters all the way from Vesta to Ceres to pick me up and turn off the distress call Forty-niner had been beaming out on the broadband frequencies for all those weeks.

It was only a milliwatt signal, didn't cost us a piffle of electrical power, but that teeny little signal got picked up at the Lunar Farside Observatory, where they had built the big SETI radio telescope. When they first detected our distress call the astronomers went delirious: they thought they'd found an intelligent extraterrestrial signal, after more than a century of searching. They were sore as hell when they realized it was only a dinky old waterbot in trouble, not aliens trying to say hello.

They didn't give a rat's ass of a hoot about Forty-niner and me, but as long as our Mayday was being beamed out their fancy radio telescope search for ETs was screwed. So they bleeped to the International Astronautical Authority, and the IAA complained to corporate headquarters, and Donahoo got called on the carpet at Vesta and told to get to *JRK49N* and turn off that damned distress signal!

And that's how we got rescued. Not because anybody cared about an aged waterbot that was due to be scrapped or the very junior dumbass riding on it. We got saved because we were bothering the astronomers at Farside.

Donahoo made up some of the cost of his rescue mission by selling off what was left of Forty-niner to one of the salvage

outfits at Ceres. They started cutting up the old bird as soon as
we parked it in orbit there.

But not before I put on a clean new spacesuit and went aboard
JRK49N one last time.

I had forgotten how big the ship was. It was huge, a big massive collection of spherical tanks that dwarfed the fusion drive
thruster and the cramped little pod I had lived in all those weeks.
Hanging there in orbit, empty and alone, Forty-niner looked
kind of sad. Long, nasty gashes had been ripped through the water tanks; I thought I could see rimes of ice glittering along their
ragged edges in the faint starlight.

Then I saw the flickers of laser torches. Robotic scavengers
were already starting to take the ship apart.

Floating there in weightlessness, my eyes misted up as I approached the ship. I had hated being on it, but I got teary-eyed
just the same. I know it was stupid, but that's what happened, so
help me.

I didn't go to the pod. There was nothing there that I wanted,
especially not my cruddy old spacesuit. No, instead I worked my
way along the cleats set into the spherical tanks, hand over
gloved hand, to get to the heart of the ship, where the fusion reactor and power generator were housed.

And Forty-niner's CPU.

"Hey, whattarya doin' there?" One of the few humans direct-
ing the scavenger robots hollered at me, so loud I thought my
helmet earphones would melt down.

"I'm retrieving the computer's hard drive," I said.

"You got permission?"

"I was the crew. I want the hard core. It's not worth anything
to you, is it?"

"We ain't supposed to let people pick over the bones," he said.
But his tone was lower, not so belligerent.

"It'll only take a couple of minutes," I said. "I don't want anything else; you can have all the rest."

"Damn right we can. Company paid good money for this scrap pile."

I nodded inside my helmet and went through the open hatch that led down to $JRK49N$'s heart. And brain. It only took me a few minutes to pry open the CPU and disconnect the hard drive. I slipped the palm-sized metal oblong into a pouch on the thigh of my suit, then got out. I didn't look back. What those scavengers were chopping up was just a lot of metal and plastic. I had Forty-niner with me.

The corporation never assigned me to a waterbot again. Somebody in the front office must've taken a good look at my personnel dossier and figured I had too much education to be stuck in a dumb job like that. I don't know, maybe Donahoo had something to do with it. He wouldn't admit to it, and I didn't press him about it.

Anyway, when I finally got back to Vesta they assigned me to a desk job. Over the years I worked my way up to chief of logistics and eventually got transferred back to Selene City, on the Moon. I'll be able to take early retirement soon and get married and start a family.

Forty-niner's been with me all that time. Not that I talk to him every day. But it's good to know that he's there and I can ease off the stresses of the job or whatever by having a nice long chat with him.

One of the days I'll even beat him at chess.

INTRODUCTION TO
"MOON RACE"

It matters not whether you win or lose, but how you play the game.

Yeah, maybe.

"Moon Race" is set on the Moon, at a time when that airless, barren little world is the frontier of human expansion beyond Earth.

It's a hard and dangerous frontier. As one insightful man once put it, "Pioneering boils down to inventing new ways to get yourself killed."

But even on the most arduous and demanding of frontiers, the human spirit will invent new forms of entertainment, too. No human community has ever been all work and no play.

Each form of entertainment has its own particular rules. Breaking the rules, even bending them, can get a player disqualified.

It doesn't matter whether you win or lose? The hell it doesn't!

MOON RACE

John Henry said to his Captain,
"A man ain't nothin' but a man,
And before I'll let your steam drill beat me down
I'll die with this hammer in my hand, Lord, Lord
I'll die with this hammer in my hand."

USUALLY, GAZING OUT across the crater floor to the weary old ringwall mountains with the big, blue, beautiful Earth hanging in the black sky above—usually it fills my heart with peace and calm.

But not today.

My palms are sweaty while I wait for the "go" signal. There are six of us lined up in our lunar buggies, ready to race out to the old *Ranger 9* site and back again to Selene's main airlock. Two hundred and some kilometers, round trip. If I follow the path the race officials have laid out.

I'm sitting at the controls of a five-meter-tall, six-legged lunar vehicle that we've nicknamed Stomper. We designed it to haul freight and carry cargo over rough ground, not for racing. The five other racers are also converted from working lunar vehicles, but they're either wheeled or tracked: they can zip along at speeds up to thirty klicks per hour, if you push them.

I've got to win this race or get sent back to dirty, dangerous, overcrowded Earth.

See, Harry Walker and I started this design company, Walker's Walkers, while I was still his student at Selene University. Put every penny we had into it. Now we've built our prototype, Stomper, and we've got to prove to everybody that a legged vehicle

can work out on the Moon's surface as well or better than anything with wheels or tracks.

So we entered the race. Harry's a paraplegic. If we win, he'll
be able to afford stem cell therapy to rebuild his legs. If we don't
win, Walker's Walkers goes bust, he stays in his wheelchair, and I
get sent back Earthside. It's Selene's one hard rule: if you don't
have a job, you get shipped out. You either contribute to Selene's
economy or you're gone, man, gone. There's no room for free-
loaders. No charity. No mercy.

The light on my control board flashes green and I push Stomper's throttle forward carefully. We're off with a lurch and a
bump.

Stomper's six legs start thumping along as I edge the throttle
higher. But Zeke Browkowski zips out ahead of the rest of the
pack, just like I figured he would.

"So long, slowpokes," he sings out as he pulls farther in front.
"Hey, Taylor," he calls to me, "why don't you get out and push?"
I can hear him laughing in my headphones.

Zeke's in Dash-nine, the newest buggy in Selene, of course.
His older brother runs the maintenance section and makes certain he does well by Zeke.

Even though Stomper's cabin is pressurized, I'm suited up,
helmet and all. It's uncomfortable, but if I have to go outside for
emergency maintenance during the race I won't have to take the
time to pull on the cumbersome suit.

Selene City is built into the base of Mount Yeager, the tallest
mountain in the ringwall of the giant crater Alphonsus. Two-
thirds of the way across the crater floor lie the remains of *Ranger
9*, one of the early unmanned probes from back in the days before Armstrong and Aldrin landed over in the Sea of Tranquility.

There's been some talk about expanding Selene beyond Alphonsus's ringwall, going out onto the Mare Nubium and even
farther. But so far it's only talk. Selene is restricted to Alphonsus,
for now.

I figure the run out to the *Ranger 9* site and back to Selene's main airlock should take on the order of ten hours. Zeke Browkowski will try to make it faster, of course. Knowing him, I'll bet he's souped up Dash-nine with extra fuel cells, even though that's against the race rules.

Harry teaches mechanical design at the university, from his wheelchair. He had the ideas for Walker's Walkers and I did his legwork, so to speak. I've got to win this race and show everybody what Stomper can do. Harry can keep his professorship at the university even if we lose. But I'll have to go back to Detroit, Michigan, USA, Earth. I've worked too long and too hard to go back to that cesspool.

I need to win this race!

Stomper's lumbering along like some monster in a horror vid. Sitting five meters above the ground, I can see Zeke's Dash-nine pulling farther ahead of us, kicking up a cloud of dust as it rolls across the crater floor on its big springy wheels. In the Moon's low gravity the dust just hangs there like a lazy cloud.

"Come on, Stomper," I mutter to myself as we galumph past the solar-cell farms spread out on the crater floor "It's now or never." I nudge the throttle a notch higher.

Stomper's six legs speed up, but not by much. It's like sitting on top of a big mechanical turtle with six heavy metal feet. I have to be careful: if I push too hard I could burn out a bearing. Stomper's slow enough on six legs; if we lose one we'll be out of it altogether.

Zeke's pulling farther ahead while ol' Stomper's six feet pound along the dusty bare ground. Lots of little pockmark craterlets scattered across the floor of Alphonsus, and plenty of rocks, some big as houses. Stomper's automated guidance sensors walk us around the more dangerous ones, but I get a kick out of smashing the smaller stones into powder.

It's a real hoot, sitting five meters tall with Stomper's control panel spread out in front of me, feeling all that power, watching the rock-strewn ground go by. Harry would love to be up here, I bet, in control even though his own legs are useless.

Stomper has a lot of power, all right, but not enough speed to catch Dash-nine or even the slower vehicles. Like the turtle against a quintet of hares. But I have a plan. I'm going to take a shortcut.

The race's official course from Selene's main airlock to the *Ranger 9* site is a dogleg shape, because the buggies have to detour around the hump of rugged hills in the center of Alphonsus. I figure that ol' Stomper can climb those hills, thread through 'em and get to the *Ranger 9* site ahead of everybody else. Then I'll come back the same way and win the race!

That's my plan.

For now I follow the trail of lighted poles that mark the race course. Dash-nine is so far ahead that all I can see of Browkowski is a cloud of dust near the short horizon. Three of the other vehicles are ahead of me, too, but I see that the fourth one of them is stopped dead, its two-man crew outside in their suits, bending over a busted track.

I flick to the suit-to-suit frequency and get a blast of choice language from the pair of 'em.

"You guys all right?" I call to them.

Moans and groans and elaborate profanity. But neither one of them is hurt and Selene's already sending a repair tractor to pick them up.

I push on. I can see the tired old slumped hills of the crater's central peak rising just over the horizon. I turn Stomper toward them.

Instantly my earphones sing out, "Taylor Reed, you're veering off course." Janine's voice. She sounds upset.

"I'm taking a shortcut," I say.

"That's not allowed, Taylor."

The race controller is Janine Al-Jabbar, as sweet and lovely a lady as you could find. But now she sounds uptight, almost fearful.

"I've studied the rules," I tell her, keeping my voice calm, "and there's nothing in 'em says you *have to* follow the course they've laid out."

"It's a safety regulation," she answers, sounding even more worried. "You can't go off on your own."

"Janine, there's no problem with safety. Ol' Stomper can—"

A man's voice breaks in. "Taylor Reed, get back on course or you're disqualified!"

That's Mance Brunner, the director of the race. He's also chancellor of Selene University. Very important person, and he knows it.

"Disqualified?" My own voice comes out as a mouse squeak. "You can't disqualify me just because—"

"Get back on course, Reed," says Brunner, less excited but harder, colder. "Otherwise I'll have no option except to disqualify you."

I take a deep breath, then I reply as calmly as I can, "Sir, I am continuing on my own course. This is not a safety risk, nor is it grounds—"

He doesn't even hear me out. "You're disqualified, Reed!"

"But—"

"Attention all vehicles," Brunner announces. "Taylor Reed in vehicle oh-four is hereby disqualified."

None of the other racers says a word, except for Zeke Browkowski, who snickers, "Bye-bye, turtle guy."

To say I am pissed off is putting it very mildly. Brunner never did like me, but what he's just done is about as low and rotten as you can get. And there's no way around it, he's the race director. There's no court of appeals. If he says I'm out, I'm *out*.

Stomper's still clunking along, but I reach for the control yoke to turn us around and head back to Selene.

But I hesitate. Disqualify me, huh? Okay, so I'm disqualified. I'm not going to let that stop me. Brunner can yell all he wants to, I'm going to push through those hills and prove my point, even if it's just to myself.

Janine's voice comes back in my earphones, low and kind of sad. "I'm sorry, Tay. He was standing right over my shoulder. There was nothing I could do."

"Not your fault, Janine," I tell her. "You didn't do anything to feel sorry about."

But in the back of my mind I realize that if I have to go back Earthside I'll never see her again.

Well, disqualified or not, I head out for the *Ranger 9* site by the most direct route: across the central hills.

They look like dimples in the satellite imagery, but as ol' Stomper gets closer to them, those rounded slumped hills rise up in front of me like a real barrier. They're not steep, and not really all that high, but those slopes are worn almost as smooth as glass. There's no air on the Moon, you know, and for eons micrometeorites the size of dust motes have been falling in from space and sandpapering the hills.

I start to wonder if Stomper can really climb across them. There aren't any trails or passes, just a jumbled knot of rocks rising up from the plain of the crater floor. Sigurdsen tried going up them in a wheeled buggy back before Selene became an independent nation; he found the going too treacherous and turned back. Nobody's bothered since then. There's nothing in those bare knobby hills that's worth the effort.

I throttle down and shift to a lower gear.

"Easy does it, Stomper," I mutter. "You can do it. I know you can."

One step at a time, like a turtle on tiptoes, we pick our way through the jumbled rocks. I'm pouring sweat by the time we get near the top. Inside the spacesuit you can boil in your own juices, you know.

"Are you singing?" Janine's voice asks me.

"What?"

"Sounds like you were singing to yourself, Tay," she says, sounding kind of concerned.

I realize I must have been humming to myself, sort of. An old folk song my grandfather used to sing, about a railroad worker named John Henry.

"I'm okay," I tell her.

"Dr. Brunner's really hacked at you," Janine says. "He's sore you haven't turned back."

"He's gonna have to be sore a while longer," I answer tightly.

Stomper clomps along up the worn old rocks and we get to the top. Off in the distance I can see the crumpled wreckage of *Ranger 9*. I have to be even more careful going downhill, making sure each one of Stomper's six feet are solidly planted with each step. No slipping, no sliding.

Easing my way down the hills is even scarier than going up. Ol' Stomper lurches hard; for an instant I'm scared that we're going to tip over. But Stomper plants those big feet of his solidly and we're okay. Still, my hands are slippery with perspiration as I jiggle the throttle and the gear shifts.

We get down, back on the crater floor, and start thumping along as fast as we can to the *Ranger 9* wreckage. Out on the horizon to my left I spot a hazy cloud of dust heading my way. It's Zeke, in Dash-nine. The turtle has beaten the hare!

"Vehicle oh-four reporting," I sing into my lip microphone. "I'm approaching the *Ranger* site."

"Pay no attention to Taylor Reed," Brunner's icy voice answers immediately. "He's been disqualified."

Bastard! I walk Stomper right up to the crumpled remains of *Ranger 9*, under its protective dome of clear glassteel, and use the external arms to plant my marker by the old wreckage. Then I turn around and start for home.

I ought to slow down, I know. I can't win the flicking race, I've been disqualified. So what's the difference? But then I hear Zeke call, "Dash-nine at *Ranger* site. Starting my return leg."

And again I remember that old, old folk song my grandfather used to sing when things got really bad. About John Henry, a black man who refused to give up. And I thought, I'll be damned if I let Zeke Browkowski or Mance Brunner or anybody else beat me. I'll die with a hammer in my hands, Lord, Lord.

"Come on, you ol' turtle," I mutter to Stomper. "Let's get home before Zeke does."

Stomper weaves through the hills again and we're back down on the flat. We clomp along at a pretty fair clip, but then I see Browkowski off to my right, a cloud of dust coming around the hills and heading straight for home.

It's turning into a two-car race. I'm way ahead but Zeke is catching up fast. I can see him in the rearview screen, a cloud of dust that's getting closer every second.

I'm pushing too hard. Stomper's middle left leg starts making a grinding noise. My control panel shows a blinking yellow light. The leg's main bearing is starting to overheat.

I shut down the middle left leg altogether; just keep it locked up and off the ground. Stomper limps the rest of the way back to Selene's main airlock. It's a rough, jouncing ride but we get there a whole two minutes, eighteen seconds ahead of Zeke.

Who is proclaimed the official winner of the race, of course.

I limp Stomper through the main airlock and into Selene's big, cavernous garage, power down, and duck through the hatch. Five meters high, I can see the crowd gathering around Browkowski and Dash-nine: Brunner and Zeke's older brother, the chief of maintenance, a bunch of other people. Even Janine.

Nobody's waiting for me at the bottom of Stomper's ladder except Harry, sitting in his powerchair and grinning up at me.

I'll die with this hammer in my hand. The words to that old song kept ringing in my mind. I was dead, all right. Just like ol' John Henry.

Once I plant my boots on the garage's concrete floor, I slide my helmet visor up and take a look at Stomper. His legs are covered with dust, even the middle left one, which is still hanging up there like some ponderous mechanical ballet dancer doing a pose.

"Better keep your distance," I tell Harry. "My coveralls are soaked with perspiration. I'm gonna smell pretty ripe when I peel off this suit."

He's grinning at me, big white teeth sparkling against his dark skin. "I'll go to the infirmary and get some nose plugs," he says.

He rolls his chair alongside me as I clump to the lockers where the suits are stored. I take off the helmet and then sit wearily on the bench to remove my big, thick-soled boots. As I start to worm my arms out of the sleeves, Janine shows up.

I stand up, my arms half in the suit's sleeves. Janine looks pretty as ever, but kind of embarrassed.

"I'm sorry you were disqualified, Tay," she says.

"Not your fault," I mumble.

She tries to smile. "There's a sort of party over at the Pelican Bar."

"For Zeke. He's the winner."

"You're invited, too."

Before I can refuse, Harry pipes up. "We'll be there!"

Janine's smile turns genuine. "Good. I'll see you there, okay?" And she scampers off.

I scowl at Harry. "Why'd you say yes? I don't feel like partying. 'Specially for Zeke."

"Chill out, Taylor," Harry tells me. "All work and no play, you know."

So we go off to the Pelican Bar—after I take a quick shower and pull on a fresh set of coveralls. The Pelican's owned by some fugitive from Florida; he's got the place decorated with statues of pelicans, photographs of pelicans, painting of pelicans. Behind the bar there's a big screen display of Miami, the way it looked before the greenhouse floods covered it over. Lots of pelicans flying over the water, diving for fish.

The place is jammed. Bodies three, four deep around the long bar. Every booth filled. Noise like a solid wall. I take two steps inside the door and decide to turn around and leave.

But Harry grabs my wrist and tows me through the boisterous crowd, like a tractor dragging some piece of wreckage.

He takes me right up to Zeke Browkowski, of all people, who's standing at the bar surrounded by admirers. Including Janine.

"Hey, here's the turtle guy!" Zeke yells out, grinning at me. My hands clench into fists but I don't say anything.

To my total shock, Zeke sticks out his hand to shake. "Taylor, you beat me. You broke the rules, but you beat me, man. Congratulations."

Surprised, I take his hand and mutter, "Lotta good it's done me."

Still grinning, Zeke half turns to the guy standing next to him. He's an Asian man: older, grayer, wearing a regular suit instead of coveralls, like the rest of us.

"Taylor, this is Hideki Matsumata. He designed Dash-nine."

Matsumata bows to me. On reflex, I bow back.

"You have made an important contribution, Mr. Reed."

"Me?"

Smiling at me, Matsumata says, "I was certain that my Dash-nine couldn't be beaten. You proved otherwise."

I can't figure out why he was smiling about it. I hear myself say, "Like Zeke says, I broke the rules."

"You bent the rules, Mr. Reed. Bent them. Sometimes rules need to bent, stretched."

I didn't know what to say.

Glancing down at Harry, in the powerchair beside me, Matsumata says, "Today you showed that walking vehicles can negotiate mountainous territory that wheeled or tracked vehicles cannot."

"That's what walkers are all about," says Harry. "That's what I was trying to tell you all along."

"You have proved your point, Professor Walker," Matsumata says. But he's looking at me as he says it.

Harry laughs and says, "Soon's we get that bad bearing replaced, Tay, you're going to take Stomper up to the top of Mount

Yeager. And then maybe you'll do a complete circumnavigation of the ringwall."

"But I don't have a job."

"Sure you do! With Walker's Walkers. I haven't fired you."

"The company's not busted?"

Harry's big grin is my answer. But Matsumata says, "Selene's governing council has wanted for some time to build a cable-car tramway over the ringwall and out onto Mare Nubium. Walking vehicles such as your Stomper will make that project possible."

"We can break out of the Alphonsus ringwall and start to spread out," Harry says. "Get down to the south polar region, where the ice deposits are."

My head's spinning. They're saying that I can stay here on the Moon, and even do important work, valuable work.

Zeke claps me on the shoulder. "You done good, turtle guy."

"By breaking the rules and getting disqualified," I mutter, kind of stunned by it all.

Janine comes up and slips her hand in mine. "What was it you were singing during the race? Something about dying with a hammer in your hand?"

"John Henry," I mumble.

"Wrong paradigm," says Harry, with a laugh.

"Whattaya mean?"

"The right paradigm for this situation is an old engineer's line: Behold the lowly turtle, he only makes progress when he sticks his neck out."

INTRODUCTION TO "SCHEHERAZADE AND THE STORYTELLERS"

Now we cross the frontier of time, going back to ancient Baghdad at its most magnificent, in the time of turbaned sultans and the beautiful, clever, and courageous Scheherazade of *The Thousand and One Nights*.

But was she really that clever and courageous?

SCHEHERAZADE AND THE STORYTELLERS

"I NEED A new story!" exclaimed Scheherazade, her lovely almond eyes betraying a rising terror. "By tonight!"

"Daughter of my heart," said her father, the grand vizier, "I have related to you every tale that I know. Some of them, best beloved, were even true!"

"But, most respected father, I am summoned to the sultan again tonight. If I have not a new tale with which to beguile him, he will cut off my head in the morning!"

The grand vizier chewed his beard and raised his eyes to Allah in supplication. He could not help but notice that the gold leaf adorning the ceiling in his chamber was peeling once more. I must call the workmen again, he thought, his heart sinking.

For although the grand vizier and his family resided in a splendid wing of the sultan's magnificent palace, the grand vizier was responsible for the upkeep of his quarters. The sultan was no fool.

"Father!" Scheherazade screeched. "Help me!"

"What can I do?" asked the grand vizier. He expected no answer.

Yet his beautiful, slim-waisted daughter immediately replied, "You must allow me to go to the Street of the Storytellers."

"The daughter of the grand vizier going into the city! Into the bazaar! To the street of those loathsome storytellers? Commoners!

Little better than beggars! Never! It is impossible! The sultan would never permit you to leave the palace."

"I could go in disguise," Scheherazade suggested.

"And how could anyone disguise those ravishing eyes of yours, my darling child? How could anyone disguise your angelic grace, your delicate form? No, it is impossible. You must remain in the palace."

Scheherazade threw herself onto the pillows next to her father and sobbed desperately, "Then bid your darling daughter farewell, most noble father. By tomorrow's sun I will be slain."

The grand vizier gazed upon his daughter with true tenderness, even as her sobs turned to shrieks of despair. He tried to think of some way to ease her fears, but he knew that he could never take the risk of smuggling his daughter out of the palace. They would both lose their heads if the sultan discovered it.

Growing weary of his daughter's wailing, the grand vizier suddenly had the flash of an idea. He cried out, "I have it, my best beloved daughter!"

Scheherazade lifted her tear-streaked face.

"If the Prophet—blessed be his name—cannot go to the mountain, then the mountain will come to the Prophet!"

The grand vizier raised his eyes to Allah in thanksgiving for his revelation, and he saw once again the peeling gold leaf of the ceiling. His heart hardened with anger against all slipshod workmen, including (of course) storytellers.

AND SO IT was arranged that a quartet of burly guards was dispatched that very morning from the sultan's palace to the street of the storytellers, with orders to bring a storyteller to the grand vizier without fail. This they did, although the grand vizier's hopes fell once he beheld the storyteller the guards had dragged in.

He was short and round, round of face and belly, with big round eyes that seemed about to pop out of his head. His beard was ragged, his clothes tattered and tarnished from long wear.

The guards hustled him into the grand vizier's private chamber and threw him roughly onto the mosaic floor before the grand vizier's high-backed, elaborately carved chair of sandalwood inlaid with ivory and filigrees of gold.

For long moments the grand vizier studied the storyteller, who knelt trembling on the patched knees of his pantaloons, his nose pressed to the tiles of the floor. Scheherazade watched from the veiled gallery of the women's quarters, high above, unseen by her father or his visitor.

"You may look upon me," said the grand vizier.

The storyteller raised his head, but remained kneeling. His eyes went huge as he took in the splendor of the sumptuously appointed chamber. Don't you dare look up at the ceiling, the grand vizier thought.

"You are a storyteller?" he asked, his voice stern.

The storyteller seemed to gather himself and replied with a surprisingly strong voice, "Not merely *a* storyteller, oh mighty one. I am *the* storyteller of storytellers. The best of all those who "

The grand vizier cut him short with, "Your name?"

"Hari-ibn-Hari, eminence." Without taking a breath, the storyteller continued, "My stories are known throughout the world. As far as distant Cathay and the misty isles of the Celts, my stories are beloved by all men."

"Tell me one," said the grand vizier. "If I like it you will be rewarded. If not, your tongue will be cut from your boastful throat."

Hari-ibn-Hari clutched at his throat with both hands.

"Well?" demanded the grand vizier. "Where's your story?"

"Now, your puissance?"

"Now."

NEARLY AN HOUR later, the grand vizier had to admit that Hari-ibn-Hari's tale of the sailor Sinbad was not without merit.

"An interesting fable, storyteller. Have you any others?"

"Hundreds, oh protector of the poor!" exclaimed the story-teller. "Thousands!"

"Very well," said the grand vizier. "Each day you will come to me and relate to me one of your tales."

"Gladly," said Hari-ibn-Hari. But then, his round eyes narrowing slightly, he dared to ask, "And what payment will I receive?"

"Payment?" thundered the grand vizier. "You keep your tongue! That is your reward!"

The storyteller hardly blinked at that. "Blessings upon you, most merciful one. But a storyteller must eat. A storyteller must drink, as well."

The grand vizier thought that perhaps drink was more important than food to this miserable wretch.

"How can I continue to relate my tales to you, oh magnificent one, if I faint from hunger and thirst?"

"You expect payment for your tales?"

"It would seem just."

After a moment's consideration, the grand vizier said magnanimously, "Very well. You will be paid one copper for each story you relate."

"One copper?" squeaked the storyteller, crestfallen. "Only one?"

"Do not presume upon my generosity," the grand vizier warned. "You are not the only storyteller in Baghdad."

Hari-ibn-Hari looked disappointed, but he meekly agreed, "One copper, oh guardian of the people."

SIX WEEKS LATER, Hari-ibn-Hari sat in his miserable little hovel on the Street of the Storytellers and spoke thusly to several other storytellers sitting around him on the packed-earth floor.

"The situation is this, my fellows: the sultan believes that all women are faithless and untrustworthy."

"Many are," muttered Fareed-al-Shaffa, glancing at the only

female storyteller among the men, who sat next to him, her face boldly unveiled, her hawk's eyes glittering with unyielding determination.

"Because of the sultan's belief, he takes a new bride to his bed each night and has her beheaded the next morning."

"We know all this," cried the youngest among them, Haroun-el-Ahson, with obvious impatience.

Hari-ibn-Hari glared at the upstart, who was always seeking attention for himself, and continued, "But Scheherazade, daughter of the grand vizier, has survived more than two months now by telling the sultan a beguiling story each night."

"A story stays the sultan's bloody hand?" asked another storyteller, Jamil-abu-Blissa. Lean and learned, he was sharing a hookah with Fareed-al-Shaffa. Between them, they blew clouds of soft gray smoke that wafted through the crowded little room.

With a rasping cough, Hari-ibn-Hari explained, "Scheherazade does not finish her story by the time dawn arises. She leaves the sultan in such suspense that he allows her to live to the next night, so he can hear the conclusion of her story."

"I see!" exclaimed the young Haroun-el-Ahson. "Cliffhangers! Very clever of her."

Hari-ibn-Hari frowned at the upstart's vulgar phrase, but went on to the heart of the problem.

"I have told the grand vizier every story I can think of," he said, his voice sinking with woe, "and still he demands more."

"Of course. He doesn't want his daughter to be slaughtered."

"Now I must turn to you, my friends and colleagues. Please tell me your stories, new stories, fresh stories. Otherwise the lady Scheherazade will perish." Hari-ibn-Hari did not mention that the grand vizier would take the tongue from his head if his daughter was killed.

Fareed-al-Shaffa raised his hands to Allah and pronounced, "We will be honored to assist a fellow storyteller in such a noble pursuit."

Before Hari-ibn-Hari could express his undying thanks, the

bearded, gnomish storyteller who was known throughout the bazaar as the Daemon of the Night, asked coldly, "How much does the sultan pay you for these stories?"

THUS IT CAME to pass that Hari-ibn-Hari, accompanied by Fareed-al-Shaffa and the gray-bearded Daemon of the Night, knelt before the grand vizier. The workmen refurbishing the golden ceiling of the grand vizier's chamber were dismissed from their scaffolds before the grand vizier asked, from his chair of authority:

"Why have you asked to meet with me this day?"

The three storytellers, on their knees, glanced questioningly at one another. At length, Hari-ibn-Hari dared to speak.

"Oh, magnificent one, we have provided you with a myriad of stories so that your beautiful and virtuous daughter, on whom Allah has bestowed much grace and wisdom, may continue to delight the sultan."

"May he live in glory," exclaimed Fareed-al-Shaffa in his reedy voice.

The grand vizier eyed them impatiently, waiting for the next slipper to drop.

"We have spared no effort to provide you with new stories, father of all joys," said Hari-ibn-Hari, his voice quaking only slightly. "Almost every storyteller in Baghdad has contributed to the effort."

"What of it?" the grand vizier snapped. "You should be happy to be of such use to me—and my daughter."

"Just so," Hari-ibn-Hari agreed. But then he added, "However, hunger is stalking the Street of the Storytellers. Starvation is on its way."

"Hunger?" the grand vizier snapped. "Starvation?"

Hari-ibn-Hari explained, "We storytellers have bent every thought we have to creating new stories for your lovely daughter—

blessings upon her. We don't have time to tell stories in the bazaar anymore—"

"You'd better not!" the grand vizier warned sternly. "The sultan must hear only new stories, stories that no one else has heard
before. Otherwise he would not be intrigued by them and my
dearly loved daughter would lose her head."

"But, most munificent one," cried Hari-ibn-Hari, "by devot-
ing ourselves completely to your needs, we are neglecting our
own. Since we no longer have the time to tell stories in the bazaar, we have no other source of income except the coppers you
pay us for our tales."

The grand vizier at last saw where they were heading. "You want
more? Outrageous!"

"But, oh far-seeing one, a single copper for each story is not
enough to keep us alive!"

Fareed-al-Shaffa added, "We have families to feed. I myself
have four wives and many children."

"What is that to me?" the grand vizier shouted. He thought
that these pitiful storytellers were just like workmen everywhere,
trying to extort higher wages for their meager efforts.

"We cannot continue to give you stories for a single copper
apiece," Fareed-al-Shaffa said flatly.

"Then I will have your tongues taken from your throats. How
many stories will you be able to tell then?"

The three storytellers went pale. But the Daemon of the Night,
small and frail though he was in body, straightened his spine and
found the strength to say, "If you do that, most noble one, you
will get no more stories and your daughter will lose her life."

The grand vizier glared angrily at the storytellers. From her
hidden post in the veiled gallery, Scheherazade felt her heart sink.
Oh father! she begged silently, Be generous. Open your heart.

At length the grand vizier muttered darkly, "There are many
storytellers in Baghdad. If you three refuse me I will find others
who will gladly serve. And, of course, the three of you will lose

your tongues. Consider carefully. Produce stories for me at one copper apiece, or be silenced forever."

"Our children will starve!" cried Fareed-al-Shaffa.

"Our wives will have to take to the streets to feed themselves," wailed Hari-ibn-Hari.

The Daemon of the Night said nothing.

"That is your choice," said the grand vizier, as cold and unyielding as a steel blade. "Stories at one copper apiece or I go to other storytellers. And you lose your tongues."

"But magnificent one—"

"That is your choice," the grand vizier repeated sternly. "You have until noon tomorrow to decide."

IT WAS A gloomy trio of storytellers who wended their way back to the bazaar that day.

"He is unyielding," Fareed-al-Shaffa said. "Too bad. I have been thinking of a new story about a band of thieves and a young adventurer. I think I'll call him Ali Baba."

"A silly name," Hari-ibn-Hari rejoined. "Who could take seriously a story where the hero's name is so silly?"

"I don't think the name is silly," Fareed-al-Shaffa maintained. "I rather like it."

As they turned in to the Street of the Storytellers, with ragged, lean, and hungry men at every door pleading with passersby to listen to their tales, the Daemon of the Night said softly, "Arguing over a name is not going to solve our problem. By tomorrow noon we could lose our tongues."

Hari-ibn-Hari touched reflexively at his throat. "But to continue to sell our tales for one single copper is driving us into starvation."

"We will starve much faster if our tongues are cut out," said Fareed-al-Shaffa.

The others nodded unhappily as they plodded up the street and stopped at Fareed's hovel.

"Come in and have coffee with me," he said to his companions. "We must think of a way out of this problem."

All four of Fareed-al-Shaffa's wives were home, and all four of them asked the storyteller how they were expected to feed their many children if he did not bring in more coins.

"Begone," he commanded them—after they had served the coffee. "Back to the women's quarters."

The women's quarters were nothing more than a squalid room in the rear of the hovel, teeming with noisy children.

Once the women had left, the three storytellers squatted on the threadbare carpet and sipped at their coffee cups.

"Suppose this carpet could fly," mused Hari-ibn-Hari.

Fareed-al-Shaffa hmphed. "Suppose a genie appeared and gave us riches beyond imagining."

The Daemon of the Night fixed them both with a somber gaze. "Suppose you both stop toying with new story ideas and turn your attention to our problem."

"Starve from low wages or lose our tongues," sighed Hari-ibn-Hari.

"And once our tongues have been cut out the grand vizier goes to other storytellers to take our place," said the Daemon of the Night.

Fareed-al-Shaffa said slowly, "The grand vizier assumes the other storytellers will be too terrified by our example to refuse his starvation wage."

"He's right," Hari-ibn-Hari said bitterly.

"Is he?" mused Fareed. "Perhaps not."

"What do you mean?" his two companions asked in unison.

Stroking his beard thoughtfully, Fareed-al-Shaffa said, "What if all the storytellers refused to work for a single copper per tale?"

Hari-ibn-Hari asked cynically, "Would they refuse before or after our tongues have been taken out?"

"Before, of course."

The Daemon of the Night stared at his fellow storyteller. "Are you suggesting what I think you're suggesting?"

"I am."

Hari-ibn-Hari gaped at the two of them. "No, it would never work. It's impossible!"

"Is it?" asked Fareed-al-Shaffa. "Perhaps not."

THE NEXT MORNING the three bleary-eyed storytellers were brought before the grand vizier. Once again Scheherazade watched and listened from her veiled gallery. She herself was bleary-eyed as well, having spent all night telling the sultan the tale of Ala-al-Din and his magic lamp. As usual, she had left the tale unfinished as the dawn brightened the sky.

This night she must finish the tale and begin another. But she had no other to tell! Her father had to get the storytellers to bring her fresh material. If not, she would lose her head with tomorrow's dawn.

"Well?" demanded the grand vizier as the three storytellers knelt trembling before him. "What is your decision?"

The three of them had chosen the Daemon of the Night to be their spokesperson. But as he gazed up at the fierce countenance of the grand vizier, his voice choked in his throat.

Fareed-al-Shaffa nudged him, gently at first, then more firmly.

At last the Daemon said, "Oh, magnificent one, we cannot continue to supply your stories for a miserable one copper per tale."

"Then you will lose your tongues!"

"And your daughter will lose her head, most considerate of fathers."

"Bah! There are plenty of other storytellers in Baghdad. I'll have a new story for my daughter before the sun goes down."

Before the Daemon of the Night could reply, Fareed-al-Shaffa spoke thusly, "Not so, sir. No storyteller will work for you for a single copper per tale."

"Nonsense!" snapped the grand vizier.

"It is true," said the Daemon of the Night. "All the storytellers have agreed. We have sworn a mighty oath. None of us will give you a story unless you raise your rates."

"Extortion!" cried the grand vizier.

Hari-ibn-Hari found his voice. "If you take our tongues, oh most merciful of men, none of the other storytellers will deal with you at all."

Before the astounded grand vizier could reply to that, Fareed-al-Shaffa explained, "We have formed a guild, your magnificence, a storytellers' guild. What you do to one of us you do to us all."

"You can't do that!" the grand vizier sputtered.

"It is done," said the Daemon of the Night. He said it softly, almost in a whisper, but with great finality.

The grand vizier sat on his chair of authority getting redder and redder in the face, his chest heaving, his fists clenching. He looked like a volcano about to erupt.

When, from the veiled gallery above them, Scheherazade cried out, "I think it's wonderful! A storytellers' guild. And you created it just for me!"

The three storytellers raised their widening eyes to the balcony of the gallery, where they could make out the slim and graceful form of a young woman, suitably gowned and veiled, who stepped forth for them all to see. The grand vizier twisted around in his chair and nearly choked with fury.

"Father," Scheherazade called sweetly, "is it not wonderful that the storytellers have banded together so that they can provide stories for me to tell the sultan night after night?"

The grand vizier started to reply once, twice, three times. Each time no words escaped his lips. The three storytellers knelt before him, staring up at the gallery where Scheherazade stood openly before them—suitably gowned and veiled.

Before the grand vizier could find his voice, Scheherazade said, "I welcome you, storytellers, and your guild. The grand vizier, the most munificent of fathers, will gladly pay you ten coppers for each story you relate to me. May you bring me a thousand of them!"

Before the grand vizier could figure how much a thousand stories would cost, at ten coppers per story, Fareed-al-Shaffa smiled up at Scheherazade and murmured, "A thousand and one, oh gracious one."

THE GRAND VIZIER was unhappy with the new arrangement, although he had to admit that the storytellers' newly founded guild provided stories that kept the sultan amused and his daughter alive.

The storytellers were pleased, of course. Not only did they keep their tongues in their heads and earn a decent income from their stories, but they shared the subsidiary rights to the stories with the grand vizier once Scheherazade had told them to the sultan and they could then be related to the general public.

Ten coppers per story was extortionate, in the grand vizier's opinion, but the storytellers' guild agreed to share the income from the stories once they were told in the bazaar. There was even talk of an invention from far-off Cathay, where stories could be printed on vellum and sold throughout the kingdom. The grand vizier consoled himself with the thought that if sales were good enough, the income could pay for regilding his ceiling.

The sultan eventually learned of the arrangement, of course. Being no fool, he demanded a cut of the profits. Reluctantly, the grand vizier complied.

Scheherazade was the happiest of all. She kept telling stories to the sultan until he relented of his murderous ways, much to the joy of all Baghdad.

She thought of the storytellers' guild as her own personal creation and called it Scheherazade's Fables and Wonders Association.

That slightly ponderous name was soon abbreviated to SFWA.

The story was written as my contribution to *Gateways*, a story collection honoring Frederik Pohl on his ninetieth birthday, edited by his wife, Elizabeth Anne Hull.

The storytellers are all based on fellow writers of science fiction, their names thinly disguised by pseudo-Arabic monikers.

In addition to being a masterful storyteller himself, and a good and dear friend, Fred Pohl was a Grand Master of the Science Fiction and Fantasy Writers of America—a slightly ponderous name that is usually abbreviated as SFWA.

INTRODUCTION TO
"DUEL IN THE SOMME"

The frontier in this story is a frontier of technology. *Virtual reality* is the name commonly given to an electronic method of presenting sensory inputs to a person. A VR user sees, hears, even feels a simulation of the real world. VR allows you to *experience* a scene, instead of merely reading or watching or listening to it, a scene that actually exists only in the circuitry of the virtual reality system.

Although VR technology hasn't gone as far as it is presented in "Duel in the Somme," the day is coming when virtual reality systems will offer a complete digital hallucination; the user will not be able to tell the difference between the VR simulation he (or she) is experiencing and the real world.

Which opens some intriguing possibilities . . .

DUEL IN THE SOMME

THE CRISIS CAME when Kelso got on my butt in that damned Red Baron triplane of his and started shooting the crap out of my Spad. I mean, I knew this was just a simulation, it wasn't really real, but I could see the fabric on my wings shredding, and the plane started shaking so hard my teeth began to rattle.

I kicked left rudder and pushed on the stick as hard as I could. Wrong move. The little Spad flipped on its back and went into a spin, diving toward the ground.

It's only a simulation! I kept telling myself. It's not real! But the wind was shrieking and the ground spinning around and around and coming up fast and I couldn't get out of the spin and simulation or not I puked up my guts.

I knew I was going to die. Worse, Kelso would get to take Lorraine to the ski weekend and tell her all about what a wuss I am. While they were in bed together, most likely. Rats!

How did I get myself into this duel? All because of Lorraine, that's how. Well, that's not really true. I can't blame her. I went into it with my eyes wide open. I even thought this would be my best chance to beat Kelso.

Yeah. Fat chance.

I mean, it was all weird from the beginning.

There I was, taking the biggest risk I'd ever taken, sitting at my workstation and using my BlackBerry to text message sweet Lorraine: GOT RSRVS FR ASPEN COMING WKND. JOIN ME? EL ZORRO.

I mean, everybody in the company was after Lorraine. She was beautiful, smart, elegant, kind, beautiful, sweet, independent, and beautiful.

Me, I was just one of the nerds in the advanced projects department, a geekboy stuck in one of those cubicles like Dilbert. Not that I was repulsive or tongue-tied. I mean, I wasn't as slick and handsome as Kelso, but I didn't crack mirrors or frighten babies with my looks. Lorraine always smiled at me whenever we passed each other in the corridor. I sat with her in the cafeteria a few times and we had very pleasant conversations.

She even called me Tom. Not Thomas. Tom. I mean, even in school everybody called me by my last name, Zepopolis. The few friends I had called me Zep. When I first started working at the company guys like Kelso called me Zeppelin, but one glance from Lorraine and I started dieting. She even complimented me on how I was slimming down. Talk about incentive!

But I didn't have the nerve to sign my real name to the invitation I sent her. I thought it might add an air of mystery to the invite, maybe get her thinking romantic thoughts and wondering who her secret admirer might be. Zorro, the masked swordsman. The dashing hero. Yeah, right.

Kelso saw right through me in a microsecond.

"Zepopolis," he snapped, leaning over the top of my cubicle wall. He was tall enough to stand head and shoulders above the cubicle's flimsy partition.

I jumped like I'd been shot. Dropped my no-fat doughnut on the floor, nearly sloshed the coffee out of my Star Wars insulated mug.

"Yes, sir!" I blurted, leaping to my feet as I swiveled my chair around to face him. Kelso was the department head, a position he'd obtained by hard work, intelligence, and a powerful personality. Plus the fact that his father was founder, CEO, and board chairman of Kelso Electronics, Inc.

DUEL IN THE SOMME

See, Kelso was after Lorraine, major league. Flowers, gifts, taking her out dancing, to the theater—he even sat through an entire opera with her, according to the office rumor mill. So far, she had been pleasant to him, polite and friendly, but that's as far as it went. Again, according the office vibes.

I figured she might welcome a little competition, a little mystery and romance. I figured I might even have a chance with her. Kelso figured otherwise.

He looked me over with a jaundiced eye. "You the hump who sent that weird invitation to Lorraine?" he demanded.

I could have denied it and that would be the end of it. I could have admitted it and apologized and *that* would be the end of it.

Instead I drew myself up to my full five-nine and said, "That's right. I'm waiting for her answer."

"Her answer is no," Kelso said, with some heat.

I heard myself say, "I'll have to hear that from her." I mean, I *talked back* to him!

Kelso just stared at me for about half a minute (seemed like half a year), his fingers gripping the partition so hard they left permanent dents. Kelso was big enough to snap me in half; he played handball every lunch hour (for him, lunch was two hours, of course). He took boxing lessons at a downtown gym. He even played polo, for crying out loud.

His voice went murderously low, "I'm telling you, Greek geek, Lorraine isn't going on any ski weekend with you or Zorro or anybody else except me."

"Don't I have something to say about that?"

We both turned at the sound of her voice, and there was Lorraine, like a vision of an angel dressed in hip-hugging jeans and a blouse that clung to her like Saran Wrap. She was standing in the entrance of my cubicle, her beautiful face set in a very soulful expression.

I sputtered at the sight of her. "Lorraine, I—"

"Are you El Zorro?" she asked, a slight smile breaking out.

"He's El Deado if he's not careful," Kelso growled.

Lorraine arched her brows and asked, "Are you two fighting over me?"

"It wouldn't be much of a fight," Kelso sneered. "Two blows struck: I hit Zorro and he hits the floor."

"Neanderthal," I heard myself say. That's stupid! I told myself. Don't get him sore enough to start punching!

"Geek," he replied.

Lorraine said, "I won't have you fighting. I'm not a prize to be awarded to the winner. Besides, it's no way to settle this."

That's when the Great Idea hit me.

"Wait a minute," I said. "What if we fight a duel? An actual duel, like they did in the old days?"

"A duel?" she asked.

Kelso grouched, "Dueling's been outlawed for two hundred years. More."

I pulled out my trump card. "But what if we fight a duel in a virtual reality simulation?"

"Virtual reality?" Lorraine echoed.

"Simulation?" Kelso's heavy brows knit together. "Like we use to train pilots?"

"Yeah. We've got VR systems that give the user a complete three-dimensional simulation: you see, touch, hear a world that exists only in the computer's chips."

"And it's interactive, isn't it? You can manipulate that world while you're in it," Lorraine chimed in. I told you she was smart as well as gorgeous.

"That's right," I said enthusiastically. "You can move in the simulated environment and make changes in it."

Kelso was frowning puzzledly. "You mean we could fight a duel in a virtual reality setting . . . ?"

"Right," I said. "Share a VR world, whack the hell out of each other, and nobody gets really hurt."

A slow smile crept across his devilishly handsome face. "Whack the hell out of each other. Yeah."

I didn't like the sound of that.

"Winner takes all?" Kelso asked.

I nodded.

"Oh no you don't," Lorraine snapped. "I'm not some prize you win in a video game. I don't want anything to do with this macho bullflop!"

And she flounced off without a backward look at us, her long dark hair bouncing off her shoulders. We both stared at her as she just about stomped down the corridor.

Rats, I thought. Here I wanted her to fall for the romance of it all, and all she did was get sore. Double rats.

I shrugged. "Well, it was an idea, anyway."

"A good idea," said Kelso.

"Whattaya mean?"

He gave me a narrow-eyed look. "This is between you and me, Zepopolis."

"But Lorraine—"

"You and me," Kelso repeated. "We fight our duel and the loser swears he won't go after Lorraine ever again."

"But she—"

"Lorraine won't know anything about it. And even if she does, what can she do? I'll whip you in the duel and you stop bothering her. Got it?"

"Got it," I muttered. But I thought that maybe—just maybe—I'd beat Kelso's smug backside and he'd be the one to stop sniffing after Lorraine.

So that night, after even the most gung-ho of the techies had finally gone home, Kelso and I went down to the VR lab and started programming the system there for our duel. I knew the lab pretty well; I used it all the time to check out the cockpit simulations we created for the Air Force and Navy. It wouldn't take much to modify one of the sims for our duel, I thought.

The lab was kind of eerie that late at night: only a couple of desk lights on, pools of shadows everywhere else. The big simulations chamber was like an empty metal cave, except for the wired-up six-degree chairs in its middle.

Kelso and I talked over half a dozen ideas for scenarios—a medieval joust with lances and broadswords, an old-fashioned pistol
duel aboard a Mississippi steamboat, jungle warfare with assault
rifles and hand grenades, even a gladiatorial fight in ancient Rome.

I slyly suggested an aerial dogfight, World War I style. I didn't
tell Kelso that I'd spent hours and hours playing WWI air battle
computer games.

"You mean, like the Red Baron and Snoopy?" he asked, breaking into a wolfish grin.

"Right."

"Okay. I'll be the Red Baron."

I tried to hide my enthusiasm. "That makes me Snoopy, I
guess."

"Flying a doghouse!" Kelso laughed.

"No," I replied as innocently as I could muster. "I'll fly a Spad
XIII."

"Okay with me." Kelso agreed too easily, but I didn't pay any
attention to it at the time.

"We'll start with an actual scenario out of history," I suggested,
"a battle between the Red Baron's squadron and a British squadron,
over the Somme sector in—"

"A duel in the Somme!" Kelso punned. "Get it? Like that old
movie, *Duel in the Sun*." He laughed heartily at his own witticism.

Me, I smiled weakly, disguising my elation. I had him where I
wanted him. I had a chance to beat him, a damned good chance.
So I thought.

It wasn't cosmically difficult to plug the WWI scenario I had
used so often into the VR circuitry. I got the specs on the Spad
XIII and the Fokker Dr. 1 triplane easily enough through the
Web. The tough part was to get the VR system to accept two inputs from two users at the same time without shorting itself into
a catatonic crash. I spent all night working on it. Kelso quit around
midnight.

"I've got to get my sleep and be rested for the weekend's exer-
tions," he said as he left. "With Lorraine."

He went home. I continued programming, but my mind filled with a beautiful fantasy of Lorraine and me together in the ski lodge, snuggling under a colorful warm quilt.

That was before I found out that Kelso flew *real* airplanes and was a member of a local stunt flying organization. Good thing I didn't know it then; I'd have slit my throat and gotten it over with.

So the next night, after a quick takeout salad (with low-cal dressing), I headed down to the VR lab. I bumped into Kelso, also heading for the sim chamber. With Lorraine! They had eaten dinner together, he informed me with a vicious smile. And there were almost a dozen techies trailing along behind them.

"But I thought—"

"You thought I didn't know," Lorraine said to me. "Like anybody can keep a secret in this jungle gym for nerds."

That hurt.

"I still think you two are acting like a couple of macho creeps," she said. "But if you're going to go through with this duel the least I can do is watch you making Looney Tunes of your selves."

The geek squad behind her and Kelso got a laugh out of that as they followed after us down to the VR lab. The word about our duel had well and truly leaked out.

"We're going to have a great time in Aspen," Kelso said to Lorraine.

She didn't reply.

He was walking down the corridor at her side. I was on her other side, all three of us striding toward the VR lab like soldiers on parade. The rest of the onlookers shambled along behind us. I mean, techies aren't the slickest-looking people. They looked like a collection of pudgy unwashed refugees and smelled like stale pepperoni pizza.

Lorraine finally spoke. "Just because you two heroes have decided to fight this duel over me doesn't mean that I'll go anywhere with either of you."

My heart clutched beneath my ribs. She's found out about the duel! If she backs out of this, what's the sense of fighting it?

"You've got to!" I blurted.

"No I don't," she insisted. "This duel is between the two of you. You guys and your macho fantasies. Don't include me in it."

Kelso isn't the sharpest pencil in the box, but he quickly said, "You're right, Lorraine. This is between the Greek geek and me. The loser stops bothering you." He looked down at me. "Right, Zepopolis?"

I looked at Lorraine. The expression on her face was unfathomable. I mean, she looked sort of irritated, intrigued, sad, and excited all at the same time. I can handle computer programming at its most arcane, but I couldn't figure out what was going through Lorraine's mind. I mean, if she didn't want to have anything to do with our duel, why'd she come down to the VR lab with us?

Well, we got to the lab. While the rest of the guys leaned over my shoulder and made seventeen zillion suggestions on how to do it better, I powered up the simulation program and checked it out. Kelso stood off in a shadowy corner with Lorraine. No touchy games between them; she was watching me intently while Kelso fidgeted beside her.

It was time to enter the simulations chamber. Kelso marched in like a conquering hero and picked up the helmet waiting on his chair.

"Gloves first," I said.

"Yeah. Right."

So we wormed our hands into the sim gloves. Their insides were studded with sensors, and a slim optical fiber line trailed from them to the connectors built into the chamber wall. They felt fuzzy, tingly.

Then I pulled the helmet over my head, but kept the visor up. The helmet had its own power batteries and linked to the computer wirelessly.

I sat down. Kelso sat down. In a few minutes, I knew, we'd be seeing and feeling World War I fighter planes in combat over the Somme. I licked my lips. Nervous anticipation, big time.

"You ready?" I asked Kelso, raising my voice to hide the tremor that was quivering inside me.

"Ready," he said, his voice muffled a bit by the helmet.

The computer was set for remote activation. Once I started the simulation program everything went automatically. I looked down at the armrests of my chair and leaned on the button that turned on the sim program. Then I slid my visor down over my eyes.

The computer's voice sounded in my helmet earphones, "Simulation will begin in ten seconds . . . nine . . . eight . . ."

I couldn't see a thing with the visor over my eyes. What if I goofed the programming? I suddenly thought, I should've gone to the bathroom before—

Abruptly the rattling roar of a 220-horsepower Hispano-Suiza engine shook my molars, and I was wedged into the cockpit of a Spad XIII bouncing along in the wake of three other Spads up ahead of me. The wind was blowing fiercely in my face. The altimeter on my rudimentary control panel flopped around between 4,000 and 4,200 feet. It should've been in meters, I know, but I had programmed it so I could understand it without dividing by 0.3048 every time I wanted to know how high I was.

The noise was shattering, and the engine was spitting a thin spray of castor oil over my windscreen and into my face. I wiped at my goggles with a gloved hand. The sim program couldn't handle odors; good thing, the smell of castor oil would've started me retching, most likely.

I looked up over my left shoulder; the sky was clear blue and empty up there. Twisting in the other direction, my heart did a double-thump. There were eight Fokker triplanes above me, diving at us from out of the sun, led by one painted fire-engine red. Kelso.

I started waving frantically to the Spads up ahead of me, but they plowed on like lambs to the slaughter. No radio, of course.

So I yanked back on the stick and pulled my nimble little fighter into a steep climb, rushing headfirst into the diving triplanes.

Their first pass wiped out my squadronmates. As I looped over and started diving, I could see all three of them spinning toward the shell-pocked ground, trailing smoke and flame. I was alone against Kelso and his whole squadron.

The other triplanes flew off; the Red Baron and I were alone in the sky. One on one. *Mano a mano.* I got on his tail, but before I could open up with my Vickers machine guns Kelso stood that goddam triplane on its tail and climbed toward heaven like a homesick angel. When I tried to climb after him it was like I was carrying an elephant on the Spad's back.

Kelso flipped the triplane into an inside loop, and I lost him in the sun's glare. I leveled off and kept squinting all around to spot him again. And there he was! Diving down behind me. I nosed over and dived away; the triplane could climb better than I could, but when it tried to dive it just sort of floated downward. My Spad went down like a stone with an anvil tied to it.

But I couldn't dive forever, and when I pulled up, Kelso got right on my tail, shooting my plane to shreds. I twisted, banked, turned left and then right. He stayed right behind me, blazing away. My Spad was starting to look like Swiss cheese. That's when I nosed over again and accidentally flipped the plane into a spin. And upchucked.

I couldn't pull the Spad out of its spin. I was going to crash and burn, and it was all my own fault. Kelso didn't have to shoot me down, I was going to screw myself into the ground. No parachute, either: the Royal Flying Corps wasn't allowed to use them.

So I did the only thing I could think of. I twisted my body back toward where Kelso's red triplane was circling above me, and I put my right hand to my brow. I who am about to die salute you.

I crashed. I burned. I died.

And just like that I was back in the sim chamber, with a gutful of stinking vomit smeared inside my helmet and dripping down my shirt. I almost upchucked again.

Kelso got up from his chair with a grin bright enough to light up Greater Los Angeles. He strode out of the chamber to the cheers of the geek squad waiting outside in the control room. Me, I pulled off the smelly helmet and looked around for something to clean up the mess I'd made.

It took quite a while to clean up. By the time I was finished the VR lab was dark and quiet. Good thing, too. I didn't need anybody there to jeer at what a complete catastrophe I'd created for myself.

"Do you need some help?"

Lorraine's voice! I turned and there she was, at the entrance to the sim chamber, with a mop and pail in her hands.

I just gaped at her. When I finally found my voice I asked her, "Where's Kelso?"

She made a face. "Down at the nearest bar with the rest of the guys, celebrating his great victory."

"You didn't go with him?"

"I'm more interested in you," she said.

In me!

Then she added, "This dueling idea of yours. Could you turn it into a package that could be sold retail?"

I blinked. "Yeah, I guess so. But—"

She smiled at me. "We could market this, Tom. We could sell millions of them."

"We?"

"We'll have to raise some capital, form our own company. I know a few people who could help us."

"Leave Kelso Electronics?"

"Of course. We're going to get rich, Tom. You and me."

I told you she was smart, as well as beautiful. We never did get to Aspen that weekend. We were too busy creating VR Duels, Inc.

But there were lots of other weekends, later on.

AFTERWORD TO
"DUEL IN THE SOMME"

This story was inspired by my novelette "The Perfect Warrior," published in *Analog* in May 1963 and later incorporated into my 1969 novel, *The Dueling Machine*.

INTRODUCTION TO
"BLOODLESS VICTORY"

Exploring the frontier of virtual reality a little further, suppose VR systems got so good that people could fight duels to the death in them, without being harmed in the slightest?

Instead of taking someone to court over a dispute and waiting while the wheels of justice grind away (and the lawyers' fees mount up), fight a duel against the person you're at odds with. Swords, pistols, fighter planes, flamethrowers, custard pies—whatever the two parties agree on.

It would be much more satisfying than dragging a suit through the courts, even if you lose. At least it would be quick.

But how could you get a state legislature to agree to allow VR duels to be legally binding? After all, most of those legislators are lawyers themselves, aren't they? To say nothing of the members of Congress.

How, indeed.

BLOODLESS VICTORY

FOUR LAWYERS SAT huddled around a table in the Men's Bar of the Carleton Club.

Actually, one of them was a state supreme court justice, another a former psychologist, the third a patent attorney—which the judge disdained despite the man's lofty assertion that he dealt with "intellectual properties."

"Do you think it's wise?" asked John Nottingham, the only man at the table whom the judge deemed to be a real lawyer; Nottingham practiced criminal law, dressed in properly conservative dark suits, and affected a bored Oxford accent.

"Fight a duel in a virtual reality machine," mused Rick Gorton, the patent lawyer, "and have its results count just the same as a decision by a court of law." Intellectual properties or not, Gorton shook his head in disbelief and took another gulp of his scotch. Gorton always wore a boyish grin on his round, florid face. And his suits always looked as if he'd slept in them.

"I think it's the wave of the future," said Herb Franklin, the ex-psychologist who was now an assistant district attorney.

Randolph Halpern was the judge, and he had always thought that Franklin had taken his law degree and passed the bar exam merely so that he could be accepted into the Carleton Club.

The Carleton was the capital city's poshest and most exclusive of private clubs. Only lawyers and political officeholders were allowed membership. Since virtually every political officeholder also possessed a law degree, only the occasional outsider gained membership to the Carleton, and he was almost always encouraged to resign by subtle yet effective snubs and discourtesies.

Franklin was one of those outsiders, in Halpern's view, and the judge was inwardly incensed that the man could sit beside him in the dark mahogany paneling of the Men's Bar just as if he truly belonged here. Franklin was a round, jolly fellow with a snow-white beard that made him look like Santa Claus. But Justice Halpern still could not accept Franklin as an equal. The man was an outsider and always would be, in the judge's view. A psychologist! And now he was advocating this ridiculous idea of letting virtual reality duels serve as valid legal suits!

"It's never been done before!" protested Justice Halpern. "There's no precedent for it. Absolutely none."

Randolph Halpern was slim as a saber, his head shaved totally bald, although he wore the same pencil-thin moustache he had sported since his college days. His suit was impeccably tailored, dark gray. A solid maroon tie was knotted perfectly at his lean, wattled throat.

Gorton rubbed his reddish nose and said, "Well, by golly, it sounds like a fun idea to me." He signaled to the Hispanic waiter for a refill of his scotch.

"Fun," Halpern sneered, thinking, Of course an intellectual properties lawyer would favor this kind of gadgetry. And Franklin, sitting next to him and smiling like a benevolent Father Christmas. Psychologist. A lawyer should be a *serious* man, filled with gravitas. Yet Franklin sat there with that maddening grin on his bearded, chubby face and a mug of ale in his fist.

"I'll grant you it could be exciting, Rick," Franklin said to the patent attorney. "But it's more serious than that. Court calendars all over the state are jammed so badly that it takes months, sometimes years, for a case to be heard. That's a long time to wait for justice."

"Lucrative, though," observed Nottingham laconically. Halpern nodded at the man. *He's a real lawyer. He knows billable hours from balderdash.*

"That's another point," said Franklin. "Lots of citizens can't afford to take a case to court."

"They're too cheap to pay the piper," Halpern countered.

Franklin shook his head. "They're denied justice because it's too expensive. And too slow. The dueling machine could allow them to obtain closure swiftly and at a reasonable cost."

Gorton took another sip of scotch and mused, "You have a difference with somebody. Instead of suing the guy and having your case drag through the courts for God knows how long—"

Franklin interjected, "And paying through the nose for every phone call and trip to the men's room that your attorney makes."

Nodding amiably, Gorton went on, "Yeah. Instead of that, you go to one of VR Duels, Inc.'s facilities. You and your opponent agree on the setting for the duel and the weapons to be used, then you whack the hell out of each other in virtual reality. Nobody gets hurt and you abide by the results of the duel just as if it was legally binding."

"It would be legally binding," Nottingham pointed out, "if the state supreme court rules favorably on the matter." He cast a questioning eye toward Justice Halpern.

Before the judge could say anything, Franklin added, "And it would be much more satisfying emotionally to the participants in the duel. Much more satisfying than having a judge or jury or court-appointed mediator decide on your case."

Justice Halpern objected, "Now, really . . ."

"Yes, really," Franklin insisted. "Psychological studies have shown that even the losers in a VR duel feel more satisfied with the results than they would with a verdict handed down by a court of law."

"Those studies were funded by VR Duels, Inc., were they not?" Nottingham asked drily.

"It doesn't matter," Halpern said flatly. "The supreme court will *not* allow virtual reality duels to have the same legal standing as a court's decision. Not if I have anything to do with it!"

Nottingham nodded as if satisfied. Gorton looked a trifle abashed. Franklin's habitual smile faded for a moment but quickly returned to his bearded face once again.

Justice Halpern downed the last of his brandy and soda, then pushed away from the table.

"This dueling-machine business is one thing," he said as he got to his feet. "But I have a *really* important problem to deal with."

As the other three got up from their chairs, Franklin asked, "A really important problem?"

"Yes," said Halpern. "The board's been petitioned to open the Men's Bar to female members."

Gorton's eyes went wide. "The Men's Bar? But they can't do that! Can they?"

His lean, austere face showing utter distaste, Justice Halpern said, "I knew we should never have allowed women to become members of the Club."

"Had to, didn't we?" Franklin asked. "It's the law. Equal rights and all that."

His expression going from distaste to outright disgust, Halpern said, "Yes, we had to, according to the law of the land. But we agreed to keep the Men's Bar sacrosanct! *They* agreed to it! But now those aggressive, loud-mouthed feminists are going back on the agreement. They've petitioned the board to 'liberate' the Men's Bar."

"The board won't go for that, will they?" Gorton asked, looking worried.

"They certainly shouldn't," said Nottingham, with some heat. "We need someplace on God's green Earth where we can be away from them."

Justice Halpern nodded. "The board's appointed a committee to study the matter. We're meeting in ten minutes to plot out our strategy and make a recommendation to the full board when it meets on the first of the month." With that, he strode out of the Men's Bar, leaving the other three standing at their table.

"He's going to give himself a heart attack," Gorton mused as he sat down again and reached for his drink.

Franklin shook his head. "No. The judge is the kind of man who doesn't get a heart attack, he gives them."

Nottingham chuckled. "But he seems dead set against this dueling-machine proposition."

"And he's the swing vote on the supreme court, from what I hear," said Gorton.

Franklin beckoned to the waiter for another mug of ale, then hunched forward in his chair like a conspirator about to reveal his plans.

"About the dueling machine," he said, his voice lowered.

"Yes?"

"You remember Martin Luther King's famous line, 'I have a dream?'"

"Yes."

"Well, I have a scheme."

Thus it was arranged that Rick Gorton, amiable Pooh-bear of a man, would challenge Justice Halpern to a duel. It was all done in a very friendly way, of course. The next afternoon, when the four men met again at the club, Halpern was in a smiling mood.

Gazing around the warm dark paneling of the Men's Bar, the judge said with some satisfaction, "Well, at least I got the committee to agree that we should dig in our heels and recommend that the board reject the women's petition out of hand."

"D'you think the board will have the guts to follow your recommendation?" Gorton asked.

"They caved in to the women before," Nottingham recalled, clear distaste in his voice and face.

"They haven't been particularly famous for their courage," Franklin added.

With tight-lipped determination, Justice Halpern said, "The board will follow my rec—er, I mean, the committee's recommendation, never fear." He looked admiringly around the soothingly dark, pleasingly quiet room. "This old place will remain a male bastion."

Franklin nodded knowingly, remembering that several key members of the club's board had cases pending before Justice Halpern.

"That's good news," Franklin murmured.

"Indeed it is," said Halpern, with a self-satisfied smile. He signaled the barkeep for his usual brandy and soda.

Franklin glanced at Gorton, who glanced in turn at Nottingham.

When neither of them said a word, Franklin spoke up. "When will the supreme court decide on the dueling-machine proposal?"

Halpern gave him a sharp look. "In two weeks, when we open the year's hearings."

Very gently, Franklin stepped on the toe of Gorton's nearer shoe.

The patent attorney took the hint. "Y'know, your honor, it doesn't seem right to make a decision on the case without trying a duel yourself."

"Me?" The judge looked alarmed. "Fight a duel?"

"In virtual reality," Gorton said. "Nobody gets hurt."

"It's all nonsense," the judge grumbled.

Franklin nudged Gorton under the table again, harder, and the patent attorney said, "I could be your challenger. You could pick any setting you like. Choose your weapons."

Halpern gave Gorton one of his well-known icy stares.

Nottingham came in with the line they had rehearsed earlier in the day. "You would be the only member of the court who has experienced the dueling machine. The other justices would have to look up to you, follow your example."

"It's all nonsense," Halpern repeated.

Franklin nodded sagely. "I understand. It's a little scary, fighting a duel—even in virtual reality."

"You told me no one gets hurt," the judge said.

"Nobody does," Gorton said. "I've fought three duels so far. They're fun!"

"Three duels?" Halpern asked.

With a pleasant grin, Gorton said, "Once I was a fighter pilot in a World War I biplane. And I was a knight fighting in a tournament, armor and lances and all that." He added sheepishly, "I lost that one."

"Your opponent unhorsed you?" Nottingham asked, on cue.

"He killed me," Gorton said, still grinning. "Skewered me with his lance, right through my shield and armor and all."

Halpern looked aghast. "You died?"

"In the VR simulation. Opened my eyes and I was back in the dueling machine booth, safe and sound. No blood."

"That . . . that's interesting," said the judge.

"If you fought a duel," Franklin asked, his bearded face all innocent curiosity, "what setting would you choose? What weapons?"

Trained psychologist that he was, Franklin had assessed Halpern wisely. It took only a few days of sophisticated arm-twisting to get the judge to agree to face Rick Gorton in a duel—under the conditions that Justice Halpern picked.

THE ONLY SIGN of apprehension that Halpern showed as the four men entered the VR Duels, Inc. facility was a barely discernable throbbing of the blue vein in his forehead, just above his left eye.

Gorton seemed perfectly at ease, his round face displaying his usual easygoing, lopsided smile. Franklin was quiet and very serious; Nottingham stiffly formal.

The dueling-machine office was located in a busy, noisy

shopping mall, set between a music store thronged with teenagers and a pharmacy that catered to Medicare patients. Once the four men had pushed through the facility's front doors, the place looked more like a medical clinic than the kind of gaming arcade that Halpern had expected. There was a small anteroom, its walls all hospital white and bare. Through an open doorway he could see a larger room that was filled with a row of booths, also in sterile white décor.

A pleasant-faced young man was sitting at the desk in the anteroom. He wore a white tunic and slacks, with a stylized pair of crossed sky-blue scimitars on the breast of the tunic.

"Justice Halpern?" said the young man, his smile showing perfect gleaming teeth. "Precisely on time."

As the young man gestured them to the curved plastic chairs in front of his desk, a pair of slim young women stepped into the anteroom and stood on either side of the open doorway. They also wore white tunics with the blue crossed scimitars, and slacks. They too were smiling professionally.

"And you must be Mr. Richard Gorton, Esquire," said the young man. Looking at Franklin and Nottingham, his expression grew a bit more serious. "And you gentlemen?"

"We are friends of the combatants," said Nottingham.

"Seconds," Franklin said.

"I see," said the young man. "Well, we really have no need of seconds, but if you'd like to remain during the duel we have a seating area inside the main room."

The man identified himself as the duel coordinator and briefly outlined the procedure: each of the duelists would be placed in a soundproofed, windowless booth, where the young women—who were simulations technicians—would help them into their sensor suits and helmets.

With a glance at the computer screen on his desk, the coordinator said, "I see that you have chosen the Battle of Waterloo as the setting for your duel. Your weapons are sabers and lances."

"Correct," Halpern said, his voice brittle with tension. Gorton merely rubbed his nose and nodded.

"Very well, gentlemen," said the coordinator, rising from his desk. "If you will simply follow the technicians, they will prepare you for your duel. Good luck to each of you."

Halpern waited for him to say *May the better man win*, but the coordinator refrained from that cliché.

He followed the slim young woman on his right into the inner room; she stopped at the first booth in the row that lined its wall. Gorton was led into the next booth, beside it.

"You'll have to take off your outer clothing, sir," said the technician, still smiling, "and put on the sensor suit that's hanging inside the booth. You can call me when you're ready."

Halpern felt some alarm. No one had told him he'd have to strip. He glared at the young woman, who remained smilingly unperturbed as she held open the door to the booth.

Reluctantly, grumbling to himself, Justice Halpern stepped into the booth. Once the woman closed its door and he himself clicked its lock, he saw that the booth's curving walls were bare. The only furniture inside was a stiff-backed chair. A set of what looked like old-fashioned long johns was hanging against the wall.

Justice Halpern scanned the claustrophobic little booth for a sign of hidden cameras. With some trepidation, he peeled down to his underwear as quickly as he could and pulled on the gray, nubby outfit. It felt fuzzy against his bare arms and legs, almost as if it were infested with vermin.

"Are you ready, sir?" came the technician's voice through a speaker grill set into the ceiling of the booth.

Halpern nodded, then, realizing that she couldn't see him (hoping that she couldn't, actually), he said crisply, "I'm ready."

The lock clicked and the door swung open. The young woman stepped inside and suddenly the booth felt very crowded to Halpern. He smelled the delicate scent of her perfume.

She was carrying a plastic helmet under one arm. It looked like a biker's helmet to Halpern. Resting the helmet on the chair, she pulled a white oblong object from her tunic pocket, about the size and shape of a TV remote controller, and ran it up and down Halpern's fuzzy-suited body.

Nodding, she said, "Your suit is activated. Good."

"No wires?" he asked.

Her smile returning, she replied, "Everything is wireless, sir."

Halpern wished she wouldn't call him *sir*. It made him feel a hundred years old.

She picked the helmet off the chair and handed it to him. "Put it on and pull down the visor. When the duel begins the visor will go totally black for a moment. Don't panic. It's only for a moment or two while we program the duel for you. When it clears you'll see the place where your duel is set."

Halpern wordlessly put on the helmet. It felt heavy, cumbersome.

"Now pull down the visor, please."

He did. It was tinted, but he could see her clearly enough.

She looked him up and down one final time, then said, "Okay, you're ready for your duel. You can sit down." She turned to the door, stepped through, gave him a final gleaming smile, and closed the booth's door.

Halpern sat down.

"Halpern-Gorton duel commencing in ten seconds," came a man's voice in his helmet earphones.

Then everything went black.

BEFORE HE COULD do anything more than gulp with fright, the darkness vanished in a swirl of colors and then the rolling hills of a green countryside appeared.

A trace of a cold smile curled Randolph Halpern's thin lips. He was sitting astride his favorite mount, the chestnut mare that the Iron Duke himself had given him.

Gorton and the rest of them think they're going to make a fool of me, Halpern said to himself as he patted the mare's neck, gentling her. They don't know that I've studied every aspect of the Battle of Waterloo since I was in prelaw.

Behind him, screened by the thick forest, the entire brigade was lined up and waiting eagerly for Halpern's order to charge. It all seemed so very real! The smell of the grass, the distant rumble of artillery, even the warmth of the sun on his shoulders, now that the morning rain had drifted away. The simulation is well-nigh perfect, Halpern had to admit. Virtual reality, as seemingly real as the genuine thing.

He could hear his men's horses snuffling impatiently, sense their eagerness to come to grips with their wily foe. Up on the sparsely wooded ridge ahead Halpern could see Bonaparte's Frenchies, pennants flying from their lances, as they trotted toward the distant town of Waterloo.

He pulled his saber from its scabbard with the clean whisper of deadly steel, and a hundred other sabers slid from their scabbards behind him.

"England expects every man to do his best!" Halpern shouted. Then he pointed his saber at the enemy and spurred his mount into a charge.

The French lancers were caught completely by surprise, as Halpern had planned. His brigade charged into their flank in a wild screaming melee of flashing steel and dust and blood. Within moments it was over. The French had been routed.

All except their leader, who sat panting and sweating on his devil's black stallion, gripping his bloodied lance in one big-knuckled hand and staring at Halpern, his chest heaving beneath his gaudy uniform.

It was Gorton, of course, big easy-going Rick Gorton, looking more like a frightened oversized child than one of Napoleon's brave lancers.

"He's mine, lads," Halpern cried, and he charged straight at his opponent.

Who stood his ground and casually skewered the incautious Halpern on his lance. The pain was monumental. Halpern fought to remain conscious, to raise his saber, to strike the detested enemy in the name of God, Harry, and Saint George. Instead, he slipped into darkness.

And opened his eyes in the booth of the dueling machine. The same young technician had opened the booth's door and was lifting the virtual reality helmet off Halpern's bald head, which was glistening with perspiration.

"I'm afraid you lost, sir," said the young woman, her earlier smile replaced by a sorrowful countenance. "Better luck next time."

"YOU WEREN'T SUPPOSED to beat him," Herb Franklin growled.

Rick Gorton looked embarrassed. "I didn't mean to, by golly. He just ran onto my lance."

The two lawyers were sitting in a corner of the Men's Bar. Franklin was scowling like a Santa Claus confronting a naughty boy.

"Now he'll never vote in favor of making duels legally binding. Never."

Gorton shrugged helplessly and ordered another scotch.

As the waiter brought his drink, John Nottingham entered the bar, scanned the mostly empty tables, and made straight for them.

"How's the Sword of Justice this morning?" Franklin asked dismally.

"He's busy persuading the other members of the board to turn down the women's petition," Nottingham said as he slid into the chair between the two men.

"What about the dueling machine?"

Nottingham shrugged elaborately. "I think that's a hopeless cause. He fought a duel and lost. Got himself killed."

Franklin shot a scowl toward Gorton.

"He's certainly not going to decide in favor of allowing duels to be legally valid," Nottingham concluded.

"Well, don't blame me," Gorton said. "I didn't expect him to charge right into my lance."

Franklin sank back in his chair, his normally jolly face clouded with thought. Nottingham ordered his usual rye and ginger ale while Gorton sat staring into his scotch like a little boy who'd been caught poaching cookies.

At last Franklin straightened up and asked, "When does the board vote on the women's petition?"

"First of the month," said Nottingham. "Monday."

"And when does the supreme court hand down its decision about the dueling machine?"

"The fifteenth."

Franklin nodded. His old smile returned to his bearded face, but this time there was something just the slightest bit crafty about it.

A CHILLY WIND was driving brittle leaves down the street as Justice Halpern left the Carleton Club. He bundled his topcoat around his body and peered down toward the taxi stand on the corner. No cabs, of course: during the rush hour they were all busy.

Standing at the top of the club's entryway steps, wishing he hadn't given his chauffeur the afternoon off, Halpern thought he might as well go back inside and have the doorman phone for a taxi. It would take at least a half hour, he knew. I'll wait in the Men's Bar, he thought.

But as he stepped through the glass front door and into the club's foyer a tiny slip of a woman accosted him.

"Justice Halpern," she said, as if she was pronouncing sentence over him.

Suppressing a frown, Halpern said frostily, "You have the advantage over me, miss."

"Roxanne Harte, Esquire," she said. "*Ms.* Roxanne Harte." She pronounced the *Ms.* like a colony of bees swarming.

"How do you do?" Halpern noticed that Ms. Harte couldn't have been out of law school for very long. She was a petite redhead, rather pretty, although her china-blue eyes seemed to be blazing with some inner fury.

"You are a member here?" he asked, feeling nettled.

"As much a member as you are, sir. And I'm very unhappy with you, your honor."

"With me?"

"With you, sir."

Halpern looked around the foyer. The uniformed doorman was standing by the cloakroom, chatting quietly with the attendant there. No one else in sight. Or earshot.

"I don't understand," he said to Ms. Harte. "Why should you be unhappy with me? What have I done—"

"You're trying to convince the board to reject our petition."

Halpern's eyes went wide. "You're one of—of those?"

"One of the women who want to end the chauvinistic monopoly you maintain over the Men's Bar, yes, that's me."

Feeling almost embarrassed at this little snip of a woman's arrogance, Halpern said, "This isn't the place to discuss club matters, young lady."

"I agree," she snapped. "I know a much better way to settle this issue, once and for all."

"How do you propose—"

She never let him finish his question. "I challenge you to a duel, sir."

"A duel?"

"Choose your weapons!"

"This is nonsense," Halpern said. He began to turn away from her.

But Roxanne Harte grabbed him by the sleeve and with her other hand delivered a resounding slap to Halpern's face.

"Choose your weapons," she repeated.

Halpern stood there, his cheek burning. The doorman and cloakroom attendant were staring at him. John Nottingham came through the door from the club's interior and stopped, sensing instinctively that something was wrong.

"Well?" Ms. Harte demanded.

"I can't fight a duel with you," Halpern said. "You're only a woman."

"That's the attitude that makes this duel necessary, isn't it?" she said, practically snarling.

Drawing himself up to his full height, Halpern said, "I have every advantage over you. I am taller, heavier, stronger. You couldn't stand up to me in a duel."

"What about pistols?" Ms. Harte replied immediately. "Back in the Old West they called the Colt six-gun the Equalizer. How about a duel with pistols?"

Halpern was about to point out to her that he was the club's champion pistol shot for the past three years running. But he stopped himself. *Why should I tell her? She wants to fight a duel against me. She's the one who suggested pistols.*

Nodding, Justice Halpern said through clenched teeth, "Very well, then. Pistols it will be." And he added silently, *You little fool.*

NEWS OF THE duel spread through the club almost instantly, of course. By the following afternoon, as Justice Halpern stepped into the Men's Bar for his customary libation, every man there got to his feet and applauded.

Halpern tried to hide the pleasure he felt as he made his way across the room to the table where Franklin, Gorton, and Nottingham were sitting.

"The defender of our rights and privileges," Franklin said, beaming, as the judge sat down.

"By golly," said Gorton, "I've got to hand it to you, your honor. It's high time somebody stood up for what's right."

Nottingham was a bit more subdued. "From what I understand, you have agreed that the outcome of this duel will decide whether or not the women's petition will be accepted."

"That's right," Halpern said, as the Hispanic waiter placed his brandy and soda in front of him. "If she wins, the Men's Bar will be opened to women."

"But she won't win," Gorton said. Then he added, "Will she?"

"How could she," Franklin said, "against the club's best shot?"

"You've agreed on the setting?" Nottingham asked.

"A frontier saloon in the Old West," said Halpern as he reached for his drink. With a smile that was almost a smirk he added, "She'll have to come in through the ladies' entrance, I expect."

THE FOLLOWING MORNING Halpern had his chauffeur drive him back to the shopping mall where the VR Duels, Inc. facility was. Franklin, Gorton, and Nottingham were already there, even though he arrived scrupulously on time. Ms. Harte was nowhere to be found.

Typical woman, Halpern said to himself. Late for the appointment. Then he thought, Maybe she won't show up at all. The idea pleased him immensely.

Franklin and the others looked very serious as they stood in the anteroom waiting for his opponent.

"Relax," Halpern told them. "The purity of the Men's Bar will not be defiled."

At that moment Ms. Harte burst into the room, looking rather like a worried high school student who'd been sent down to the principal's office for discipline.

"Sorry I'm late," she said, avoiding Halpern's stern gaze.

Halpern felt growing impatience as the same bright-smiling technician carefully went over each and every detail of the duel, the sensor suit, and the helmet he would have to wear. Get on with it! he railed at her silently. But he kept his face and demeanor perfectly polite, absolutely correct. He allowed himself to show no hint of impatience.

"You'll have to stand on your feet for this duel," said the technician just before she closed the door of the booth, leaving Halpern clothed in the nubby sensor suit and unwieldy biker's helmet. The helmet felt heavy, and he couldn't get over the feeling that some kind of loathsome bugs were worming their way under his skin.

The technician shut the door at last. Halpern stood alone for a long moment that seemed to stretch indefinitely. The booth was narrow, confining, its walls smooth and bare.

"Okay," he heard a man's voice in his helmet earphones. "Activating Halpern-Harte duel."

The world went completely dark for an instant, then a brief flare of colors swirled before his eyes and he heard a muted rumbling noise.

Abruptly he was standing at the bar of an Old West frontier saloon, crowded with rough-looking men, bearded and unwashed, smelly. Over in one corner a man who looked suspiciously like Rick Gorton was banging away at a tinny-sounding piano. It can't be Gorton, Halpern said to himself. Looking at the piano player more closely, Halpern saw that he had a bushy red beard and his fingernails were cracked and dirty.

"What're you having, Judge?"

Halpern turned and saw the bartender smiling at him. The man looked a little like Herb Franklin, but much younger, more rugged, his beard darker and rather bedraggled. A badly stained apron was tied around his ample middle.

"Judge?" the bartender prompted.

"Brandy and soda," said Halpern.

The bartender's bushy brows hiked up. "You want to put sarsaparilla in your brandy, Judge?"

Halpern thought a moment, then shook his head. "No. Water. Brandy and a glass of water. No ice."

The bartender gave him a puzzled look, then reached for a bottle, muttering to himself, "Ice?"

Halpern looked up at his reflection in the mirror behind the bar. He saw that he was wearing a long black frock coat and a black, wide-brimmed hat. On his right hip he felt the weight of a heavy pistol. A Colt six-shooter, he surmised. Not the sleek, well-balanced Glock automatic he used at the target range in the club's basement. This thing felt like a cannon.

"Brandy and water," the bartender said, slapping two glasses onto the surface of the bar. Some of the water splashed onto the polished wood.

Halpern took a cautious sip. It was awful. Like vinegar mixed with battery acid, he thought.

Turning, he surveyed the crowded barroom. Lots of dusty, unshaven, grubby men in boots and grimy clothes lining the bar. Others sitting at tables. Looked like an intense game of poker was going on in the farthest corner. Everybody carried a gun; some of the men had two. He almost expected to see John Wayne come sauntering through the swinging doors. Or Clint Eastwood, at least.

The swinging doors did indeed bang open, and a tiny, almost elfin figure stepped in. Wearing scuffed cowboy boots, faded Levis, an unbuttoned leather vest over a checkered shirt, and a beat-up brown Stetson pulled low. Gritty with trail dust. She had a Colt revolver strapped to her hip.

Halpern recognized Ms. Harte, just barely. He saw the blazing anger in those china-blue eyes.

She took five steps into the barroom and stopped, facing Halpern.

"Judge," she called across the crowded saloon, "you hanged my kid brother for cattle rustlin' that he didn't do."

The barroom went totally silent. Instinctively Halpern pushed the edge of his frock coat away from the butt of the pistol holstered at his hip.

"The jury found him guilty," he said, surprised at the quaver in his voice.

"'Cause you threw out the evidence that would've cleared him, you sneaky polecat."

"That's not true!"

"You callin' me a liar? Go for that hawgleg, Judge."

With that Ms. Harte started to draw the six-shooter from her holster. Halpern fumbled for his gun. It was huge and heavy, felt as if it weighed ten pounds.

To his credit, he got off the first shot. The plate glass window behind Ms. Harte shattered. She fired once, twice. He heard glassware smashing on the bar behind him. Men were diving everywhere to get out of the line of fire. Halpern saw the piano player spin around on his little stool, eyes wide, a lopsided grin on his thickly bearded face.

He fired again and a chair two feet to Ms. Harte's left went clattering across the floor. This isn't like target shooting! Halpern realized. Not at all.

A bullet tore at his frock coat, and Halpern felt a sudden need to urinate. He fired at his unmoving opponent and her hat flew off her head. She didn't even wince. She shot again and more glassware exploded behind him.

Gripping his cumbersome long-barreled pistol in both hands, Halpern fired once again.

Ms. Harte toppled over backward, her smoking pistol flying from her hand. Her bright blue eyes closed forever.

For a moment Halpern was plunged into utter darkness. Then he felt the VR helmet being lifted off his head. The young woman smiled at him warmly.

"You won, Justice Halpern. You won the duel."

Halpern licked his lips and then smiled back at the technician. "Yes, I did, didn't I? I shot her dead."

On shaky legs he stepped out of the virtual reality booth. Ms. Harte was coming out of the booth on the other side of the room. She smiled weakly at him.

"Touché," she called across the chamber.

Halpern bowed graciously. Perhaps there is something to this dueling-machine business, after all, he thought.

———

IT WAS A seafood restaurant: small, slightly tatty, and completely on the other side of the city from the supreme court's building and the Carleton Club.

Herb Franklin smiled as he got to his feet to welcome his luncheon guest. He had barely had a chance to sit at the table; she was right on time.

"Congratulations," he said to Roxanne Harte, Esq.

Ms. Harte smiled prettily as she took the chair that Franklin held for her.

"It did come out pretty well, didn't it?" she said.

Franklin took his own chair as he said, "The supreme court handed down its decision this morning. Duels in properly registered dueling-machine facilities are now recognized as legally binding. First state in the union to go for it."

"A precedent," said Ms. Harte, as she picked up the menu that lay atop her plate.

"This state is a trendsetter." Franklin was beaming.

"Justice Halpern voted with the majority?" she asked.

Nodding vigorously, Franklin told her, "He wrote the majority opinion, no less."

Ms. Harte smiled prettily. "I'll bet VR Duels, Inc. will declare a dividend."

"Very likely," Franklin agreed happily. "Very likely."

They both ordered trout, and Franklin picked a dry white wine to go with the fish.

"I really want to thank you," Franklin said, once they had sipped at the wine. "I know it was quite a sacrifice for you."

"Sacrifice?"

"The club's board turned down your petition about the Men's Bar."

Ms. Harte shrugged prettily. "It wasn't *my* petition. I don't care about your old Men's Bar."

"Oh," said Franklin. "When I first talked to you about it, I thought—"

"I'm not a radical feminist. The petition was just the bait for your trap. And it worked."

Franklin nodded, a little warily, and turned his attention to the trout.

She said, "So now the good citizens of this state can settle their differences with a duel in virtual reality."

"Under the specified conditions. Both parties have to sign a formal agreement to make the results of the duel binding on them."

She took another sip of wine, then said. "It's funny. You told me that Justice Halpern was a champion pistol shot, but he was worse than I am."

"There's a big difference between shooting at a target and firing at someone who's shooting back at you," Franklin said. "And that Dragoon's revolver we gave him is a lot different from the Glock he's accustomed to."

"I suppose," Ms. Harte agreed faintly. "But boy, he was a really rotten shot, you know. I deliberately missed him four times and I still had to pretend to be hit; he never came close to me."

Franklin hissed, "For God's sake don't let anyone else know that! If it ever gets back to him . . ."

"Don't worry, my lips are sealed," she replied. "After all, an assistant district attorney has got to have some discretion."

With a relieved chuckle, Franklin said, "You'll get the next opening in the DA's office. It's all set. We just have to wait a few months so Halpern doesn't start putting two and two together."

She nodded, but then asked, "So why did you go through all this? Why are you so intent on getting VR duels accepted as legally binding?"

Franklin eyed her carefully for a long, silent moment. At last he answered, "Several reasons. First, it will help people get their differences settled without waiting for months or even years for a court to come to a decision for them."

"Uh-huh."

"Second, it will unclog court calendars. A lot of petty nuisance suits will disappear. People will fight duels instead of calling for lawyers."

"Lawyers' incomes will go down, you know."

"Yes, but it's all for the best," Franklin said loftily. "It will make our society better. Healthier. People will take out their aggressions in harmless but emotionally satisfying virtual reality duels. As a former psychologist, I'm certain that it will be a great benefit to society."

"Really?"

"So some lawyers won't make as much money," he went on. "They won't have as many ambulances to chase. So what? Money isn't everything. We have to think of the greater good."

"I see." Ms. Harte broke into a knowing grin. "And just how much money have you invested in VR Duels, Inc.?"

Franklin tried to keep a straight face but failed. Smiling like a true lawyer, he replied, "Quite a bit, Roxanne, my dear. Quite a healthy goddamned bit."

INTRODUCTION TO
"MARS FARTS"

First, I should apologize for the somewhat vulgar title. But, as you will see, it really is appropriate.

Satellites placed in orbit around the planet Mars have detected occasional whiffs of methane gas in the thin Martian atmosphere. They seem to appear seasonally, in the springtime.

Methane is a compound of carbon and hydrogen. The gas is quickly broken up into its constituent elements by solar ultraviolet radiation. The freed hydrogen presumably wafts to the top of the atmosphere and eventually boils away into space.

So the methane is destroyed almost as soon as it is produced. Yet something produces fresh methane every year.

On Earth, microbes living deep underground use the energy of our planet's hot core to drive their metabolism. They eat rock or iron and excrete methane.

Could such methanogenic bacteria be producing the methane found in the Martian atmosphere?

Here is a frontier to be explored!

MARS FARTS

"A CATHOLIC, A Jew, and a Muslim are stuck in the middle of Mars," said Rashid Faiyum.

"That isn't funny," Jacob Bernstein replied, wearily.

Patrick O'Connor, the leader of the three-man team, shook his head inside the helmet of his pressure suit. "Laugh and the world laughs with you, Jake."

None of them could see the faces of their companions through the tinting of their helmet visors. But they could hear the bleakness in Bernstein's tone. "There's not much to laugh about, is there?"

"Not much," Faiyum agreed.

All around them stretched the barren, frozen, rust-red sands of Utopia Planita. Their little hopper leaned lopsidedly on its three spindly legs in the middle of newly churned pockmarks from the meteor shower that had struck the area overnight.

Off on the horizon stood the blocky form of the old *Viking 2* lander, which had been there for more than a century. One of their mission objectives had been to retrieve parts of the *Viking* to return to Earth, for study and eventual sale to a museum. Like everything else about their mission, that objective had been sidelined by the meteor shower. Their goal now was survival.

A barrage of tiny bits of stone, most of them no larger than dust motes. Once they had been part of an icy comet, but the ice had melted away after God-knew-how-many trips around the sun, and now only the stones were left when the remains of the comet happened to collide with the planet Mars.

One of the rare stones, almost the size of a pebble, had punctured the fuel cell that was the main electrical power source for the three-man hopper. Without the electrical power from that fuel cell, their rocket engine could not function. They were stranded in the middle of the frozen, arid plain.

In his gleaming silvery pressure suit, Faiyum reminded O'Connor of a knight in shining armor, except that he was bending into the bay that held the fuel cell, his helmeted head obscured by the bay's upraised hatch. Bernstein, similarly suited, stood by nervously beside him.

The hatch had been punctured by what looked like a bullet hole. Faiyum was muttering, "Of all the meteoroids in all the solar system in all of Mars, this one's got to smack our power cell."

Bernstein asked, "How bad is it?"

Straightening up, Faiyum replied, "All the hydrogen drained out during the night. It's dead as a doornail."

"Then so are we," Bernstein said.

"I'd better call Tithonium," said O'Connor, and he headed for the ladder that led to the hopper's cramped cockpit. "While the batteries are still good."

"How long will they last?" asked Bernstein.

"Long enough to get help."

It wasn't that easy. The communications link back to Tithonium was relayed by a network of satellites in low orbit around Mars, and it would be another half hour before one of the comm-sats came over their horizon.

Faiyum and Bernstein followed O'Connor back into the cockpit, and suddenly the compact little space was uncomfortably crowded.

With nothing to do but wait, O'Connor said, "I'll pressurize the cockpit so we can take off the helmets and have some breakfast."

"I don't think we should waste electrical power until we get confirmation from Tithonium that they're sending a backup to us."

"We've got to eat," O'Connor said.

Sitting this close in the cramped cockpit, they could see each other's faces even through the helmet visors' tinting. Faiyum broke into a stubbly-chinned grin.

"Let's pretend its Ramadan," he suggested, "and we have to fast from sunup to sundown."

"Like you fast during Ramadan," Bernstein sniped. O'Connor remembered one of their first days on Mars, when a clean-shaven Faiyum had jokingly asked which direction Mecca was. O'Connor had pointed up.

"Let's not waste power," Bernstein repeated.

"We have enough power during the day," Faiyum pointed out. "The solar panels work fine."

Thanks to Mars's thin, nearly cloudless atmosphere, just about the same amount of sunshine fell upon the surface of Mars as upon Earth, despite Mars's farther distance from the sun. Thank God for that, O'Connor thought. Otherwise we'd be dead in a few hours.

Then he realized that, also thanks to Mars's thin atmosphere, those micrometeoroids had made it all the way down to the ground to strafe them like a spray of bullets, instead of burning up from atmospheric friction, as they would have on Earth. The Lord giveth and the Lord taketh away, he told himself.

"Tithonium here," a voice crackled through the speaker on the cockpit control panel. All three of them turned to the display screen, suddenly tight with expectation.

"What's your situation, E-3?" asked the face in the screen. Ernie Roebuck, they recognized: chief communications engineer.

The main base for the exploration team was down at Tithonium

Chasma, part of the immense Grand Canyon of Mars, more than three thousand kilometers from their Excursion 3 site.

O'Connor was the team's astronaut: a thoroughly competent Boston Irishman with a genial disposition who tolerated the bantering of Faiyum and Bernstein—both geologists—and tried to keep them from developing a real animosity. A Muslim from Peoria and a New York Jew: how in the world had the psychologists back Earthside ever put the two of them on the same team, he wondered.

In the clipped jargon of professional fliers, O'Connor reported on their dead fuel cell.

"No power output at all?" Roebuck looked incredulous.

"Zero," said O'Connor. "Hydrogen all leaked out overnight."

"How did you get through the night?"

"The vehicle automatically switched to battery power."

"What's the status of your battery system?"

O'Connor scanned the digital readouts on the control panel. "Down to one-third of nominal. The solar panels are recharging 'em."

A pause. Roebuck looked away, and they could hear voices muttering in the background. "All right," said the communicator at last. "We're getting your telemetry. We'll get back to you in an hour or so."

"We need a lift out of here," O'Connor said.

Another few moments of silence. "That might not be possible right away. We've got other problems, too. You guys weren't the only ones hit by the meteor shower. We've taken some damage here. The garden's been wiped out and E-1 has two casualties."

Excursion 1 was at the flank of Olympus Mons, the tallest mountain in the solar system.

"Our first priority has to be to get those people from E-1 back here for medical treatment."

"Yeah. Of course."

"Give us a couple of hours to sort things out. We'll call you back at noon, our time. Sit tight."

O'Connor glanced at the morose faces of his two teammates, then replied, "We'll wait for your call."

"What the hell else can we do?" Bernstein grumbled.

Clicking off the video link, O'Connor said, "We can get back to work."

Faiyum tried to shrug inside his suit. "I like your first suggestion better. Let's eat."

With their helmets off, the faint traces of body odors became noticeable. Munching on an energy bar, Faiyum said, "A Catholic, a Muslim, and a Jew were showering together in a YMCA . . ."

"You mean a YMHA," said Bernstein.

"How would a Muslim get into either one?" O'Connor wondered.

"It's in the States," Faiyum explained. "They let anybody in."

"Not women."

"You guys have no sense of humor." Faiyum popped the last morsel of the energy bar into his mouth.

"This," Bernstein countered, "coming from a man who was named after a depression."

"El-Faiyum is below sea level," Faiyum admitted easily, "but it's the garden spot of Egypt. Has been for more than three thousand years."

"Maybe it was the garden of Eden," O'Connor suggested.

"No, that was in Israel," said Bernstein.

"Was it?"

"It certainly wasn't here," Faiyum said, gazing out the windshield at the bleak, cold Martian desert.

"It's going to go down near a hundred below again tonight," Bernstein said.

"The batteries will keep the heaters going," said O'Connor.

"All night?"

"Long enough. Then we'll recharge 'em when the sun comes up."

"That won't work forever," Bernstein muttered.

"We'll be okay for a day or two."

"Yeah, but the nights. A hundred below zero. The batteries will crap out pretty soon."

Tightly, O'Connor repeated, "We'll be okay for a day or two."

"From your mouth to God's ear," Bernstein said fervently.

Faiyum looked at the control panel's digital clock. "Another three hours before Tithonium calls."

Reaching for his helmet, O'Connor said, "Well, we'd better go out and do what we came here to do."

"Haul up the ice core," said Bernstein, displeasure clear on his lean, harsh face.

"That's why we're here," Faiyum said. He didn't look any happier than Bernstein. "Slave labor."

Putting on a false heartiness, O'Connor said, "Hey, you guys are the geologists. I thought you were happy to drill down that deep."

"Overjoyed," said Bernstein. "And here on Mars we're doing areology, not geology."

"What's in a name?" Faiyum quoted. "A rose by any other name would still smell."

"And so do you," said Bernstein and O'Connor, in unison.

The major objective of the Excursion 3 team had been to drill three hundred meters down into the permafrost that lay just beneath the surface of Utopia Planita. The frozen remains of what had been an ocean billions of years earlier, when Mars had been a warmer and wetter world, the permafrost ice held a record of the planet's history, a record that geologists (or aerologists) keenly wanted to study.

Outside at the drill site, the three men began the laborious task of hauling up the ice core that their equipment had dug. They worked slowly, carefully, to make certain that the fragile, six-centimeter-wide core came out intact. Section by section they unjointed each individual segment as it came up, marked it carefully, and stowed it in the special storage racks built into the hopper's side.

"How old do you think the lowest layers of this core will be?"

Bernstein asked as they watched the electric motor slowly, slowly lifting the slender metal tube that contained the precious ice.

"Couple billion years, at least," Faiyum replied. "Maybe more."

O'Connor, noting that the motor's batteries were down to less than fifty percent of their normal capacity, asked, "Do you think there'll be any living organisms in the ice?"

"Not hardly," said Bernstein.

"I thought there were supposed to be bugs living down there," O'Connor said.

"In the ice?" Bernstein was clearly skeptical.

Faiyum said, "You're talking about methanogens, right?"

"Is that what you call them?"

"Nobody's found anything like that," said Bernstein.

"So far," Faiyum said.

O'Connor said, "Back in training they told us about traces of methane that appear in the Martian atmosphere now and then."

Faiyum chuckled. "And some of the biologists proposed that the methane comes from bacteria living deep underground. The bacteria are supposed to exist on the water melting from the bottom of the permafrost layer, deep underground, and they excrete methane gas."

"Bug farts," said Bernstein.

O'Connor nodded inside his helmet. "Yeah. That's what they told us."

"Totally unproven," Bernstein said.

"So far," Faiyum repeated.

Sounding slightly exasperated, Bernstein said, "Look, there's a dozen abiological ways of generating the slight traces of methane that've been observed in the atmosphere."

"But they appear seasonally," Faiyum pointed out. "And the methane is quickly destroyed in the atmosphere. Solar ultraviolet breaks it down into carbon and hydrogen. That means that *something* is producing the stuff continuously."

"But that doesn't mean it's being produced by biological processes," Bernstein insisted.

"I think it's bug farts," Faiyum said. "It's kind of poetic, you know."

"You're crazy."

"You're a sourpuss."

Before O'Connor could break up their growing argument, their helmet earphones crackled, "Tithonium here."

All three of them snapped to attention. It was a woman's voice, and they recognized whose it was: the mission commander, veteran astronaut Gloria Hazeltine, known to most of the men as Glory Hallelujah. The fact that Glory herself was calling them didn't bode well, O'Connor thought. She's got bad news to tell us.

"We've checked out the numbers," said her disembodied radio voice. "The earliest we can get a rescue flight out to you will be in five days."

"Five days?" O'Connor yipped.

"That's the best we can do, Pat," the mission commander said, her tone as hard as concrete. "You'll have to make ends meet until then."

"Our batteries will crap out on us, Gloria. You know that."

"Conserve power. Your solar panels are okay, aren't they?"

Nodding, O'Connor replied, "They weren't touched, thank God."

"So recharge your batteries by day and use minimum power at night. We'll come and get you as soon as we possibly can."

"Right." O'Connor clicked off the radio connection.

"They'll come and pick up our frozen bodies," Bernstein grumbled.

Faiyum looked just as disappointed as Bernstein, but he put on a lopsided grin and said, "At least our bodies will be well preserved."

"Frozen solid," O'Connor agreed.

The three men stood there, out in the open, encased in their pressure suits and helmets, while the drill's motor buzzed away as if nothing was wrong. In the thin Martian atmosphere, the drill's drone was strangely high pitched: more of a whine than a hum.

Finally, Bernstein said, "Well, we might as well finish the job we came out here to do."

"Yeah," said Faiyum, without the slightest trace of enthusiasm.

The strangely small sun was nearing the horizon by the time they had stored all the segments of the ice core in the insulated racks on the hopper's side.

"A record of nearly three billion years of Martian history," said Bernstein, almost proudly.

"Only one and a half billion years," Faiyum corrected. "The Martian year is twice as long as Earth years."

"Six hundred eighty-seven Earth days," Bernstein said. "That's not quite twice a terrestrial year."

"So sue me," Faiyum countered, as he pulled an equipment kit from the hopper's storage bay.

"What're you doing?" O'Connor asked.

"Setting up the laser spectrometer," Faiyum replied. "You know, the experiment the biologists want us to do."

"Looking for bug farts," Bernstein said.

"Yeah. Just because we're going to freeze to death is no reason to stop working."

O'Connor grunted. Rashid is right, he thought. Go through the motions. Stay busy.

With Bernstein's obviously reluctant help, Faiyum set up the laser and trained it at the opening of their bore hole. Then they checked out the Rayleigh scattering receiver and plugged it into the radio that would automatically transmit its results back to Tithonium. The radio had its own battery to supply the microwatts of power it required.

"That ought to make the biologists happy," Bernstein said, once they were finished.

"Better get back inside," O'Connor said, looking toward the horizon where the sun was setting.

"It's going to be a long night," Bernstein muttered.

"Yeah."

Once they were sealed into the cockpit and had removed their helmets, Faiyum said, "A biologist, a geologist, and Glory Hallelujah were locked in a hotel room in Bangkok."

Bernstein moaned. O'Connor said, "You know that everything we say is being recorded for the mission log."

Faiyum said, "Hell, we're going to be dead by the time they get to us. What difference does it make?"

"No disrespect for the mission commander."

Faiyum shrugged. "Okay. How about this one: a physicist, a mathematician, and a lawyer are each asked, 'How much is two and two?'"

"I heard this one," Bernstein said.

Without paying his teammate the slightest attention, Faiyum plowed ahead. "The mathematician says, 'Two and two are four. Always four. Four point zero.' The physicist thinks a minute and says, 'It's somewhere between three point eight and four point two.'"

O'Connor smiled. Yes, a physicist probably would put it that way, he thought.

"So what does the lawyer answer?"

With a big grin, Faiyum replied, "The lawyer says, 'How much is two and two? How much do you want it to be?'"

Bernstein groaned, but O'Connor laughed. "Lawyers," he said.

"We could use a lawyer here," Bernstein said. "Sue the bastards."

"Which bastards?"

Bernstein shrugged elaborately. "All of them," he finally said.

The night was long. And dark. And cold. O'Connor set the cockpit's thermostat to barely above freezing, and ordered the two geologists to switch off their suit heaters.

"We've got to preserve every watt of electrical power we can. Stretch out the battery life as much as possible," he said firmly.

The two geologists nodded glumly.

"Better put our helmets back on," said Bernstein.

Faiyum nodded. "Better piss now, before it gets frozen."

The suits were well insulated, O'Connor knew. They'll hold our body heat better than blankets, he told himself. He remembered camping in New England, when he'd been a kid. Got pretty cold there. Then a mocking voice in his mind answered, But not a hundred below.

They made it through the first night and woke up stiff and shuddering and miserable. The sun was up, as usual, and the solar panels were feeding electrical power to the cockpit's heaters.

"That wasn't too bad," O'Connor said, as they munched on ration bars for breakfast.

Faiyum made a face. "Other than that, how did you like the play, Mrs. Lincoln?"

Bernstein pointed to the control panel's displays. "Batteries damned near died overnight," hc said.

"The solar panels are recharging them," O'Connor replied.

"They won't come back a hundred percent," said Bernstein. "You know that."

O'Connor bit back the reply he wanted to make. He merely nodded and murmured, "I know."

Faiyum peered at the display from the laser they had set up outside. "I'll be damned."

The other two hunched up closer to him.

"Look at that," said Faiyum, pointing. "The spectrometer's showing there actually is methane seeping out of our bore hole."

"Methanogens?" mused Bernstein.

"Can't be anything else," Faiyum said. With a wide smile, he said, "We've discovered life on Mars! We could win the Nobel Prize for this!"

"Posthumously," said Bernstein.

"We've got to get this data back to Tithonium," said O'Connor. "Let the biologists take a look at it."

"It's being telemetered to Tithonium automatically," Bernstein reminded him.

"Yeah, but I want to see what the biologists have to say."

The biologists were disappointingly cautious. Yes, it was methane gas seeping up from the bore hole. Yes, it very well might be coming from methanogenic bacteria living deep underground. But they needed more conclusive evidence.

"Could you get samples from the bottom of your bore hole?" asked the lead biologist, a Hispanic American from California. In the video screen on the control panel, he looked as if he were trying hard not to get excited.

"We've got the ice core," Faiyum replied immediately. "I'll bet we've got samples of the bugs in the bottom layers."

"Keep it well protected," the biologist urged.

"It's protected," O'Connor assured him.

"We'll examine it when you bring it in," the biologist said, putting on a serious face.

Once the video link was disconnected, Bernstein said morosely, "They'll be more interested in the damned ice core than in our frozen bodies."

All day long they watched the spikes of the spectrometer's flickering display. The gas issuing from their bore hole was mostly methane, and it was coming up continuously, a thin invisible breath issuing from deep below the surface.

"Those bugs are farting away down there," Faiyum said happily. "Busy little bastards."

"Sun's going down," said Bernstein.

O'Connor checked the batteries' status. Even with the solar panels recharging them all day, they were barely up to seventy-five percent of their nominal capacity. He did some quick arithmetic in his head. *If it takes Tithonium five days to get us, we'll have frozen to death on the fourth night.*

Like Shackleton at the South Pole, he thought. *Froze to death, all of 'em.*

They made it through the second night, but O'Connor barely

slept. He finally dozed off, listening to the soft breeze wafting by outside. When he awoke, every joint in his body ached, and it took nearly an hour for him to stop his uncontrollable trembling.

As they chewed on their nearly frozen breakfast bars, Bernstein said, "We're not going to make it."

"I can put in a call to Tithonium, tell 'em we're in a bad way."

"They can see our telemetry," Faiyum said, unusually morose. "They know the batteries are draining away."

"We can ask them for help."

"Yeah," said Bernstein. "When's the last time Glory Hallelujah changed her mind about anything?"

O'Connor called anyway. In the video screen, Gloria Hazeltine's chunky blond-haired face looked like that of an implacable goddess.

"We're doing everything we can," she said, her voice flat and final. "We'll get to you as soon as we can. Conserve your power. Turn off everything you don't need to keep yourselves alive."

Once O'Connor broke the comm link, Bernstein grumbled, "Maybe we could hold our breaths for three, four days."

But Faiyum was staring at the spectrometer readout. Methane gas was still coming out of the bore hole, a thin waft, but steady.

"Or maybe we could breathe bug farts," he said.

"What?"

Looking out the windshield toward their bore hole, Faiyum said, "Methane contains hydrogen. If we can capture the methane those bug are emitting . . ."

"How do we get the hydrogen out of it?" O'Connor asked.

"Lase it. That'll break it up into hydrogen and carbon. The carbon precipitates out, leaving the hydrogen for us to feed to the fuel cell."

Bernstein shook his head. "How're we going to capture the methane in the first place? And how are we going to repair the fuel cell's damage?"

"We can weld a patch on the cell," O'Connor said. "We've got the tools for that."

"And we can attach a weather balloon to the bore hole. That'll hold the methane coming out."

"Yeah, but will it be enough to power up the fuel cell?"

"We'll see."

With Bernstein clearly doubtful, they broke into the equipment locker and pulled out the small, almost delicate, welding rod and supplies. Faiyum opened the bin that contained the weather balloons.

"The meteorologists aren't going to like our using their stuff," Bernstein said. "We're supposed to be releasing these balloons twice a day."

Before O'Connor could reply with a choice *Fuck the meteorologists*, Faiyum snapped, "Let 'em eat cake."

They got to work. As team leader, O'Connor was glad of the excuse to be doing something. Even if this is a big flop, he thought, it's better to be busy than to just lie around and wait to die.

As he stretched one of the weather balloons over the bore hole and fastened it in place, Faiyum kept up a steady stream of time-worn jokes. Bernstein groaned in the proper places and O'Connor sweated inside his suit while he laboriously welded the bullet-hole-sized puncture of the fuel cell's hydrogen tank.

By midafternoon the weather balloon was swelling nicely.

"How much hydrogen do you think we've got there?" Bernstein wondered.

"Not enough," said Faiyum, serious for once. "We'll need three, four balloons full. Maybe more."

O'Connor looked westward, out across the bleak frozen plain. The sun would be setting in another couple of hours.

When they finished their day's work and clambered back into the cockpit, O'Connor saw that the batteries were barely up to half their standard power level, even with the solar panels recharging them all day.

We're not going to make it, he thought. But he said nothing. He could see that the other two stared at the battery readout. No one said a word, though.

The night was worse than ever. O'Connor couldn't sleep. The cold *hurt*. He had turned off his suit radio, so he couldn't tell if the other two had drifted off to sleep. He couldn't. He knew that when a man froze to death, he fell asleep first. Not a bad way to die, he said to himself. As if there's a good way.

He was surprised when the first rays of sunlight woke him. I fell asleep anyway. I didn't die. Not yet.

Faiyum wasn't in the cockpit, he saw. Looking blearily through the windshield he spotted the geologist in the early morning sun fixing a fresh balloon to the bore hole, with a big round yellow balloon bobbing from a rock he'd tied it to.

O'Connor saw Faiyum waving to him and gesturing to his left wrist, then remembered that he had turned his suit radio off. He clicked the control stud on his wrist.

". . . damned near ready to burst," Faiyum was saying. "Good thing I came out here in time."

Bernstein was lying back in his cranked-down seat, either asleep or . . . O'Connor nudged his shoulder. No reaction. He shook the man harder.

"Wha . . . what's going on?"

O'Connor let out a breath that he hadn't realized he'd been holding.

"You okay?" he asked softly.

"I gotta take a crap."

O'Connor giggled. He's all right. We made it through the night. But then he turned to the control panel and saw that the batteries were down to zero.

Faiyum and Bernstein spent the day building a system of pipes that led from the balloon's neck to the input valve of the repaired fuel cell's hydrogen tank. As long as the sun was shining they had plenty of electricity to power the laser. Faiyum fastened the balloon's neck to one of the hopper's spidery little landing legs and connected it to the rickety-looking pipework. Damned contraption's going to leak like a sieve, O'Conner thought. Hydrogen's sneaky stuff.

As he worked he kept up his patter of inane jokes. "A Catholic, a Muslim, and a Jew—"

"How come the Jew is always last on your list?" Bernstein asked, from his post at the fuel cell. O'Connor saw that the hydrogen tank was starting to fill.

Faiyum launched into an elaborate joke from the ancient days of the old Soviet Union, in which Jews were turned away from everything from butcher's shops to clothing stores.

"They weren't even allowed to stand in line," he explained as he held the bobbing balloon by its neck. "So when the guys who've been waiting in line at the butcher's shop since sunrise are told that there's no meat today, one of them turns to another and says, 'See, the Jews get the best of everything!'"

"I don't get it," Bernstein complained.

"They didn't have to stand in line all day."

"Because they were discriminated against."

Faiyum shook his head. "I thought you people were supposed to have a great sense of humor."

"When we hear something funny."

O'Connor suppressed a giggle. Bernstein understood the joke perfectly well, he thought, but he wasn't going to let Faiyum know it.

By the time the sun touched the horizon again, the fuel cell's hydrogen tank was half full and the hopper's batteries were totally dead.

O'Connor called Tithonium. "We're going to run on the fuel cell tonight."

For the first time since he'd known her, Gloria Hazeltine looked surprised. "But I thought your fuel cell was dead."

"We've resurrected it," O'Connor said happily. "We've got enough hydrogen to run the heaters most of the night."

"Where'd you get the hydrogen?" Glory Hallelujah was wide-eyed with curiosity.

"Bug farts," shouted Faiyum, from over O'Connor's shoulder.

They made it through the night almost comfortably and spent

the next day filling balloons with methane, then breaking down the gas into its components and filling the fuel cell's tank with hydrogen.

By the time the relief ship from Tithonium landed beside their hopper, O'Connor was almost ready to wave them off and return to the base on their own power.

Instead, though, he spent the day helping his teammates and the two-man crew of the relief ship attach the storage racks with their previous ice core onto the bigger vehicle.

As they took off for Tithonium, five men jammed into the ship's command deck, O'Connor felt almost sad to be leaving their little hopper alone on the frigid plain. Almost. We'll be back, he told himself. And we'll salvage the *Viking 2* lander when we return.

Faiyum showed no remorse about leaving at all. "A Jew, a Catholic, and a Muslim walk into a bar."

"Not another one," Bernstein groused.

Undeterred, Faiyum plowed ahead. "The bartender takes one look at them and says, 'What is this, a joke?'"

Even Bernstein laughed.

INTRODUCTION TO
"A PALE BLUE DOT"

Galileo wrote, "Astronomers . . . seek to investigate the true constitution of the universe—the most important and most admirable problem that there is."

Looking across the frontier of space, astronomers have found in recent years thousands of planets orbiting other stars. But so far, none of these exoplanets resembles Earth very closely. No one has yet found a "pale blue dot" like our own planet out among the stars.

Not yet.

But the search goes on, year by patient year, using constantly better instruments and ideas. Sky-scanning telescopes dot mountaintops all across our world. Telescopes have been placed in space, to look farther and better.

And as the frontiers of knowledge and discovery move on, the search for a pale blue dot continues.

The most important and most admirable problem that there is.

A PALE BLUE DOT

TOM DANIELS TIPTOED down the shadowy concrete corridor toward the door marked STAFF ONLY.

This is cool, he said to himself. Like a spy or a detective or something.

He was celebrating his fifteenth birthday in his own way. All summer long he'd been stuck here at the observatory. His father had said it would be fun, but Tom wished he'd stayed back home with Mom and all his friends. There weren't any other kids at the observatory, nobody his own age anywhere nearby. And there wasn't much for a bright, curious fifteen-year-old to do, either.

He remembered last summer, when he'd stayed home with Mom. At least at home I could go out in the backyard at night and look at the sky. He remembered the meteor shower that had filled the night with blazing streaks of falling stars.

No meteor showers here, he thought. Not this summer. Not ever.

Sure, Dad tried to find busywork for him. Check the auxiliary battery packs for the computers. Handle the e-mail going back to the university. If that was fun, Tom thought, then having pneumonia must be hysterical.

There was one time, though, when Dad let him come into the

telescope control center and look at the images the big 'scopes
were getting. That was way cool. Stars and more stars, big groady
clouds of glowing gas hanging out there in deep space. Better
than cool. Radical.

That was what Tom wanted. To be in on the excitement. To
discover something that nobody had ever seen before.

But Dad was too busy to let Tom back into the control center
again. He was in charge of building the new telescope, the one
that everybody said would be powerful enough to see Earth-
sized planets orbiting around other stars. Other worlds like
Earth.

All the observatory's telescopes were searching for planets
circling around other stars. They had found plenty of them, too:
giant worlds, all of them much bigger than Earth. None of them
had an ocean of blue water. None had fleecy white clouds and an
atmosphere rich with oxygen. No "pale blue dot" like Earth.

Dad said this new 'scope just might be able to find a pale blue
dot out there among the stars: a pale blue dot like Earth.

So Tom tiptoed to the locked steel door, all alone in the middle of the night, determined to celebrate his birthday in his own
way.

He had memorized the lock's electronic code long ago. Now
he tapped the keypad set into the concrete wall and heard its
faint beeps. For a moment nothing happened, then the door
clicked open.

What if somebody's in the control center? Tom asked himself.
What if Dad's in there? I'm supposed to be asleep in my bunk.

He shook his head. None of the astronomers worked this late
at night unless something special was going on. The big telescopes outside were all automated; the computers collected the
images they saw and recorded all the data. Only if something unusual happened would anybody get out of bed and come down
here.

He hoped.

Pushing through the heavy steel door, Tom saw that the control center really was empty. Even the ceiling lights were off; the only light in the cramped little room came from the computer screens, flickering off the walls in an eerie greenish glow.

The big display screen on the wall showed the telescopes outside, big spidery frameworks of steel and aluminum pointing out at the black night sky.

His heart thumping faster than usual, Tom went straight to the console where the new telescope was controlled. He sat in the little wheeled chair, just as his father would. For a moment he hesitated, then, licking his lips nervously, he booted up the computer.

"Happy birthday to me," Tom whispered as the screen lit up and showed a display of icons.

Dad's going to be pretty sore when he finds out I used the new 'scope before anybody else, Tom thought. But if I discover something, something new and important, maybe he won't get so mad. Maybe I can find the pale blue dot he's been looking for.

Tom knew the telescope was already focused on a particular planet orbiting a distant star. He leaned forward in his chair and pecked at the keyboard to get some pictures on the screen. Up came an image of the planet that was being observed by the new telescope: a big slightly flattened sphere covered with gaudy stripes and splotches of color. Along the bottom of the screen a data bar showed what the telescope's sensors had determined: the planet's size, its density, the chemical elements it was made of.

Tom saw that the planet was a lot like Jupiter, but much bigger. A huge gas giant of a planet, without even a solid surface to it. So very different from Earth. Seven hundred light years away. He calculated quickly in his head: That's forty-two trillion miles. I'm seeing this planet the way it looked seven hundred years ago; it's taken light that many years to cross the distance from there to here.

Then his breath caught in his throat. From behind the curve of the planet's rim, Tom saw something new appearing.

A moon, he realized. It had been hidden behind the planet's huge bulk. Glancing at the data bar he saw that this moon was almost the same size as Earth. And it gleamed a faint, soft blue.

A pale blue dot! As the distant moon moved clear of the planet it orbited, Tom saw a world that looked like Earth.

He yanked the phone from its holder and punched out his father's number. "Dad! Come quick! Quick!"

Before his father could ask a question Tom hung up, bent forward in his chair, staring at this distant blue world.

Then he looked again at the data bar. This world showed no water. No oxygen. The blue color was from methane, a deadly unbreathable gas.

His father burst into the data center. "What is it, Tom? What's wrong?"

Feeling almost ashamed, Tom showed him the display screen. "I thought I'd found a world like Earth," he said, crushingly disappointed.

"What are you doing in here?" his father demanded. "You ought to be in bed, asleep."

"I . . ." Tom took a deep breath. "I'm celebrating my birthday."

"Your birthday? That's not until tomorrow."

"It's past midnight, Dad."

Dad's frown melted slowly into a smile. "Yes, so it is. Well, happy birthday, son."

"Thanks, Dad."

"I had a surprise party arranged for you," Dad said, almost wistfully. "With a videophone call arranged from your mother and sister."

Tom tried not to laugh. "I guess I surprised you, instead."

"I guess you did."

Dad spent almost half an hour studying Tom's discovery.

"Well, it's not like Earth is *now*," he said at last, "but Earth had a lot of methane in its atmosphere a few billion years ago."

"It did?" Tom brightened a little.

"Yes, back when life first began on our world."

"So this world is like ours was, way back then?"

"Perhaps," his father said. "You've made a real discovery, Thomas. This is the first world we've found that could become Earthlike, in a few billion years. By studying this world we might be able to learn a lot more about our own."

"Really?"

Dad was grinning broadly now. "We'll have to write a paper for the journal about this."

"We? You mean, us?"

"You made the discovery, didn't you? Daniels and Daniels, co-authors."

"Wow!"

The two of them worked side by side for several more hours, using the telescope's sensors to measure as much as they could about this distant new world.

Finally, as the morning shift started coming into the center, Tom asked, "Have you ever made a big discovery, Dad?"

His father shook his head and smiled sorrowfully. "Can't say that I have, Tom. I've put my whole life into astronomy, but I've never made what you could call a big discovery."

Tom nodded glumly.

"But here you are, fifteen years old, and you've already made a significant discovery. You're going to make a fine astronomer, my boy."

"I don't know if I want to be an astronomer," Tommy said.

His father looked shocked. "Why not?"

"I don't know," said Tom. "I was lucky tonight, I guess. But is it really worth all the work? Night after night, day after day? I mean, you've spent your whole life being an astronomer, and it hasn't made you rich or famous, has it?"

"No, it hasn't," his father admitted.

"And it keeps you away from Mom and us kids a lot of the time. Far away."

"That's true enough."

"So what good is it? What does astronomy do for us?"

Dad gave him a funny look. Getting up from the computer, he said, "Let's take a walk outside."

"Outside?" That surprised Tom.

He followed his father down the bare concrete corridor and they struggled into their outdoor suits.

"Science is like a great building, Tom," Dad said as he opened the inner hatch. "Like a cathedral that's still being built, one brick at a time. You added a new brick tonight."

"One little brick," Tom mumbled.

"That's the way it's built, son. One little brick adds to all the others."

Dad swung the outer hatch open. "But there's always so much more to learn. The cathedral isn't finished yet. Perhaps it never will be."

They stepped outside onto the barren dusty ground. Through the visor of his helmet Tom saw the spidery frameworks of the Lunar Farside Observatory's giant telescopes rising all around them. And beyond stretched the universe of stars, thousands, millions of stars glowing in the eternal night of deep space, looking down on the battered face of the Moon where they stood.

Tom felt a lump in his throat. "Maybe I'll stick with astronomy, after all," he said to his father. And he thought it might be fun to add a few more bricks to the cathedral.

AFTERWORD TO
"A PALE BLUE DOT"

This story was inspired by Jocelyn Bell Burnell, who in 1967 discovered the first pulsar while she was doing "grunge work" as a graduate student at Cambridge University. Pulsars are collapsed stars that emit powerful pulses of radio energy.

In this story we again breach the frontier of time travel.

Traveling into the past or the future is not forbidden by the known laws of physics, and what is not forbidden might one day be accomplished by determined human minds and hands.

When H. G. Wells first published his novella *The Time Machine*, Albert Einstein was sixteen years old. William Thomson, newly made Lord Kelvin, was the grand old man of physics, and a stern guardian of the orthodoxy who proclaimed that physicists had discovered just about everything that there was to know. The frontier of knowledge was closing, according to him.

Wells's idea of time as a fourth dimension that we might be able to travel through would have been anathema to Kelvin, but it would have lit up young Albert's mind. Was Einstein inspired by Wells? Did a science fiction tale lead to Einstein's concept of relativity?

Hence this story of Wells, Kelvin, teenaged Einstein, and a time traveler.

And one other person, as well.

INSPIRATION

HE WAS AS close to despair as only a lad of seventeen can be.

"But you heard what the professor said," he moaned. "It is all finished. There is nothing left to do."

The lad spoke in German, of course. I had to translate it for Mr. Wells.

Wells shook his head. "I fail to see why such splendid news should upset the boy so."

I said to the youngster, "Our British friend says you should not lose hope. Perhaps the professor is mistaken."

"Mistaken? How could that be? He is a famous man! A nobleman! A baron!"

I had to smile. The lad's stubborn disdain for authority figures would become world-famous one day. But it was not in evidence this summer afternoon in A.D. 1896.

We were sitting in a sidewalk café with a magnificent view of the Danube and the city of Linz. Delicious odors of cooking sausages and bakery pastries wafted from the kitchen inside. Despite the splendid warm sunshine, though, I felt chilled and weak, drained of what little strength I had remaining.

"Where is that blasted waitress?" Wells grumbled. "We've been here half an hour, at the least."

"Why not just lean back and enjoy the afternoon, sir?" I suggested tiredly. "This is the best view in all the area."

Herbert George Wells was not a patient man. He had just scored a minor success in Britain with his first novel and had decided to treat himself to a vacation in Austria. He came to that decision under my influence, of course, but he did not yet realize that. At age twenty-nine, he had a lean, hungry look to him that would mellow only gradually with the coming years of prestige and prosperity.

Albert was round-faced and plumpish; still had his baby fat on him, although he had started a moustache as most teenaged boys did in those days. It was a thin, scraggly black wisp, nowhere near the full white brush it would become. If all went well with my mission.

It had taken me an enormous amount of maneuvering to get Wells and this teenager to the same place at the same time. The effort had nearly exhausted all my energies. Young Albert had come to see Professor Thomson with his own eyes, of course. Wells had been more difficult; he had wanted to see Salzburg, the birthplace of Mozart. I had taken him instead to Linz, with a thousand assurances that he would find the trip worthwhile.

He complained endlessly about Linz, the city's lack of beauty, the sour smell of its narrow streets, the discomfort of our hotel, the dearth of restaurants where one could get decent food—by which he meant burnt mutton. Not even the city's justly famous linzer torte pleased him. "Not as good as a decent trifle," he groused. "Not as good by half."

I, of course, knew several versions of Linz that were even less pleasing, including one in which the city was nothing more than charred radioactive rubble and the Danube so contaminated that it glowed at night all the way down to the Black Sea. I shuddered at that vision and tried to concentrate on the task at hand.

It had almost required physical force to get Wells to take a walk across the Danube on the ancient stone bridge and up the Pöstlingberg to this little sidewalk café. He had huffed with anger when we had started out from our hotel at the city's central square, then soon was puffing with exertion as we toiled up the steep hill. I was breathless from the climb also. In later years a tram would make the ascent, but on this particular afternoon we had been obliged to walk.

He had been mildly surprised to see the teenager trudging up the precipitous street just a few steps ahead of us. Recognizing that unruly crop of dark hair from the audience at Thomson's lecture that morning, Wells had graciously invited Albert to join us for a drink.

"We deserve a beer or two after this blasted climb," he said, eying me unhappily.

Panting from the climb, I translated to Albert, "Mr. Wells . . . invites you . . . to have a refreshment . . . with us."

The youngster was pitifully grateful, although he would order nothing stronger than tea. It was obvious that Thomson's lecture had shattered him badly. So now we sat on uncomfortable cast-iron chairs and waited—they for the drinks they had ordered, me for the inevitable. I let the warm sunshine soak into me and hoped it would rebuild at least some of my strength.

The view was little short of breathtaking: the brooding castle across the river, the Danube itself streaming smoothly and actually blue as it glittered in the sunlight, the lakes beyond the city and the blue-white snow peaks of the Austrian Alps hovering in the distance like ghostly petals of some immense unworldly flower.

But Wells complained, "That has to be the ugliest castle I have ever seen."

"What did the gentleman say?" Albert asked.

"He is stricken by the sight of the Emperor Friedrich's castle," I answered sweetly.

"Ah. Yes, it has a certain grandeur to it, doesn't it?"

Wells had all the impatience of a frustrated journalist. "Where is that damnable waitress? Where is our beer?"

"I'll find the waitress," I said, rising uncertainly from my iron-

hard chair. As his ostensible tour guide, I had to remain in character for a while longer, no matter how tired I felt. But then I saw
what I had been waiting for.

"Look!" I pointed down the steep street. "Here comes the
professor himself!"

William Thomson, First Baron Kelvin of Largs, was striding
up the pavement with much more bounce and energy than any of
us had shown. He was seventy-one, his silver-gray hair thinner
than his impressive gray beard, lean almost to the point of looking frail. Yet he climbed the ascent that had made my heart thun-
der in my ears as if he were strolling amiably across some campus
quadrangle.

Wells shot to his feet and leaned across the iron rail of the café.
"Good afternoon, your Lordship." For a moment I thought he
was going to tug at his forelock.

Kelvin squinted at him. "You were in my audience this morning, were you not?"

"Yes, m'lud. Permit me to introduce myself: I am H. G. Wells."

"Ah. You're a physicist?"

"A writer, sir."

"Journalist?"

"Formerly. Now I am a novelist."

"Really? How keen."

Young Albert and I had also risen to our feet. Wells introduced
us properly and invited Kelvin to join us.

"Although I must say," Wells murmured as Kelvin came round
the railing and took the empty chair at our table, "that the service here leaves quite a bit to be desired."

"Oh, you have to know how to deal with the Teutonic tem-
perament," said Kelvin jovially as we all sat down. He banged the
flat of his hand on the table so hard it made us all jump. "Service!"
he bellowed. "Service here!"

Miraculously, the waitress appeared from the doorway and
trod stubbornly to our table. She looked very unhappy—sullen,
in fact. Sallow pouting face with brooding brown eyes and down-

turned mouth. She pushed back a lock of hair that had strayed across her forehead.

"We've been waiting for our beer," Wells said to her.

"And now this gentleman has joined us—"

"Permit me, sir," I said. It *was* my job, after all. In German I asked her to bring us three beers and the tea that Albert had ordered and to do it quickly.

She looked the four of us over as if we were smugglers or criminals of some sort, her eyes lingering briefly on Albert, then turned without a word or even a nod and went back inside the café.

I stole a glance at Albert. His eyes were riveted on Kelvin, his lips parted as if he wanted to speak but could not work up the nerve. He ran a hand nervously through his thick mop of hair. Kelvin seemed perfectly at ease, smiling affably, his hands laced across his stomach just below his beard; he was the man of authority, acknowledged by the world as the leading scientific figure of his generation.

"Can it be really true?" Albert blurted at last. "Have we learned everything of physics that can be learned?"

He spoke in German, of course, the only language he knew. I immediately translated for him, exactly as he asked his question.

Once he understood what Albert was asking, Kelvin nodded his gray old head sagely. "Yes, yes. The young men in the laboratories today are putting the final dots over the *i*'s, the final crossings of the *t*'s. We've just about finished physics; we know at last all there is to be known."

Albert looked crushed.

Kelvin did not need a translator to understand the youngster's emotion. "If you are thinking of a career in physics, young man, then I heartily advise you to think again. By the time you complete your education there will be nothing left for you to do."

"Nothing?" Wells asked as I translated. "Nothing at all?"

"Oh, add a few decimal places here and there, I suppose. Tidy up a bit, that sort of thing."

Albert had failed his admission test to the Federal Polytechnic in Zurich. He had never been a particularly good student. My goal was to get him to apply again to the Polytechnic and pass the exams.

Visibly screwing up his courage, Albert asked, "But what about the work of Röntgen?"

Once I had translated, Kelvin knit his brows. "Röntgen? Oh, you mean that report about mysterious rays that go through solid walls? X-rays, is it?"

Albert nodded eagerly.

"Stuff and nonsense!" snapped the old man. "Absolute bosh. He may impress a few medical men who know little of science, but his X-rays do not exist. Impossible! German daydreaming."

Albert looked at me with his whole life trembling in his piteous eyes. I interpreted:

"The professor fears that X-rays may be illusory, although he does not as yet have enough evidence to decide, one way or the other."

Albert's face lit up. "Then there is hope! We have not discovered *everything* as yet!"

I was thinking about how to translate that for Kelvin when Wells ran out of patience. "Where *is* that blasted waitress?"

I was grateful for the interruption. "I will find her, sir."

Dragging myself up from the table, I left the three of them, Wells and Kelvin chatting amiably, while Albert swiveled his head back and forth, understanding not a word. Every joint in my body ached, and I knew that there was nothing anyone in this world could do to help me. The café was dark inside and smelled of stale beer. The waitress was standing at the bar, speaking rapidly, angrily, to the stout barkeep in a low venomous tone. The barkeep was polishing glasses with the end of his apron; he looked grim and, once he noticed me, embarrassed.

Three seidels of beer stood on a round tray next to her, with a single glass of tea. The beers were getting warm and flat, the tea cooling, while she blistered the bartender's ears.

I interrupted her vicious monologue. "The gentlemen want their drinks," I said in German.

She whirled on me, her eyes furious. "The *gentlemen* may have their beers when they get rid of that infernal Jew!"

Taken aback somewhat, I glanced at the barkeep. He turned away from me.

"No use asking him to do it," the waitress hissed. "We do not serve Jews here. *I* do not serve Jews and neither will he!"

The café was almost empty this late in the afternoon. In the dim shadows I could make out only a pair of elderly gentlemen quietly smoking their pipes and a foursome, apparently two married couples, drinking beer. A six-year-old boy knelt at the far end of the bar, laboriously scrubbing the wooden floor.

"If it's too much trouble for you," I said, and started to reach for the tray.

She clutched at my outstretched arm. "No! No Jews will be served here! Never!"

I could have brushed her off. If my strength had not been drained away I could have broken every bone in her body and the barkeep's, too. But I was nearing the end of my tether and I knew it.

"Very well," I said softly. "I will take only the beers."

She glowered at me for a moment, then let her hand drop away. I removed the glass of tea from the tray and left it on the bar. Then I carried the beers out into the warm afternoon sunshine.

As I set the tray on our table, Wells asked, "They have no tea?"

Albert knew better. "They refuse to serve Jews," he guessed. His voice was flat, unemotional, neither surprised nor saddened.

I nodded as I said in English, "Yes, they refuse to serve Jews."

"You're Jewish?" Kelvin asked, reaching for his beer.

The teenager did not need a translation. He replied, "I was born in Germany. I am now a citizen of Switzerland. I have no religion. But, yes, I am a Jew."

Sitting next to him, I offered him my beer.

"No, no," he said with a sorrowful little smile. "It would merely upset them further. I think perhaps I should leave."

"Not quite yet," I said. "I have something that I want to show you." I reached into the inner pocket of my jacket and pulled out the thick sheaf of paper I had been carrying with me since I had started out on this mission. I noticed that my hand trembled slightly.

"What is it?" Albert asked.

I made a little bow of my head in Wells's direction. "This is my translation of Mr. Wells' excellent story, *The Time Machine*."

Wells looked surprised, Albert curious. Kelvin smacked his lips and put his half-drained seidel down.

"Time machine?" asked young Albert.

"What's he talking about?" Kelvin asked.

I explained, "I have taken the liberty of translating Mr. Wells's story about a time machine, in the hope of attracting a German publisher."

Wells said, "You never told me—"

But Kelvin asked, "Time machine? What on Earth would a time machine be?"

Wells forced an embarrassed, self-deprecating little smile. "It is merely the subject of a tale I have written, m'lud: a machine that can travel through time. Into the past, you know. Or the, uh, future."

Kelvin fixed him with a beady gaze. "Travel into the past or the future?"

"It is fiction, of course," Wells said apologetically.

"Of course."

Albert seemed fascinated. "But how could a machine travel through time? How do you explain it?"

Looking thoroughly uncomfortable under Kelvin's wilting eye, Wells said hesitantly, "Well, if you consider time as a dimension—"

"A dimension?" asked Kelvin.

"Rather like the three dimensions of space."

"Time as a fourth dimension?"

"Yes. Rather."

Albert nodded eagerly as I translated. "Time as a dimension, yes! Whenever we move through space we move through time as well, do we not? Space and time! Four dimensions, all bound to-gether!"

Kelvin mumbled something indecipherable and reached for his half-finished beer.

"And one could travel through this dimension?" Albert asked. "Into the past or the future?"

"Utter bilge," Kelvin muttered, slamming his emptied seidel on the table. "Quite impossible."

"It is merely fiction," said Wells, almost whining. "Only an idea I toyed with in order to—"

"Fiction. Of course," said Kelvin, with great finality. Quite abruptly, he pushed himself to his feet. "I'm afraid I must be go-ing. Thank you for the beer."

He left us sitting there and started back down the street, his face flushed. From the way his beard moved I could see that he was muttering to himself.

"I'm afraid we've offended him," said Wells.

"But how could he become angry over an idea?" Albert won-dered. The thought seemed to stun him. "Why should a new idea infuriate a man of science?"

The waitress bustled across the patio to our table. "When is this Jew leaving?" she hissed at me, eyes blazing with fury. "I won't have him stinking up our café any longer!"

Obviously shaken, but with as much dignity as a seventeen-year-old could muster, Albert rose to his feet. "I will leave, madam. I have imposed on your so-gracious hospitality long enough."

"Wait," I said, grabbing at his jacket sleeve. "Take this with you. Read it. I think you will enjoy it."

He smiled at me, but I could see the sadness that would haunt his eyes forever. "Thank you, sir. You have been most kind to me."

He took the manuscript and left us. I saw him already reading it as he walked slowly down the street toward the bridge back to Linz proper. I hoped he would not trip and break his neck as he ambled down the steep street, his nose stuck in the manuscript.

The waitress watched him too. "Filthy Jew. They're everywhere! They get themselves into everything."

"That will be quite enough from you," I said as sternly as I could manage.

She glared at me and headed back for the bar.

Wells looked more puzzled than annoyed, even after I explained what had happened.

"It's their country, after all," he said, with a shrug of his narrow shoulders. "If they don't want to mingle with Jews there's not much we can do about it, is there?"

I took a sip of my warm flat beer, not trusting myself to come up with a properly polite response. There was only one timeline in which Albert lived long enough to make an effect on the world. There were dozens where he languished in obscurity or was gassed in one of the death camps.

Wells's expression turned curious. "I didn't know you had translated my story."

"To see if perhaps a German publisher would be interested in it," I lied.

"But you gave the manuscript to that Jewish fellow."

"I have another copy of the translation."

"You do? Why would you—"

My time was almost up, I knew. I had a powerful urge to end the charade. "That young Jewish fellow might change the world, you know."

Wells laughed.

"I mean it," I said. "You think that your story is merely a piece of fiction. Let me tell you, it is much more than that."

"Really?"

"Time travel will become possible one day."

"Don't be ridiculous!" But I could see the sudden astonishment in his eyes. And the memory. It was I who had suggested the idea of time travel to him. We had discussed it for months back when he had been working for the newspapers. I had kept the idea in the forefront of his imagination until he finally sat down and dashed off his novella.

I hunched closer to him, leaned my elbows wearily on the table. "Suppose Kelvin is wrong? Suppose there is much more to physics than he suspects?"

"How could that be?" Wells asked.

"That lad is reading your story. It will open his eyes to new vistas, new possibilities."

Wells cast a suspicious glance at me. "You're pulling my leg."

I forced a smile. "Not altogether. You would do well to pay attention to what the scientists discover over the coming years. You could build a career writing about it. You could become known as a prophet if you play your cards properly."

His face took on the strangest expression I had ever seen: he did not want to believe me and yet he did; he was suspicious, curious, doubtful and yearning—all at the same time. Above everything else he was ambitious, thirsting for fame. Like every writer, he wanted to have the world acknowledge his genius.

I told him as much as I dared. As the afternoon drifted on and the shadows lengthened, as the sun sank behind the distant mountains and the warmth of day slowly gave way to an uneasy deepening chill, I gave him carefully veiled hints of the future. A future. The one I wanted him to promote.

Wells could have no conception of the realities of time travel, of course. There was no frame of reference in his tidy nineteenth-century English mind of the infinite branchings of the future. He was incapable of imagining the horrors that lay in store. How could he imagine them? Time branches endlessly, and only a few, a precious handful of those branches manage to avoid utter disaster.

Could I show him his beloved London obliterated by fusion bombs? Or the entire northern hemisphere of Earth depopulated by man-made plagues? Or a devastated world turned to a savagery that made his Morlocks seem compassionate?

Could I explain to him the energies involved in time travel or the damage they did to the human body? The fact that time travelers were volunteers sent on suicide missions, desperately trying to preserve a timeline that saved at least a portion of the human race? The best future I could offer him was a twentieth century tortured by world wars and genocide. That was the best I could do.

So all I did was hint, as gently and subtly as I could, trying to guide him toward that best of all possible futures, horrible though it would seem to him. I could neither control nor coerce anyone; all I could do was to offer a bit of guidance. Until the radiation dose from my trip through time finally killed me.

Wells was happily oblivious to my pain. He did not even notice the perspiration that beaded my brow despite the chilling breeze that heralded nightfall.

"You appear to be telling me," he said at last, "that my writings will have some sort of positive effect on the world."

"They already have," I replied, with a genuine smile.

His brows rose.

"That teenaged lad is reading your story. Your concept of time as a dimension has already started his fertile mind working."

"That young student?"

"Will change the world," I said. "For the better."

"Really?"

"Really," I said, trying to sound confident. I knew there were still a thousand pitfalls in young Albert's path. And I would not live long enough to help him past them. Perhaps others would, but there were no guarantees.

I knew that if Albert did not reach his full potential, if he was turned away by the university again or murdered in the coming Holocaust, the future I was attempting to preserve would disappear in a global catastrophe that could end the human race forever. My task was to save as much of humanity as I could.

I had accomplished a feeble first step in saving some of humankind, but only a first step. Albert was reading the time-machine tale and starting to think that Kelvin was blind to the real world. But there was so much more to do. So very much more.

We sat there in the deepening shadows of the approaching twilight, Wells and I, each of us wrapped in our own thoughts about the future. Despite his best English self-control, Wells was smiling contentedly. He saw a future in which he would be hailed as a prophet. I hoped it would work out that way. It was an immense task that I had undertaken. I felt tired, gloomy, daunted by the immensity of it all. Worst of all, I would never know if I succeeded or not.

Then the waitress bustled over to our table. "Well, have you finished? Or are you going to stay here all night?"

Even without a translation Wells understood her tone. "Let's go," he said, scraping his chair across the flagstones.

I pushed myself to my feet and threw a few coins on the table. The waitress scooped them up immediately and called into the café, "Come here and scrub down this table! At once!"

The six-year-old boy came trudging across the patio, lugging the heavy wooden pail of water. He stumbled and almost dropped it; water sloshed onto his mother's legs. She grabbed him by the ear and lifted him nearly off his feet. A faint tortured squeak issued from the boy's gritted teeth.

"Be quiet and do your work properly," she told her son, her voice murderously low. "If I let your father know how lazy you are . . ."

The six-year-old's eyes went wide with terror as his mother let her threat dangle in the air between them.

"Scrub that table good, Adolph," his mother told him. "Get rid of that damned Jew's stink."

I looked down at the boy. His eyes were burning with shame and rage and hatred. Save as much of the human race as you can, I told myself. But it was already too late to save him.

"Are you coming?" Wells called to me.

"Yes," I said, tears in my eyes. "It's getting dark, isn't it?"

INTRODUCTION TO
"THE LAST DECISION"

One of the things that make science fiction such a vital and vivid field is the synergy that manifests itself among the writers. Whereas in most other areas of contemporary letters the writers appear to feel themselves in competition with each other (for headlines, if nothing else), the writers of science fiction have long seen themselves as members of a big family. They share ideas, often work together, and they help each other whenever they can.

A large part of this synergy stems from the original Milford Writers' Conference, which used to be held annually in Milford, Pennsylvania. Everlasting thanks are due to Damon Knight, James Blish, and Judith Merril, who first organized the conferences. For eight days out of each June, a small and dedicated group of professional writers—about evenly mixed between old hands and newcomers—ate, slept, breathed and talked about writing. Lifelong friendships began at Milford, together with the synergy that makes two such friends more effective working together than the simple one-plus-one equation would lead you to think.

I met Gordon R. Dickson at the first Milford I attended, back in the early 1960s, and we became firm friends right until Gordy's death. We collaborated on a children's fantasy, *Gremlins, Go*

Home, some years later, and even though we lived half a continent apart it was rare six months when we didn't see each other.

"The Last Decision" is an example of the synergy between writers. Gordy wrote a marvelous story, "Call Him Lord," which stuck in my mind for years. In particular, I was haunted by the character of the Emperor of the Hundred Worlds. As powerful a characterization as I have found anywhere, even though he was actually a minor player in Gordy's story. I wanted to see more of the Emperor, and I finally asked Gordy if he would allow me to use the characters in a story of my own. He graciously gave his permission.

The result is "The Last Decision," a story about the frontiers of space, time, knowledge, and—above all else—the kind of friendship that outlasts even death.

THE LAST DECISION

1

THE EMPEROR OF the Hundred Worlds stood at the head of the conference chamber, tall, gray, grim-faced. Although there were forty other men and women seated in the chamber, the Emperor knew that he was alone.

"Then it is certain?" he asked, his voice grave but strong despite the news they had given him. "Earth's Sun will explode?"

The scientists had come from all ends of the empire to reveal their findings to the Emperor. They shifted uneasily in their sculptured couches under his steady gaze. A few of them, the oldest and best-trusted, were actually on the Imperial Planet itself, only an ocean away from the palace. Most of the others had been brought to the Imperial Planetary System from their homeworlds and were housed on other planets in the system.

Although holographic projections made them look as solid and real as the Emperor himself, there was always a slight lag in their responses to him. The delay was an indication of their rank within the scientific order, and they even arranged their seating in the conference chamber the same way: the farther away from the Emperor, the lower in the hierarchy.

Some things cannot be conquered, the Emperor thought to himself as one of the men in the third rank of couches, a roundish, bald, slightly pompous little man, got to his feet. *Time still reigns supreme. Distance we can conquer, but not time. Not death.*

"Properly speaking, sire," the bald little man was saying, "the Sun will not explode. It will not become a supernova. Its mass is too low for that. But the eruptions it will suffer will be of sufficient severity to heat Earth's atmosphere to incandescence. It will destroy all life on the surface. And, of course, the oceans will be drastically damaged; the food chain of the oceans will be totally disrupted."

Good-bye to Earth, then, thought the Emperor.

But aloud he asked, "The power satellites and the shielding we have provided the planet—they will not protect it?"

The scientist stood dumb, waiting for his Emperor's response to span the light-minutes between them. *How drab he looks*, the Emperor noted. *And how soft*. He pulled his own white robe closer around his iron-hard body. He was older than most of them in the conference chamber, but they were accustomed to sitting at desks and lecturing to students. He was accustomed to standing before multitudes and commanding.

"The shielding," the man said at last, "will not be sufficient. There is nothing we can do. Sometime over the next three to five hundred years the Sun will erupt and destroy all life on Earth and the inner planets of its system. The data are conclusive."

The Emperor inclined his head to the man, curtly, a gesture that meant both "thank you" and "be seated." The scientist waited mutely for the gesture to reach him.

The data are conclusive. The integrator woven into the neurons of the Emperor's cerebral cortex linked his mind with the continent-spanning computer complex that was the Imperial memory.

Within microseconds he reviewed the equations and found no flaw with them. Even as he did so, the other hemisphere of his brain was picturing Earth's daystar seething, writhing in a fury of pent-up nuclear agony, then erupting into giant flares. The Sun calmed afterward and smiled benignly once again on a blackened, barren, smoking rock called Earth.

A younger man was on his feet, back in the last row of couches.

The Emperor realized he had already asked for permission to speak. Now they both waited for the photons to complete the journey between them. From his position in the chamber and the distance between them, he was either an upstart or a very junior researcher.

"Sire," he said at last, his face suddenly flushed in embarrassed self-consciousness or, perhaps, the heat of conviction, "the data may be conclusive, true enough. But it is *not* true that we must accept this catastrophe with folded hands."

The Emperor began to say, "Explain yourself," but the intense young man never hesitated to wait for an Imperial response. He was taking no chances of being commanded into silence before he had finished.

"Earth's Sun will erupt only if we do nothing to prevent it. A colleague of mine believes that we have the means to prevent the eruptions. I would like to present her ideas on the subject. She herself could not attend this meeting." The young man's face grew taut, angry. "Her application to attend was rejected by the Coordinating Committee."

The Emperor smiled inwardly as the young man's words reached the other scientists around him. He could see a shock wave of disbelief and indignation spread through the assembly. The hoary old men in the front row, who had chosen the members of the Coordinating Committee, went stiff with anger.

Even Prince Javas, the Emperor's last remaining son, roused from his idle daydreaming where he sat at the Emperor's side and seemed to take an interest in the meeting for the first time.

"You may present your colleague's proposal," said the Emperor. *That is what an Emperor is for*, he said silently, looking at his youngest son, seeking some understanding on his handsome untroubled face. *To be magnanimous in the face of disaster.*

The young researcher took a fingertip-sized cube from his sleeve pocket and inserted it into the computer slot in the arm of his couch. The scientists in the front ranks of the chamber glowered and muttered to each other.

The Emperor stood lean and straight, waiting for the information to reach him. When it did, he saw in his mind a young dark-haired woman whose face might have been seductive if she were not so intensely serious about her subject. She was speaking, trying to keep her voice dispassionate, but almost literally quivering with excitement. Equations appeared, charts, graphs, lists of materials and costs; yet her intent, dark-eyed face dominated it all.

Beyond her, the Emperor saw a vague, star-shimmering image of vast ships ferrying megatons of equipment and thousands upon thousands of technical specialists from all parts of the Hundred Worlds toward Earth and its troubled Sun.

Then, as the equations faded and the starry picture went dim and even the woman's face began to pale, the Emperor saw the Earth, green and safe, smelled the grass and heard birds singing, saw the Sun shining gently over a range of soft, rolling, ancient wooded hills.

He closed his eyes. *You go too far, woman*. But how was she to know that his eldest son had died in hills exactly like these, killed on Earth, killed *by* Earth, so many years ago?

2

HE SAT NOW. The Emperor of the Hundred Worlds spent little time on his feet anymore. *One by one the vanities are surrendered*. He sat in a powered chair that held him in a soft yet firm embrace. It was mobile and almost alive: part personal vehicle, part medical monitor, part communications system that could link him with any place in the Empire.

His son stood. Prince Javas stood by the marble balustrade that girdled the high terrace where his father had received him. He wore the blue-gray uniform of a fleet commander, although he had never bothered to accept command of even one ship. His wife, the princess Rihana, stood at her husband's side.

They were a well-matched pair, physically. Gold and fire. The prince had his father's lean sinewy grace, golden hair, and star-flecked eyes. Rihana was fiery, with the beauty and ruthlessness of a tigress in her face and tawny eyes. Her hair was a cascade of molten copper tumbling past her shoulders, her gown a metallic glitter.

"It was a wasted trip," Javas said to his father, with his usual sardonic smile. "Earth is . . . well," he shrugged, "nothing but Earth. It hasn't changed in the slightest."

"Ten wasted years," Rihana said.

The Emperor looked past them, beyond the terrace to the lovingly landscaped forest that his engineers could never quite make the right shade of terrestrial green.

"Not entirely wasted, daughter-in-law," he said at last. "You only aged eighteen months."

"We are ten years out of date with the affairs of the court," she answered. The smoldering expression on her face made it clear that she believed her father-in-law deliberately plotted to keep her as far away from the throne as possible.

"You can easily catch up," the Emperor said, ignoring her anger. "In the meantime, you have kept your youthful appearance."

"I shall always keep it! *You* are the one who denies himself rejuvenation treatments, not me."

"And so will Javas, when he becomes Emperor."

"Will he?" Her eyes were suddenly mocking.

"He will," said the Emperor, with the weight of a hundred worlds behind his voice.

Rihana looked away from him. "Well, even so, I shan't. I see no reason why I should age and wither when even the foulest shopkeeper can live for centuries."

"Your husband will age."

She said nothing.

And as he ages, the Emperor knew, *you will find younger lovers. But of course, you have done that already, haven't you?*

He turned toward his son, who was still standing by the balustrade.

"Kyle Arman is dead," Javas blurted.

For a moment, the Emperor failed to comprehend. "Dead?" he asked, his voice sounding old and weak even to himself.

Javas nodded. "In his sleep. Heart seizure."

"But he's too young . . ."

"He was your age, Father."

"And he refused rejuvenation treatments," Rihana said, sounding positively happy. "As if he were royalty! The pretentious fool! A servant . . . a menial . . ."

"He was a friend of this House," the Emperor said.

"He killed my brother," said Javas.

"Your brother failed the test. He was a coward. Unfit to rule." *But Kyle passed you*, the Emperor thought. *You were found fit to rule . . . or was Kyle ashamed of what he had done to my firstborn?*

"And you accepted his story." For once, Javas's bemused smile was gone. There was iron in his voice. "The word of a backwoods Earthman."

"A pretentious fool," Rihana gloated.

"A proud and faithful man," the Emperor corrected. "A man who put honor and duty above personal safety or comfort."

His eyes locked with Javas's. After a long moment in silence, the Prince shrugged and turned away.

"Regardless," Rihana said, "we surveyed the situation on Earth, as you requested us to do."

Commanded, the Emperor thought. *Not requested.*

"The people there are all primitives. Hardly a city on the entire planet! It's all trees and huge oceans."

"I know. I have been there."

Javas said, "There are only a few million living on Earth. They can be evacuated easily enough and resettled on a few of the frontier planets. After all, they *are* primitives."

"Those 'primitives' are the baseline of our race. They are the pool of genetic material against which our scientists constantly measure the rest of humanity throughout the Hundred Worlds."

Rihana said, "Well, they're going to have to find another primitive world to live on."

"Unless we prevent their Sun from exploding."

Javas looked amused. "You're not seriously considering that?"

"I am . . . considering it. Perhaps not very seriously."

"It makes no difference," Rihana said. "The plan to save the Sun—to save your precious Earth—will take hundreds of years to implement. You will be dead long before the first steps can be brought to a conclusion. The next Emperor can cancel the entire plan the day he takes the throne."

The Emperor turned his powered chair slightly to face his son, but Javas looked away, out toward the darkening forest.

"I know," the Emperor whispered, more to himself than to her. "I know that full well."

3

HE COULD NOT sleep. The Emperor lay on the wide expanse of warmth, floating a single molecular layer above the gently soothing waters. Always before, when sleep would not come readily, a woman had solved the problem for him. But lately not even lovemaking helped.

The body grows weary but the mind refuses sleep. Is this what old age brings?

Now he lay alone, the ceiling of his tower room depolarized so that he could see the blazing glory of the Imperial Planet's night sky.

Not like the pale sky of Earth, with its bloated Moon smiling inanely at you, he thought. This was truly an Imperial sky, brazen with blue giant stars that studded the heavens like brilliant sapphires. No moon rode in that sky; none was needed. There was never true darkness on the Imperial Planet.

And yet Earth's sky seemed so much friendlier. You could pick out old companions there: the two Bears, the Lion, the Twins, the Hunter, the Winged Horse.

Already I think of Earth in the past tense. Like Kyle. Like my son.

He thought of Earth's warming Sun. How could it turn traitor? How could it . . . begin to die? In his mind's eye he hovered above the Sun, bathed in its fiery glow, watching its bubbling, seething surface. He plunged deeper into the roiling plasma, saw filaments and streamers arching a thousand Earthspans into space, heard the pulsing throb of the star's energy, the roar of its power, blinding bright, overpowering, ceaseless merciless heat, throbbing, roaring, pounding . . .

He was gasping for breath and the pounding he heard was his own heartbeat throbbing in his ears. Soaked with sweat, he tried to sit up. The bed enfolded him protectively, supporting his body.

"Hear me," he commanded the computer, his voice cracking.

"Sire?" answered a softly female voice in his mind.

He forced himself to relax. Forced the pain from his body. The dryness in his throat eased. His breathing slowed. The pounding of his heart diminished.

"Get me the woman scientist who reported at the conference on the Sun's explosion ten years ago. She was not present at the conference; her report was presented by a colleague."

The computer needed more than a second to reply, "Sire, there were four such reports by female scientists at that conference."

"This was the only one to deal with a plan to save the Earth's Sun."

4

MEDICAL MONITORS WERE implanted in his body now. Although the Imperial physicians insisted that it was impossible, the Emperor could feel the microscopic implants on the wall of his beating heart, in his aorta, alongside his carotid artery. The Imperial psychotechs called it a psychosomatic reaction. But since his mind was linked to the computers that handled all the information on the planet, the Emperor knew what his monitors were reporting before his doctors did.

They had reduced the gravity in his living and working areas of the palace to one-third normal and forbade him from leaving those areas, except for the rare occasions of state when he was needed in the Great Assembly Hall or another public area. He acquiesced in this: the lighter gravity felt better and allowed him to be on his feet once again, free of the powerchair's clutches.

This day he was walking slowly, calmly, through a green forest of Earth. He strolled along a parklike path, admiring the lofty maples and birches, listening to the birds and small forest animals' songs of life. He inhaled the scents of pine and grass and sweet clean air. He felt the warm sun on his face and the faintest cool breeze. For a moment he considered how the trees would look in their autumnal reds and golds. But he shook his head.

No. There is enough autumn in my life. I'd rather be in springtime.

In the rooms next to the corridor he walked through, tense knots of technicians worked at the holographic systems that produced the illusion of the forest, while other groups of white-suited meditechs studied the readouts from the Emperor's implants.

Two men joined the Emperor on the forest path: Academician Bomeer, head of the Imperial Academy of Sciences, and Supreme Commander Fain, chief of staff of the Imperial Military Forces. Both were old friends and advisors, close enough to the Emperor to be housed within the palace itself when they were allowed to visit their master.

Bomeer looked young, almost sprightly, in a stylish robe of green and tan. He was slightly built, had a lean, almost ascetic face that was spoiled by a large mop of unruly brown hair.

Commander Fain was iron gray, square-faced, a perfect picture of a military leader. His black and silver uniform fit his muscular frame like a second skin. His gray eyes seemed eternally troubled.

The Emperor greeted them and allowed Bomeer a few minutes to admire the forest simulation. The scientist called out the correct names for each type of tree they walked past and identified several species of birds and squirrels. Finally the Emperor

asked him about the young woman who had arrived on the Imperial Planet the previous month.

"Sire, I have discussed her plan thoroughly with her," Bomeer
said, his face going serious. "I must say that she is dedicated, en-
ergetic, close to brilliant. But rather naïve and overly sanguine
about her own ideas."

"Could her plan work?" asked the Emperor.

"Could it work?" the scientist echoed. He had tenaciously held
on to his post at the top of the scientific hierarchy for nearly a
century. His body had been rejuvenated more than once, the
Emperor knew. But not his mind.

"Sire, there is no way to tell if it could work! Such an operation
has never been attempted before. There is no valid data. Mathe-
matics, yes. But even so, there is no more than theory. And the
costs! The time it would take! The technical manpower! Stag-
gering."

The Emperor stopped walking. Fifty meters away, behind the
hologram screens, a dozen meditechs suddenly hunched over their
readout screens intently.

But the Emperor had stopped merely to repeat to Bomeer,
"Could her plan work?"

Bomeer ran a hand through his boyish mop, glanced at Fain
for support and found none, then faced the Emperor again. "I . . .
there is no firm answer, sire. Statistically, I would say that the
chances are vanishingly small."

"Statistics!" The emperor made a disgusted gesture. "A refuge
for scoundrels and sociotechs. Is there anything scientifically
impossible in what she proposes?"

"Nnn . . . not *theoretically* impossible, sire," Bomeer replied
slowly. "But in the practical world of reality, it . . . it's the *magni-
tude* of the project. The costs. Why, it would take half of Commander Fain's fleet to transport the equipment and material."

Fain seized his opportunity to speak. "And the Imperial Fleet,
sire, is spread much too thin for safety as it is."

"We are at peace, Commander," said the Emperor.

"For how long, sire? The frontier worlds grow more restless every day. And the aliens beyond our borders—"

"Are weaker than we are. I have reviewed the intelligence assessments, Commander."

"Sire, the relevant factor in those reports is that the aliens are growing stronger and we are not."

With a nod, the Emperor resumed walking. The scientist and the commander followed him, arguing their points unceasingly.

Finally they reached the end of the long corridor, where the holographic simulation showed them Earth's Sun setting beyond the edge of an ocean, turning the restless sea into an impossible glitter of opalescence.

"Your recommendations, then, gentlemen?" the Emperor asked wearily. Even in one-third gravity his legs felt tired, his back ached.

Bomeer spoke first, his voice hard and sure. "This naïve dream of saving Earth's Sun is doomed to fail. The plan must be rejected."

Fain added, "The fleet can detach enough squadrons from its noncombat units to initiate the evacuation of Earth whenever you order it, sire."

"Evacuate them to an unsettled planet?" the Emperor asked.

"Or resettle them on existing frontier worlds. The Earth residents are rather frontierlike themselves; they've purposely been kept primitive. They would get along well with some of the frontier populations. They might even serve to calm down some of the unrest on the frontier worlds."

The Emperor looked at Fain and almost smiled. "Or they might fan that unrest into outright rebellion. They are a cantankerous lot, you know."

"We can deal with rebellion," said Fain.

"Can you?" the Emperor asked. "You can kill people, of course. You can level cities and even render whole planets uninhabitable. But does that end it? Or do the neighboring worlds become fearful and turn against us?"

Fain stood as unmoved as a statue. His lips barely parted as he asked, "Sire, may I speak frankly?"

"Certainly, Commander."

Like a soldier standing at attention as he delivers an unpleasant report to his superior officer, Fain drew himself up and intoned, "Sire, the main reason for unrest among the frontier worlds is the lack of Imperial firmness in dealing with them. In my opinion, a strong hand is desperately needed. The neighboring worlds will respect their Emperor if—and only if—he acts decisively. The people value strength, sire, not meekness."

The Emperor reached out and laid a hand on the Commander's shoulder. Fain was still iron-hard under his uniform.

"You have sworn an oath to protect and defend this realm," the Emperor said. "If necessary, to die for it."

"And to protect and defend you, sire." The man stood straighter and firmer than the trees around them.

"But this empire, my dear Commander, is more than blood and steel. It is more than any one man. It is an *idea*."

Fain looked back at him steadily, but with no real understanding in his eyes. Bomeer stood uncertainly off to one side.

Impatiently, the Emperor turned his face toward the ceiling hologram and called, "Map!"

Instantly the forest scene disappeared and they were in limitless space. Stars glowed around them, overhead, on all sides, underfoot. The pale gleam of the galaxy's spiral arms wafted off and away into unutterable distance.

Bomeer's knees buckled. Even the Commander's rigid self-discipline was shaken.

The Emperor smiled. He was accustomed to walking on the face of the deep.

"This is the empire, gentlemen," he lectured in the starlit shadows. "A handful of stars, a pitiful scattering of worlds set apart by distances that take years to traverse. All populated by human beings, the descendents of Earth."

He could hear Bomeer breathing heavily. Fain was a ramrod

outline against the glow of the Milky Way, but his hands were outstretched, as if seeking balance.

"What links these scattered dust motes? What preserves their ancient heritage, guards their civilization, protects their hard-won knowledge and arts and sciences? The Empire, gentlemen. We are the mind of the Hundred Worlds, their memory, the yardstick against which they can measure their own humanity. We are their friend, their father, their teacher and helper."

The Emperor searched the black starry void for the tiny yellowish speck of Earth's Sun while continuing:

"But if the Hundred Worlds decide that the Empire is no longer their friend, if they want to leave their father, if they feel that their teacher and helper has become an oppressor . . . what then happens to the human race? It will shatter into a hundred fragments, and all the civilization that we have built and nurtured and protected over these centuries will be destroyed."

Bomeer's whispered voice floated through the darkness. "They would never . . ."

"Yes. They would never turn against the Empire because they know they have more to gain by remaining with us than by leaving us."

"But the frontier worlds," Fain said.

"The frontier worlds are restless, as frontier communities always are. If we use military might to force them to bow to our will, then other worlds will begin to wonder where their own best interests lie."

"But they could never hope to fight against the Empire!"

"They could never hope to *win* against the Empire," the Emperor corrected. "But they could destroy the Empire and themselves. I have played out the scenarios with the computers. Widespread rebellion *is* possible, once the majority of the Hundred Worlds becomes convinced that the Empire is interfering with their freedoms."

"But the rebels could never win," Commander Fain insisted. "I have run the same wargames myself, many times."

"Civil war," said the Emperor. "Who wins a civil war? And once we begin to slaughter ourselves, what will your aliens do then, my dear Fain? Eh?"

His two advisors fell silent. The forest simulation returned, in deep twilight shadow now. The three men began to walk back along the path, which was softly illuminated by luminescent flowers.

Bomeer clasped his hands behind his back as he walked. "Now that I have seen some of your other problems, sire, I must take a stronger stand and insist—yes, sire, *insist*—that this young woman's plan to save the Earth is even more foolhardy than I had at first thought it to be. The cost is too high, the chance of success is much too slim. The frontier worlds would react violently against such an extravagance. And," with a nod to Fain, "it would hamstring the fleet."

For several moments the Emperor walked down the simulated forest path without speaking a word. Then, slowly, "I suppose you are right. It is an old man's sentimental dream."

"I'm afraid that's the truth of it, sire," said Fain.

Bomeer nodded sagaciously.

"I will tell her. She will be disappointed. Bitterly."

Bomeer gasped. "She's here?"

The Emperor said, "Yes. I had her brought here to the palace. She has crossed the Empire, given up more than two years of her life to make the trip, lost a dozen years of her career over this wild scheme of hers . . . just to hear that I will refuse her."

"In the palace?" Fain echoed. "Sire, you're not going to see her in person? The security—"

"Yes, in person. I owe her that much." The Emperor could see the shock on their faces. Bomeer, who had never stood in the same building with the Emperor until he had become Chairman of the Academy, was trying to suppress his fury with poor success. Fain, sworn to guard the Emperor as well as the Empire, looked worried.

"But sire," the Commander said, "no one has personally seen

the Emperor, privately, outside of his family and closest advisors," Bomeer bristled visibly, "in years . . . decades!"

The Emperor nodded but insisted, "She is going to see me. I owe her that much. An ancient ruler on Earth once said, 'When you are going to kill a man, it costs nothing to be polite about it.' She is not a man, of course, but I fear that our decision will kill her soul."

They looked unconvinced.

Very well, then, the Emperor said to them silently. *Put it down as the whim of an old man . . . a man who is feeling all his years . . . a man who will never recapture his youth.*

5

SHE IS ONLY *a child.*

The Emperor studied Adela de Montgarde as the young astrophysicist made her way through the guards and secretaries and halls and anterooms toward his own private chambers. He had prepared to meet her in the reception room, changed his mind and moved the meeting to his private office, then changed it again and now waited for her in his study. She knew nothing of his indecision; she merely followed the directions given her by the computer-informed staff of the palace.

The study was a warm old room lined with shelves of private disks that the Emperor had collected over the years. A stone fireplace big enough to walk into spanned one wall; its flames soaked the Emperor with life-giving warmth. The opposite wall was a single broad window that looked out onto the real forest beyond the palace walls. The window could also serve as a hologram frame; the Emperor could have any scene he desired projected from it.

Best to have reality this evening, he told himself. *There is too little reality in my life these days.* So he eased back in his powerchair and watched his approaching visitor on the display screen above the fireplace of the richly carpeted, comfortably paneled old room.

He had carefully absorbed all the computer's dossier about Adela de Montgarde: born of a noble family on Gris, a frontier world whose settlers were slowly, painfully transforming from a ball of rock into a viable habitat for human life. He knew her face, her life history, her scientific accomplishments and rank. But now, as he watched her approaching on the display screen built into the stone fireplace, he realized how little knowledge had accompanied the computer's detailed facts.

The door to the study swung open automatically, and she stood uncertainly, framed in the doorway.

The Emperor swiveled his powerchair around to face her. The display screen immediately faded and became indistinguishable from the other stones of the fireplace.

"Come in, come in, Dr. Montgarde."

She was tiny, the smallest woman the Emperor remembered seeing. Her face was almost elfin, with large curious eyes that looked as if they had known laughter. She wore a metallic tunic buttoned to the throat and a brief skirt. Her figure was childlike.

The Emperor smiled to himself. *She certainly won't tempt me with her body.*

As she stepped hesitantly into the study, her eyes darting all around the room, the Emperor said:

"I'm sure that my aides have filled your head with all sorts of nonsense about protocol—when to stand, when to bow, what forms of address to use. Forget it all. This is an informal meeting, common politeness will suffice. If you need a form of address for me, call me sire. I shall call you Adela, if you don't mind."

With a slow nod of her head, she answered, "Thank you, sire. That will be fine." Her voice was so soft that he could barely hear it. He thought he detected a slight waver in it.

She's not going to make this easy for me, he said to himself. Then he noticed the stone she wore on a slim silver chain about her neck.

"Agate," he said.

She fingered the stone reflexively. "Yes . . . it's from my homeworld . . . Gris. Our planet is rich in minerals."

"And poor in cultivable land."

"True. But we are converting more land every year."

"Please sit down," the Emperor said. "I'm afraid it's been so long since my old legs have tried to stand in full gravity that I'm forced to remain in this powerchair . . . or lower the gravitational field in this room. The computer files said that you are not accustomed to low-G fields."

She glanced around the warm, richly furnished room.

"Any seat you like. My chair rides like a magic carpet."

Adela picked the biggest couch in the room and tucked herself into a corner of it. The Emperor glided his chair over to her.

"It's very kind of you to keep the gravity up for me," she said.

He shrugged. "It costs nothing to be polite. But tell me, of all the minerals that Gris is famous for, why did you choose to wear agate?"

She blushed.

The Emperor laughed. "Come, come, my dear. There's nothing to be ashamed of. It's well known that agate is a magical stone that protects the wearer from scorpions and snakes. An ancient superstition, of course, but it could possibly be significant, eh?"

"No! It's not that!"

"Then what is it?"

"It . . . agate also makes the wearer . . . eloquent in speech."

"And a favorite of princes," added the Emperor.

Her blush had gone. She sat straighter and almost smiled. "And it gives one victory over her enemies."

"You perceive me as your enemy?"

"Oh no!" She reached out toward him, her small, childlike hand almost touching his.

"Who then?"

"The hierarchy. The old men who pretend to be young and refuse to admit any new ideas into the scientific community."

"I am an old man, Adela."

"Yes . . ." She stared frankly into his aged face. "I was surprised when I saw you a few moments ago. I've seen holographic images, of course . . . but you . . . you've *aged*."

"Indeed."

"Why can't you be rejuvenated? It seems like a useless old superstition to keep the Emperor from using modern biomedical therapies."

"No, no, my child. It is a very wise tradition. You complain of inflexible old men at the top of the scientific hierarchy. Suppose you had an inflexible old man on the Emperor's throne? A man who would live not merely six or seven score years, but many centuries? What would happen to the Empire then?"

"Ohh. I see." And there was real understanding in her eyes. And sympathy.

"So the king must die, to make room for new blood, new ideas, new vigor."

"It's sad," she said. "You are known everywhere as a good Emperor. The people love you."

He felt his eyebrows rise. "Even on the frontier worlds?"

"Yes. They know that Fain and his troops would be standing on our necks if it weren't for the Emperor. We are not without our sources of information."

He smiled. "Interesting."

"But that isn't why you called me here to see you," Adela said.

She grows bolder. "True. You want to save Earth's Sun. Acadamecian Bomeer and all my advisors tell me that it is either impossible or foolish. I fear they have powerful arguments on their side."

"Perhaps," she said, "But I have the facts."

"I have seen your presentation, I understand the scientific basis of your plan."

"We can do it!" Adela said, her hands suddenly animated. "We can! The critical mass is really minuscule compared to . . ."

"Gigatons are minuscule?"

"Compared to the effect they will produce, yes."

And then she was on her feet, pacing the room, ticking off

points on her fingers, lecturing, pleading, cajoling. The Emperor's powerchair nodded back and forth, following her intense, wiry form as she paced.

"Of course it will take vast resources! And time—more than a century before we know to a first-order approximation if the initial steps are working. I'll have to give myself up to cryosleep for decades at a time. But we *have* the resources! And we have the time . . . just barely. We can do it, if we want to."

The Emperor said, "How can you expect me to divert half the resources of the Empire to save Earth's Sun?"

"Because Earth is *important*," she argued back, a tiny fighter standing alone in the middle of the Emperor's study. "It's the baseline for all the other worlds of the Empire. On Gris we send biogenetic teams every twenty-five years to check our own mutation rate. The cost is enormous for us, but we do it. We have to."

"We can move Earth's population to another G-type star. There are plenty of them."

"It won't be the same."

"Adela, my dear, believe me, I would like to help. I know how important Earth is. We simply cannot afford to try your scheme now. Perhaps in another hundred years or so . . ."

"That will be too late."

"But new scientific advances . . ."

"Under Bomeer and his ilk? Hah!"

The Emperor wanted to frown at her, but somehow his face would not compose itself properly. "You are a fierce, uncompromising woman," he said.

She came to him and dropped to her knees at his feet. "No, sire. I'm not. I'm foolish and vain and utterly self-centered. I want to save Earth because I know I can do it. I can't stand the thought of living the rest of my life knowing that I could have done it, but never had the chance to try."

Now we're getting to the truth, the Emperor thought.

Adela continued, "And someday, maybe a million years from now, maybe a billion . . . Gris's sun will become unstable. I want to be able to save Gris, too. And any other world whose star threatens it. I want all the Empire to know that Adela de Montgarde discovered the way to do it!"

The Emperor felt the breath rush out of him.

"Sire," she went on, "I'm sorry if I'm speaking impolitely or stupidly. It's just that I know we can do this thing, do it successfully, and you're the only one who can make it happen."

But he was barely listening. "Come with me," he said, grasping her slim wrists and raising her to her feet. "It's time for the evening meal. I want you to meet my son."

6

JAVAS PUT ON his usual amused smirk when the Emperor introduced Adela. *Will nothing ever reach past his everlasting façade of polite boredom?* Rihana, at least, was properly enraged. He could see the anger on her face: A virtual barbarian from some frontier planet. Daughter of a petty noble. Practically a commoner. Dining with them!

"Such a young child to have such grandiose schemes," said the princess once she realized who Adela was.

"Surely," said the Emperor, "you had grandiose schemes of your own when you were young, Rihana. Of course, they involved lineages and marriages rather than astrophysics, didn't they?"

Neither of them smiled.

The Emperor had ordered dinner out on the terrace, under the glowing night sky of the Imperial Planet. Rihana, who was responsible for household affairs, always had sumptuous meals spread for them: the best meats and fowl and fruits of a dozen prime worlds. Adela looked bewildered at the array placed before her by the human servants. Such riches were obviously new to her. The Emperor ate sparingly and watched them all.

Inevitably the conversation returned to Adela's plan to save

Earth's Sun. And Adela, subdued and timid at first, slowly turned tigress once again. She met Rihana's scorn with coldly furious logic. She countered Javas's skepticism with:

"Of course, since it will take more than a century before the outcome of the project is proven, you will probably be the Emperor who is remembered by all the human race as the one who saved the Earth."

Javas's eyes widened slightly. *That hit home*, the Emperor noticed. *For once something affected the boy. This girl should be kept at the palace.*

But Rihana snapped, "Why should the crown prince care about saving Earth? His brother was murdered by an Earthman."

The Emperor felt his blood turn to ice.

Adela looked panic-stricken. She turned to the Emperor, wide-eyed, open-mouthed.

"My eldest son died on Earth," he told her. "My second son was killed putting down a rebellion on a frontier world. My third son died of a strange viral infection that *some* tell me was assassination." He stared at Rihana. "Death is a constant companion in every royal house."

"Three sons . . ." Adela seemed about to burst into tears.

"I have not punished Earth, nor that frontier world, nor sought to find a possible assassin," the Emperor went on, icily. "My only hope is that my last remaining son will make a good Emperor despite his . . . handicaps."

Javas turned very deliberately in his chair to stare out at the dark forest. He seemed bored by the antagonism between his wife and his father. Rihana glowered like molten lava.

The dinner ended in dismal, bitter silence. The Emperor sent them all away to their rooms while he remained on the terrace and stared hard at the stars strewn so thickly across the sky.

He closed his eyes and summoned a computer-assisted image of Earth's Sun. He saw it coalesce from a hazy cloud of cold gas and dust, saw it turn into a star and spawn planets. Saw it beaming out energy that allowed life to grow and flourish on some of those planets. And then he saw it age, blemish, erupt, swell, and finally collapse into a dark cinder.

Just as I will, thought the Emperor. *The Sun and I have both reached the age where a bit of rejuvenation is needed. Otherwise . . . death.*

He opened his eyes and looked down at his veined, fleshless, knobby hands. *How different from hers! How young and vital she is.*

With a touch on one of the control studs set into the arm of his powerchair, he headed for his bedroom.

I cannot be rejuvenated. It is wrong even to desire it. But the Sun? Would it be wrong to try? Is it proper for puny men to tamper with the destinies of the stars themselves?

Once in his tower-top bedroom he called for her. Adela came to him quickly, without delay or question. She wore a simple knee-length gown tied loosely at the waist. It hung limply over her childlike figure.

"You sent for me, sire." It was not a question but a statement. The Emperor knew her meaning: *I will do what you ask, but in return I expect you to give me what I desire.*

He was already reclining in the soft embrace of his bed. The texture of the monolayer surface felt soft and protective. The warmth of the water beneath it eased his tired body.

"Come here, child. Come and talk to me. I hardly ever sleep anymore; it gives my doctors something to worry about. Come and sit beside me and tell me all about yourself . . . the parts of your life story that are not on file in the computers."

She sat on the edge of the huge bed; its nearly living surface barely dimpled under her spare body.

"What would you like to know?" she asked.

"I never had a daughter," the Emperor said. "What was your childhood like? How did you become the woman you are?"

She began to tell him. Living underground in the mining settlements on Gris. Seeing sunlight only when the planet was far enough from its too-bright star to allow humans to walk on the surface safely. Playing in the tunnels. Sent by her parents to other worlds for schooling. The realization that her beauty was not physical. The few lovers she had known. The astronomer who had championed her cause to the Emperor at that meeting nearly fifteen years ago. Their brief marriage. Its breakup when he realized that being married to her kept him from advancing in the hierarchy.

"You have known pain too," the Emperor said.

"It's not an Imperial prerogative," she answered softly. "Everybody who lives knows pain."

By now the sky was milky white with the approach of dawn. The Emperor smiled at her.

"Before breakfast everyone in the palace will know that you spent the night with me. I'm afraid I have ruined your reputation."

She smiled back, impishly. "Or perhaps *made* my reputation."

He reached out and grasped her by her shoulders. Holding her at arm's length, he searched her face with a long, sad, almost fatherly look.

"It would not be a kindness to grant your request. If I allow you to pursue this dream of yours, have you any idea of the enemies it would make for you? Your life would be so cruel, so filled with envy and hatred."

"I know that," Adela said evenly. "I've known that from the beginning."

"And you are not afraid?"

"Of course I'm afraid! But I won't turn away from what I must do. Not because of fear. Not because of envy or hatred or any other reason."

"Not even for love?"

He felt her body stiffen. "No," she said. "Not even for love."

The Emperor let his hands drop away from her and called out to the computer, "Connect me with Prince Javas, Academician Bomeer, and Commander Fain."

Almost instantly the three holographic images appeared on separate segments of the farthest bedroom wall. Bomeer, halfway across the planet in late afternoon, was at his ornate desk.

Fain appeared to be on the bridge of a warcraft. Javas, of course, was still in bed. It was not Rihana who lay next to him.

The Emperor's first impulse was disapproval, but then he wondered where Rihana was sleeping.

"I am sorry to intrude on you so abruptly," he said to all three men, while they were still staring at the slight young woman sitting on the bed with their Emperor. "I have made my decision on the question of trying to save Earth's Sun."

Bomeer folded his hands on his desktop. Fain, on his feet, shifted uneasily. Javas arched an eyebrow and looked more curious than anything else.

"I have listened to your arguments and find that there is much merit in them. I have also listened carefully to Dr. Montgarde's arguments, and find much merit in them, as well."

Adela sat rigidly beside him. The expression on her face was frozen: she feared nothing and expected nothing. She neither hoped nor despaired. She waited, hardly breathing. She waited.

"We will move the Imperial throne and all the court to Earth's only Moon," said the Emperor.

They gasped. All of them.

"Since this project to save the Sun will take many human generations, we will want the seat of the Empire close enough to the project so that the Emperor may take a direct view of its progress."

"But you can't move the entire capital!" Fain protested. "And to Earth! It's a backwater . . ."

"Commander Fain," the Emperor said sternly. "Yesterday you were prepared to move Earth's millions. I ask now that the Fleet move the court's thousands. And Earth will no longer be a backwater once the Empire is centered once again at the original home of the human race."

Bomeer sputtered. "But . . . but what if the plan fails? The Sun will erupt . . . and . . . and . . ."

"That is a decision to be made in the future."

The Emperor glanced at Adela. Her expression had not changed noticeably, but she was breathing rapidly now. The excitement had hit her body, it hadn't yet penetrated her emotional defenses.

"Father," said Javas, "may I point out that it takes *five years* in realtime to reach Earth from here? The Empire can't be governed without an Emperor for five years."

"Quite true, my son. You will go to Earth before me. Once you've set up everything there, you will become acting Emperor while I make the trip."

Javas's mouth dropped open. "Acting Emperor? For five years?"

"With a little luck," the Emperor said, grinning slightly, "old age will catch up with me before I reach Earth and you will be the full-fledged Emperor for the rest of your life."

"But I don't want—"

"I know, Javas. But you will be Emperor someday. It is a responsibility you cannot avoid. Five years of training will stand you in good stead."

The Prince sat up straighter in his bed, his face serious, his eyes meeting his father's steadily.

"And, son," the Emperor went on, "to be Emperor—even for five years—you must be master of your own house."

Javas nodded. "I know, Father. I understand. And I will be."

"Good."

Then the prince's knowing smile flitted across his face once again. "But tell me . . . suppose, while you are in transit toward Earth, I decide to move the Imperial court elsewhere? What then?"

His father smiled back at him. "I believe I will just have to trust you not to do that."

"You would trust me?" Javas asked.

"I always have."

Javas's smile took on a new pleasure. "Thank you, Father. I will be waiting for you on Earth's Moon. And for the lovely Dr. Montgarde, as well."

Bomeer was still livid. "All this uprooting of everything . . . the costs . . . the manpower . . . over an unproven theory!"

"Why is the theory unproven, my friend?" the Emperor asked.

Bomeer's mouth opened and closed like a fish's, but no words came out.

"It is unproven," said the Emperor, "because our scientists have never gone so far before. In fact, the sciences of the Hundred Worlds have not made much progress at all in several generations. Isn't that true, Bomeer?"

"We . . . sire, we have reached a natural plateau in our understanding of the physical universe. It has happened before. Our era is one of consolidation and practical applications of already acquired knowledge, not new basic breakthroughs."

"Well, this project will force some new thinking and new breakthroughs, I warrant. Certainly we will be forced to recruit new scientists and engineers by the shipload. Perhaps that will be impetus enough to start the climb upward again, eh, Bomeer? I never did like plateaus."

The academician lapsed into silence.

"And I see you, Fain," the Emperor said, "trying to calculate in your head how much of your fleet strength is going to be wasted on this old man's dream."

"Sire, I had no—"

The Emperor waved him into silence. "No matter. Moving the capital won't put much of a strain on the fleet, will it?"

"No, sire. But this project to save Earth . . ."

"We will have to construct new ships for that, Fain. And we will have to turn to the frontier worlds for those ships." He glanced at Adela. "I believe that the frontier worlds will gladly join the effort to save Earth's Sun. And their treasuries will be enriched by our purchase of thousands of new ships."

"While the Imperial treasury is depleted."

"It's a rich Empire, Fain. It's time we shared some of our wealth with the frontier worlds. A large shipbuilding program will do more to reconcile them with the Empire than anything else we can imagine."

"Sire," the Commander said bluntly, "I still think it's madness."

"Yes, I know. Perhaps it is. I only hope that I live long enough to find out, one way or the other."

"Sire," Adela said breathlessly, "you will be reuniting all the worlds of the Empire into a closely knit human community such as we haven't seen in centuries!"

"Perhaps. It would be pleasant to believe so. But for the moment, all I have done is to implement a decision to *try* to save Earth's Sun. It may succeed, it may fail. But we are sons and daughters of planet Earth, and we will not allow our original homeworld to be destroyed without striving to our uttermost to save it."

He looked at their faces again. They were all waiting for him to continue. *You grow pompous, old man.*

"Very well. You each have several lifetimes of work to accomplish. Get busy, each of you."

Bomeer's and Fain's images winked off immediately. Javas's remained.

"Yes, my son? What is it?"

Javas's ever-present smile was gone. He looked serious, even troubled. "Father . . . I am not going to bring Rihana to Earth with me. She wouldn't want to come, I know—at least, not until all the comforts of the Court were established there for her."

The Emperor nodded.

"If I'm to be master of my own house," Javas went on, "it's time we ended this farce of a marriage."

"Very well, son. That is your decision to make. But, for what it's worth, I agree with you."

"Thank you, Father." Javas's image disappeared.

For a long moment the Emperor sat gazing thoughtfully at the wall where the holographic images had appeared. At last he turned to Adela.

"I believe I will send you to Earth on Javas's ship. I think he likes you, and it's important that the two of you get along well together."

Adela looked almost shocked. "What do you mean by 'get along well together'?"

The Emperor grinned at her. "That is for the two of you to decide."

"You're scandalous!" she said. But she was smiling too.

He shrugged. "Call it part of the price of victory. You'll like Javas, he's a good man. And I doubt that he's ever met a woman quite like you."

"I don't know what to say . . ."

"You'll need Javas's protection and support, you know. You have defeated my closest advisors, and that means that they have become your enemies. Powerful enemies. That is also part of the price of your triumph."

"Triumph? I don't feel very triumphant."

"I know," said the Emperor. "Perhaps that's what triumph really is: not so much glorying in the defeat of your enemies as weariness that they couldn't see what seemed so obvious to you."

Abruptly, Adela moved to him and put her lips to his cheek. "Thank you, sire."

"Why, thank you, child."

For a moment she stood there, holding his old hands in her tiny young ones.

Then she said, "I . . . have lots of work to do."

"Of course. We might never see each other again. Go do your work. Do it well."

"I will," she said. "And you?"

He leaned back into the enfolding embrace of the bed. "I've finished my work. I believe that now I can go to sleep." And with a smile he closed his eyes.

ABOUT THE AUTHOR

Ben Bova is a six-time winner of the Hugo Award, a former editor of *Analog*, a former editorial director of *Omni*, and a past president of both the National Space Society and the Science Fiction Writers of America. Bova is the author of more than a hundred and thirty works of science fact and fiction. He lives in Florida.

WWW.BENBOVA.NET